A Justice of Ehrylan

John Douglas Day

Copyright © 2012 by John Douglas Day

All rights reserved.

ISBN: 1508435693

ISBN-13: 978-1508435693

No part of this book may be used for any purpose other than personal use. Reproduction, modification, storage in a retrieval system or retransmission, in any form or by any means, electronic, mechanical or otherwise, for reasons other than personal use, is strictly prohibited without prior written permission of the publishers. A reasonable use exception is granted for excerpts needed for review.

3 2 1

This work is dedicated to my father and to Nancy Taylor. Without their relentless encouragement and help, it would not have come to light.

Contents

MAP OF EHRYLAN v
MAP OF THE BEND vi
REGIONS OF EHRYLAN vii
1. MEETINGS 1
2. BEGINNINGS 17
3. ALTERCATION IN THE BENDWOOD 42
4. THE OLD ONES 73
5. THE MESSAGE 104
6. THE CHOOSING 120
7. DREAMER 138
8. TOWER MILL 170
9. REVELATIONS 203
10. STRIKING DAWN 222
11. ERRANTRY 248
12. SILVER SAILING 278
13. UNMASKED 291
14. MANY PARTINGS 318
15. THE THIRD BATTLE 335
16. A SHELTERING PLACE 353
17. THE BATTLE OF THE BEND 379
18. AFTERMATH 407
19. PARTINGS 424
ABOUT THE AUTHOR 438
OTHER WORK 439

MAP OF EHRYLAN

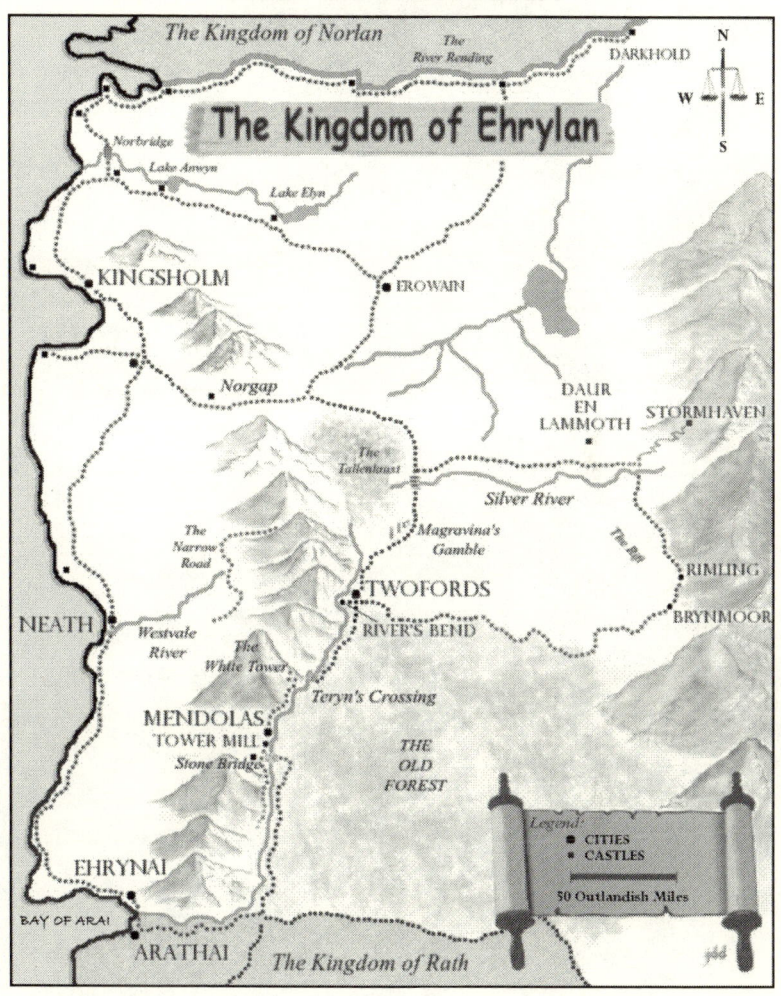

MAP OF THE BEND

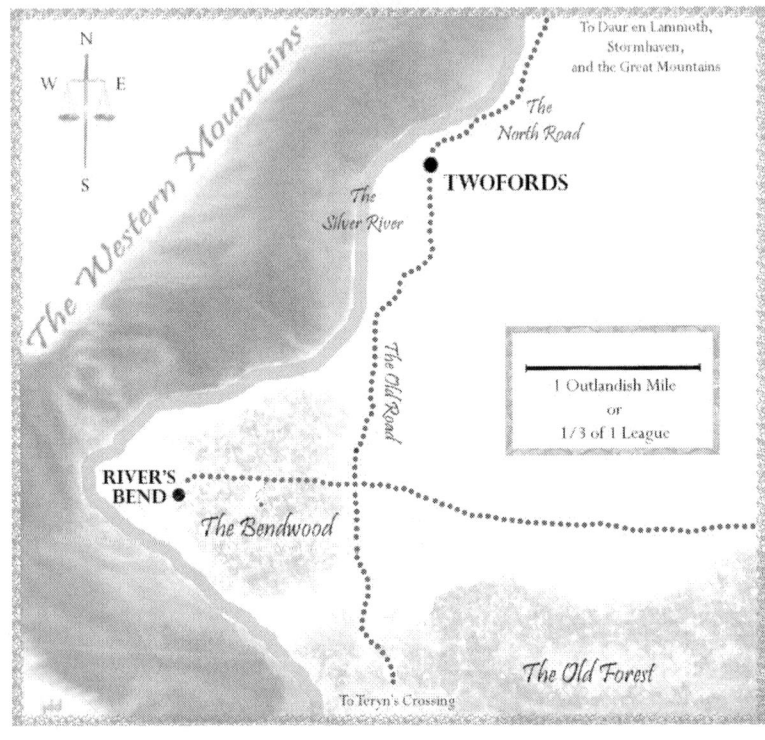

REGIONS OF EHRYLAN

100 Outlandish Miles

The Tallenlaust and the Old Forest are not strictly considered part of Ehrylan.

1. MEETINGS

I.

The note was on the table near the hilt of my sword. Five sets of eyes peered at it through the candle light, desperate to know what it said. Was it to be more waiting? Was it war at last? Once I divulged the decoded message, there would be disappointment, frustration, even bitterness. But now, for them, there was still room for hope.

"What are you waiting for? Don't keep us in suspense!"

The man who had spoken eyed me suspiciously. He must have suspected what I already knew. In this group, he was known only as 3. The others were 1, 2, 4, and 5. As the unit commanders, they would take the news to their people, the men and women who would fight and die for their city and the kingdom of Ehrylan once the war to regain our freedom began in earnest.

I sighed. "There's to be no action. We wait."

Even in their disappointment, the three men and two women kept discipline, holding their voices down as well as their emotions. 3 did as well as the others, though his mumbled complaints were audible. Whether or not he grumbled too loudly was never an issue. At that moment, far too soon to be a response to his words, the alarm sounded.

The soft ringing brought all six of our heads around. The bell, which had been muffled to dampen the sound, was hidden in the shadows that pooled in one corner of the chamber. A cord ran along hidden paths to the main rooms of the inn. That bell meant only one thing—trouble, big trouble, coming soon.

We hung transfixed, nailed to our seats as our minds attempted to fix on the calamity and what we had to do. Faces turned toward me with fear-stretched eyes. Yes, I saw fear in those eyes, even though these men and women had been hand-picked to be the leaders of the revolution in Twofords. That fear was justified, but it was dwarfed by an unbending determination that spread like liquid gold on their faces, dismay turning to resolve.

I was on my feet before the bell stopped vibrating. The others were not much slower. There was a general scurrying as each of us performed prearranged assignments. If any of us were caught, if any of the documents we carried were found and decoded, the lives of hundreds of people would be put in jeopardy. The fate of the revolution would be darkened, set back substantially, maybe fatally.

"Hurry!" My encouragement was wholly unnecessary.

I watched as 2, still stuffing a sheaf of parchment into a satchel, vanished into her bolt hole. It led to fortified doorways that would be sealed to delay the pursuit. Behind one of those doors was a window that gave on to a secret escape route.

Casting a final glance at me, 3 lurched into one of the back rooms, lugging his haul of damaging intelligence to the hidden door he would use. 1 followed after him, then 5. Last but for me was 4. He chased 2 into the bolt hole. As I pushed a chest over the trap door, I could hear the stout timber being slid into its restraints on the underside. Good. That was done!

The first blow fell on the outer door to our chamber. The door shuddered. The hallway must have been flooded with

Dauroth's soldiers. I looked around for anything we might have missed, saw nothing. The second blow fell. The door shuddered again. Still it held. It was very stout.

I grabbed my sword and the note from the table. The third blow came with a sick, tearing sound. I fled. From the corner of my eye, I saw the lintel bow inward. The final blow threw the door back from the fractured wall. I heard the scream of breaking timber and the growl of stone falling in on itself.

Then I was out through my own bolt hole, this one leading to the inn's roof. I hastened to shut the hatch and secure it. Bending low to avoid being seen from below, I ran for my life.

II.

I took my time returning to Twofords, which was home. It was only a modest city, though one of the largest in the Southland. The event at the inn had occurred elsewhere. It was my policy not to meet with my assembled unit at home. We had been fortunate at the inn; no one was caught. More than a month had passed. I had finally managed to convince myself that we had gotten away cleanly and was going about my other life, the one that occupied my time and attention when I wasn't plotting rebellion.

I emerged from the alley's shade, pausing to let my eyes adjust to the afternoon light. The sound of laughing filled the air, not joyful laughter, but a mocking, derisive exhalation that was not pleasant to hear. The sound wasn't improved by the quick, snapping echo that jumped back from the stone walls of the square.

At the center of the open quadrangle, four boys were grouped in a ragged circle. There was a single child in the center of the group, younger than the others; perhaps he'd seen ten summers, maybe eleven. The others were older, bigger. The perimeter of the circle was moving, the older boys demonstrating a jerky procession around the figure within. I stopped, melting a step back into the shadows with unconscious habit.

"Ya, ya, yahhh," jeered one of the older boys. "Look what the dogs dragged in!" He waded in toward the center of the circle, advancing on the child with the branch of a willow tree held in one hand like a sword.

The child held his ground, then skipped nimbly to the side when the willow branch descended, cutting the air with a strident whoosh. The other boys shifted, keeping the enclosing circle intact. Now it was three around two. The child adjusted his position as well, not letting any of them close enough to make a grab for him. He staggered slightly, and I saw that one of his knees was badly skinned. A trickle of blood mixed with sweat ran down his shin like an exposed vein. His tunic was ripped at the neck.

This wasn't innocent play.

The boy with the willow branch attacked again. The child jumped aside. The circle shifted, smaller now, the older boys closing in. One of them stooped and picked up a rock.

"The dogs dragged in a dog," he exclaimed, "a dirty little puppy from outside the walls. We can't have that, can we?" He hurled his missile. It whistled through the distance, missing the child's head by a hand span. The stone struck a wall with such force that it shattered with a crack and a puff of dust.

No, this was not play at all.

One of the encircling attackers cried, "Good one, Pruis!"

It seemed that Pruis was the leader of this gang. The other three all turned toward him, laughing. I recognized him, though I did not know him personally. His father was a merchant who supplied goods to the garrison. I'd seen them in the market and throughout the city.

While the bullies were occupied with their own self-admiration, my eye caught a swift, furtive movement. The child leapt forward, snatching at the branch in his enemy's hand. He came away with it too, and things went from bad to worse. The older boy, having been temporarily bested by the younger, was not pleased. Forgetting caution, he advanced on the child with two quick steps.

The child danced back. His feet flowed smoothly, never leaving the broken flagstones. He came to rest for an instant, turned his shoulder toward the pursuing youth and, holding the branch in both hands, extended it exactly as a man well-versed in the arts of the sword would do. Then, he shuffled back, keeping the branch between them, retreating as the older boy came on. When his opponent was in mid-stride, the child erupted with a blaze of unexpected energy. He sprang forward and brought the branch down in a blow that caught the older boy in the center of his forehead with a resounding crack.

The limb, as long as my arm and as thick as my thumb, must have been green. It did not break. The stricken boy staggered back, collapsing on his buttocks with a surprised look that was nearly comical. He looked like a toddler learning to walk. The child sprang past him, pivoted, and delivered a savage blow across one ear from behind. The smitten boy shrieked in pain and crumpled to the ground in a ball.

The child slid sideways, exploiting a temporary vulnerability in the circle. There were no alleys near his position. He had nowhere to run. He was quickly surrounded again. The movement had, however, placed the beaten youth outside the perimeter. Now it was one against three.

I was amazed. How did such a waif learn to move so like a warrior?

The three remaining attackers, now enraged, tightened their circle. The child turned to face each of them alternately, exactly as an experienced soldier might have done in a similar situation. He was valiant, this one, but I could see that it would be soon over. Three against one, particularly when the three are all almost twice as big as the one, are long odds.

He was not finished yet. He whirled on the balls of his feet, swinging the branch, just as one of the older boys was about to grab him from behind. The blow glanced off the attacker's upper arm with a smack.

The child brandished the branch at the two remaining attackers. He managed to drive them back two or three steps, the hunted becoming the hunter. Was this possible? I stood watching, transfixed by the spectacle. My interest swelled like the expectant inhalation of the forest before a storm.

The two boys who had been hit were back in the fray now; the limb was sturdy, but too light to inflict real damage. The attackers pressed in relentlessly. The small child pushed them back with his branch, which might have been burning with bright fire for the respect they paid it. For a moment, the five of them were at a stand-off. Four circled one, a wheel of hate searching for satisfaction. Pruis pushed one of his compatriots forward. The boy lurched toward the center of the circle, toward the prey.

Dodging aside, the child's foot went awry. He may have slipped on a pebble or even a patch of blood. Whatever the reason, his bare foot slid to one side. He had to put both hands out to avoid falling completely to the ground. The older boys sprang forward, burying him under the press of their bodies.

There was a brief, confused scuffle. Two of the older boys heaved the child up by his arms. They all stood in place for a moment, five chests heaving with exertion. Pruis moved to face the child, but not near enough to be within reach.

"That's it for you, puppy. I am tired of playing with you," he said. He glanced around. "Where's Demus?"

"Here," said the pudgy boy who had originally held the willow branch. He was standing two paces back. He was sheltering in Pruis' lee.

"You first." Pruis jerked his head toward the child, who was struggling against restraint.

Demus took a position in front of the child. He pulled his balled fist back. Before he could strike, the child lashed out with a violent kick. The foot struck the older boy where no one wants to be struck. Demus slumped once more to the ground. He started to moan and whine.

The child sank down also, but much quicker. He lifted both feet off the ground. The boys restraining him were pulled down and in, their heads colliding. The contact was not hard enough to be disorienting, but it did surprise them. The child tore himself free, leapt away. Unfortunately, he bounded straight at Pruis who, stepping aside at just the right moment, shoved him sideways.

The child tumbled, head over heels, landing spread eagle on his back, his head smacking the ground solidly. The three remaining attackers drew their circle around him. They were practically dancing with fury. There was death on their faces. I saw it as clearly as I could see their shadows against the flagstones.

Realization came to me suddenly. I had seen enough.

"Four to one is not fair sport, even if the one is armed with a willow wand." I made the proclamation loudly enough to be sure they all heard me. Four heads jerked around at the sound of my voice. I stepped out of the shadows and moved forward into the square. The child, scrambling to his feet, did not take his eyes off the nearest attacker, even for an instant.

"My sport is not your business," returned Pruis defiantly. He glared at me with the outrage of an offended nobleman's son. I had been in this land long and long. I knew his family was not noble. Not now, not ever.

"I'll agree with you on that." I walked forward unhurriedly, pausing in front of him, fixing him with my stare. He was tall for his age, perhaps a forehead shorter than my six feet. Then, pushing by him close enough to ensure my upper arm brushed his shoulder, I said, "Your sport is not my business, but injustice is."

There was a tense moment. As I continued toward their prey, my back was exposed to two of them. The patch of skin between my shoulder blades twitched, and I missed the sword that would have been at my side if I had been more prepared for an altercation. As I closed the distance, I showed my battle eyes to the two miscreants facing me from the far side of the child. That froze them to their spots. When I reached the child, I stopped and turned back slowly, theatrically.

I gave the leader my most baleful glare, hoping to conceal my concern that he would simply laugh at me and proceed with this ugly business. Now I was within their circle as well. Times had not yet grown so bad in Twofords that a healthy man need fear a small gang of youngsters, though such days were not far off. Yet, there was a nasty feeling here, a sense that at least one or two of the attacking youth were indifferent to the consequences of the evil they were committing. Even in that situation, my mind cried out. When did death become a game for the young? How had Dauroth ruined us so quickly?

My concern was unfounded. The young ruffian snarled at me, then turned on his heel. He took two quick steps, then turned back and spat on the ground where he had been standing. He stalked off into one of the alleys that led from the square. His companions scurried after him, one moving more slowly than the others.

Dismissing them from my mind, I turned to the boy they'd been harassing. He retreated from me far enough to make an easy escape should I prove troublesome. I shook my head.

"Nay, lad. Don't fear me. I want nothing of you."

He did not reply; his eyes fixed, almost unblinking, on my shoulders. Another sign that he's seen training, I thought. The curiosity that had piqued my interest grew, expanding as an autumn breeze grows stronger, catching up fallen leaves, moving them down the woodland path.

When I made no move toward him, he risked a glance behind and to either side before returning to his scrutiny of me.

"Will you talk with me a while?"

No answer.

We stood in silence for a breath or two—my breaths, that is. His chest was still heaving. His eyes flicked right, left, looking for the best escape route. I knew if I didn't do something—the right thing—quickly, he'd soon be gone.

By chance, or so it seemed at the time, a drop of blood falling from his elbow caught my eye.

"You're hurt," I said, casting about for the right bait, not knowing why I was fishing but knowing that this was a fish I had to catch. "I can help with that. I'm no healer, but I've learned a thing or two over the years."

Still no answer. His front foot shifted ever so slightly, as if he'd taken weight off it in preparation. He turned his head again. I saw how thin he was, how his neck muscles stood out like ropes, how the tunic hung from his shoulders like an empty sack. It's now or never, I thought in growing and irrational alarm.

"While I patch you up, you can eat."

His head jerked around, eyes widening involuntarily.

"I've a fine stew simmering. Fresh-killed venison, new potatoes, carrots, peas. And bread. The bread is not as fresh, but it goes nicely with the stew."

III.

He followed me through the stone lanes, but not closely. He came with me as if it were contrary to his better judgment. I continued to speak to him, attempting to assuage his fear, wondering of what he was afraid.

My efforts to get him to talk had been fruitless until, at last, he answered the simplest question imaginable. Perhaps a father would have asked such an obvious question immediately. A father would have known instinctively that it was the right question. I had not the wisdom for so simple a puzzle.

"What's your name?" I was not expecting a response.

"Boy," he said.

I'd stopped. His momentum carried him almost to my heels before he came to a halt. He scurried away.

"Boy is not a name; it's a ..." I was unable to come up with something that might be humorous. I finished lamely, "... well, it's not a name."

He stared at his feet. "Boy. That's my name."

"I'd rather not call you that."

He said nothing, taking little half-steps backward to increase the distance between us as if I were giving off an uncomfortable heat.

I stood looking down at him, thinking what to say. He raised an arm to wipe something from his forehead. A large, half-clotted drop of blood fell from the elbow. It bloomed, clear and distinct against the stones, a tiny rose.

"Come," I said, setting off again before finishing the statement, "I am wasting time."

We were wrapped in silence as we came to my home in the section of Twofords known as the Stone Gate. I pushed the door open, waved him in. He backed away, looking at the doorway as if he'd seen it in some oft-recurring nightmare.

There was little else to do, so I threw a raised eyebrow at him over my shoulder and went inside. I crossed to the hearth before looking to see if he'd followed. The doorway stood empty, a portal of light in the dark expanse of the rough stone wall. It crossed my mind that he might have fled, vanishing back into the sorrow from where he had so recently and unexpectedly emerged. That thought alarmed me.

My heart beat four times, each thump stronger than the last as I watched. Just as I was considering bolting back out in chase, I saw the toe of his bare foot inch past the door stop. Craned forward on an extended neck, the top of his head came through enough for his eyes to pass the threshold. He stood there looking like a frightened doe, turning his head this way and that, inspecting the premises while his eyes adjusted to the dimness.

I think it was the smell of food that finally defeated his caution. His head turned toward the hearth. At one side, I'd built an oven of sorts, not nearly so large as the ovens in a rich man's house, or the house of a king, but nice enough for me. I was a single man of small needs. On top of the oven rested a clay pot filled halfway to the brim with venison stew new-made yesterday. I'd set it there to warm over the dying embers this morning before venturing out. The aroma of the simmering meat—a rare luxury to many in this troubled time—painted the air with fragrant color. The child who had caught my attention raised his face in my direction. I read a question in his eyes. I smiled and nodded. Hesitantly, he moved through the door and into my home for the first time.

I gestured toward the table. The boy crossed the space

silently, carefully, seeming to watch me without taking his eyes off the pot.

"Sit and be welcome." I said this softly, not wanting to scare away the rabbit. I decided to address his cuts, scrapes, and other trophies of the recent scuffle after the meal when he might have developed more trust.

He risked a glance at the chair. Dragging it out from the table with a suggestion from his foot, he sat down. His knees, toes, and shoulders faced the open door in preparation for a quick retreat.

"I mean you no harm, child. Look, I will bring you food. I am going to get a plate and a spoon. Then I am going to put some stew on the plate, ok?"

He looked from me to the oven, then to the door and back to me. He nodded.

"Yes? I am going to move now. Don't be afraid."

He fastened his gaze on me, watching suspiciously as I fulfilled my promise. I was careful to move away from him first. I crossed to a wooden shelf near the oven, gathered a plate, a spoon, and a hunk of stale, but eminently edible bread. I paused to open the wooden shutters. A cascade of sunlight brightened the place considerably.

Not that there was much to see. Apart from the oven—which, though I am no stone smith, I had made myself—there was only a table, a cabinet, and some shelves. It was a simple kitchen, though superior to the accommodation afforded by most of the city's residents. Many of even the nicer homes inside the city walls had no indoor oven. Sadly, I felt sure that many of the residence did not eat every day, either.

This had not always been the case. It was only since the overthrow of the previous king, some three decades before, that need had replaced plenty. Under King Brand and his fathers before him, the families of Ehrylan had supported each other. There had been a prevailing sense of community. Now, in less than a man's span of years, depravation had wrought dramatic change on the Ehrylain, which is what we call ourselves.

Though I did not know at the time, this was only the beginning of the hardest years.

I pulled down the ladle and hefted a generous portion of stew onto the wooden plate. I almost stepped toward him but reconsidered at the last moment. Instead, I looked at him and raised my eye brows with a questioning tilt of my head. He responded by turning his back on me for the first time and bellying up to the table.

So does the timid doe give over caution for hunger's sake. In this case, it did not matter. I had no ill intentions for the boy. Just wanted to help. I was hoping he would sense that.

IV.

I tried to converse with him as he ate. I asked the small questions, not really looking for answers, expecting none, hoping he would grow used to my voice. Gradually, after wading through a bog of yes and no answers, it became clear that he lived outside the walls of Twofords, and even beyond the encroaching confusion of wooden structures that sprawled outside its perimeter. There were two other children, though they were not his brother or sister. The woman who kept them all was not his mother. His only description of her was "she."

He ate like a young dog, gulping the food as if it might yet get away. Occasionally, he glanced sideways, seemingly wary of an attack. When he'd nearly vanquished the two ladles of stew I'd deposited in front of him, I asked if he wanted more. He didn't look up from his plate. He just shook his head from side to side in two quick jerks, mopping at a puddle of gravy with the last of the bread. After that was gone, he sat fidgeting, his eyes moving here and there about the surface of the table and into the far corners of the room.

"Enough?"

He nodded.

"Good. May I take a look at your wounds now?"

He looked at me, cocking his head toward the far shoulder

just a little, giving the impression of a silent, "Can I trust you?"

"I can't promise it won't hurt, you understand, but I am sure I can help."

"I am not afraid of pain," he said.

I almost jumped at his unexpected voice.

"Good. Good! Just a moment."

I carried one of the chairs to a place adjacent the open window. I set it there in a pool of light, and fetched a shallow pan from one of the wall pegs.

"I am going to get some water and a few other things. Will you be alright?"

He nodded.

With some trepidation, I left the main room to gather what I needed. I remember thinking he would flee the moment I was out of the room. I also remember wondering why I cared so much. Much to my relief, he was still seated at the table when I returned.

I motioned him into the chair near the window. He came without reluctance, I was pleased to see, though he was slow and stiff arising.

He had a small bruise above his left breast; I could see it through the rip in his tunic. There were no broken ribs, but I did find a large bruise, budding with an enraged purple, on the outside of his right thigh. He had severe scratches on all his appendages. Little, angry rivers of partially scabbed blood glared at me insolently wherever I looked. A knot on the back of his head was the last of it. On the whole, he had done quite well for himself. I judged he would be recovered sooner than at least one of his attackers.

After I washed and cleaned his scrapes, I applied a salve from a small stone pot I kept in a cool place beneath my house. It was made from plants that grew far to the south in the deserts of Yar. The salve had restorative graces, especially on burns, and some ability to sooth pain.

I started to bandage his knee, but he balked at that. Nor did he allow me to stitch together his tunic.

"Why? What's the harm?"

"She'll see," he answered matter-of-factly. "She'll see. There will be trouble. Trouble for me."

I told him I understood, though that was somewhere short of the truth. I had many questions. As he was less than talkative, I was looking at disappointment square in the face. Still, there was one thing I wanted to know most of all.

"It looked to me like you have some experience with the long blade."

This struck him somewhere sensitive. He jumped in his seat hard enough that the legs of the chair grumbled against the floor.

He swallowed hard. "I've never held a sword. I've had knives, but she always finds them and takes them away. Or the others do, the other children, the bigger ones." He paused for breath, looked me in the eye before adding almost casually, "Not her children. The gangs, you know?"

"Yes. I think I do." I changed course. "Have you trained with a wooden sword?"

"No." His voice was flat. I saw the muscles in his jaw jump and his fingers clench into a fist. "Who would teach me? I've no father, and I've no sword."

"Ah. I am sorry. I can't imagine how hard that is for you. My father died when I was about twenty. I know he loved me dearly, as I loved him."

I took one of the other chairs from the table. He did not seem to notice.

I did not want to push the boy, but that curious commotion within me would not abate. I had learned long ago from a very wise man to trust my intuition, to listen to that quiet, babbling mind-voice that would not shut up. So I pressed on.

"I'll not let this rest until I have what I want, though you owe me nothing. You can leave at any time. Or, you can have some more venison." I gestured to the pot on the hearth. He shook his head. "What I want to know is this. How did you know how to swing that branch, how to turn your shoulder into your opponent, how to shift your feet close to the ground without lifting them? Where did you learn to move like that?"

Despite his refusal of more stew, he put two fingers to his mouth and sucked them briefly before he answered. "I watch the soldiers. Sometimes, when I can get away, I hide in the edge of the clearing where they practice."

"Ah. And what do you see?"

"They break up into groups. The older soldiers train the younger ones."

"What do they show them?"

"Sometimes they do the same movements over and over again. The teachers call that drills. 'Defensiff drills' and 'offensiff drills,' or something like that. I don't know what it means, but that's what they shout at the young soldiers. They stand a certain way, one foot forward and one back, and swing their swords. Then they practice stepping forward one step and swinging. They practice stepping backwards and swinging. Then to each side. Then it's two steps and swing.

"Other times, the old soldiers, they teach… I don't know what to call it. It looks like they are dancing with their swords, fighting invisible opponents. You know?"

"Yes," I said again, "I do know. Those are sword forms. They are practicing against invisible opponents, just as you say."

He was growing more excited now, more animated and alive. He shifted in his chair, turned toward me, full on, looked into my face.

"Sometimes they practice those…whadgya callem'? Sword forms? … against each other. They use wooden swords, I guess so they don't hurt each other. That's where I got the idea to practice with a stick." He was nodding to himself, unconscious of the action. "So I watch and watch, trying to rememberize what they do. Then I go off somewhere alone and try to do it myself. Today was the first time I used it against somebody else for reals. I didn't even know I was doing it, you know?"

"Yes, I know," I said once more. "That's exactly the way it is supposed to work. The forms and drills teach your body how to act so that when the time comes to fight, you don't really have to think about swinging or moving at all. It just happens. My teacher used to tell me that it is better to act than to react."

He made no reply to this. In fact, he was looking increasingly uneasy, his eyes flicking to the window and the door intermittently. Yet this subject seemed interesting to him.

"Will you stay yet for a while? We can talk more about sword forms. There's plenty for supper."

"No," he answered. "I have to go. But, I thank you for your help. You've been… kind." The last word fell from his lips like he was unsure of its meaning.

"You are welcome." I wanted to push him to stay, but that annoying inner voice was chanting a warning. So instead I said, "I hope you'll come again."

"You do? Why? What am I to you?"

"Why?" I chuckled loud enough that he heard and almost smiled himself, almost, but not quite. "Why? I don't really know the answer to that myself. But I hope you will. Anytime. Supper time is the best. I am usually here then."

"I'll remember that." He stood up and moved toward the door.

"Is there anything you need? How can I help you?"

He considered. I thought that was an excellent sign.

"I'm thirsty."

Not a parent, indeed! I had never poured him a drink, not before, during, or after his meal. I got him a cup of water. He gulped it down at a single draught after I assured him it was safe to drink. I refilled it. He finished this one more slowly.

"I thank you again. I am going now." With that, he pulled the door open and gazed out into the full light of late afternoon. He looked back at me once.

"Good bye," he said, and vanished through the door, pulling it closed after him. I had to fight the urge to rush to the window and watch him leave.

2. BEGINNINGS

I.

He didn't come the next day, or the day after. As time passed, my curiosity was chased away by the real work. Teaching children was a cover. I was building a war. It is, perhaps, understandable that I neglected to remember him. What was the boy to me? I saw a dozen such waifs every day. The poor were to be found in all corners of the city, save only on Castle Hill, an area we common folk avoided. It is true that the child had demonstrated peculiar skills, and his terse reticence had an odd, endearing quality. But, my vocation as a teacher brought me often into contact with the gifted and engaging. There was nothing to discriminate the boy from the rest, apart from the way he had faced down four older, larger bullies

On the third day, I had to deliver a message to one of my associates in the Resistance. She would pass it on to her contacts, and so on down the line. We were still recovering from the near disaster of the previous month. No one had been caught, but the fact that we had been tracked to a roadside inn was troubling. Only planning and rehearsal had saved us. And luck.

My contact was to meet me in the Shambles, a complication of wood, mud, and turmoil that laid hold of the wall encircling the city. It was almost a village in itself. I didn't go there often. City dwellers were not overly welcomed in that dim, pulsing world. The same could be said of the denizens of the Shambles, and even the villagers from River's Bend, which was a morning's walk to the south. Their presence was accepted within the Twofords only because they fulfilled necessary functions. The two groups, insiders and outsiders, tolerated each other just enough for commerce to proceed.

The situation was totally at odds with the state of our society only a generation before. The small castle atop the single hill within the walls had, at one time, served the community as a haven of justice. Since the coming of Dauroth from the Outlands, the moat had been filled with dirt, and the castle had been filled with foreign soldiers who cared for their own comfort a great deal and for justice not at all. Life throughout the kingdom of Ehrylan had taken a hard turn for the worst when we were conquered by men from distant lands.

The Shambles proper was away from the two gates. Near the gates, the adjacent space was relatively open and unobstructed. As the distance from the gates and their guards increased, so did the presence of stalls, shops, pins, and people until, at last, even the full summer sun could not penetrate interconnecting constructions.

As one moved farther from the gates and deeper into the Shambles, tolerance for city dwellers decreased. Twofords' council, a group of officious foreigners and turncoat locals who served the invaders rather than the townsfolk, did not take offense. Occasionally, a show of force was staged, a response to some imagined riot or illegal gathering. Most of us believed these were prearranged affairs, orchestrated solely for the purpose of political expedience rather than real need. Dauroth's purpose was ever to divide, to pull down, and to destroy. Nowhere could his success be seen more completely than in the separation of the good folk of Twofords, the

Shambles, and River's Bend.

It was into this profusion of structures, streets, and flesh that I had to go to meet my contact. The exchange of the message went well. I bumped into her. We both dropped packages we were holding. The packages were intentionally similar to one another. If one or two wound up in the wrong hands, who would know? Once that was done, we drifted apart.

I was careful to conduct other business, too. In truth, I spent more time shopping than I did war mongering that day. I exchanged a few pennies for herbs, and a silver crescent for a fist-sized chunk of tenur root. When I was done with that, I hid away my money pouch and moved back toward the Old Road. Though I had bought the right to linger a while, it did not pay to remain in the Shambles when you had showed coin.

That night, I fell asleep watching the glow of the moon around the knuckles of the shutters. That night, I had the dream again. It was a familiar dream, one I had suffered through many times in the last three decades. It had, for me, all the qualities of a nightmare; but it wasn't. The dream was a sleeping remembrance of real events, a reliving of the first time I had ever killed a man.

My friend and I had been on a hunting expedition. Neither of us had yet seen sixteen summers. We had our hunting knives and bows, but not our swords. This occurred in the last month before the Outlanders started their invasion in earnest. But for my friend and me, the invasion started that night.

We were walking back to camp, deep within our homeland, unaware of the peril that waited around the next turn of the forest path. Tired—and more than a little dispirited—from the fruitless chase a wily buck had led us, we were not talking as would have been more usual. That, more than anything else, is what saved us from blundering right into the midst of Ehrylan's enemies. Something caught my friend's ear, or maybe it was his nose. He stopped dead in his tracks, held up a hand. I thought he had seen another deer.

Once we stopped, I heard the voices. They were chanting.

My friend and I looked at each other, the implications tumbling through our minds. Our hearts began to race as we stared at each other across the dusky light of a tree-dimmed evening. The more we listened, the more we knew there could be no mistake. Those voices were not speaking with any of the languages prevalent in the kingdoms of the Crescent, and they were certainly not singing praises to the All Father.

Adopting a stalking aspect, we crept closer to the twisted singing. We melted into the forest, approaching under the shelter of its trees. It took a long time to get close enough to make out what was going on. By then, darkness had laid hold of the mountains.

The chant swelled in a crescendo. A single voice lifted above the rest, shouting a command. At once, a storm of flame bellowed upward from the center of a clearing. We froze, my friend and I, partly from not being able to see with our fire-blinded eyes, mostly because we were too scared to move. Truth to tell, I thought we might be seen straight away. I was ready to bolt.

There was a smattering of talking, orders, answers, and the like. We were still several paces from the edge of the clearing. In it was a ring of figures. Four of them were soldiers of some sort. The others wore black robes. Even in the darkness, their hoods were pulled over their heads, hiding their faces.

My mind screamed, "Dryhm!" I almost gasped with the fear that swelled within me. How could Dryhm be here, so deep within Ehrylan? Neither my friend nor I had ever seen one of these Outlandish priests before, but we had heard plenty. They were said to be inhumanly cruel.

Between the circle of eight and the fire, three men were bound hand and foot in kneeling positions. They were gagged. Each of them wore the cloaks and insignia of Ehrylan's warriors. They were King Brand's men! The hostages were our countrymen.

Next to the captured Ehrylain—that is what we call ourselves in the Old Tongue, not Ehrylanners as the Common Tongue would have it—stood another Dryhm. He was obviously the leader of this group of... what? Spies? Raiders? He signaled to one of the robed men. That man dragged one of the bound Ehrylain to an altar near the fire.

When the prisoner had been secured to the altar, the leader stepped forward. He took the gag out of the man's mouth. In heavily accented Common Tongue, the robed figure said, "Call to your god. Beg. He cannot deliver you from the Dryhm. Tonight, your blood shall slake the moon's thirst, and ours, as well. Blood and thirst are real things. Your god is not."

The threatened man did no cry out for freedom or even for salvation. After spitting to clear his mouth, he growled, "You won't get away with this. Maybe you will kill me and my friends, but justice has a way of pursuing murderers. Soon enough, you and your armies will be cast back into the Outlands where you belong."

"Soon enough, you say? It will not be soon enough for you. You will die tonight. By the next full moon, our armies will be streaming across your borders. A month or two after that, my master will sit atop the marble stool your feeble king calls a throne."

The Dryhm held up a crooked knife. From where we were, my friend and I could not see the moon, but its light gleamed off the cruel blade. Finally, I understood what was happening. My blood seemed to freeze within me. They were going to sacrifice these men!

We were a hard day's ride from anyone that could do something useful to help. The thought of rushing back to tell our fathers what we had seen raced across my mind. That would mean we had to leave these men to die. I could not do that.

Careful not to make a sound, I turned to my friend. Our eyes met. The truth of it struck us both at the same time. We had to free these men. I sat as if dazed while I looked at the problem. But not my friend; he turned inward. I had seen him do it so many times it was a familiar occurrence to me. He was thinking, designing a solution. In a moment, he signaled that he was going to make his way around the circle to some other quarter. I knew he would not go directly across, because then his arrows might hit me. Had not our fathers drilled that lesson into us? Never shoot your bow in the direction of something you don't want to kill. There was another wisdom in my friend's tactic. By splitting up, we might make the enemy think they were being attacked by a larger force, and not just by two boys barely old enough to hunt on their own.

As he moved away, I thought about what had to be done. I was about to take lives, perhaps give my own. I had never killed a man before. That thought, and the notion that all that was about to change, echoed between my ears. But that part is never in the dream. In the dream, as soon as my friend moves away, the screaming begins. It is always the same. First comes the fire, then comes the gleaming knife, then come the screams.

What really happened, what the dream does not show, is that the head Dryhm incanted for some time in a language I had never heard before. Foul, in the extreme, it seemed to me. When he was done with that, he bent over the sacrificial prisoner and sliced open the man's tunic, baring his chest. Then, once more, the Dryhm held the crooked knife high so that the moonlight glanced off the metal blade

Both hands still held above his head, the priest said in the Common Tongue, "The blade will drink, we will drink, and the moon will drink. Only the cold stone goes thirsty, for she is not with us. Die now, and take this message to your god. The Dryhm are come, and with us comes the Faceless. All will serve the Faceless and despair." Having delivered himself of that soliloquy, the priest left his hands in the air a moment longer, turning the blade so that he could stab downward with it.

This was, as I have said, the first time I had ever seen a Dryhm. I was almost cowed by the visceral presence of the man, the command of his voice. The strength of his convictions threatened to overwhelm me as I stared open-mouthed at him, my bow ready but forgotten in my hands.

My friend's first arrow took him full in the chest. I saw it come all the way through and vanish with a sputter into the fire. The head Dryhm staggered back a step, then collapsed, gasping a spray of blood. Before he hit the ground, a second arrow hit one of the priests who had taken a station near the other two prisoners. That is when the screaming began. That is when I remembered myself. I got off two shots, though not so quickly as my friend. Two soldiers fell, the first clutching at the hole my arrow had made in his throat and the other grasping at the shaft that had sprouted from his chest. That left five more enemies, all of whom were screaming. The young night was suddenly old with profanity.

These men, though they were Outlanders, were not cowards. They charged straight for me. Why all of them made for me and none for my friend, I never found out. At that moment, it did not matter. I had to draw them off far enough for my friend to get into the clearing and free the prisoners. Then the odds would be much better.

I stood up and turned to flee. My foot hit a snag. I fell hard. There was no time to get to my feet, so I rolled over. A dark form reared above me. There was only just enough light for me to see the staff in his hands. It was raised for a killing blow. As he brought it crashing down, I rolled again. He leapt closer and struck. Then there were two men above me, each poking at me viciously with their weapons. I kept rolling. They kept stabbing down at me. It may seem like a funny scene, but there was nothing fun about it, not in real life back when I was a boy, not when, as a full-grown man, I suffered through the dream time and again.

There were too many of them trying to get at me amidst the thick cluster of trees. Three of them got caught in a tangle of arms, staves, swords, and branches. I had enough time to climb to my feet. The fourth man, a soldier rushing toward me with a drawn sword, was upon me before I could turn and scamper away through the forest. Somehow, I had managed to keep hold of my bow. I swung it at him with all my might. It connected with his head. He fell to his knees.

Then the fifth man was on me. He was also a soldier. I

swung at him, but he blocked my attack easily with his sword. With a quick twist, he caught my elbow with the haft of his weapon. Agony shot up my arm. The bow fell from my hand. I looked into the eyes of my opponent. He smirked, and pushed me back a step so he could kill me. Behind him, I could see the outlines of the other three men.

Desperately, I groped for my hunting knife. It was where it should have been, a welcome friend at need. The familiar whisper of its metallic voice as the blade slid from the leather scabbard was a calming balm. I did not pause to see what my opponent was doing. Blindly, I slammed my knife into the space where I thought his stomach should be. It was there. I twisted the blade and jerked to the side as I pulled it out. A gush of warm stink splashed on the ground at our feet. Then I was off.

Back then, more than thirty years ago, they had pursued me, those other three Outlanders. They caught me, but not until I led them full circle into the arms of my friend and our liberated countrymen. Uncharacteristically, the dream I had the night after venturing into the Shambles took a different turn. Never in all the long years had the dream carried me into unfamiliar and unreal territory. But that happened now.

I was running through the forest, desperately trying to get back to the relative safety of my friends. On the verge of collapse—more from haste than exhaustion—I crashed through the trees at what should have been the edge of the clearing. But that is not where I found myself. Sprawling in an uncontrolled slide, I found myself on an open plain. Even in the dream, I knew this was something new.

In the midst of the flatlands grew a single willow tree. Somehow knowing that there was security for me under its sheltering branches, I dashed across the open ground. Then, in the way that dreams have, I was there, and all sense of peril was gone. The tree was immense, its branches arching above me, shielding me from the eyes of my enemies.

Beside me was a large, white boulder. Its bottom half was buried in the ground near the base of the tree, and a little spring bubbled up from beneath it. There was something carved on the face of the rock, an inscription. I could see it, but could not make sense of it. An urgency descended on me. It seemed very important that I get a better look at that inscription. I could not move a muscle. The harder I fought, the more firmly I was held. I struggled until, at last, utterly exhausted, I sank into oblivion.

When I awoke the next morning, I was uncommonly muzzy, too dull even to wonder at the general malaise. I washed my face and neck with cool water. There was basket of apples near the table. I took one and sat on the hearth. Cutting the fruit into pieces, I ate them one by one. While I was sucking the juice from my fingers, I remembered the dream.

It is not every day that a boy kills for the first time. Many relive that experience in their dreams, where the spirits of sorrow and delight contest. I wondered how many relived it so faithfully. With that thought, I remembered the new part of the dream—the willow, the boulder, and the spring. I sat and pondered, but there were no answers on my hearth.

Why had the recurrent hound of my slumber popped up now? The simple fact that I had been on an errand for the Resistance might account for that. As for the rest? Maybe it was nothing at all.

II.

More than a week after my encounter with the boy, I was sitting at the table, examining a scroll that purported to be an account of the history of the Crescent. Books had long ago replaced scrolls, and this document showed every sign of being quite old. The shutters were open, allowing me to use the afternoon's natural sunlight to illuminate the yellowed calf skin. I was completely engrossed when I heard a shuffling outside my doorway. I looked that way, listening for the knock.

The fingers of two small hands slid over the sill of the window. His head popped up. He looked around the room, sight of me.

"Busy?" He asked casually, as if announcing oneself through an open window was the most common thing in the world.

"Yes, but not too," I replied, trying to sound less surprised than I was. "Would you like to come in or shall we chat this way?"

"Oh, I'll come in, I guess." The head disappeared, the fingers vanished, and I heard the crunch of feet on earth.

I dropped the scroll on the table less delicately than it deserved and moved to the door. I closed my eyes and took a deep breath, letting it out slowly. Here we go, I thought, and pulled the door open.

There he was, looking up at me, not smiling, not frowning. I looked back at him, speechless.

"Well," I said finally, "If you're coming in, in you must come." I stepped back and aside, remembering his reluctance to let me near him.

"Yes," he said, and stepped into my home for the second time.

He took only a single step, not even moving far enough so that I could shut the door. I waited. One breath. Two. Three.

"In or out?" I asked.

He shot a look up at me. "In, I guess." He took three more steps, these toward the table. Familiar ground, I judged.

"Good." I swung the door closed. It shut more resolutely than I'd intended, loud and absolute. I thought he might jump or become alarmed, but he did not notice. I wondered then if I misjudged his demeanor. Perhaps what I took as fear was something else entirely.

"Would you like to sit?"

"Yes." He made no movement.

"At the table, perhaps?"

"Ok." He looked at the table, then at the chair in which I had been sitting so recently. It was out and ready to receive him. He settled into it awkwardly, not as if he was in pain, but as if the chair was an unaccustomed event.

I crossed the room and picked up the scroll, placing it in its case.

His eyes followed my hands. "What's that?"

"A scroll."

"Why are you putting it away?"

I was suddenly conscious of the fact that he was asking me questions, initiating conversation. His voice was unemotional in a way that was almost unnerving, but he was talking to me. And then, considering how best to answer him, I became quite uncomfortable.

"It's... well... valuable."

"I'm not going to steal it."

"Steal it?" The two words broke cover and ran across the space between us, squealing like a wounded pig. "I didn't... I wouldn't..." I stopped, took a breath, continued more calmly. "That's not what I meant at all. It never occurred to me that you might want to steal it... or anything else for that matter."

His eyes widened as if to say, "I steal lots of things. Don't you know?" But he didn't say that. He said, "Why did you say it was valuable?"

I considered for a moment. "I thank you for pointing that out. What I meant was that the scroll is fragile. Do you know what that means?"

He shook out a no.

"It means that if you don't treat it right, it will break or come to harm."

"Like a baby bird or an egg? Or a really young puppy?"

"Yes. Like that."

"So if I broke it, you would lose money?"

"No, that's not exactly what I meant either."

"What exactly did you mean?" He seemed to have forgotten any fear of me he might have had. I wondered which one of us would teach the other more.

"My thanks again. What I meant... mean... is that the scroll is old and can easily be broken. It has value to me, not monetary value, just personal value. I care about it like… like… how you wouldn't want to see a friend harmed."

I was going to continue on in that vein, which would have been excessively pedantic, when I realized that I did not know if this boy had friends. That stopped me long enough for him to reply.

"I understand that."

"Good." I wondered where to go from here. "Would you like to see it?"

"I've never looked at a scroll. Or a book. I've heard of them, but I've never held one, you know?"

This statement rocked me.

"Never? We can change that now." I started to pull the offending item out again, then stopped.

"Hey, boy."

"What?"

"You thirsty?"

For this, I was rewarded. He grinned so wide it looked to me like the corners of his mouth would touch the bottom of his ears.

"You bet!"

I handed him the container with the scroll in it, then brought a cup of water for him and a tankard for myself. He took a fine swallow from his cup and set it down well away from where he had placed the scroll.

"You ready to look at that scroll?"

"Yes."

I deposited the container in front of him. He looked at it dubiously for a moment, then up at me.

"Open it like this." I grasped the cylindrical case in one hand and tugged gently at the hasty knot I tied earlier.

We studied the thing for the next half hour. I tried to show him the many maps and illustrations. He was more interested in the letters and words, which were meaningless to him. I was on the verge of asking him if he'd like to learn to read when the unmistakable sound of a growling stomach announced itself.

"Ready to eat?"

"Yes!"

"Come on, give me a hand." We got up from the table, and I led him to the cupboard.

"There's no stew, but this might serve." I handed him the meat pie I'd intended to finish that evening. I grabbed two plates and two spoons and crossed back to the table. I motioned for him to sit.

I divided the pie in two, depositing the larger portion on his plate. I started to scoop out the remaining slab on the second plate then thought better of it. If I had been eating alone, I would have eaten directly from the clay container and avoided dirtying a plate. Then I second-guessed myself. Which was better to teach him, the prudence of a lazy man or proper table behavior? After a moment's hesitation during which I changed my mind several times, I finally shoveled the rest of the meat pie onto the second plate.

The boy noticed the internal struggle and asked, "What's wrong?"

"Nothing," I replied, then remembered his keen ability to detect untruths. "I was considering whether or not I should eat out of the pot to save clean the other plate."

I looked at him, wanting to see his reaction. He sat with his hands in his lap, eyes drilling into the food. The silence grew thick and expectant. I had no idea what to do, so I did the most obvious. I pulled out a chair and sat across from him. I set my plate in front of me.

"Would you like to eat now?"

"Yes."

"Then eat."

He snapped upright in his chair, grabbed the spoon, and began to gobble his food. Once again, I was reminded of a well-trained dog that stands ready to eat, salivating and twitching, awaiting the master's command, only to erupt into violent motion at the word. He thrust spoonfuls of pie into his mouth as rapidly as his chewing and swallowing would allow; the chewing was getting the short end of that stick. Bits of carrot and potato fell from the spoon with almost every bite, some on the plate, some on the table, some in his lap. As before, the pace of his eating did not abate until the food on the plate began to grow scarce. I had not yet taken a single bite from my own portion.

"More? Would you like some more?" I asked, not considering where I might get more. He looked up at me, then down at my plate. He shook his head. He seemed to draw in on himself, eyes down, looking as if he wanted to vanish, a dog anticipating the master's harsh word and perhaps harsher hand. Suddenly I understood.

Though I no longer felt any need to eat, I spooned some pie into my mouth. I chewed and swallowed, forcing myself through the familiar acts. I didn't want the food. I only wanted to set him at his ease, to somehow recall the young boy that had only moments before been looking at the scroll with me with a selflessness only a child can achieve. After a few bites, I pushed the plate back.

"Did you get enough? I've plenty and to spare."

"Yes." He was absently picking at the carrots and potatoes in his lap, carefully gathering them one at a time and placing them in his mouth.

"Sure?"

"Yes."

"May I ask you a question?"

"Yes." No hesitation, no disclaimer.

I paused, mulling over the recent insight.

When I did not speak immediately, he looked up at me. His eyebrows rose in an unspoken inquiry.

"You are not afraid... of me?"

He shook his head, a single jerk to each side.

"I thank you. I think I understand now," I said.

"Understand what?"

"The woman, when you eat, you have to wait for her to tell you to start, is that right?"

He agreed. "We don't eat together. I mean, not at the same time. They eat, the children and her. I have to wait until they are done. After they go away from the table, I can eat what's left on their plates. Sometimes, when there is extra, she puts food on my plate before they start, but I still have to wait."

"I am sorry," I said. What else was there?

"Sorry? Don't be. Soon I'll be big enough, and I will leave. I am waiting for that."

"How old are you?"

"I don't know."

"When is your birthday?"

"I don't know that either."

These admissions seemed of no great importance to him. His next comment helped me realize how close to his secret pain I was getting.

He looked at me out of the corner of his eye. "You ask a lot of questions."

"Do I?" I waited to see if he'd caught the joke. He hadn't.

"Yes."

"Does that bother you?"

"No. I am just not used to it. I mean, not used to your sort of questions." He stopped, perhaps considering, then continued. "She asks me lots of questions. Where are you going? What are you doing? Where have you been? That sort of thing. Your questions, they're different. Like you are interested, I guess."

"Maybe I am. Would that be so bad?"

He didn't answer that. I could feel a growing threat of uncomfortable strain in the room; the air felt scarce. I retreated to the previous subject.

"A boy's got to have a birthday, you know. How else will he know when he comes of age? That's important."

He plucked an imaginary scrap of food from his plate. After what seemed a long time, he said, "Important for city dwellers, maybe, and for some of the richer folk in the Shambles. But not for the poor. When there's nothing to come into, coming of age isn't so important."

True enough. I looked him up and down, seeing the worn tunic with its roughly repaired rip at the throat. I noted his bare feet. These things I had seen before. There was something new this time, a certain quality I could not identify. I wondered if he might be older than I had thought, maybe he was as old as twelve. Though there were lapses in vocabulary, he was quite well spoken. Then I realized I was walking through a hay stack, an expression we Ehrylain use to describe someone who'd forgotten he was in the middle of a conversation.

"We can pick a day to be your birthday."

He nodded.

"You could pick a day famous in history, like the day Selmer slew the dragon, or the day King Brand…"

He interrupted me. This was not something that ever became frequent. I've always remembered this particular occasion because it was the first time he did it.

"The day I leave her for the last time will be my birthday."

"That sounds excellent. Where will you go?"

"I am not sure yet. Maybe that's why I still go back there. I am still a kid, you know?" He looked up at me to make sure I was taking him seriously. I was.

"Yes, you are, but an interesting one. I'd like to get to know you better. Is that ok?"

"Yes."

"Shall we be friends?"

"Yes." And to my great surprise, he held up his right hand, palm out, and extended it slightly toward me. It was the greeting a man gives a friend he has not seen in a long time. I held up my left hand, pressing the palm to his.

Just like that, we were friends.

III.

I examined his wounds. The salve had done its work, and youth, too, which is another salve. I saw no tell-tale redness to betray the onset of the Red Death. He let me tend him again, though I could see he thought the whole procedure unnecessary.

I repeated the question I had asked him. "Where will you go when you leave?"

"I've thought about just walking away and seeing what I might see. But that is a little scary. I mean, even though things are not nice at that place, at least I get some food most days. Once I leave, I can catch food in the country and ..." He looked at me carefully. "I can steal food in the city. But I don't know what things are like ... out there. I've never been more than a day's walk from the Bend."

"Ah. I have. Shall I tell you something important?"

He nodded.

"Things are just the same no matter where you go, and also quite different."

He laughed at that, and winced as I rubbed harder at the crusty scab on his elbow. It was a prodigious trophy.

"You're going to tear my arm off?"

"Not today, I think. But one never knows."

"Just be careful. I am fragle."

"Fragle?"

"You know, fragle....like a puppy? Fragle."

I laughed, long and hard. I tried to stop, but that only made me laugh harder. I had to end my ministrations because my eyes were filling with tears.

"Fragile. The word is fragile. Fraj...eye..el." I wasn't sure even that was clear through my spasmodic laughter.

"Fragile," he repeated, quite seriously. "Why are you laughing at me?"

That sobered me up in an instant. Did I just loose myself in mirth for a moment and throw away everything I had gained?

"Please don't think that. What you said was funny, at least to me. But I was not laughing at you. When you said fragle, it just struck me as cute. Then I realized you were actually trying to be funny, to be facetious, which was even better."

I paused there, considering. Facetious—there's another word to learn sometime, but not now. "Irony makes me laugh, at least sometimes, when it does not hurt too much."

"What's irony?"

What had I gotten myself into? To buy some time, I stood up and moved back to the table. He pulled his chair across the space and climbed back on it. Almost immediately he began to inspect his plate again.

I plucked an apple from the pile and gave it to him. He smiled at me and sank his teeth into it, tearing away a mouthful with a crisp crunch.

"Irony." The word floated between us. "That's when you say one thing but really mean the opposite, like when the wind is blowing really hard, maybe hard enough to blow your hat off, and you say 'I sure am glad the wind's not blowing.'"

He nodded. I could see he understood.

"It was funny to me, you saying you were fragile. I would not describe you as fragile."

"How would you describe me?" He looked me right in the eye, almost insolent, and took another huge bite out of the apple.

I was getting into more trouble with every statement.

"You? Hmmm. Now let's see. You. You're resilient."

"Resilient? What's that?" He swallowed, then added, "And don't say 'resilient is the opposite of fragile.'"

I was astounded, since it was exactly what I had intended to say. My opinion of his intellect climbed another notch. It wasn't just that he might be older than he appeared; there was something else. I felt that wind again, the one that had whipped up my interest at our first meeting.

"Resilient means tough, rough, maybe even bendable. That's how I think of you, tough and bendable, like a young willow tree." I was watching to see what he thought of that when I remembered the dream. I swallowed hard, choking on my own saliva.

He looked at me sideways. "Can I ask you a question?"

"Yes. You may always ask me a question."

"Is resilient irony for fragile?"

I gazed at him, trying to determine if he was exercising rather sophisticated wit. But there was no humor in his eyes, only an avid desire to learn. It was a look to which I soon became accustomed.

"That, my boy, is a great question. Those two words are opposites. If you used them correctly, you might be using irony. The irony is not in the words, but in how you use them. That's how most things are, not just words. It's not things that are important, but what you do with them. Understand?"

"Well... maybe. I think so."

"You like words don't you?"

"I never thought of it that way, but, yes, I guess so. When I hear people talking and they use words I don't understand, I wish I had some way to learn them. The words, I mean."

"I noticed you liked the scroll. You seemed interested in the writing." I knew what he would say before I finished the sentence, and just how he would say it.

"Yes."

My heart quickened. It felt like I was watching my line twitch with the nibble of a fish. I was eager to haul on the pole, terrified I'd miss the bite. I had no reason to care about this child, one in a hundred or more in this out-of-the-way city. But there was something special in him, something I wanted to see.

Did this young boy remind me of the person my own son might have grown into if he had not been killed so early on, so long ago? I did not know. But I knew this felt like the most important moment of my life. I put both hands on the table and leaned across it.

As delicately as I could, I said, "Would you like to learn to read?"

"Yes!" He nearly came out of his seat. His plate flipped over and landed clattering on the floor. Instantly, almost as violently, he shrank back into his chair. He wrapped both hands around his apple, inspecting it suspiciously. He seemed to draw into himself again, to diminish.

I didn't know what to do, so I grabbed an apple for myself and took a bite, chewed, swallowed—repeated. I leaned forward again and set the apple on the table.

"I'm a teacher, you know." My words sounded false, the claim of a seller of frog bile cures and worthless potions.

He looked up. "Everyone knows that. You teach letters and numbers. You teach reading and writing. You taught the miller's son the Old Tongue."

"Yes, I do those things."

I started to move on and broach the idea of teaching him to read when what he'd said made it through the anticipation that had cast a fog about my mind. I stopped dead in my verbal tracks and thought of the repercussions, recognizing implications of which he could have no idea. Serious implications. My skin abruptly became clammy.

"Everyone knows that? Who's everyone? I did not know I was famous."

"The people in my world. I don't know what the people in your world know. You are the only stone dweller I've spent time with."

I unclenched my balled fists and rose out of my chair. I stepped around the end of the table and picked up the plate.

"How do your people know about me at all?"

His mouth wrinkled, and his brow furrowed. He looked the perfect caricature of someone who was thinking, "Art thou a fool?"

"You teach the orphans in River's Bend, don't you? At least once every moon." River's Bend was the name for the area within a crook in the Silver River just southwest of Twofords. It was also the name of the village there, a collection of huts, houses, and farmsteads that squatted on the plain within the river's curving bank.

"That's true. I do that."

"Do you think we are blind and dumb? Do you think we don't talk among ourselves?"

"No, child, never that. You are right. I was being foolish. I asked the wrong question. I was mostly wondering how you knew I taught the miller's son."

"Then why didn't you ask that? Why do you always ask two questions before you get to the one you really want to ask?"

Now it was my turn to shrink. "I think it is because I'm concerned I'll offend you. Listen, I want you to know this. I don't do it because I think you are stupid, or that you won't understand, ok?"

"Yes," he answered, nodding.

"Believe me?"

"Yes."

"Good. Maybe we can make a deal. How about if I teach you to read and you teach me to ask better questions? Or maybe it's that I need to ask questions better?"

He stared at me, attempting to see if I were making fun of him. Then he said, "A deal, huh?"

"Never mind about that. If you want to learn, I'll teach you to read, or write, or add, or subtract even if you won't help me. I suspect I have as much to learn as you do, at least in some ways. But what I really want to know—need to know, actually—is how you know I taught the miller's son the Old Tongue?"

"Why is that so important?"

I had to fight hard not to scream in frustration. I rubbed my hand over my face and took a bite of my apple. He took the opportunity to rip another chunk from his. After I swallowed, I started again, opening his first history lesson. I account this as the first of learning sessions we had, sessions where I frequently benefited as much as he did.

"Child, who speaks the Old Tongue now? Do you know?"

"The Old Ones, of course, the Children of the Forest. We don't see them often, but, when we do, they talk to us in the Common Tongue and to each other in the Old Tongue. I think it might be their language, you know?"

"Yes. Who are they, do you know?"

"Marn says they are the rimmints of the people who were here before the soldiers came."

"Remnants," I said. "Remnants."

"Remnants," he said. "It means what's left over, right?"

"Right. And Marn is correct. The Children of the Forest are the descendants of the folk that lived here before the soldiers came, and even before King Brand's ancestors first ruled this kingdom. They helped King Brand fight against the invaders and refuse to give up the fight to this very day. But there are so few that they can't make open war, and they don't leave the Old Forest, which is where they have always lived. They are the reason it is not safe for the soldiers in the Old Forest."

"So why does it matter what language they speak?"

"Dauroth made it against the law to speak the Old Tongue. They are breaking the law, his law, anyway."

"And you are breaking the law by teaching it!" He looked happy with the revelation, but the look dissolved again just as quickly. "So why did you teach the Old Tongue to Marc, the miller's son?"

"Because the miller asked me to. He has not forgotten the days of King Brand. And he does not want his son to be ignorant of them. Keeping the language alive is one way of not forgetting. Old legends do the same thing. But this is dangerous knowledge. The miller, his son, me, we all could be put to death if the authorities found out. That's why it's important."

"Oh." He hung his head, spoke without looking up. "You don't trust me."

I thought, "Trust you? I don't even know your name!"

What I said was, "Maybe. Maybe not. I didn't know it was common knowledge that I taught Marc that language. I thought they would keep it more secret."

"Maybe they trust me more than you do." He stopped. "They know me better than you do."

"Yes, that is certainly true. When you were so free in talking about Marc's lessons, I was caught off guard, caught with my sword down."

"Free with my tongue? Is that what you are worried about?"

"Um… yes, I think so."

I readied for the lash of his words. In my experience, even the ridicule of an angry adult cannot equal the remonstration of a child who knows they've been wronged. I was considering the placations I might use in defense when he broke in on my thought.

"You don't have to worry about that. I only brought it up because we are alone. I was pretty sure you already knew you had taught Marc to speak the Old Tongue, what with you being there."

I looked at him, sure I heard humorous reproach in his voice. I was right. He was grinning.

IV.

The boy showed interest in the history of Ehrylan from the beginning. He knew the soldiers of the garrison were invaders from foreign lands. He knew of King Brand, whom Dauroth had overthrown. He may have heard stories from someone that had actually been alive during that time; the miller was one of those. I was certain he had never had access to someone with my knowledge of the Outlands—the world beyond the Crescent. I shared with him some of my perspective of the war, the memories of one who saw it and lived through it first-hand. That perspective had been dearly bought. The price I paid was the loss of my friends and my family, all of them, every one.

He knew of the Five Battles, could name them in fact. I told him details he could not have heard before, details that may not be remembered by anyone now alive save me alone. He listened attentively, asking questions, as was his way, at every turn. He showed a broad familiarity with the calamities that had befallen King Brand's kingdom. But he knew very little of the other six of the Crescent's kingdoms. His knowledge of the world beyond them was almost non-existent, as if the boundaries of humanity stopped at the shores of the ocean to the west and the Great Mountains to the east. Perhaps that was to be expected. His life would not benefit from such knowledge. He had little room for useless facts.

I brought out the scroll again. I showed him drawings depicting the historic events we were discussing, and maps of Ehrylan and the other six kingdoms where those events occurred. I read him some of the shorter entries and pointed out common words that were easy to recognize: it, and, the, a, him, her, king. Though this was not a lesson on reading, I used the opportunity to grease the wagon wheel, as we say.

Eventually, like all long-winded teachers, I puttered to a halt in my discourse. My mouth was dry, and I wanted a drink. I stood up, stretching, listening to the bones in my knees and ankles snap and pop like dry twigs. Looking out the window, I thought I had best close the shutters and light the lamps against the growing darkness. I moved to do so.

"It's getting dark," I said, stating the obvious, a thing I have found both equally annoying and useful in my long life. This time, it proved valuable.

"Oh! I have to go. Right now! I have to go." He was already headed for the door.

"Why?"

He stopped dead in his tracks and gave me that look again, the look of someone attempting to reason with the village idiot.

"You know I have to be outside the gates by dark." There was reproof in the words.

Outsiders, particularly those without the trappings of wealth, were not permitted to remain inside the walls after dark unless they were in the company of a resident or had a paying berth in one of the taverns and inns. This, like many of the ordinances created by the Council, was enforced only sporadically, usually when some ulterior motive was served. When the rule was enforced, those caught within were punished with beatings, incarceration, or, if they could pay, fines. In some cases, the Outsider simply vanished. No explanation was offered; no inquiry was entertained.

The gates were shut promptly at sunset and opened promptly at sunrise. As was the case with almost every responsibility that belonged to the garrison, promptly meant the events occurred generally within an hour or so of the stated time. That was well in this case, for it yielded some hope that the child could make it out, if not before the darkness fell, at least before the gates did.

He reached the door, pulled it open.

"Will you come again? I mean, I hope you will come again."

"I'll come again." He looked out at the darkening street and then back at me. "But one thing. Something I've wanted to ask you all afternoon."

"Yes?" My mind stormed with a thousand possible questions. In the instant I waited, I calculated an answer for each of them. When it came, his question was not among those I had considered.

"That meat pie," he said, a statement rather than a question.

"Yes?" I waited, breathless.

"It's just stew in a crust, isn't it? Like stew, but in a box you can eat."

My mouth opened and closed repeatedly, like a fish, as I struggled to make an answer. I need not have bothered. He was gone. This time he left the door open. I stepped forward to close it, expecting to see his form vanishing down the stone lane. I saw only the lengthening shadows. My mind held the image of him just before he'd darted out, clear as sunlight dancing on a freshly polished blade. He'd thrown me a sidelong glance, looking at me from the corner of his eye as a dog will when it does not want you to know it is looking at you. Just in the instant before he fled, he'd smiled that face-splitting smile.

3. ALTERCATION IN THE BENDWOOD

I.

The next time he came, it happened the same way. It became a ritual for us as time progressed.

His face in the window. "Busy?"

"Yes. But not too. Would you like to come in or shall we chat this way?"

"I'll come in."

We acted this out many times over the next few weeks. Eventually I convinced him to knock on the door. Later, we forwent even that ritual, and he began to let himself in. By that time, we'd established set meeting times. Not regular times, mind you, but days and times we agreed to in advance.

I tired of referring to him as boy or child and decided to take the elk by the ears and fix the situation. By then, he was well on his way to reading. He had already learned his letters, could recognize many words, and sound out those he did not. I'd started him on numbers that morning. I waited until he was deep within his lesson, setting numbered tiles we'd made in the correct order, 0 through 9, before approaching the subject.

"I've a question for you, child."

He looked up at me, his tongue poking out of the corner of his mouth in his effort to correctly cipher the oh-so-cryptic number line. He didn't speak.

"I asked you this before. I want to ask you again. What is your name?"

He considered this, setting the tile he was holding, a crudely drawn 8, on the table. He put it in the correct place.

"She calls me boy. But…" He seemed to fight an internal struggle. "But my friends, they call me Gammin."

"Gammin. That's splendid."

"What's splendid?"

"Gammin. Your name, I think it's a good name for you."

"No. What does splendid mean?"

"Oh, sorry. Splendid means wonderful and grand."

"Why didn't you just say wonderful and grand?"

"Ha! Good question. The truth is, that's just how I talk. Another time, I might have done just that, said grand and wonderful, that is. But not this time. This time I thought splendid, so that's what I said."

There was silence. He reached down, his fingers hovering over the 8 tile, then retreating without touching it. He looked up at me. "Would you like to call me Gammin?"

"Yes. I'll call you Gammin. It is a very good name. It's a word from the Old Tongue, and I like the sound."

"A word? From the Old Tongue? What does it mean?"

"It means tadpole."

"Tadpole? Like the frog?"

"Yes. Like the frog, or more accurately, like a very young frog, before it grows legs."

"Why is that a good name for me? It doesn't seem very nice."

"No? Well then, you are to consider this. There are a lot of tadpoles in the pond at first, but only a few are strong enough to grow to adulthood. Fewer still, maybe only one or two in several generations, grow up to become the frog that rules the roost, so to speak. Another way to think of it is this: Even the frog that rules the pond was once a tadpole. You must learn to think this way, to think a circle around every problem."

He was silent, perhaps considering the implications of what I'd said. He was still thinking when I told him my name, Annen. I did not volunteer that *annen* was also a word from the Old Tongue, but it did not matter. He asked me if it was, saying that it had the same sort of sound. I told him it meant luck, hope, or sometimes even servant, depending on the usage. That sparked another discussion of how one word or sound can have more than one meaning. What I did not tell him was that, in another land and another language, *annen* meant lost wanderer.

Eventually, we exhausted his interest in homonyms. He started to work on the number line again. I let him adjust a tile or two before interrupting.

"Tell me about your friends, the ones who call you Gammin."

He looked up as if I had startled him.

"You know I run with Marc, the miller's son. The miller and his wife are friends too, that's for sure. There's Dara and Marn, and Marin and Arica. I guess those are most of them, most of the people that would claim me as friend."

Claim me as friend. He said it as if he had no right to declare the friendship himself.

"Dara, Marn, Marin and Arica? Who are they? Those are old names."

"They live in the forest near River's Bend. Dara and Marn are the parents. Marin and Arica are brother and sister. Marin, that's the brother, he's my best friend."

He finished lining up the numbers correctly on the first try. This was an exceptional achievement. He'd only learned them as we made the tiles earlier that day. He was quick that way and, yet, sometimes frustratingly slow.

I never learned to predict when he might be which.

II.

In the sixth month of the year—Middle Moon as it is called in Ehrylan—a specter of fear began to grow in Twofords. There was no uncertainty as to the cause. From the highest to the lowest, we knew what was coming and when. The only uncertainty was upon whom the weight of the shadow would drop.

Gammin's visits had become more frequent as summer approached. Though we still talked a good deal, more of the time was spent each session in the pursuit of knowledge—letters and numbers mostly, but also geography and history. On some occasions, I took him with me as I moved about Twofords completing the various chores and tasks that accompany living.

One day, I took Gammin to the butcher with me. I did not, as a rule, allow him to accompany me when I was on Resistance business. That day was an exception. There could be no harm in it. He could not have known what I was about. We dropped off the carcass of a doe I had killed earlier that morning. Secreted in the meat was a small stone vial. In the vial was an encoded message.

After the butcher, we headed back to my home in the Stone Gate. As we made our way, the boy saw someone on the far side of the busy market street.

"Is that a Gatherer?"

"Yes. Don't stare. Don't look at him at all. Just ignore him." I quickened my pace, putting myself between the boy and the fiend.

Ignoring the figure seemed to be the order of the day. The current of people on his side of the street parted like water flowing around a large rock in a small stream. People cast their eyes down or looked anywhere but toward him. The closer we got, the quieter it became. When we were abreast of him, there was near silence.

The Gatherer was clad in a hooded robe that encased him head to foot. On his breast was a silver broach in the form of a wolf's head with ruby eyes. The figure held a staff. He stood motionless, his face hidden within the confines of his hood.

We hurried past, relieved, like everyone else, when the course took us out of his sightline. Gammin started to question me. I stilled him with a gesture of my hand. He seemed to understand and remained mute the rest of the way.

Middle Moon is a time of clear skies and moderate temperatures in the Southland. It is difficult in such agreeable weather to remain somber. By the time we reached my door, we were recovered.

The house was cool and dark. I opened the shutters, spilling in a lake of sunlight. Gammin fetched me a tankard of water and a smaller cup for himself. Placing them on the table, he settled into the chair I now thought of as his and waited for me. I splashed water from the basin on my face and ran my fingers through my hair before taking my own place across from him.

"I was going to teach you more about sums today, but there's a more important matter to discuss."

"The Gatherers?"

"Yes, and about the Tax. What do you know of the Gatherers?"

This was something I had been planning to discuss with him, not knowing if he was aware of the evil on the horizon. Most parents talked about this unpleasant subject with their children by their seventh year, but Gammin's situation made such a disclosure improbable.

"Last night at supper I heard the woman talking to Kam and Kami." Those two were the brother and sister with whom Gammin shared the small farmstead he never called home. "Kam saw one of the Gatherers at the gate, another in the Shambles. He asked her about them."

"What did she tell Kam?"

"She said that they were the king's men come to take children away. Not all the children, just some. You know?"

"Yes, I know, and it is time you knew as well. Would you like something to eat first?"

"No," he answered, surprising me. He seldom declined an offer of food. "I want to know about the Gatherers and the Tax."

"I will tell you."

The pacing started before the telling. There was so much to say, too much for Gammin's young ears. I could not find a place to start until I remembered one of King Brand's many sayings. Things can't work out for the best if you don't start from the beginning. So I did.

"In the first years after King Brand fell, there was calm in the kingdom. At least, it was calm compared to the years of war we'd just lived through. The armies of Ehrylan had been defeated. Most of the able-bodied fighters had been killed or deported as slaves. Many fled with their families to one of the other kingdoms. Some saved themselves by swearing fealty to the Dauroth, the invader from the Outlands."

I stopped to give Gammin a chance to ask questions. None came.

"Some loyalists—that's what we call folks who hold true to King Brand—took their families and melted into the forests, mountains, and swamps of Ehrylan."

Gammin nodded. He said, "The Old Ones."

"I am not talking about the Old Ones—they refer to themselves as Children of the Forest. They have been in the Old Forest since before there was an Ehrylan. I am talking about the subjects of King Brand before Dauroth came, those who refuse to submit to his rule. According to Dauroth's law, it is death even to speak with them."

I waited for more from him, but he was silent again. That was unusual. He was typically a font of questions.

"Dauroth sent soldiers to areas that held strategic importance or to regions that hosted pockets of resistance. Twofords wasn't either of those, but, eventually, a garrison came to the castle that guards the two fords across the Silver River."

Gammin gave me a questioning look. "Is there a Gatherer in this story?"

"Yes, I am coming to that right now. When Dauroth's tax began. The people paid willingly enough; there had always been a tax, even in the days of King Brand. At first the levy was simple, gold or some equivalent measure of goods or services. Then the Gatherers arrived and read Dauroth's decree."

Gammin exclaimed, "There must be an awful lot of them to go to every city in the kingdom at the same time!"

"No, child. The Tax takes place in different months in different regions of Ehrylan. In this region, the Southland, it takes place during Harvest Moon, the tenth month. In Kingsholm, far north where Dauroth holds court, the Tax occurs during War Moon, the eighth month. In Darkhold, it's in the seventh month, Fire Moon."

"In the eighth year of Dauroth, the Gatherers began to steal our children. It was just another tax, they said."

"Didn't the people of Ehrylan resist?"

"Of course. There was bloodshed throughout the land. Even now, more than two decades later when most people can't recall life before the Tax, it's not unheard-of for folk to take arms and rise up against the Gatherers. When that happens, the whole village or city suffers. Farms are burned and…"

I had to stop there. My mind flooded with images of children being wrested from the dead arms of their parents while fields and farmhouses crumbled to nothing under the weight of howling flames. I took a long pull at my tankard. I finished the water, but there was no relief. My thirst was a parched heart. Crossing to a cask set into a niche in the wall, I filled the tankard with local ale, brown and rich. I downed that potion in a series of angry swallows and refilled before returning to the table.

"The children are taken into Dauroth's service. They become soldiers, or scholars, or engineers, or carpenters. A few are selected for the service of Dauroth's gods; those few become Dryhm. There's no set number for the Tax, or if there is, it's never declared publicly. The Gatherers take a few each year from each area. They call the event a Choosing. I've heard of as many as twelve being taken from one village during a Choosing. Twice, I was in a village when no one was taken. Even then, even though they took no one away, the Gatherers came.

"They come and go for weeks and sometimes months before the Choosing, always accompanied by armed escorts. They do their choosing at the first full moon of the harvest."

I swallowed more ale.

"The Tax follows a seven-year cycle. Girls between the ages of twelve and sixteen are carried away the first year. Then, for two years, boys between thirteen and sixteen are taken. The cycle is repeated for the fourth, fifth, and sixth year—girl, boy, boy. On the seventh year, there is no Tax. That has become known as the Fallow Year, though I hate to see such a blessed term applied to such foulness. That is Dauroth's way. He takes what is good and wraps it in spite to make it hurtful."

My voice was beginning to break. I drained the tankard and slammed it down on the table. It shattered in a storm of splinters. The Tax, more than any other demonstration of Dauroth's hideous strength, assured that the Ehrylain would continue as a conquered people.

We were in the sixth year of the cycle. Next year, Twofords would rest in the Fallow Year. This year, we would give up our sons to the conqueror. And summer was upon us. The young danced and played in whatever scant time their daily chores left them. Mothers and fathers looked on, watching, waiting, wondering.

I made sure Gammin understood that this was not the natural order. He asked me to tell him more about the Gatherers themselves, but there was little more I could contribute. The Gatherers could be either men or women. They came and went with impunity. They were Dryhm, the acolytes who served the Faceless, Dauroth's foreign god. The Dryhm kept what they called sacred temples in most settlements large enough to be called a city. Twofords had its own nest of Dryhm. Their stronghold was high up on Castle Hill, in the Grove.

Gammin asked the question at which I had been worrying. "Will they take me?"

"I do not think so. Not this year. You look too young and there is no one to mark the year of your birth. Next year you are also safe; it will be Fallow then. The year after is for girls. After that, for the next two years you are certainly at risk."

"That's not what I meant. Will they take me, a fatherless boy, a poor boy?"

"The Gatherers... no... Dauroth takes the rich and the poor. The Tax takes the brightest and the best, the strongest, the most promising."

"The king would want the best in his armies, wouldn't he?"

"Please do not refer to Dauroth as king. But, yes, you are correct. Any ruler wants the best servants he or she can get. That's not why he takes whom he takes."

"Why, then?"

I started to answer, changed what I had been going to say. "You tell me. Why would he do that?"

He considered, but not for very long. "I don't know."

"Come with me. I will show you."

I took him out through the one of the doors that opened off the main room. This let on to a hallway. Half way down the hall, I opened a door on the right and led him into the central courtyard of my home.

"Wow! I never... you didn't...do all the houses in Twofords have this?" He tossed his arm out, indicating the tiny collection of trees and stones that comprised my courtyard.

"I don't know. I haven't been in most of them."

I led him to my piled fire wood. "Gammin, look at the pile. How is it laid?"

He barely glanced at it before he spoke. "Marn, that's Marin's father, he's a woodcutter. He lets us pile the wood he brings back from the forest."

"I imagine so," I said drily.

"What do you mean by that?"

This child did not miss anything. "I was thinking he probably welcomed the help of your strong arms."

"I am not strong, at least not compared to Marin. Anyway, Marn, the woodcutter, he taught us to pile the big pieces along the bottom and the smaller pieces on top."

"Did he tell you why?"

"If you put the small ones on the bottom and the big ones on the top, the pile falls over."

"Yes."

"What does that have to do with the Tax and the Gatherers?"

"You asked why Dauroth would take the smartest and strongest children if it were not because he wanted them for himself. I asked you to look at the wood pile. Does the answer not suggest itself?"

We stood in silence while he considered. I enjoyed the fresh air and the breeze, but not nearly as much as I enjoyed teaching the boy. Finally, he shrugged his shoulders and said, "I don't know, Annen."

"Ah," I replied. I clasped my hands in front of me. They made a soft plopping sound as they met. "Perhaps later. Let's go back inside and do some reading."

He looked at me quite perplexed, then began to follow. I stopped as soon as he stepped after me. "Oh. I was forgetting. Will you please grab some kindling?" He obediently retrieved an armful of twigs from the top of the pile. "Maybe we'll need some logs too. Here, give me that small stuff. You grab those two logs." I pointed to pieces of wood about half way down the pile. He looked at me again, even more perplexed, then handed over the twigs and branches.

Gammin put a hand each on the two logs and looked back at me. "These?" He asked with his eyes. I nodded.

"I'll need to move the wood on top to get to these," he said. His eyes flicked momentarily to the side of the pile where large logs were already lying exposed. It was from there that any sane person would take the next piece.

"No, pull those two out. Those are the ones I want."

Without further comment, he tugged firmly and quickly at the two logs in the middle of the pile. They came out. The logs above fell in to fill the void. That started a cascade. Within a single breath, that section of the woodpile collapsed into a muddle.

When the last log had settled into its bed of chaos, Gammin looked back at me, perhaps thinking I would scold him for his carelessness. I was fortunate enough to see his eyes the instant question turned to realization.

He stood right in front of me and looked up. His eyes shined like stars. They were winter-grey. "Dauroth takes the strong because, without them, we can't hold together."

"Yes, Gammin. You've done very well." He smiled a swift smile. It lit his face, a bolt of lightning, and fled as quickly away.

"I thank you," he answered, starting to move back into the house. I stopped him.

"The wood larder is full; didn't you notice? The night will be fine in any case. There's no need of more wood." I dropped my load of kindling on the small sea of firewood, motioned for him to do the same, and walked away.

III.

Next morning, he came early. It was uncommon for him to appear two days in a row. I requested it in advance, so he was able to make whatever arrangements he needed to make.

After he'd conquered an army of fruit and porridge, I slipped the sling of a water bag over my shoulder and tossed him an empty pack, really just a sack with two arm straps. My plans included a covert message drop. They did not account for the violence that lurked just out of sight.

The day began pleasantly. We picked up the deer we had dropped off at the butcher. I loaded the meat, wrapped and ready for transport, into the pack.

I led the way toward the orphanage. It was the only one in town, and it was in one of the less-prosperous parts of the city. The market street took us down to the wide avenue that ran along the interior of the city wall. There we turned west and walked to the dilapidated building that was called, by those who loved it, the Step. Those who lived their often called it Stepholm.

In the time before Dauroth, the predicament of orphans was the concern of all good people. They were cared for by guardians appointed by the king's administration. The laws of guardianship were ancient. Dauroth had no such compunctions. Orphans received no special attention. There was no consideration for the welfare of the poor and helpless either. Consequently, the care of the poor, homeless, and orphaned fell to those who remembered and followed the old ways.

The Step was similar to my house, four wings surrounding a courtyard. It was about the same size. Unlike mine, this structure was constructed almost entirely of wood. The roof was thatched with rushes from the wetlands adjacent the nearby river. The building and grounds were tattered like a threadbare cloth, not from lack of care, but from long use. On the whole, the place gave the impression of a garment that had been worn away through constant care.

Even before we turned off the wall street, I heard a sharp cry. This was followed by a chorus of delighted squeals. The door burst open. A frenzy of children rushed to meet me. Gammin took two quick steps back. There was no time for me to turn and tell him to stand easy. Before I could even glance over my shoulder, the river of arms, legs, and squeals broke over me. I was engulfed.

I need not have worried for Gammin. He was ignored completely. Eventually, I found the time to look back over the tops of heads and upstretched hands. Our eyes met. I'll never forget that look. It took me quite by surprise. The tadpole was not alarmed. He was amused.

I lifted my eyes from the sea of smiles and looked at the

doorway to the house. This was filled with the form of Merelina, the proprietress of the Step, and the guardian of these children. She was definitely not tall. Her body was slender. Yet, when I was in her presence, I had the feeling I was with a large, stout woman whose embrace would be warm, welcoming, and all-encompassing.

Merelina leaned against the side of the doorway, one foot crossed in front of the other. Her hair, black with a single streak of grey at the front, was pulled back in a tail and held with a piece of leather that had been dyed blue. Her long dress was neat and clean. It was so old and often-mended that the original color was impossible to tell. When our eyes met she smiled, looked down at her hands, and shook her head slowly.

"You again?"

"Yes, me again. You always were observant." I pushed the words out as a shield, tried to hide behind them. Merelina could take my breath away with a single look.

She laughed openly. I saw the flash of fine, white teeth. She smiled a smile that was pleasant to see and shook her head a second time.

"Children, children! Let the poor man in."

At her word, the soup of children boiling about my legs parted.

With a toss of my head, I told Gammin to follow and walked through the gate, up the path, and into the Step. The children waited for me to go in first. Merelina motioned toward one of the three large tables that filled the room. Before I could take my place, she threw her arms around me. My arms encircled her automatically.

"It's good to see you, Annen."

"And you, Lina. It's good to see you."

She placed her hands on my chest where her face had just rested, and pushed herself away.

"Sit. You want water."

In those days, water in Twofords could be a risky thing. The ducts and channels that had for centuries delivered water had fallen into disrepair since the coming of Dauroth. Most city dwellers contented themselves with ale or juice. Those who could afford them drank wine or canella, a non-intoxicating, softly flavored brew made from crushed leaves. Others drank kef, a hot beverage brewed from ground, roasted beans. Canella and kef were less risky to drink than water. Boiling of the water made it more wholesome, not any special attribute of the leaves. This knowledge was not widely held in Ehrylan at the time, having been forgotten along with so much of the Healer's lore.

I had no fear of Merelina's water. It was filtered and boiled. I accepted the dipper and sat down on one of the rough-hewn benches that bordered the tables. There were no chairs.

She sat next to me. I handed the dipper back to her and she delicately finished the contents, gazing at Gammin. He was standing just inside the door in a pool of children. Most of them were even smaller than him. I think Merelina was going to ask me about him. Before she could, a boy that was a full head shorter than Gammin stepped boldly up to him.

"Who are you?"

Gammin answered, "I am nobody."

"Everybody's somebody; that's what Temay says. What's your name?"

"Shouldn't you tell me yours first?" Gammin looked over to me. I wondered if he was thinking of a time not so long ago when I had failed to honor this time-honored protocol. I also wondered at the comfort and ease with which he was dealing with this situation. He seemed to be a book of many pages.

Pushing out his chest pugnaciously, the small child exclaimed "I'm Max!"

"Max. Hello Max. My name is Gammin."

"Gammin," stated the youngster with finality. Then, without another word, he turned, leapt across the space between us, and flung himself into my lap. I was pushed back against the table, knocking it back a hand's breadth. I let out a groan, only half of which was in jest, and tousled Max's short-cropped hair. I gave him an affectionate squeeze before lifting him down.

"Hello, Max. Good to see you. You be kind to my friend Gammin."

"He's your friend? Then he's my friend too!" With that, Max marched back to Gammin and engaged him in a conversation that soon involved several others.

I took back the dipper from Merelina and moved off to return it to the bucket. On my way, I caught sight of a young man sitting by himself on the hearth. Instead of replacing the dipper as I had intended, I filled it half full and took it to the boy.

"Temay! It's good to see you. Are you thirsty?" I held out the dipper.

The boy was larger and older than the other children. He did not look at me, though he began to speak almost immediately. With the first word, he began to nod his head repeatedly, as if tapping out a steady beat with his chin.

"It's you again. That's what she said. I can see that. We can see it is you, and you are here again. It's obviously you when you come because, otherwise, it would be someone else. What would we do then? We would say 'It's you again' again because it would be them and they would be you. At least to them. Yes, that is right. Absolutely right."

The rapid cascade of words came to an abrupt halt as the boy's hand shot out toward me.

Without looking up, he continued. "Yes. I am thirsty. I am always thirsty. But you know that. You know that I am always thirsty because it's you, and I am always thirsty when you are here. Does that mean that you make me thirsty? I don't think so. I am thirsty when you are not here. Yes. I am thirsty."

When his head finally stopped bobbing, he turned toward me. It was a sharp, jerking motion that brought his face up for just enough time to meet my eyes. Then he returned to the study of the ground at his feet. I put the dipper in his hand, knowing he would spill it. Merelina was already fetching the mop.

He did better than usual and got most of the water into his mouth.

"May I sit next to you, Temay?" I did not wait for the answer, knowing it would be a long one.

"Of course you can sit. You must have learned to sit. Didn't your mother teach you to sit? She must have. Yes, she must have. You know how to sit. But you said you wanted to sit next to me. That's what you said. I know it is. I remember that. I may not remember your name, but I remember you wanted to sit next to me the last time you were here. Yes. You can sit next to me. You can sit next to me again because you are here again and it's you and you want to sit next to me. Sit."

"You know my name, Temay. I've told it to you before. You have a good memory, an excellent memory. You remember a lot of things." I intentionally fell into his habit of speech, his tendency to repeat things. It was an effective way to converse with him. He was certainly worth conversing with.

"I remember lots of things. Lots of things. I can't remember how many things I can't remember. But I know your name. I know your name because you come here and you are here again. I know your name. I just don't remember it. Of course I know your name."

"How are you, Temay? How's your foot?" Last time I saw him, his foot had been bandaged. No one knew how he had cut it, and he would not tell. He was always hurting himself, was Temay.

"How am I, Temay? I was thirsty, but I am not thirsty any more. My foot is fine too. My foot does not hurt, and I am not thirsty. I am fine."

In the instant before I spoke, I realized Temay had just stated the secret to a happy life. I am not in pain. I am not thirsty. I am fine. It is the simple and the children who are wisest, so King Brand used to say. The older I got, the more I understood he had the right of it.

"That's good, Temay. I'd like you to meet someone." I turned to look for Gammin. He was standing at my shoulder. Behind him, in an unfamiliar silence that was almost reverent, a crowd of young boys and girls stood watching us. I got up. Twenty sets of eyes and twenty chins followed me in hushed unison, like so many bemused kittens watching a bird take flight.

"Temay, this is my friend. His name is Gammin. Gammin, this is my friend, Temay."

Gammin stepped forward. As I feared, Temay looked down at his feet stubbornly. His head moved up and down, a silent affirmation to some unknown question. He did not say a word. In truth, Temay spoke only to a few people—myself, Merelina, and a couple of his fellow orphans. He refused to speak to others and, usually, would not even look at strangers. My concern swelled as I waited for Gammin to respond. If he felt rejected even here, among the outcast of the city, his self-esteem might be damaged, and it would be my fault.

I had yet to learn that Gammin, in some imponderable twist of fate, knew how to hold on to his own self-worth. The opinion of someone else meant very little to him. He pointed to a tray I had not noticed.

"What do you have there? Did you draw those?"

Temay's head jerked toward the tray. His hands snaked out and grabbed it, pulling it into his lap where he clutched it protectively. A few of the sheets crinkled. Temay put them down again on the hearth, smoothed them carefully, then returned them to their proper place in the stack. He sat nodding his head fitfully, staring into his lap as if counting. Then he looked at me.

"They are mine. I collected them, and they are mine."

Temay was an amazing artist, but he never referred to having painted or drawn his pictures. To his mind, he collected them; they were always exacting copies of whatever he was attempting to capture. They were always brilliant.

"I don't think he wants them, Temay. He just asked you about them. They are very nice."

"He can keep his words to himself. That's how I keep my collections, to myself. They are mine."

"It's all right, Temay," said Gammin. "I was just wondering. Anyway, we are going out to play Cross the Creek. Would you like to come?"

Temay did not answer. He stared at his lap.

Gammin turned and poked Max in the chest. "You're it!" He scampered through the doorway into the courtyard beyond. A cloud of shrieks filled the room as the herd stampeded out.

I looked at Temay, wishing I could help him. He was special. I did not see the role he would play in the great events to come, but I knew he had one. It was a premonition of sorts. I have those, sometimes, as you will see.

I stood walking through the hay stack as I pondered his puzzle. I smelled lavender. Merelina slid between us and swept the mop across the floor at Temay's feet.

IV.

We stayed longer than I had planned, though the time was well spent. I talked with Merelina for a good while, mostly about her charges and the difficulties they faced. The lady downplayed the difficulties and emphasized the small, everyday triumphs. I helped her with chores that would have been difficult for a single adult. We mended some furniture, moved others. We re-hung a shutter.

My real goals had been accomplished early on when I'd given her more than half the meat and a small package that contained the tenur root. I had prepared the latter by slicing it into small slivers and pickling them in a special solution. This was a delicacy that Temay loved in a singular way. Tenur root, even pickled, is too pungent and sour for most palates. But the boy, if allowed, would consume the whole batch in one sitting. That would be disastrous. The root, when regularly administered in the proper proportion, had medicinal qualities that seemed to ease Temay's distrust and other odd behaviors. However, like any beneficial substance, too much tenur root can kill a man by sending him into a long, slowly-progressing sleep that ends in death.

Merelina thanked me with a smile and a kind word. She touched my hand. "You are not teaching them today?"

I was making ready to depart.

"Not today. But we will come again, Gammin and I, sooner rather than later."

"Gammin, yes. I'd like to know more of him. Do you intend that he should come and stay with us here?"

"I am not at all sure my intentions matter. I've no hold on the boy and he owes me nothing. He comes and goes at his pleasure, not mine."

"You do have a soft spot. I have noticed. And the children notice. Where did you meet him?"

I told her as quickly as I could, sharing the details of how we met and the times we'd had together since. I had not discussed these things with anyone else and doing so, I found, brought relief to a sore spot I'd not known was there.

We took our leave as morning ended, after helping Merelina serve up the midday meal of rye bread and a thick soup of onions, garlic, nuts, and spinach. The new supply of fresh meat allowed her to be more liberal than was usual; she produced a hunk of cheese and shared this out between the hungry children. Though each child received only a small portion, they accepted it with much thanks.

Gammin and I made our partings with the children, promising to return before the new moon. I led him back the way we had come. We shouldered through the crowd at the gate. Once out of the city, we wasted no time with the Shambles. My business was in River's Bend.

The Old Road ran south from Twofords. It mostly followed the river through the Old Forest on its way to the river port, Mendolas. That was a perilous and uncertain passage. Dauroth's reach did not extend into the Old Forest. Few accounted it safe.

Our journey did not lead us into that particular peril, though danger waited along our route, unexpected and made more hazardous thereby. It was an hour's walk—one league as King Brand counted it—from the city to the village in the bend of the river. We turned west on Bend Road, which crossed the Old Road a mile from the Forest.

The river encompassed the village of River's Bend on three sides. To the east, a wood stood from one side of the bend to the other. The wood, Bendwood, was not a finger of the Old Forest. The trees were entirely different. We entered Bendwood without hesitation. It was a pleasant place, as open and light as the forest was dark and dense. Branches danced in sunlight.

We turned off on a short spur trail near the center of the wood. It led to a clearing. Near one edge of the clearing, a large fist of stone jutted from the hillside. A spring emerged from a glistening crack. The water tumbled into a shallow cistern. The cistern was supported on a pillar of granite. Both were covered with rough carvings. The carvings, once clear and distinct, were worn away by the passage of time.

A fragile curtain of water fell from the edge of the cistern and pooled about the base of the pillar. This was carried away in a rill that wandered to the edge of the clearing, where it vanished into the earth. A plaque set into the outcropping above the spring had born an inscription. "Come, traveler. Satisfy your thirst. Take this water. Be blessed." The well-known verse had been blotted out by Dauroth's chisels.

We stopped here, as ever I did when coming this way. The water was clear and wonderfully cool. I asked Gammin to drink first, but he refused. I pressed him; he stubbornly insisted.

I bathed my hands and face with handfuls of water, relishing the oft-repeated, ever-delightful feeling. I filled our water bag after drinking long and deep. Much refreshed, I offered Gammin a slight bow and stepped back.

As my tadpole began to enjoy the water, I moved off. Attempting to appear nonchalant, I sat on one of the stone benches that lined the perimeter. I waited until the boy was distracted with his ablution, using the time to make sure we were unobserved. I slid a hand into my pocket and closed my fingers around a tube the size of one of my fingers. I opened my arms wide to the sun in a stretch that was as much real as feigned. As casually as I could, I glanced over at Gammin. He was still involved in his refreshment.

After a final check of the clearing, I leaned forward and slid the tube into a shallow hole beneath the grass and leaves at the base of one of the bench's supports. Without looking—long practice had made the use of my eyes unimportant—I located the small rock that was laid by and pressed it into the remaining space, effectively sealing and hiding the opening. I sat for a while before rising. Then, once again moving with what I hoped appeared to be random indifference, I strolled around the perimeter of the clearing stopping to rest briefly on each of the two other benches.

I was sitting on the bench nearest the spring when Gammin began to look around for me. He trotted over and deposited himself next to me without a word. He had taken no notice of my activities, which was all the better for both of us. We sat in silence until he spoke.

"I love this place."

"So do all who revere Ea."

He made no reply. We had not discussed his beliefs, but I had no concern that he might have devoted himself to the foreign gods that were now compulsory. Few outside the city walls pledged themselves to that distant pantheon of harsh-sounding names and dubious reputations, at whose head stood a god without a face. Old timers like me remembered when the worship of Ea was open and free. We were not tempted.

I drank another mouthful from the spring and gave silent thanks to Ea, who made us all—Ehrylain and Outlander—before we set out on the last stage of the short journey.

V.

Emerging from the west edge of the wood, we came to the green on the outskirts of the village of River's Bend. The feeling here was markedly different than that of Twofords. Laughter spilled often around corners and out of open doorways. Children chased each other in games, worked together in shared labor. I would have made my home there if the work of my life did not require otherwise. But I could not. I could only invest my hope in a future where these folk could live free from the oppressor's shadow, a future where the Ehrylain would once again grow strong and vibrant. This seemed the least I could do, given my part in the events that led to this sad state of affairs.

We did not have to venture far into the village on this trip. The orphanage sat hard by the periphery of the wood. There was not much village, in any case; most of the people lived in nearby farms and ranches. Here were the inns, shops, and work yards of those who provided services to others—smith, wood wright, stone mason. The miller's wife sold delightfully rustic baked goods in a shop that always smelled amazing. This smattering of local merchants, though the title of merchant did not apply well, occupied wooden structures on either side of the wide country road. The orphanage occupied one end of what could be called, accurately though somewhat facetiously, the business district of River's Bend.

There was no rush of children to greet us as we entered the yard of this orphanage. They were busy with the wood wright, working on a building at the far side of the enclosure. Likewise, the guard dog was of no use in raising the alarm. He knew me well. He knew Gammin even better, I soon discovered. His name was Bilious. Anyone who spent time around him could attest why. Bilious, a large, one-eyed hound with floppy ears and an irascible disposition, was curled on the raised porch. When he caught our wind, he raised his head and pushed himself slowly to his feet, shifting tentatively from one side to the other in favor of his age-twisted hips. As he sauntered over to us, I was considering offering a warning to Gammin. Old Bil did not tolerate strangers. The dog ignored me completely until he'd greeted and been greeted by the boy.

"Old friends, " I said.

"Yes." Gammin, who was busy scratching the dog's ear, presented me a look that said as plain as day 'What were you expecting?' I had not put much thought into the boy's place in this community. I associated his life with the woman who, at least nominally, cared for him on a farmstead south of the village.

I started to move past. As my foot landed on the first step, Old Bil uttered a grumpy woof. In previous years, he would have planted his paws on my chest and stood wagging his tail as I tried to keep his tongue from giving me an unwanted facial cleansing. In his old age, he was unable to do so. His ingrained habit resulted only in a half-hearted maneuver that raised his front paws a hand's breadth off the ground before the pain cut it short. I bent down and made my greetings. When he was satisfied, Bil gave my hand a lick, depositing a copious amount of dog slobber that I wiped off with undisguised haste. As Gammin followed me into the building, the old fellow curled into a comfortable ring of fur, teeth, and claws and went promptly to sleep.

The room at the front of the house was adorned with sturdy chairs and a stone fireplace. All, including the shutters that stood open on either side of the door, had been constructed by masters in their craft. The rooms beyond included two dormitories, a dining hall, and a well-appointed kitchen. There were storage and work rooms. This facility had been built as a refuge for parentless children so long ago that even the memory of its construction was lost.

I rang the bell. A woman's voice answered, "Coming!"

The door leading to the girls' quarters opened revealing the pleasant face of Eanna, guardian of the orphans of the River's Bend. Before I could introduce Gammin, she reached out and tousled his hair. He responded by hugging her about the hips, a gesture that was indicative of great familiarity. Once more, I was taken by surprise though, by now, I should have contrived to understand that the boy was no stranger here.

"Greetings, young Gammin. It's long since you visited. What, not once in the last half moon?"

"I've been busy." His eyes flicked in my direction. Whether the look was accusing or thankful, I could not tell. Perhaps it was both.

"The children will be happy to see you. And you as well, Master Annen."

"It's good to be back," I replied.

Gammin gave the rest of the deer meat to her. She thanked him without the relief Lina had shown. The Bend cared for their own better than the increasingly divided and competitive lot within the city walls. There were fewer children here, perhaps only a dozen, though the facility could accommodate three times that number. Eanna and the villagers fed the children without my help.

Eanna motioned Gammin towards the back door. He headed off with the almost inexhaustible energy of youth. I did not see him again until it was too late. My mind was on Eanna and the children.

I chatted with the lady while we waited for the carpenter to have his time. It was his turn this month to teach the orphans, just as next month the miller or the stone mason or the seamstress would have his or hers. The people of the Bend had continued the long practice of teaching orphans the rudiments of various trades. Such exposure and instruction facilitated a place for them in the community, assured they had opportunity. These children had no mother or father to look to their future, no hope of assuming the family trade as was the normal way.

Eanna told how things had been in the Bend since my last visit, generally good with some troublesome events related to soldiers and other undesirable visitors from Twofords. This latter included the Gatherers, of course, for they roamed the countryside with a keen knowledge of where children lived. But the Gatherers were not yet giving any physical difficulty; that would come at harvest. It was mostly the soldiers that caused distress in the village and, sometimes, bored young adults from the city. These, usually two or three at a time or as many as ten, might stop on their way along the Old Road for refreshment or for simple mayhem at River's Bend. The trouble might take the form of drunken behavior all the way up to and including the physical abuse of village people. The folk were long accustomed to such happenings, and knew that there was no satisfaction to be gained from the Council. The occurrences were becoming more frequent and more egregious with each passing moon. Even today, Eanna told me, a small group of obnoxious young men had been lurking in the vicinity, throwing money and insults around in equal quantity.

Eanna also told me how she knew Gammin. He came from time to time, to play with the other children. He'd been known to share their table. I asked her about his living situation. She was considering an answer when the door to the room opened, and in came the wood wright.

We greeted each other, and shared a quick embrace. A few words passed between us, but each knew the other had business that needed attending. We soon parted. I left him to Eanna and headed out.

The children were strewn about the yard in groups, some still playing at the woodworking. As they caught sight of me, the groups converged, and I was once again submerged in a sea of children. I asked them what they'd been learning. The less bashful were happy to explain.

I started to settle in for the enjoyable time to come. Spending time with these children was a true joy. I could be far too long describing this happy place—the village, the people, and the love I always found there. The memory is strong, the sorrow of its loss terrible. But I must proceed to the matters that concern the boy, for this is his story. I will have it remembered as it occurred.

What the carpenter taught them evolved into a discussion of metallurgy and the desire to tailor the hardness of the metal to the needs of the tool. Someone asked why a softer blade would ever be more desirable. I was deep inside the answer when I heard the first scream.

It came to me in the instant my head jerked up. Gammin was nowhere to be seen. Another shriek. On the heels of this came Gammin's voice clear and urgent, "Run, Arica!"

I bolted in the direction of the screams.

VI.

As I charged into the Bendwood, a girl, incoherent with urgency, almost ran into me. She was looking back over her shoulder as she fled. At the last instant, she saw me and skidded to a halt, emitting a startled screech. I recognized it as the blood relative of the others I'd heard. Her chest was heaving, her eyes wide as saucers. Then she was gone. I was left with the fleeting image of a young girl a little older than Gammin.

I followed the trail back the way she'd come. Then, guided by angry voices, I changed course, abandoning the trail, and headed directly toward them. Branches ripped my skin and grasped at my clothing. I recognized at least two voices in addition to Gammin's. My apprehension grew.

I heard the words "gonna kill" and "last time."

Gammin screamed in pain.

I heard Pruis, the leader of the gang from which I had rescued Gammin. "He's not here to…"

There were other words and other sounds, blows and exhalations of pain. There was laughter, the disdainful cackle I'd heard before. Then I was upon them.

The clearing was only the size of a room, maybe twelve paces from one side to the other. What I saw stopped me in my tracks. Metal gleamed in Pruis' hand. He held a dagger at Gammin's throat. Another boy held Gammin's head back, dragging on his hair.

"Hold him still, Toram. I'm gonna cut this filthy peasant's throat," urged Pruis, "No one will even miss him."

"Wait, Pru! Not yet." This was from Demus, the boy Gammin had kicked in the groin the last time they'd met. He was keeping his distance from the danger. "Don't kill him yet. I owe him something."

An ugly frown splashed Pruis' face. He turned toward Demus with a look of frustration. Then, what the boy had said sunk past the throbbing layer of hate. His face changed, and a malicious smile infected his lips.

"I guess you do, at that. I'll pay it for you. What else are friends for?" Pruis looked back at the boy holding Gammin, said, "You got him, Toram? Hold him good and tight. I don't want him to get away this time."

"I got him," replied Toram, wrenching Gammin's head back even farther.

Pruis stepped back and slid the knife into its sheath. I saw silver on the leather, and on the haft of the knife. As soon as the blade was sheathed, Gammin gave a ferocious heave, but it was no use. Toram, far bigger and far stronger, simply laughed and thrust his knee against Gammin's lower back. Gammin cried out in pain as his hips were forced forward. I might have been able to put a stop to this madness, but I was too slow. Someone else was faster.

Pruis pulled back his foot. I could see the kick coming. My mind jumped ahead, visualizing the impact so clearly that I could already hear the sickening thud and see Gammin reel in pain. At just that moment, in the instant between the kick's preparation and release, everything changed. It was as if lightning struck.

A swift shape arrowed from the shadows at the edge of the clearing. I thought it was a bear, then saw it was too small and too ferocious for that. It was only a young boy. He slammed into Pruis from behind, shoulder to hip, pitching him forward violently. The sound of the impact, a muted wallop, arrived in my ear just before Pruis' surprised grunt. The two boys flew through the air, a pair of mating dragons, two bodies but one form. Toram shrank back, but not quickly enough to avoid being accidentally pummeled by Pruis' right arm. It caught him square on the chin. Someone's knee plowed into Toram's midsection as the mass of bodies hit the ground. Toram collapsed insensible. Gammin tumbled free.

I stood rooted, a few steps outside the perimeter of the clearing. My eyes followed Gammin as he rolled away. Toram lay unmoving. My young friend pushed himself up on his knees and shook his head, forcing away the effects of the beating he'd taken. I started to call his name, but the sounds of a fierce scuffle caught us both by the attention.

Pruis was on his back, and he had his hands full. The boy straddling his chest was at least a full head shorter, but it was all Pruis could do to keep from having his head and face caved in. The smaller boy, whom I had first thought was a bear, was raining blows down in the truest sense of the phrase, fist after fist, hammering Pruis with a powerful intensity that did not seem credible to one so young. Pruis lunged from side to side, pushing outstretched hands against his assailant's torso and neck. This worked against him. The smaller boy, the bear boy, fastened his teeth on one of the hands as it pushed against his chin. Bear boy began to shake his head violently from side to side. I was reminded of the sharks I'd seen in the days of my youth, long ago during my wanderings to the lost island of Lupoa, where the dragons are. The sharks used the same side-to-side motion to rip chunks of meat from their prey, turning the ocean red with the purpose of their savage hunger.

Pruis shrieked in a manner that would have been accounted unmanly coming from a child half his age. Perhaps the cry voiced frustration as much as pain. He summoned himself, gave up on the attempts to block the shower of fists. He bucked his hips and arched his back, simultaneously rolling to one side and ripping his hand from the bear boy's clenched teeth.

The maneuver was effective. Bear boy toppled off. He rolled on his shoulder and popped up, spitting out blood and a grizzly bite of flesh. Pruis sprang to his feet. His unmarked left hand reached for the knife at his belt.

I heard a groan from the other side of the clearing, turned just in time to see Demus clamber to his feet in front of Gammin. Demus! I had forgotten him. It was obvious that the two had tussled and Demus had lost. He glanced fearfully at Gammin, then flung a quick look around the clearing and saw that Pruis was consumed in his own conflict. His eyes slid over the form of Toram, who was only now just lifting his head and pushing himself upright. Then Demus saw me. He whirled on his heel to scamper away from the clearing. I stood like a fool watching him vanish into the wood until a savage yell broke my trance. At last, I rushed into the clearing.

Pruis was still engaged with the bear boy. He'd drawn his knife and was attempting to stab downward at his opponent. Bear boy, who must have been strong for his youth and size, was holding off the stroke with his left hand and clutching Pruis throat with his right. The thumb and fingers were digging at the exposed throat.

Gammin was nearby, a stout limb dangling menacingly from one hand. He was trying to get behind Pruis. I could see that; so could Pruis. What the older boy could not see was the murder in Gammin's eyes.

I leapt into the center of the clearing and shouted, "Stop!"

To my great surprise, they did.

Pruis jumped back, landing in a crouch with the knife extended in front of him. It was a nice move. If bear boy had pursued, he'd have been impaled for sure. There was no possibility of that. Released suddenly from the pressure Pruis had been applying, bear boy fell forward, sprawling on his belly. He was completely exposed. It was a deadly moment. It would be the work of an instant for Pruis to leap forward and strike a fatal blow. But bear boy was not exposed for long. Gammin stepped between them, perilously close to the business end of the knife.

I cried "Stop, Gammin!"

I moved toward them. Gammin did not look at me; his eyes were fastened on Pruis. The branch in his hand hovered between them, as did the point of the blade.

For several breaths, nothing happened. With the enhanced senses that are sometimes given to one in an emergency, minute details loomed large. Pruis held the knife extended toward Gammin, its tip wavering slightly in the space between them. Large drops of blood fell from his other hand. I could hear them strike the carpet of leaves in the perfect silence that engulfed us. There was blood on Gammin's face. His mouth was painted with it so that his teeth, exposed in a fierce grimace, glowed with unnatural whiteness. Where he'd been struck on his cheeks and neck, large red welts stood out against a layer of dirt mixed with sweat.

Pruis and Gammin were poised like arrows on bows drawn to the point of breaking. It seemed that the slightest disturbance would set them off in a storm of rage and death. We all floated for a timeless moment, human dust suspended in the dreamy sunlight of a late afternoon.

Toram broke the spell. Rising groggily to his feet, he murmured, "Where's Demus?" He was unaware of the spectacle before him.

Pruis moved first. His eyes swept the clearing. As soon as Pruis' eyes shifted, bear boy erupted to his feet and gave Gammin a mighty push, propelling him into my arms. Then he stepped back two paces and stood facing Pruis.

Gammin tore at the leather of my jerkin in his desperation to arise. I reached down and handed him up. He immediately stepped to one side and squared off with Toram, not sparing a single look at bear boy or Pruis. Toram was still recovering his wits and was in no position to threaten anyone. As I watched, he bent forward, and put his hands on his thighs. I looked at Gammin and our eyes met, understanding passing between us.

"Good. Now everyone. Everyone take a step back. Do it now." And we all did, all accept Toram, who retched loudly and vomited on his feet.

There was a moment when the boys, all except Toram, inspected the clearing. Heads swiveled, eyes darted. I took another short step back; this gave me a view of Pruis, Toram, and bear boy. I had expected Gammin to follow me, to step close to my protection. This was a measure of how little I still knew about him. I caught his flitting eye and motioned with my own. He closed the distance between us and took a position just in front of me, between me and Pruis. He was protecting me. The notion alarmed me more than it pleased me. Then he spoke into the silence of the trees and I understood at last.

"Over here, Mar." His voice was not a command or even a request. He was reciting a fact.

Bear boy backed up to us without a single look, his feet gliding along the forest floor with a sure grace that belied any fear. His eyes remained fixed on Pruis.

Mar, the boy who was not a bear, took his place next to Gammin. They made a shield between me and the two other boys. Looking at Pruis in the relative calm that enveloped us, I noted a gleam of gold at his throat and wrist. His costly garments were blotched with dirt and blood.

It was time to end this.

"The time for violence is done, Pruis, if ever there is such a time. Put away your knife."

He did no such thing. I am not sure how events would have turned if Toram had not spoken. His voice was distant and dreamy. "Where's Demus?"

"Pruis," I said, louder this time, "there will be no more fighting here today. Put away your knife. Put away your knife and help Toram."

Pruis slowly lowered the knife and, after assuring himself that we had not moved toward him, slid it into the sheath at his hip. He did not move to help Toram. That was not his bully's way. He took two steps toward me and glared over the heads of the young boys.

"No more fighting here today. But the violence is not done, teacher." He spit the last word out as if it were a curse that would have insulted a drunken sailor. "You saved him again, didn't you? You're not going to be there the next time."

"I didn't save him, Pruis. From the looks of things, I saved you. That is something you should consider."

Pruis made no reply. I could see his chest heaving as I returned his stare. He turned on Toram, gripped his arm roughly, and led him from the clearing in the same direction as Demus. We watched them until they vanished in the trees.

Gammin turned to me.

"Annen. I'd like you to greet my friend, Marin, son of Marn, the woodcutter."

A JUSTICE OF EHRYLAN

Never were two so well met.

4. THE OLD ONES

I.

The altercation in the Bendwood was the second time Gammin and Pruis fought. It was not the most violent. Each fight built upon the echoing foundations of the one before. The next time they tangled, death stilled the echoes.

    I am sometimes plagued by guilt as I recall this time. The span of bright days between the second and third confrontations arches across my memory. It is an ambivalent portrait painted in mismatched brush strokes. On one hand, it was during this time that the boy and I set in stone an enduring friendship. We grew to know and rely upon each other as if we were father and son. On the other hand, it was a terrible period for Twofords, a season when helpless hope decayed to despair. As the Tax neared, tension settled upon the city and surrounding countryside like blood-red dew.

    Gammin stayed away longer than was usual after the second battle with Pruis. Before I grew concerned, he popped in and displayed himself with a grin, seeming no worse for his adventure. He gave no sign that anything was amiss or that anything untoward had occurred.

I would have waited for him to tell me the parts of the tale about which I did not know, but I knew better. He would not volunteer it. At my request, he told me how he had happened upon Pruis and his gang in the Bendwood and what happened after I left him that afternoon.

He had been out with the children, listening to the wood wright while I was inside talking with Eanna. Gammin saw a friend heading into the wood, a young girl named Arica who was not part of the orphanage. Shortly thereafter, he saw Pruis and his band of bothers—that's the term he used for them, the bothers—hurrying to catch her. Gammin rushed to her rescue. He burst in upon them in the same clearing where I found them. Whereas I was late in arriving, the boy came in time and saved his friend from the evil the bothers would have inflicted upon her. The bullies turned their attention to Gammin. Arica fled, nearly crashing into me. As I continued on, she sped to River's Bend, found her brother, Marin, and sent him to rescue her rescuer. Then, the savvy young lady hurried to Eanna. They collected village men and met the boys and me as we made a slow procession out of the wood.

Gammin was examined toes to pate with several sets of careful eyes. He was cleaned rather more thoroughly than he liked, and bandaged more impenetrably than was strictly necessary. Aldryn, in addition to being the wood wright, functioned as village head man when one was needed. He questioned Arica, Gammin, and Marin. A handful of villagers had gathered by that time, and they discussed the matter between themselves.

I had to leave to arrive at the city gate before darkness closed them. Gammin was seated at a table, demolishing a wholesome meal. He was always hungry, that boy, and had an uncanny ability to find a meal in the most unlikely situations; I do not know how he managed to appear so thin and underfed. Yet, no one was ever more willing to share than my tadpole. In this case, he was sharing the unexpected bounty with the woodcutter's children. I watched them eating and chatting as if they had not a care in the world. Seeing them lost in their own acquaintance cheered me. I lingered, an outsider drawn to the fire of their friendship for its warmth. Eanna literally swept me through the doorway with her broom. Gammin spent that night under the care of Eanna and the alert eyes that kept watch against reprisals.

It felt good to have the boy in my home again. Already the place was starting to feel incomplete when he was not there, as if there was a task to which I was not attending. We did nothing of significance that first day, unless enjoying the renewal of oft acquaintance after what seems an extended period of absence is significant.

He left well before sunset, though he did not go alone. Instinct whispered to me that we needed to exercise more caution than before. I accompanied him to the gate. We chanced upon a group from River's Bend emerging from the Shambles. They were folk with whom the boy was acquainted.

Gammin did not look back, not even once. I saw him reach out and take a laden bucket from one of the women in the group.

His regular visits resumed and, though sometimes trying, they left me happy. He brought pockettuls of joy to replace what I had lost over the decades. Maybe it was the same joy I would have had from my own long-dead son. I think not, though. Each of us paints with our own colors.

One day, while we were eating, Gammin said through a mouthful of half-chewed food, "I noticed something funny today. Not funny.... interesting." This sentence reconstruction was no doubt the result of the day's lessons, which had focused on using the correct words in the appropriate contexts.

"I saw Toram at the gate, you know, one of the bothers? He was just sort of, whadyucallit? Loitering? Is that the word?"

"If you mean he was standing or sitting around without seeming purpose, yes, that would be a good word to describe it."

"Ok. He was loitering there. But that was not so much the interesting thing. Last time I came, I saw Demas there. The time before that, it was Toram again… or I mean, well…you know what I mean."

"Yes. I know what you mean. I thank you for mentioning it. This is important. Something has been bothering me and it does not surprise me that you noticed them watching you."

I meant to continue, but the accidental pun occurred to us at the same moment. I was silenced by that amazing grin. It split his face nearly in two. He started giggling, tried to repress it, and that made me laugh out loud. He soon followed. These little excursions into amusement were not uncommon. Our times together were pleasant, sure, but they were also intense. I took teaching seriously and he applied himself to learning even more so. The laughter we shared was an important balance. And that boy could make me laugh just by smiling.

Eventually, I was able to continue. "That is what you think, isn't it? The bothers are watching for you?"

He nodded, not speaking. He had gone from mirth to gravity in the blink of an eye, pulling me right behind. I saw what I had to do. The idea frightened me. The risks flashed in my mind like sparks reflected off bright steel. I lost all track of where I was and what we were doing. The sharp sound of the apple losing a piece of itself brought me back from the haystack. Gammin was staring at me, not with impatience or boredom, but with patience and a desire not to disturb my ruminations.

"What were you thinking, Annen?"

"I was thinking it is time for you to start learning how to defend yourself."

"Really?" He jumped to his feet with such energy that the chair smacked into the wall behind him. "I was wondering if you were ever going to get around to that! Can we start now? Will you teach me how to use a sword? Please? Please, Annen?"

"A sword? Yes, I can teach you swordsmanship. You don't really use a sword; you wield it. And if you are doing it right, the sword wields you. But that is not where we should start."

"No? Why not? What could be better than a sword?"

"Three questions; one breath. That's good even for you, my young friend. No, the sword is not the right place to start. Why not? There is a lot to learn first. And, what could be better than a sword? A fish if you are hungry, water if you are thirsty, and a friend if you are lonely. But today I can teach you something very important. I can teach you why a branch is better than a sword. Most times, anyway."

He looked at me with suspicious eyes until he decided I was not making fun of him. Once he'd made it through that door, he pondered. "Like when the branch is an arrow or a crossbow bolt?"

"That's not what I mean at all. Here, come with me; I'll show you."

I stood up. He grabbed his apple, which as yet bore only a single wound, though it was terminal. I was going to lead him out to the courtyard, but he anticipated me and ran to the door, almost capering. He so much resembled an excited puppy it would not have surprised me to hear him bark.

We moved down the short path to the rear wall of the courtyard. I stopped in front of a row of slender trees that lined the wall. In the far corner was a pair of seats I'd hacked from large stumps. I motioned for him to sit. He looked up at me with disappointment. Yet even then, when he was throbbing like a tuning fork, he remembered himself and obeyed me.

"I like swords too," I stated, leaning back against the wood and extending my legs. "I like them a lot. And knives. Anything metal, really."

He looked at me.

"But there are problems with swords. First, they're heavy. If you fall into deep water with your sword, you'll have to let it go quickly unless you are an able swimmer. And they're clumsy to tote around when you are not using them."

He just looked at me.

"Also, swords get dull when you use them, rusty when you

don't. You have to sharpen and polish your blade, or pay someone else to do it for you."

He remained silent. I wondered briefly if he was thinking that I was some kind of idiot, or if he was even listening at all. But that did not feel right. He was attending just fine.

"In many places, you can't bring your sword with you into a tavern. And if you are lucky or unlucky enough to ever appear before a king, you can't bring your sword, not unless you are a trusted servant or a special friend."

He blinked. It was good to know he was still alive.

"One last thing. A sword is expensive—expensive to buy and expensive to own." I crossed my feet at the ankles and put my hands behind my head. "But what would you say if I told you there was a weapon that didn't have any of these difficulties, a weapon you could own this very day?"

He spoke at last. "I like swords; that's what I would say."

This was not my first conversation with a clever child. I was not daunted.

"What I am telling you is that you could learn to fight with a weapon made from one of these trees."

"You want me to fight with a tree?"

"No," I said, laughing a little. I reached behind us and pulled out something I'd left there the day before when I had been practicing.

"A staff is a better weapon for you than a sword." I held it out to him, grasping it in the middle with a single hand. This was a huge moment for him, though he knew it not.

He sat for a moment, then stood up and took the thing into his hands. He looked as if he thought it might bite him. I wondered then what had ingrained him with so much caution in all aspects of his life. I decided I was glad I didn't know. I was considering these thoughts when he spoke, almost startling me.

"Sometimes they train with these. Staffs, right?"

"Yes, it is a staff. The soldiers?"

"Not soldiers. Dryhm. I've seen the Dryhm training with their staffs." He wrinkled his nose and made a distasted face.

"I don't trust them. The Dryhm I mean."

"Nor do I. You are wise to feel that way, perhaps less wise to admit it out loud."

"Were they always here? In the long ago, in the before time when… when…"

"When Brand was king and evil did not flow through the land like poison milk? There were no Dryhm here then, not in Ehrylan. They came with Dauroth. They are the priests of his god, his spies, and secret warriors. You must stay away from them, Gammin. They are entirely evil."

"No worries, teacher. You don't have to be troubled about that, especially during the Tax."

The Dryhm were the eyes, ears, and arms of the Tax. Though they were terrible enough in their own right, Dauroth sent armed soldiers as escort to forestall any thought of resistance during the Tax. Those companies tolerated no resistance; any hint of it was punished with swift, hideous strength. Whole villages were burned because a single child had been missing at the Choosing. As a result, the Ehrylain submitted their flesh and blood, the fruit of their love, with almost no resistance. These thoughts threatened to blacken my mood. I pushed them into their compartment. Reaching out, I tousled his hair.

"Good enough."

I took back the staff. It was far too large for him. We'd have to make him one for his own.

"Now. Show me that stance, the one you used when I saw you fighting the bothers that first time."

He peered at me with a puzzled look, the one he showed when he had no idea what I wanted but was trying nevertheless to deliver it. I was reminded of a dog I had when I was younger. He was a pleaser that one, always wanting to make me happy. Sometimes, when I gave him a command he did not recognize, he would turn his head and look at me from a strange angle, then lower his hind end in a perfect sit. I understood full well that he was saying, "I don't know what you want, but you usually get happy when I do this."

I raised my eyebrows. "What is wrong?"

"What do you mean, stance?"

"Ah. Forgive me. I will start closer to the beginning, though I think you know much of this already through watching the soldiers and the Dryhm. Look at my feet." I stood up and adopted the basic ready stance with my lower half, knees bent, feet positioned at the correct angle, waist and shoulders in the correct alignment to the rest.

"Fighting is every bit as much about standing still as it is about motion, about moving. In the same way, speed is the most important thing and correct distance is even more important. Every move you make, every advance, every retreat, is preceded by and followed by a stillness. In that instant of stillness, you are an immovable mountain and, at the same time, a feather moved by the slightest breath of a breeze. The foundation of that mountain is your stance. Understand?"

"No way, not even a little."

"Excellent. What's the last thing I said?"

"You said the foundation of my feather mountain was stance."

From that beginning, we began the real work, the construction, stone by stone, of his foundation. We started with the feet, then the toes, then the knees, then how to move the feet, how much weight to put on which leg. I taught him how to turn properly, first the head, then his hands and shoulders, and then his hips and feet. Later, much later, he asked me, "If you wanted me to stand like the soldiers stood with their swords, why didn't you just say so?"

"Before, you knew how a swordsman stands, yes?" He nodded. "Now you know why."

He smiled.

After our training, we took refreshment. We were sitting near the hearth, sipping apple juice and talking about swords again.

Wiping his lips, he said, "It wasn't really my first time."

"What wasn't your first time?"

He swallowed hard. "I told before, when we met, that the time with Pruis in the city square was the first time I used a branch as a sword against someone for real. Remember?"

"I remember."

"Well, I never fought anyone like that before, that was true, but I do practice with Marin, sometimes. I didn't want to tell you at first, because I didn't know you, you know?"

"But now you do?"

He reflected on this before answering, "I guess not. But I trust you. That's enough for me."

This statement, delivered so unconsciously, was like a beautiful sculpture. I wanted to observe it from various angles in different lights, like a wine that I might sip slowly of an evening, knowing it would change in character as its temperature changed. He did not allow me that luxury. He pressed on.

"I am sorry that I lied. Will you forgive me?"

"Certainly."

I considered telling him that it wasn't really a lie if, as he pointed out, that was the first time he had fought like that against an opponent bent on his harm. The phrase "for real" reminded me quite well of the previous conversation. At the time, what he had said was "for reals," which had amused me, even in that delicate situation. Annen, the silly old teacher. As I say, I could have told him it wasn't a lie for reals, but I did not want him to learn that it was permissible to dance around the keen edge of truth in the attempt to justify an action that obviously feels wrong. This is something all adults do, at least in my experience, myself included. I was not sure it was a good thing. Gammin had more years to endure before he would be ready to make those decisions. Or so I judged at the time. Time was shorter than I thought.

These thoughts captured my attention for a moment. When I reclaimed it, he was staring at me with questioning eyes.

"I am sorry, lad. What did you say?"

"I've been wanting to ask you something."

"Go on."

"I really enjoy our… you know… our time together. It's just that… Would you mind if I brought Marin, at least sometimes?"

"No, child, not at all. I was wondering if you were ever going to get around to asking."

It was his turn to laugh and he did so with gusto. I continued when he was able to listen.

"Teaching two is sometimes easier than teaching one, especially in the arts of war. But there is another reason. I think you should be careful, more careful, as you come and go from the city. Not just when you visit me, you understand; whenever you come up this way. It would be good if you came and went with Marin. Will his father and mother will permit it?"

"I think so, yes. But you can't tell. They are…uh…" He caught himself before the words came out, but allowed them to spill from his lips anyway, "They are adults, you know? Not very predicable."

"No, I suppose not," I answered without rising to the bait. This was important stuff. "I will go and see," I searched my memory, "Marn. Marn, the woodcutter, Marin's father. Can you arrange that?"

Gammin was sure he could make such a meeting happen and, with that out of the way, we carried on spending the little time we had left that day in happy conversation and silence that roamed to and fro like a feeding doe.

I never went to see Marn.

II.

I began to notice differences, at first subtle and then more overt, in the way I was treated in the town. One by one my clients withdrew their patronage; I lost more than half the students who lived within Twofords. In some cases, the proprietors of business where I conducted normal commerce let me know through myriad hints that my absence would be more welcome in their shops than my custom. I was not long in seeing the cause of these things. Pruis' father was the connection that linked them. He was a prominent merchant, made rich and powerful on his trade with the garrison. His reach was long and strong. He did not hesitate to use it to make life uneasy for those he disliked. I felt as yet no fear for my safety. I was not without friends.

With less than a score of days before the Choosing, the gloom and tension in Twofords increased with what seemed like every breath. It would have been easy to mistake this as the cause of the behavior of those associates who drifted with purpose from my circle, but I was heeding that internal whisper, the one that warned me the boy was in danger. The voice of my intuition had kept me from danger and death more times than I cared to admit. Even without the complication of adolescent enmity, the time of the Choosing always held danger aplenty for Annen, who had other tasks than the instruction of the young.

One of those tasks demanded my attention now. A trip to the butcher was in order. I hunted up a deer, a fine, fat buck. This I did alone, not telling Gammin what I was intending, for he knew that my larder was far from bare and would have questioned me with questions I did not care to answer. Not yet. I took the beast straight to my usual butcher and picked up the packages a day or two later. On each excursion, I watched for signs that I was followed, either by the merchant's men or others who might take interest in my business, but there was no sign. I dropped most of the meat off at Merelina's place and spent too much time there, so I came home later than intended. I justified that by telling myself I was staying to be with the children. Merelina and the children asked after Gammin. I gave good report, omitting the fight in the Bendwood. Max, in particular, looked glum at Gammin's absence. I fancied that even Temay showed signs of being sad, but it was difficult to tell with that one.

It was nearing dusk when I set out for home, my pack light and my steps heavy. Foolishly, I allowed my attention to lose itself in the fresh images of remembrance. I came upon the carefully laid trap less prepared than otherwise I might have been. They took me in a place where I did not expect it, where I was still as safe as I could be, save perhaps River's Bend. That is the best place for a trap.

I was musing on the scent of lavender as I rounded the corner to the lane on which my house lay, deep within the Stone Gate. Something tugged at my attention. My feet stumbled to a halt. I looked around, expecting at any moment to feel an arrow between my shoulders. None came. I did not see or hear any sign that things were other than they should have been. I tried to shrug off the imaginary tingle that coursed between my skin and muscles. It was no use. I felt my mouth go dry and tasted something like rust on my tongue, the taste of danger.

What was it? I sniffed the air; there was no unfamiliar odor, at least none I could discern above the wood smoke that flavored the chilling evening. There was no untoward sound and, more importantly, no lack of normal sounds. Dogs barked in the distance, and I heard axe on wood and the calls of children from down the lane.

I searched the shadows, which were already deepening to night in many places. I looked into my memory to see if there had been unfamiliar or suspicious faces on the way here. Sadly, that memory was sketchy at best since my eyes had been turned inward for most of the way. There was nothing, just that tingle, the old friend that had so often kept the blood in my body where it belonged. Rather than placating me as it might have done, the lack of evidence made me more wary. My hand, out of long habit, dropped to where my sword should have been. There was no sword. What need had there been for a sword inside the walls of Twofords that day? The knife at my hip was not the shiny bauble of a merchant's scion. It was a worn and trusty companion of many journeys. I tugged at it so that it rested loosely in its sheath. The antler handle felt familiar and reassuring to my hand.

I took a few slow and careful steps, paused, looked around,

listened, searched the shadows. Repeated. This is also how a hunter moves through the forest, hoping to creep up on animals whose ears and noses are worlds better than his or her own. My father described it as "hunting still."

I arrived at my front door without mishap. Before approaching, I looked all around, back in the direction from which I had just come and into the shadows farther down the lane. Nothing. Yet the tingle sang beneath my skin. I waited, looking at the door, familiar yet somehow threatening. What, who, was in there?

The breeze stirred. A tree sighed. A voice spoke behind me, low and quite.

"You must go in, teacher."

I did not turn. "Must I?"

"You are surrounded." Then more loudly, "Bennoc, show yourself."

I heard the unmistakable bending of a bow, three or four bows in fact. A shape materialized out of the shadows to my left. The man was dressed for concealment in a grey-black cloak. The hood was pulled low to his eyes, the rest of his face wrapped in dark cloth. His hands were shrouded in supple gloves. His bow was black as death and the nocked arrow was tipped with midnight, or so it seemed to me.

I asked, "What do you want?"

"Enter the house. Now."

My mind spun furiously. How could I take the initiative? How could I surprise them? What would they least expect? No answer presented itself; a victim surrounded in a lonely place by men with bows has few options. Wait. That thought presented something! I was not in a lonely place; I was in my own neighborhood. Surely if I cried out, someone would come. Yes. But what would they find? A human pin cushion? My captors would vanish as easily as they appeared and the neighbors would find a dead teacher. I thought about this for a single breath. If they wanted me dead, I would be dead already.

"Now, teacher." The imperative left little doubt that my time had run out.

Knowing that it might be my last action, I turned—so slowly that my cloak did not swirl around my legs—and faced the man behind me. Bow strings all around me protested as they were pulled to the full. The man I now faced did not move a muscle. He was not close enough so that I might attempt to assault him, but he was close enough that I could see soft light shimmering from the serrated edges of the obsidian point on the end of his arrow. I caught the murmur of sweat on the breeze. Was it mine or his? Or both? Despite the coolness of the evening, I felt a drop running down my back.

We waited in silence, floating on the edge of a razor, not knowing which way we would fall. What then, his eyes asked?

I looked left and right, moving my head, only my head, with slow, measured grace as if I were on a stage in front of a queen. I looked at each man, each bow, so that I might give myself every chance of remembering something useful if I came out of this alive. I looked at the man in front of me one more time and raised my own eyebrows. Then I turned, slowly again, holding each hand out to the side where they could see them, and entered my house.

The house was dark. As I crossed the threshold, a spark was struck to tinder. A lamp blossomed into light as the door closed behind me. When my eyes adjusted, I saw several things all at once. There was a man on either side of the door. A third man stood by the hearth. Across the room, there was a man at each end of my table. Sitting at the table, as calmly as if it were his own home and I were his friend, was the man who was obviously in charge. He was not as tall as I, though the length between his shoulders was so great the blade of a sword would scarcely span it. His gnarled hands were clasped on the table in front of him. The muscles in his arms swelled beneath his tanned skin.

There was at least one more person in the house. I could feel him. Perhaps he or they were lurking in one of other rooms. It did not matter. Six to one is little better than seven to one, at least in this case. These men were no novice cut throats, no gang of bullies come for a revenge beating. I could see they were experienced and capable. They stood at ease, yet completely ready. And there was no doubt or fear in their faces, only cold resolve.

"Sit, *shinando*."

The man at the table spoke those words. I had not been looking at him. My head snapped around. It was not the speaking that caused this; it was the speech. The word "sit" was spoken in the Common Tongue; the word *shinando* was not.

"Not just yet," I answered to buy time so that I might regain my composure. I searched his face for some clue, some sign. It was a big face, a broad face. The mouth and chin were engulfed in a thick, black beard. His ample lips and prominent nose poked out of the curly facial hair like rocks rising out of a turbulent, dark sea.

"Stand if you like. I would talk with you." His speech was clear, yet slow and careful as if he were speaking a language that, though he had completely mastered it, was not the one he spoke every day.

"You are doing that." A hundred questions hammered at my mind, trying to escape my mouth. I held my tongue. And waited.

"You may relax, *shinando*. We intend you no harm."

"This is a strange way of showing your beneficence. Men of good intent do not need such an escort to confer with me."

"I take the precautions I deem necessary. As do you, *shinando*. So we have observed."

The weight of all the nightmares in creation dropped in an instant upon my shoulders. For the first time since leaving Merelina's, I thought of the meat in my pack and the other thing that was secreted there, the small thing, the hidden thing. Panic tried to push its way in, but I controlled it. I had been thinking this was connected with Pruis, that this was retribution, payment for my involvement, as it were. Only now did I consider that this might be about the Resistance, something of much greater import, something that could mean death and destruction to…. How many? I swallowed the fear, a physical action mirroring what my mind was attempting. I noticed again the sweat running down my back. I tried to force myself to breathe normally, thought even the men outside might hear my thundering heart.

If the man at the table noticed my dramatically increased alarm, he gave no indication. After a moment's silence, he spoke again.

"I am here because of the tadpole, *shinanado*." That was a very strange sentence to hear. I took a while to piece it out. The man was using the Common Tongue yet, as I have already mentioned, *shinando* is a word from a different language, as is the word he used for tadpole—*gammin*.

I did not answer.

"Gammin asked if I would speak with you. I am..."

I cut him off in mid-sentence, the relief almost knocking me off my feet. "Marn! You are Marn, Marin's father. The woodcutter."

A tiny smile touched the corners of his lips. The tension in the room evaporated as we all relaxed. These men also were relieved to have avoided the spilling of blood. Marn nodded to the men behind me who guarded the door. One of them knocked on it, very softly, a peculiar knock that was clearly a signal they had established. It guessed it meant something like "Phase Two complete." The same man stepped down the hall, and I heard the knock again, twice. So there were at least two more, in the courtyard and in one of the rooms. The man came back as quietly as he had left and resumed his position by the door. He looked more relaxed, though I could see his vigilance was not reduced. I thought that now the men were guarding us. I wondered, briefly, from whom?

I did not give up all my guard either, but I knew that, if I did not get off my feet soon, I would either faint or fall down.

"I'll take that seat now, if it please you."

Marn nodded to a chair at the table and I almost collapsed into it. I slid the pack from my shoulder and dropped it—and the secret it contained—to the ground. I pushed it under the table with my foot to keep it out of the way. And out of sight.

"Lehman, give the *shinando* something to drink. He looks like he needs it." Marn spoke these words in the Old Tongue, with the perfect ease of a language learned at his mother's knee. From this time on, we spoke only the Old Tongue. It felt as if cleansing waters were pouring from my lips at each word.

One of the men, the one on Marn's left whose name was apparently Lehman, shifted an oblong leather bag from beneath his cloak and handed it to me. I thanked him, nodded to Marn, and unstoppered it. Though I had intended only a sip, the scent from the container brushed aside any caution I had. I took four long swallows, each greedier than the last, my mouth and throat seizing control of my will at the first taste. It was as if someone had fermented juice squeezed from diamonds, as if sunlight had been captured in pure, virgin rain drops. The liquid flowed over my tongue and down my throat with a tingle that seemed at once both deliciously warm and delightfully cool. My hands reluctantly lowered the bag and offered it to Marn, who took it, drank, and passed it on to the next man. The bag made its way to each man in the room until Lehman drank of it, stoppered it, and hid it away again. A fresh, light smell danced through the air, the scent of a pine forest after a spring shower. It was the smell of forgotten hope remembered.

"Linuvea?" I asked incredulously. "Where did you get linuvea?"

Marn did not answer, though he did smile. We were all smiling now, truth to tell. Who would not? What man, woman, or child could not but smile after a draught of that precious liquid? Linuvea was one of the old things, something from the time before Dauroth that had been lost, or so I had thought. In the time of King Brand, Ehrylan abound with healing liquids and compounds made from various herbs and leaves, rocks and soils, the saps of trees, and the like. Such ingredients, when mixed appropriately and administered correctly, were remarkably effective in keeping one healthy and in returning one to health. This craft, the domain of the *nemen*, Healers, had dwindled since the fall of our society. Most healers, few of whom called themselves *nemen*, could do little more than set a broken bone or patch a wound. To come across linuvea here, now, and to know that its secret was not lost, that was a treasure indeed.

For a good while, no one spoke. The silence suffused us as the taste of the healing drink lingered. I could feel it working, lifting my spirits, heightening my senses. I think they were waiting for me, since I would be most affected, having not partaken in so long. Eventually, and I know not how much time had passed save that it was now full dark outside, I broke the silence.

"Tell me, Marn. Why do you call me *shinando*?"

"It is appropriate."

"I hardly think so."

In the old speech, *shinando* refers to a revered teacher, someone who has trodden a long, difficult path and suffered sacrifice to attain some specific wisdom or knowledge, someone who passed that learning on to others. Literally, *shinando* means "one who has gone before." To be considered such was a high honor. It was a formal thing, a thing to be respected.

"You have been teaching our Gammin. We have watched. We have seen. We are… pleased." Marn said this with a wry smile. He was poking fun at one of the sayings the Dryhm use to intimidate the Ehrylain.

"I am pleased as well. He is a remarkable boy. He has come to a place where it would be beneficial to share his lessons with another. And there are other reasons."

"The *drachem's* son. And his friends." Marn used a word that has no direct analog in the common speech. *Drachem* means, roughly, a person who betrays his own people by trafficking with the enemy or with other unclean people. A collaborator, in a sense, though *drachem* was more derogatory. It is not a word one says to her mother.

"I am concerned that the older boys from the city mean to harm him," I said. It was a relief to finally admit that to someone. "I have considered telling him that we can no longer meet in Twofords, but I am selfish. He means a lot to me." I stopped there. Marn did not speak. He looked at me with dark, unblinking eyes. I continued.

"And now I would have your son, Marin, who has already entered the fray at least once, share that danger. Had I thought it through, I might not have asked such a thing. I ask forgiveness, Marn. I allowed my own hope... and joy... to cloud my judgment. I am sorry."

"Forgiveness asked is forgiveness. But there is no need for your sorrow or my forgiveness. We will speak of Marin later. I would speak with you of Gammin. I am not quick to lay confidence in these dark times, though I am a good judge of men. You feel right to me, yet you are more than you appear, *shinando*. There was no fear in your eyes when you came in this room; any normal man would have been afraid. A lesser man might have made a mistake that cost a life. There is much about you that does not fit a teacher of children, though you wear that vocation well. You play the part, yet you do not move like a man whose life has been devoted only to learning. You have the air of a man who has traveled far and suffered much. Very much and for long."

"All those who remember the days of King Brand with gladness have suffered much and for long." I answered, turning his question from the soft and dangerous target.

It came to me then, though I should have been much sooner in realizing. Marn was not from River's Bend as I had thought. He was one of the Old Ones. His ancestors had lived in this land even before the time of a king that ruled all the lands of the crescent that lies between the Great Mountains and the sea, the lands that later became five kingdoms, then seven. Legend told that the Old Ones assisted Andur in his battles to unify the land under a single ruler and, though they never forsook their secret homes for places in the cities and villages, they were ever friends to the king and his kingdom. In Ehrylan during the time of good King Brand, uncounted generations later, the Old Ones had been honored in the way they most preferred, left alone, unmolested, free to come and go as they wished without let or hindrance. Marn was descended from those folk, people who were now outlaws though they had been part of the land since before the living memory of any but their own kind. I looked around at the men in the room with new respect and concern. The Old Ones are a law unto themselves and would do what they judged fair and right without concern for the laws of kings they did not honor. This realization brought me not concern alone, but hope also, for I had dealt with the Old Ones, the Children of the Forest, many times.

"You say true, Old One. I am a friend of the old ways. Your heart tells you so. Is it not said among your people that when eyes cannot be trusted, heart speaks true?"

"Aye. So it is said. My eyes see a man who lives among the stones and who takes money from those who honor Dauroth to teach their children. Yet I believe you are true because my heart tells me so."

"Marn, and all you who hear these words, hear me now." I rose from my seat and took a position where I might see them all at once. "A man may teach the sons of his enemy and not be a traitor. Is it not also said among you that he who controls the minds of the young controls the future?"

A murmur stole around the room like a swift breeze.

"You know much of our ways, Stone Dweller. Maybe too much."

I made no reply to this, but sat again in my place at the table.

He laughed, throwing his head back so that his beard pointed to the ceiling. "A pack of fools we are, to sit here sparring with words when it is clear we are enemies of the same enemy. We must be done with such talk, for there are more important matters to discuss. I will speak with you of the boy. He is special."

"Yes, I had noticed that. What would you tell me, Marn, the woodcutter? There is much I would like to know."

III.

He gathered himself for a tale. Then he said, "He is not of the forest. Nor, as far as I know, is he of River's Bend. I know not if any blood from Ehrylan flows in his veins. Of his mother, I can tell you a little, nothing of his father."

He looked down at his hand and swallowed. I could not read what he was thinking or feeling. It is often like that with the Old Ones. Concealment is their way, both for their safety and their comfort.

"I came upon them in the forest. They were half way to Mendolas, where the bridge spans the river. Where Teryn crossed."

Teryn was a hero, or maybe only a heroic legend, from the days before the peoples of the Crescent had been united into one kingdom by Andur. The place to which the woodcutter referred was Teryn's Crossing, one of the few places the Silver River could be traversed in these parts and where, according to stories older than the trees, Teryn built a bridge so a small army could come upon and surprise a much larger force entrenched nearby. It is told among the Old Ones that it was with their help that Teryn accomplished the feat, and they believe the tale has been told father to son, mother to daughter, in an unbroken line since it happened. It was common to hear among the Children of the Forest such attributions as "I am Matt, son of Trem, whose ancestor was with Teryn when they built a bridge."

"In those days, I did not normally go so near the road, but the deer I was tracking led me there. My arrow stuck him low, a gut shot." It sounded like an apology; I was not sure if it was to me, to himself, or to the others in the room. Maybe it was to the deer. "Perhaps I may be excused. It was a long shot and the wind was high that morning. I do not take such shots willingly, but we were in need. The winter had lingered over long and the hunger of my family was great."

When he said family he meant his tribe, his clan, those with whom he lived in some deep and hidden glen or vale in the forest where no outsider ever came without an invitation and a guide. The Old Ones live in groups of from ten to thirty. I knew he was telling the truth when he said the shot had been difficult. There is a saying of the Old Ones, though it is not their saying: "When an arrow is loosed, a life will follow." They are known for their deadly accuracy.

"There had been a fierce battle. The dead lay all around. There were two score of Dauroth's men, all Outlanders. They had attacked half a score of Chinenyeh, the wandering folk from beyond the forest far to the south. Or, for such I took them. Their clothes were of that people, though I thought the faces looked out of place in them. Surely these were Ehrylain warriors dressed as dancers and singers. There were three wagons, ruined, smoldering still, and many dead horses. The Chinenyeh had made a way-camp; the wagons were circled. The fire pit was within. The embers were still living, which was a help to me." Marn stopped and motioned to the man by the hearth who stepped over and gave him his water bag. As Marn drank, I considered this. I could see the slight bulge beneath the cloak that indicated the man to Marn's right also had a water bag. I waited for him to finish refreshing himself, but spoke before he took up his tale again.

"The man on your left had linuvea. The man on your right, he has the poison."

Marn looked at me with surprise at first. Another look spread across his face. I could not read it.

"Yes, *shinando*. That is so. If I had judged you to be a danger, you would have drunk death from a different bag. I spoke true before. You are more than simple teacher."

I made no reply, so he continued.

"There was only one survivor, a woman; young I thought she was, but older than she looked. She was not Ehrylain. And, she was pregnant." He used a word that meant both pregnant and about to give birth on the spot. "She was pierced with many wounds and had lost much blood, too much. Her slain enemies lay all about her, and in her hands she held the instruments of their deaths, a hand axe in one and a long knife in the other. They were covered with the blood of her fallen foes.

"The baby came as I knelt by her side, as if the woman had been holding him at bay until someone was at hand to help. There was water in plenty. Fire was easy, or else I would not have been able to save the babe. I found the swaddling clothes they had made for him and two blankets that were unspoiled. I was able to deliver the child and keep him warm.

"She spoke several times, but only once in a tongue that I knew, this tongue, and I wondered at that, for what Chinenyeh would speak so? Why not the Common Tongue? She said something about her son. That part was difficult for me, because she spoke words I did not understand. I thought she was trying to tell me he was unusual. Maybe the words were from her language. I know not." He shrugged.

"She bade me keep him safe, 'away from the darkness,' is what she said. She made me promise. I do not swear vows willingly. Something in the way she entreated me prompted me to do so. When she had spoken her last, she laid a hand on my arm, lay back, and breathed no more. There was no time to lose, so I forsook the dead mother and carried the living child with all speed to my home. He was almost dead when I got there, but we were in time, as you know. I left him with my wife who took him to my *goma*—my brother's wife's sister. She lost her own child, a still birth, not a week before. I took many men and went back, weary though I was. We honored the dead Ehrylain, but left Dauroth's men to the wolves and scavengers, if even they would have them. While the other's tended the fallen, I tracked down that deer. By the time I returned with it, they were finished and had gathered what could be salvaged. The dead needed not what we took.

"I was young then, not head of the family nor even in the council, so I was not part of the decision. The elders judged that the child should stay with my *goma*. There was much wisdom in that. Her husband had been an outsider; she had left the forest to live in River's Bend to be with him." He shook his head again, this time more forcefully, as if wondering why anyone would willingly leave the forest. Yet he had done so himself.

"After four years and two children, the man died leaving his wife newly pregnant. The woman returned to the forest to be with her sister. She had been with us since. It was a great sadness when her child was born dead, but a goodness came out of it for Gammin.

"In the days after he came to us, there was much talk of what was to be done. I had spoken my word to the child's mother. All agreed we were bound to help the child if we could. When the time of nursing had passed, my wife offered to take him into our house, may the Maker bless her, but my *goma* would not have it so. He stayed with her. After two years passed, the woman quarreled with her sister and said unkind things about my brother. She left us, taking the child with her. The elders judged that it was her right. I think in her heart, my *goma* does not like the forest. She prefers the village. She would never have returned to us if she had not been with child when her husband died."

I stopped him. There was something large that I did not understand. "You say she kept the baby of her own desire? And she took him with her back to the Bend?"

"I have said it."

"Why is she so cruel to him now? If only half of what Gammin says is true, she treats him like a servant, and maybe not as well as that."

"This I have wondered myself. But who can understand the ways of a woman?" Every man in the room nodded. We all knew that men were simple and women complex. He continued, "I believe she thought to find a new husband in River's Bend, one that could keep her and her children. When that did not happen, she blamed the youngest child. That is speculation only and does not come into this part of his tale." He nodded his head, perhaps to himself or to me, signaling that he was ready to move on, which he did immediately after adjusting himself in his chair.

"When she left us, I had to consider my word; with the

approval of the elders and the head of my family, I followed my *goma*, not all the way to the village, but close enough to keep an eye on the boy. And on her."

"That is a mighty sacrifice, Marn, to uproot yourself and your wife and children for the sake of keeping true to a Chinenyeh woman long dead and an oath already fulfilled."

"True enough, *shinando*. Few things are more important than a person's word."

I reflected a moment on the recent conversation I had not had with Gammin, the one about dancing on the edges of truth.

Marn mistook my lack of response for doubt. He said, "You see much. As you perceive, there was more than one reason for my relocation. I will not speak of family business to you. Do not take offense."

"I take none. All men, even good men, must have secrets in times such as these. You keep yours. I will keep mine. We will allow the Maker to judge our hearts and our truth."

"So be it. But let that be the end of this tale, and I am overlong in the telling. For almost ten years I have been Marn the woodcutter, though Marn is not my name. I have lived in the edges of my forest and watched the child grow. From time to time, I take news of the outside to my family and there is coming and going between us, but of that I will say no more. Soon enough, the boy will reach his manhood and my word will have been fulfilled. Perhaps he may join us in the forest. I would give him that choice."

"It is a good choice," I replied. "There is much to be admired in the ways of the Children of the Forest. I know; I lived among you at whiles during my life. A man could be happy there, in the forest with your people. A woman too, for women are treated as equals among you, as it was in the days of King Brand and not like it is under the foul hand of Dauroth."

The claim that I had lived among the Old Ones did not illicit a response from Marn or his men. They passed over the statement without reaction or comment. Perhaps they knew already. It was difficult to say. They are a close-lipped people and my time among them was many years ago, in the days when the land and people of Ehrylan were still bleeding from the fresh wounds of conquering swords. Yet their memories are long and true and nothing passes in the forest without their knowledge.

Marn said, "If the boy continues as he has begun, he will have a place among us. That tale will not be told for many moons. There is much pain to suffer between this moment and that. He has suffered much already, though I have done what I could to help him. As you say, *shinando*, the woman is often cruel to him. Where she fails him, I try to make recompense. He never leaves my door without a full stomach or clothing enough. He and my son are as brothers."

"There is much I do not understand." I paused to take a breath. Marn nodded an affirmative to the confession. He agreed there was much the teacher did not understand. "Gammin would not let me fix his cloak for fear of the woman. Does she punish him for your gifts?"

"She does not deny him what I give. She dare not. She fears me. What I give him, he keeps. You must understand, *shinando*, there is a difference between what you give and what I give. You live among the stones."

"True enough, Marn. Tell me one more thing, will you?"

"If I can."

"This woman, your *goma*, what is her name?"

"You ask what I cannot give. We do not name those who have turned their faces from us. She left us in her youth. We accepted her back when she returned with the outsider's children. She left again and, in the going, treated my brother and his wife badly. She left her name in the forest; we speak it no more."

I knew, just from the short time we had been together, that I would get nothing more on that account. I had a thousand other questions, but I held them. When Marn spoke again, it was a new beginning.

"I would speak to you of the boy, and of my son, Marin."

"What would you say, Old One who is not Marn, the woodcutter?"

"Tell me what you want of the boy. Why do you teach him, an orphan with no name and no family? What have you to gain?"

Having thought on this long and long, I knew there was no real answer.

"A man may do a thing though no one else can see the value. Also, a man may do a thing that brings no value."

Marn waited, calm as stone. I might have been a tree he was appraising, trying to determine if my wood was good enough for furniture or merely for fuel to feed the fire.

"Perhaps what you have said is reason enough, Old One. He has no name and no family. He is like me. Truth to tell, I do not know why I am spending time on him or even where the time might lead. I know only that my heart is glad when he is about. Where eyes fail, the heart will lead." I paused, swallowed, took a deep breath. "If that is not enough, then what must be will be. I have no more to offer." I stopped there, intending to say no more, but something popped into my head.

"I will teach him the old ways, the ways of King Brand and Prince Branden, the ways passed down from Andur, the ways of the Maker. If I can do that, I will hold myself successful. Is that enough?"

Marn smiled, his lips parting to show teeth that were healthy and white. "That is what I hoped, *shinando*. But there is more."

"More?"

"You see the danger in all these comings and goings. My heart tells me that, whether under sun or under moon, there is no safe road for Gammin between the river and the city." He stopped, took a breath, continued. "I have come to ask a favor."

"Eh?" The word he used for favor had special meaning. It did not mean only an indulgence; it was something more akin to a significant gift, something he was requesting me to give him with no hope of equal consideration. There was no telling what this might be, but, by using that word, he had told me to expect something that could be life changing.

The thought that this man, so sure and confident, might ask a favor of me was the furthest thing from my mind at that point; I was set back on my mental heels. To buy some time, I went on the attack, albeit it was a good-natured assault couched in what I thought might be humor. "Do you always come with a branch of Silanni when you come to ask a favor?"

Silanni were the assassins of the forest, silent killers who dealt out what the Old Ones considered righteous justice to those that had wronged them or theirs. They haunted stories as old as the tales of Andur, ten centuries and more, though in the time of King Brand and his forefathers, they had receded into the darkness between the trees. Justice was not scarce in those years. Since the coming of Dauroth, the Old Forest and the lands nearby had once again become their hunting grounds. Their silence was complete and their vengeance was devastating. And not always swift. It is said that the Silanni measure time and justice with differing measures.

Marn's lip twitched. Mayhap it was the thought of a smile, some small reaction to my attempted wit. If he and his men had been the silent assassins, we would not be having this conversation; I would be growing colder and stiffer and they would be long gone, having left no trace that ever they were here. He began again without acknowledging my reference.

"I come as I come and depart as I do. Yet, still I would ask this man for a favor." He eyed me with a pointed stare, maybe daring me to quip again. I did not. Drawing a deep breath as casually as I could, I allowed myself to fall into the ancient ritual.

I said, "Ask your asking."

Marn motioned to Lehman, the man with the linuvea. I fetched two cups from a niche set in the stone work above the hearth. They were only the size of a small boy's closed fist, of a type called swallowers. Normal swallowers are used in drinking games and ceremonies such as the one we were about to perform. They contain only enough liquid for a single swallow. My swallowers were not normal. I took two of the four from the niche and rinsed them with water from a bag that hung nearby. The containers resembled opaque glass, their faint, smoky color shifting from hazy blue to misty green as the light and viewing angle changed. They were not blown like glass containers. They were carved or molded out of the gemstone known as Dragon's Eye. The Stonethanes, who work the Dragon's Eye, do not share their secrets. An extravagant gift from a man now long dead, these swallowers were very precious.

I resumed my place at the table and set the swallowers in front of Marn. His eyes flicked to mine when he saw what they were. While he carefully filled them with linuvea, the other men seemed to fade—or at least try to fade—into the shadows, giving us as much privacy as was possible. The smell of sunlight and forest rain blossomed in the air as Marn set the two filled swallowers in the center of the table between us. He placed his hands in front of him on the wooden surface. I looked at them for a moment, then placed my hands in front of me in the same way, one to either side of my body, fingers slightly splayed.

"Marn, a woodcutter of the forest, will ask this favor of Annen the teacher." He turned both his hands over so that they rested knuckles against the wood, palms to the ceiling. "Accept Gammin and his brother, Marin, into your home while you teach them the way."

I was too stunned to speak. Marn was barred from speaking again until I answered. The quiet unsounds of darkness deepening outside wrapped us in a cocoon.

I had often thought of taking Gammin into my home. The associated difficulties had repeatedly pushed that possibility from my mind. But two boys? That would indeed be a challenge. My mind raced through the possibilities and the issues.

There was no question as to what I would decide, no difficulty in coming to a decision, but the implications of that decision were huge. I would be assuming responsibility for the boys. Was living among the city dwellers—the Stone Dwellers—the best thing for them?

Much as I wanted to think this through, there was no time. I spoke, though I had to swallow three times to get my throat and mouth to work correctly. Even then, my voice came out dry and gravelly.

"This man has heard you, Marn, woodcutter of the forest." I turned my hands over, palms up, and took three deep breaths, as slowly as I could. When I was ready, I took one of the Dragon's Eye swallowers and placed it in front of me. I looked into the liquid; it appeared to glow with a vibrant energy of its own, and the Dragon's Eye seemed to pulse in response. I raised my eyes to Marn's, lifted the container to my lips, and drank it off in a single swallow. The devastatingly refreshing wave washed over me, taking my breath and thoughts with it. Was there something else, something added by the ritual, some flash of intangibility? Perhaps.

When I judged I would be able to speak clearly again, I looked at Marn and said, "What Marn asks, this man will do. As it has been asked, I will see it done. I, Annen, accept Gammin and his brother, Marin, into my home. As best I can, I will teach them the way."

Marn's face did not change as he reached out with ritual formality and retrieved the other swallower. He repeated the actions I had taken and, after swallowing his portion, placed his container back in the center of the table. To complete the ceremony, I replaced my own next to it. It was done.

IV.

There seemed endless topics for discussion, and we made a good start at reducing the list. Eventually, our desire to talk faded and we lapsed more and more into silence. After an extended period during which none of us spoke, Marn sighed heavily and heaved himself to his feet.

I asked him how he would get out of the city. The gates had been closed for almost half the night already. He told me he did not need a gate. I wondered at that; what other secrets did the simple country folks have, secrets which might give those within the city walls significant unease? When I asked him how he would avoid the patrols, he sniffed and smiled. I heard a little laugh come under his breath and saw his head shake slightly. He reached out and slapped me on the back. We were friends already.

When I moved toward the front door, Marn shook his head and headed down the hall, the other men following him in silence. The man standing nearest the door tapped on it in a rhythmic pattern, then hurried after the others. By the time I got there, the door to the courtyard was closing. I did not open it and look to see where they went. It would have been fruitless. They were gone already.

Later, as I lay pondering the events of the evening, I realized I had never seen the others, the men secreted in the rest of the house. I turned over and waited for sleep. It was just swarming over me when a thought occurred. I sat bolt upright in my bed.

The meat! It was still in my pack where I had left it in the front room. Salted, smoked, and wrapped, it would keep until the morning when I would stow it in the larder. Soon I would take it to the River's Bend orphanage—the meat, and the hidden thing, a little stone vial.

5. THE MESSAGE

I.

Good days followed. Good days are nice days. I relish the memories of those good days. There was much to do and little time to do it. I had agreed to pick up the boys in the Bend two days hence. I intended to deliver the meat to Eanna at the same time.

The first day was spent mending and cleaning and trying to determine how I would house and care for the additional guests. There was an interesting moment when I realized that, in fact, they were not to be guests; they were to be residents. That set me to wondering what it would be like if my son were still alive. Would he like his two new playmates? But I was being foolish. My son would be man now, and not even a young man. He would long since have left this house and, in all likelihood, I would now have grandchildren aplenty.

There was no bed in the extra room. I had no relatives that might come visit. There was a comfortable pile of furs and a stitched mattress full of various soft things that my infrequent guests slept on. I emptied out two trunks that had been full of useless items I had been unable to part with previously for unknowable reasons. That was the extent of my preparations for their sleeping quarters.

I filled the larder with many things I thought young boys needed and a few things I knew Gammin loved. I bought more plates and dishes and cups and mugs. Soon my home looked more like a home and less like the uncluttered cave in which I had lived for some time.

In all these activities, I consulted Merelina. But for her advice, I would not have laid in near enough bread and cheese, and we all would have been eating from the same plates. It did not take long for me to realize young boys are little more than rambunctious appetites with arms and legs that knock over everything in their path, and even things not in their path. Before the first week was up, watching them eat convinced me that I needed to work harder to provide for Merelina and her children.

On the morning after the visit of Marn and the other Old Ones, a single thought presented itself over and over as I lay abed, clearing away the web of sleep. What news? What news from the Resistance in Ehrynai?

After my normal morning routine, I checked the front door to make sure it was locked and made sure the shutters were closed. I opened the pack and took out three wrapped packages before coming to the one for which I was mining. There was no indication outwardly that this package was different from the others. I knew by its size and shape that it was the one I wanted. I unwrapped the meat and, after a look over my shoulder that was useless, I probed it with my fingers until I felt what I wanted. The vial came free; it was no larger than my forefinger.

Clearing away the pack and the meat, I turned to the business of deciphering the note. The first step in that process was finding the key that would unlock the code. I looked closely at the container, searching for any design or insignia. The key was always different, yet always the same. The important information wasn't what, but how many. I found what I was looking for, a series of tiny circles carved into the side of the vial. These were connected by a line that wrapped around the little cylinder as if it were a branch from a rosebush. I wanted to know how many blooms there were. I counted them carefully. Seven. I counted again. Seven.

I cracked the seal on the vial and shook out a sheet of thin parchment. It was covered front and back with script in a female hand. At the bottom of the back side was the imprint of a rose, identical to those lining the side of the vial. It indicated where the message started. I disliked messages that read from back to front, bottom to top. It wasn't much more difficult, but it took more time, at least for me.

I did not bother to read the note. What it said was not important, just a diversion to allay suspicion if one of us were caught carrying it. It would be a note from one lover to another, nothing that could relate to the real message. I looked at the very last word. I counted the next words, receding backwards toward the beginning. I stopped at the third word, read it, then moved on, always upward toward the beginning of the note, every third word. I read each, considering what they might indicate in the larger context. It did not take many words before I knew what the assembled message would tell me.

The device of using a numerical interval was a simple method of hiding the important words among the unimportant. We'd made it more difficult by disguising the key number, in this instance three, through the use of rudimentary math. The key to the key, known to all principals and their backups, was ten. Seven from ten leaves three, and three was the number that unlocked the first level of encryption.

Tallow light pooling about me while sunlight blazed outside, I wrote the important words on scrap. I rechecked the work for accuracy, then set the parchment aside. The words on my scrap made no sense at all, whether read backward or forward. They seemed just a collection of random verbs, nouns, and prepositions. The key to the next level of encryption was the knowledge of the secret meanings of those common words.

All of us, the major conspirators in this region of Ehrylan and our seconds, had memorized one hundred words and their interpreted meanings. These were never written down. There were an additional two hundred words that could be used, though we avoided it where possible; they were listed in a certain book of poetry we all owned, encoded in a method that required no real key. Other precautions made it even less likely that someone could break our code, including the use of words that meant "disregard everything after this word," "disregard everything before this word," and even "disregard everything in this message." Also, certain three or four word combinations held collective meanings, which overlaid their individual references.

I set about translating the message. It was as I feared. We were to wait, bide our time, and make no move. We must keep the people from rising up in protest during this Tax cycle. The time for the uprising would come, but not this year. The next communication could be expected after the Choosing in the Southland. The new password was "Many mountains, one sun" Trust in Ea.

That was all. It was not much. The bit about the password was completely irrelevant. Passwords and watch signs were not changed in this way. The inclusion of the phrase "The new password is 'Many mountains, one sun.'" was misdirection. If anyone approached us using that phrase, we would know immediately that our code had been broken and we were in imminent danger.

Wait and wait and wait again. It was always the same. We were not ready or the time was not right. There was always some excuse to do nothing but keep preparing. Some men make a life out of preparing for events they will never undertake.

I rechecked my work from beginning to end, though I knew there was no mistake. I repacked and sealed the tube, hiding it within the stones of the hearth. I'd take it with me when I fetched the boys.

Before I ventured out to begin my day's activities preparing for the new inhabitants, I locked away Annen the Conspirator. Out came Annen the Teacher.

II.

I rose just before dawn on the third day since Marn came to call. I made a steaming mug of canella and ate a scant breakfast, eyeing the accumulation of food that crowded the larder. That was just the beginning. The house smelled different, even sounded strange. Familiar echoes were deadened by new items that waited for the boys.

The real changes had not even begun.

I retrieved the vial and slid it into its accustomed place in my boot, a sleeve I'd sewn in for just that purpose. When Gammin was with me, I had put it in my pocket because he might notice me pulling something from my boot. This time, I would make the delivery at the spring before I saw him, or so I thought. Promises, plans, and predictions of the weather oft go awry is an old saying in Ehrylan. It's as true a saying as ever there was.

Setting out at last, I took extra care to determine if I was followed. At the gate, I looked at trinkets in the stalls along the road, places where city folk were most apt to find items of interest. I was not interested in trinkets, even less interested in showing coin. My interest was in seeing who was out and about, who exited the gate after I did, and with whom I would share the road to River's Bend. I detected nothing untoward and moved out behind a good-sized group of villagers. I would be able to follow them at a discrete distance all the way to the Bend.

The morning was one of those late-summer mornings that often follow the first coldish nights announcing autumn. A kind breeze, soft as combed cotton, kept the heat down and carried off dust that might have accumulated on a still day. It was a beautiful day in Ehrylan and a good day to be about my tasks.

The group ahead of me turned off on Bend Road, something not unexpected. Few travelers ventured into the Old Forest in such small groups. None did so wisely. Dauroth's minions were at particular risk, one of the things that kept Twofords and the Southland so isolated. We were cut off from much of the kingdom by mountains, swamps, and forest, all of which were refuges for outlawed people with no love for the usurper.

As soon as I saw the villagers make the right turn toward the Bendwood, I slowed my pace so that I would not have to share the spring with them. I need not have bothered. Something I saw just within the edge of the Bendwood changed my plans.

There was, in those days, a stump that sat in the first fringes of the wood. Usually, there was nothing on or near that stump. Today, plain as could be, I saw three white stones lying against its base. They looked as if they had fallen there haphazardly, but I, who carefully eyed it every time I passed by, knew better. It was exactly the sign for which I was looking, the thing I least wanted to see.

The stones meant danger. I must abort my delivery. The position of the stones, on the west side of the stump—the village side—told me that difficulty was in front of me rather than behind. It might be anything, from the least significant to the most. It might mean that my contact would be away for a few days and would not be available to receive the tube, or that there were enemy troops in the area, or even that the spring was watched. The first set of stones could not tell me such detail; other signs in the other places would.

What I saw and did not see in the branches of certain trees or at the bases of others told me that the danger was not high but that there were others about, Dauroth's folk, perhaps soldiers or even Dryhm. Since the Choosing was almost upon us, this was reasonable. The last hidden sign, just before the path that led to the spring, did not warn me off. I saw the group I'd followed leaving. I raised my sword hand in a silent greeting. Those that saw me did the same and went on their way, leaving me to my own time in the glade.

I did not find trouble. After refreshing myself in the usual way, I sat on one of the benches, resting and reflecting. I thought about the boys and the changes they would make in my life, underestimating by many magnitudes what those would be. I thought of the conversations I would have with Eanna. In short, I pushed away Annen the Conspirator and put aside every thought of the vial, which I left hidden in my boot. When I was ready, I rose, stretched, and walked without incident to River's Bend.

Old Bilious gave the first greeting. I returned him his due, rubbing his wizened muzzle and scratching behind his ears the way he liked. He smelled the meat and nosed the pack I had set down beside us as I knelt to attend him.

I made my courtesies to the mistress of the establishment, handing over the meat and accepting a package of fresh-baked barley cakes in return. We chatted about the exciting news. The relocation of the two boys was well known in the village. We discussed the Choosing. Eanna did not believe any of the children in her care were at risk this year; only two were the correct age, and neither of those showed any sign of being exceptional, a characteristic that drew Dryhm at Tax time like carrion eaters to a battle. Eventually, one of the children—Simon, who, like Temay, suffered from difficulties—came in search of Eanna. After that, the news of my arrival spread, taking with it the little island of peace we had shared. All my attention was redirected to the children, as was entirely fitting.

I was in the enclosed yard behind the main building of the orphanage playing an invigorating game of One Hop with a crowd of youngsters when Gammin, Marin, and Marn arrived. I was surprised to find a sturdy wagon waiting for us in the road. The reason for the wagon was hidden beneath a tarp. It filled the entire bed of the vehicle. As I lifted a corner of the tarp, both boys were grinning ear to ear, and why not? The woodcutter had given more thought to their comfort than I. He'd made a set of bunks, a two-sided writing desk; and two chairs.

III.

We watched Marn the woodcutter encourage his farm horse homeward. It was by no means the last time I saw that wagon. Though the topic had never come up, Marn took to delivering a load of firewood at intervals precisely aligned with our need. I believe the boys communicated the state of our wood pile on a regular basis. I did not have to purchase firewood again while I lived in the Stone Gate.

From that first evening, there seemed to be a sense of not having even a single moment to loose. Before the sun set, the boys were busy assembling their beds and trying to figure out how to make the one, large over-stuffed mattress into two smaller mattresses. This was eventually accomplished through much cutting and re-stitching, though that did not happen for a few days.

I allowed them take the lead in caring for their own needs. During the first weeks of training, when they needed staves and other wooden weapons such as practice swords, I took them into the forest, helped them find the correct trees, and guided them through the process of chopping and scraping and cutting and carving. Likewise, when clothes needed mending, we mended our own, as much as we were able, at first making a game of it and later a contest. The skills of making and mending I had learned when, as a young man, I spent much time at sea; there is no group better at making fast, sturdy repairs to garments than sailors.

I took the boys with me as I visited my remaining clients and when I went to the orphanages. They became indispensable, and I wondered soon how I ever got on without them. In time, they took over many of the sessions and I had little to do but watch.

At home, we studied the ways of thought and spear, a philosophy that emphasizes mind as well as hand. It is an old concept, as old as myth, and runs through the Tales of Andur. We spent as much time reading and writing as we did studying the arts of fighting. The boys did not mind. Truth to tell, I don't think they ever tired of either physical or mental learning.

Each day we arose early. During morning training, we concentrated on movement and on empty-handed techniques that did not involve weapons. After that, while we broke our fast, we might discuss thoughts and ideas sprouting from the morning's training. This was followed by lessons on history, mathematics, reading, writing, languages. In the afternoons, we repeated the cycle: physical training, food, mental training. The routine enfolded us like a comfortable cloak. We suffered interruptions grudgingly.

On the other hand, the boys recognized that I had business to attend. I took to scheduling my tasks during the hours just before or after the noon meal. From late-morning to mid-afternoon, they had time for other than study. It was a space the boys could use for leisure and rest.

On the third night after their arrival, there was a duty I had to perform alone. Remembering that mischief abounds when hands are idle, I set the boys to a task, suggesting they attend to the mattress situation. Marin had been sleeping on the mattress, Gammin on the furs, an arrangement they settled themselves without input from me. The bunks stood empty while both boys slept on the floor—adolescent logic at its finest. This was nothing to Gammin. He had spent his life sleeping on the floor in furs that weren't as abundant or clean as those he now used. Marin showed no sign of discomfort. This being only the first week, it was all still a big adventure.

I departed before sunset, not without concerns for their safety and the safety of the breakables in the house. It was early on yet. I had not come to trust them as I would. The same was not true for them. They trusted me completely, right from the start.

My short journey took me out of the Stone Gate, across the market street, and halfway up Castle Hill to a tavern called the Crown and Scepter. It was an ostentatious name for such an establishment, especially in hard times such as these. Crowns and scepters were the two most valuable gold and silver coins, respectively. It is unlikely that the place sold anything that cost an entire crown. A meal for several men where food and drink flowed in a river of plenty might cost a scepter. But that would be a prodigious meal.

The Crown and Scepter was clean, warm in winter, and cool in summer. The food and beer were equally fine during any season. It wasn't a large tavern as taverns go, not even for Twofords. There were nests of tables on either side of the door and clustered in front of each fireplace. Staircases ascended to the second floor from small raised landings near each hearth. Such was the Crown and Scepter in the years before war came again to Twofords.

This night, when war was but a rumor in the minds of the fearful and the hopeful, the tavern was bustling with trade. Servers scurried to meet the needs of the customers. It was not a large crowd, but the evening was early yet. I chose my table carefully, not the one that was either the most isolated or the most shadowed. With a wave at the man behind the bar, whom I knew well, I claimed one of the empty tables near the hearth. A pretty lass of half my age brought her smile my way.

"Will you be eatin' tonight, Master Annen, or will it be just the drink?"

"Just a tankard of ale, for now, Molly."

As she hurried off, I extracted one of the two objects in my pocket, a small pouch, and set it on the table in front of me. I watched the other customers casually. Some of them I recognized. After a moment, I opened the pouch and took out the pipe. I tapped it against my palm and blew into the bowl though I knew the thing was as clean as could be. I thumbed a wad of cured leaves into the pipe. That did not fill the bowl, but it was enough to fit my needs, which had nothing to do with smoking, a habit in which I seldom partook. I went to the fireplace for a light. My ale was waiting for me when I returned to the table.

I seated myself, puffing on the pipe stem just enough to make the ember glow before setting it on the table. I was almost ready. With another casual look around the tavern, I reached into my pocket and extracted the second item, an egg-sized chunk of rock that is common to the mountains near Twofords. Such rocks, which are milky-white in color and glisten with small facets, were known as milk rock by the locals. I set it next to the pipe and picked up my tankard. It was time to sit back and wait.

For a good while, nothing happened of any consequence. Molly refilled my tankard from an enormous wooden pitcher that I would have had difficulty handling. As she turned to leave with one of my coppers in her skirt pocket, she nearly collided with a man coming up behind her. He pointed to my tankard as she hurried off.

"Mind if I join you?" The man pulled out the chair across from me. His voice was rough, his accent local.

"Suit yourself." I did not offer my name. Instead, I picked up the pipe, which I had ignored a trifle too long, and coaxed it back to life. Gesturing with the stem of the pipe to the pouch on the table, I asked, "Care for a smoke?"

"Why not? I've heard smoking in company is more satisfying than smoking alone."

"I've heard the same. Perhaps it is true." I slid the pouch across the table to him.

"Perhaps," he echoed, taking out his own pipe. I watched absently as he prepared his bowl.

I had never before seen him. He might be the contact for whom I was waiting, or he might be one of Dauroth's spies, which were everywhere. The principals seldom met, and never publicly. As much as possible, we did not disclose the identities of the members of our teams. This afforded a certain level of protection. No conspirator knew more than a few other conspirators.

In the event a message drop was not possible—as had been the case three days ago—those involved knew the date and location of an alternate drop. There would be no attempt to pass a note or any physical item that could be incriminating. The whole matter would be handled in a manner that left no evidence and, hopefully, created no suspicion. If either party were intercepted before or after the drop, there would be nothing to indicate our conspiracy.

The man across from me might be just what he seemed and have nothing to do with this risky business, or he might be biding his time until he judged the time was right. In any event, the next move was his; I had done my part, setting the pipe and stone on the table. One test had already been passed: there had been no names nor any attempt in naming.

We smoked in silence until Molly brought his ale. When she did not wait for him to produce a half-copper, I learned the first thing about the man. He was no stranger here or, more correctly, he was no stranger to Molly.

The man took a long pull at his brew and set it down with a satisfied exhalation. Then he said, "As good as always."

I set my pipe down, took a drink. His eyes flicked to the rock, the white rock. My pulse quickened as he spoke.

"That stone, it's milk rock unless I miss my guess."

"Yes, milk rock. I found it the other day and put it in my pocket. I'd forgotten it until just now."

"Funny name for a rock, milk rock."

"Yes." I could see the pulse beating at my wrist. I turned my hand over.

"When I was young," he continued, "I used to throw stones at the cows, to turn them when they had gone astray. I used milk rock, when I could find it. I filled my pockets with it when I knew I was going to have to work the cattle in the field." He stopped, took another long drink, smiled. "I thought it was funny, throwing milk rocks at cows."

"Did it work?"

"Sometimes."

There was silence for a time, at least between us. All around, a profusion of sounds filled the tavern with audible paint.

"You don't say much, do you?"

"Nope." I sucked on my pipe, blew out the smoke, took a sip of ale. My reticence did not bother him at all.

He puffed, then continued, speaking almost as if to himself. "There was one really obstinate cow. We used to call her

Mistress Mule because she was so stubborn. One rock was never enough for Missy Mule."

My heart hammered in my chest. I forced myself to exhale the breath I was unconsciously holding. "No?"

"With that one, I always had to throw three rocks."

There it was. He had uttered the words for which I had been waiting—three rocks. Now, he had to wait for me to say certain words. I offered them immediately.

"Care for a game of Rocks?"

"I suppose so. It will pass the time." He reached into his pocket and pulled out a pair of dice. The man I was expecting was sure to have dice in his pocket.

Rocks was a very old gambling game. I had no desire to play at dice, whether for money or no. The game would provide the vehicle with which I would transmit the message. We would speak normally, though nothing that was said would be of any import until a certain number was thrown. Whenever the number appeared on the dice, and as long as we let it stay on the dice, we would slip in the bits of information we wanted to pass on. This allowed us to communicate our secrets even if others joined us, as could easily happen in the busy tavern. If we felt uncomfortable, we ignored the number when it came up and said nothing of import.

The number tonight was three, of course.

IV.

There was a pile of coppers and half-coppers in front of each of us. A few silver marks, coins worth ten coppers each, peeked out enticingly. We'd been playing for a while. The dice had shown three several times, but I had not started the covert communication. I decided the next three would do it and rolled. The dice totaled five, a four and a one. With that roll I lost that round. My contact retrieved the bets, leaving one copper for the before, the bet that was made to buy in to each round. I tossed a copper out and passed the dice.

He rolled a two and a five, seven. He pushed a copper in. "Seven it is," I said, taking the dice. I equaled his bet. The pile in the middle, known as the bucket, now contained four coppers.

I rolled the dice; they settled on a three and a one, four. His roll having exceeded mine, he could either take the bucket and we'd start again, or he could up the bet and roll again to beat my four. That was not important. We both looked at the three.

I said, "There it is; you win again. The time is not right. Not yet. I'll bide my time until a better arrives. Your roll." He retrieved the coins, signifying that we would start a new round.

He rolled another seven, a four and a three. I dropped a copper in the bucket. I did not pick up the dice; instead, I said, "You are rolling well. I'll just have to stay calm and wait, eh? That's what my friend in Ehrynai says."

He nodded, looking at the bucket. After a moment, he dropped in a copper. "I understand. It's frustrating when you are losing like this, but there will come a time. The people in Ehrynai are pretty clever. That's what the people in Ehrynai tell me, anyway." My contact showed his nose to the ceiling, as we say. He was mimicking the disdain Southlanders frequently received from dwellers in the big cities. That was not something Dauroth brought. Some folk search for reasons to disdain.

I rolled a nine from a five and a four. The bucket was mine, but I tossed in another copper. He could match my bet and roll again to beat my nine, but he shook his head. He picked up the dice. I gathered the bucket into my pile.

We rolled a few more times, mouthing meaningless pleasantries. Then one of us rolled a three again.

"I've heard little news from the wide world these many days," I said. "There will be more news after the Choosing, I suspect."

"You think so?"

"Yes. I think so." I swallowed ale before continuing. "I did hear one word that was passed on to me. I heard that there were many mountains but only one sun."

He chuckled. *It is wisdom that comes from tales older than Ehrylan. There are many mountains to climb, but all stand under the same sun.*

"Many mountains under one sun, eh? I learned that on my mother's knee."

"Yes," I replied. "Many mountains, one sun."

We rolled on into the night, the coins passing back and forth, drinking our way through several coppers. I reiterated the message and he affirmed it in the proper way with a prearranged system. He gave me some information. I did the same for him. It was a fruitful exchange and I learned more than I would have if I had simply dropping off the vial at the spring.

Finally, there was nothing more to impart. When Molly came by yet again to fill our tankards, I declined. I thanked her for her troubles and gave her silver for her service. She went away happy.

Standing up and stretching, I looked down at my companion. "Thank you for the game."

"And you," was all he said.

I stepped out into a stiffening breeze that groped me with cold fingers. I was halfway home before it occurred to me to wonder how my contact would exit the city. Maybe he was staying at the tavern, warm and cozy in one of the rooms on the second floor; the Crown and Scepter was a safe house of sorts for us and for all who honored Ea. Or perhaps, like Marn, the contact came and went without need of the city gates. That was his concern. I had accomplished my own business and my heart felt lighter.

I considered the message, wondering again how we would quell the just outrage of our countrymen. With every Choosing, the Resistance's position became more difficult. We continued to council passivity in the face of oppression. That raised the suspicion of the people we were trying to free. We bore that uncomfortable burden. It was just one of the many prices that had to be paid in the effort to regain freedom. Not a man or woman among us begrudged it. We held the image of a free Ehrylan before us and ran toward it as light rushes over a meadow at the rising of the sun.

I arrived home to find that the mattress had been divided and re-stitched. Nothing had been broken in the house except one pair of scissors and a leather awl. Casualties of battle, I thought as I looked at the boys tucked comfortably in their beds. I sought my own, thankful that explanations would not be required of me this late in the day.

I could not find the doorway to the slumber. I lay awake wondering how I was going to bring the kingdom to the brink of war without endangering my two wards. It makes me laugh at myself now to think of it. No one is safe in a war, and there might have been no less safe place in that war than by my side. No one in Twofords was more deeply covered in conspiracy against Dauroth than I.

As a principal in the Resistance, I led a group of seconds. The number of seconds depended on the population of the respective area. In Twofords, a small city tucked in a remote corner of Ehrylan, there were only five. My seconds each commanded five team leaders. Each team leader had a team of five. Thus, I had responsibility for about one hundred fifty men and women.

Could one hundred fifty-six properly trained and equipped warriors, in the right moment of surprise, hope to defeat the garrison? I thought so. Those same men, their ranks swollen by others who would rally to King Brand's lion banner, would lead the effort to hold the city. That would only be possible if Dauroth was forced to address many such uprisings simultaneously across the whole of Ehrylan. If we had any hope in succeeding, we had to stretch the occupying army thin, cutting off and killing the extended appendages.

6. THE CHOOSING

I.

I gaped at the list in disbelief. A week had passed since my meeting in the Crown and Scepter. Tonight's moon would be half-full. Today the community learned who was summoned to the Choosing.

The list was fastened to the city's south gate with a large iron nail. There was an identical list nailed to the village hall in the Bend. It was nearly as long as my arm, though the twenty names could have been written on a sheet the size of my hand. The script stood out stark white against parchment dyed as black as Dauroth's heart. Many believed the ink was made of the bones and teeth of the previous year's Chosen, and that the parchment was colored with the blood of Dryhm. Dryhm were purported to have black blood. Whether the ink was made from bones and teeth, and whether the parchment was dipped in Dryhm, I knew not. But one thing I did know. Dryhm had the same color blood as any other person. It was not black but red, red and thick and hot. I had spilled my fair share and more, starting when I was just a boy and the war was just a babe. Ea willing, I would add to that tally.

My plan for the afternoon had been to view the Black List and provide whatever comfort I could to those affected. I'd packed enough water and food for a trip to the Bend. I had intended to see Merelina's children on the way. The notion that I might be the one in need of support had not entered my mind. What I read on this year's Black List changed all that. There, writ large in bone-white letters against a field of black nightmare, I saw the two names I dreaded most, Gammin and Marin.

Just because someone's name appeared on the Black List did not mean that person would be chosen. Knowing that did little to restrain my anxiety. With both boys listed, my chances of loss were doubled.

On shaky legs, I hurried back up to the Stone Gate and collected the boys. They must have known what had happened; there was none of the usual banter or questions as I issued curt instructions. I led them to Marn's home on the edges of the Old Forest.

By the time we arrived, the sun was at its highest. The woodcutter was chopping wood near the entrance to his barn. He was, I found out, waiting for us, having checked the Black List in the Bend as soon as it was posted. As his wife, Dara, comforted the boys with food and wisdom, Marn and I talked across a work bench in one of his sheds. There was little to say, less to be done. I was sitting with my elbows on the work bench, head bowed with my hands entwined in my hair. He was watching me. I could feel his eyes.

We could put up no resistance, even if both the boys' names were called. To do so would bring calamity down on everyone. At a bare minimum, if I resisted, I would be killed and Gammin too. If Marn resisted, he would die and all the members of his family. Our deaths would only be the beginning. Resistance was not an option, but neither was capitulation. I would not be able to watch as either boy was led away into the depths of darkness, never to be seen again in Twofords.

When I looked up at him from within my room of sorrow, Marn caught me fast with steel-hard eyes.

"There is only one thing for us to do."

"What?" I spoke louder than I had intended.

"It is a simple thing and hardest of all."

"What?"

"We must trust the Maker. His wind blows where it wills."

"There is nothing left but trust and howling wind."

"Annen, trust in the Maker is the beginning and the end of faith and life and all there is." It was the first time the woodcutter used my name. It jolted me back into myself just as he'd intended. He was wise and sly, that Old One, with wisdom beyond his thirty or forty years. He waited, but I said nothing.

"There is more to discuss. Put aside your disquiet."

"More to discuss?"

"Consider, teacher. Both boys are too young to be on the list. The *drachem's* son is old enough. He is not listed, nor any of his pack. Three more of the twenty names, not counting your son and mine, are students of yours."

I was, for the second time that day, thunderstruck. None of these ideas had crossed my mind. I was so wrapped up in my concern that I had not allowed my mind to focus. That was very bad for one in my position.

"I did not see. I thank you. Give me a moment."

I closed my eyes and sucked in three slow, deep breaths. I took the first, giving myself up to the terror. With the second, I breathed out the fear and doubt, watching them waft away on my invisible exhalation. After the third, I locked the door against them and opened my eyes.

"Welcome back," said Marn.

"What do you make of it, Marn? How do you read this riddle?"

"It is yours to read."

Most of the boys on the list belonged to families who had yet to forsake the old ways, people such as myself. This was not unusual. A handful were students of mine. That was odd.

As far as I knew, the authorities had no reason to know of my existence. Two common boys had been listed but not Pruis, nor any of his bothers. I spun the threads into a cloth of reason.

"I think, Old One, that this is revenge for my involvement with the *drachem's* son." As the words left my mouth, I felt a mist of certainty settle across my heart. "Yes. That is it. This is all about Pruis. The merchant is avenging his son. It may be that he does not know Pruis is a bully, but I doubt that."

"Go on. Do not stop while the flame is catching." Marn leaned forward and, elbows on the table, pulled intently at his beard.

"I do not understand how the *drachem* affected the lists. I've never heard of such a thing. At least not like this."

It was not unheard of for a child to be Black Listed as the result of a parent's refusal to cooperate with the local chapter of the Dryhm or for some run-in with the Council. But the favoritism had never been so flagrant. The Choosing was always a catastrophe poised on a razor's edge. Dauroth's victory was not in provoking us to open war but in pushing us relentlessly to that place where hope was lost.

I asked, "What does the *drachem* have to offer the Dryhm?"

"When we have the answer to that, many things will become clear."

The woodcutter stopped speaking as if he assumed I would spout the answer without further thought. I watched him refining his thoughts, sanding down a rough surface to find the grain.

I was too impatient to wait for him. "What could a rich man offer in place of his son and all his son's friends? What do the Dryhm lack? They do not need money." I picked up a large mallet, then put it back, selecting a half-carved axe handle instead. That was better. It felt solid and crafty in my hands.

"Dauroth is not interested in riches." Talking more to myself now, I paced back and forth in the shed, occasionally poking at something with the axe handle. "Dauroth wants to smother the works of Ea. The gathering of wealth for wealth's sake is not important to him. The *drachem* is already loyal to Dauroth. Why take from him? I think, Marn, that the merchant did not buy his son off the list. It was something else."

"You seem pleased with this conclusion, teacher."

"I have eliminated the biggest, most obvious potential. That is something."

"Good." He punctuated the word with a nod. "Something occurs to me, now you mention the ways of the evil one. By attacking you and the children you teach, the Dryhm begin the process of separating you."

I whirled around, for I had been pacing away from him. The axe handle came down on the cross member of a sawhorse with a loud thwack. Two birds erupted from the rafters and arrowed out into the light. "Yes! You have it. This is an attack against me. As it becomes known that the families of those I teach are targeted, my friends will vanish. And who could blame them?"

Marn was silent. He glanced at the sawhorse.

"There is something more, woodcutter. The idea explains why five names appear on the list, but not why Pruis and his friends do not."

"Perhaps it is coincidence. For every name on the list, there are at least ten other children, maybe twice that. Perhaps it is reward for the *drachem's* allegiance."

"I see your point, Marn. You make good sense. Yet that is not the reason. There is a thing, a gift you might call it, something I have had from a very young age. At times, I see things very clearly that to others seem blurred."

"You have a gifting? This explains much."

"It does not happen often. When it does, it is unmistakable. This is like that. I can't see why Pruis' name is not on the list, but I know there is a reason and we have not yet hit upon it."

"I will not question a gifting from the Maker, but this day wears on. Though all the fear and calamity in the world press upon my doorstep, I must feed my family and the animals that keep us. We will leave this for now. You will stay for supper. I have a task that needs more hands than I have now that my son is gone. Your help would be welcome."

There was no denying such requests, not between the two of us. It was his way of bringing us back to the real world, where our hearts beat and those we loved waited nearby. He stood up and crossed to where I was standing, taking the splintered ax handle out of my hands. He grunted and walked out of the shed, tossing the handle on the wood pile. I heard him say, low and quiet in a rumbling exhalation, "A teacher, indeed."

II.

The days passed too quickly, the nights too slowly. I met once more with Marn before the day we paid the Tax, that time without the boys. We said little then, for there was little to say. Neither of us had attended a Choosing, so we had heard only rumors of what to expect, tales told by unfortunate parents from previous years.

Those tales spoke of a black chamber, cold despite numerous flames. These emanated not only from an enormous fireplace in the front wall, but also from the mouths of stone dragons. The dragons were life-sized, or so it was said. That was unlikely. Unless there was some Dryhm magic about the Choosing Hall that made it larger on the inside than on the outside, the building was not large enough to hold more than a single dragon.

We would be first to see the latest crop of youngsters who were joining the Dryhm of their own choice. This was the last time we would see them with their faces exposed, for the Dryhm do not reveal their countenances willingly. We, who were at risk to lose our loved ones to the servitude of Dauroth, would be the last to see the faces of those who freely sacrificed their lives to his service.

The day dawned bright and gay, contrasting with the heaviness we felt in our hearts. I wanted to give the boys words of wisdom to steel them, or words to ease the passing of time until the event was upon us. Instead, we ate in silence, looking at each other as if this might be the last time we would share a meal. Marn and his good wife were there. They'd come the day before and stayed with us through that bitter night.

Before dawn, I arose from my sleepless bed and cleansed myself carefully before dressing. It is a habit among those who go to war, this special attention to the external body before battle. The ablutions mirrored the need to still the mind and clean it of conflicting thought, to focus intention so that intention becomes mindfulness and mindfulness becomes unmindedness. I failed utterly.

I was still undecided as to how I would respond if either of my two charges was taken. Either alternative was intolerable. I could not resist the Dryhm and bring destruction down upon the community. Nor could I sit by as one of boys was taken. I could not find the inner peace that is much vaunted at times such as these, so I took pains to appear outwardly composed. That, at the least, I must do for the boys.

There was more to be done in the darkness before dawn, preparations to make. I strapped a dagger to each of my thighs. As I put on my tunic, I concealed another weapon, something seldom seen in Ehrylan or the other kingdoms of the Crescent. The weapon was a two-stick. It consisted, not surprisingly, of two wooden dowels connected at one end by a chain or slender rope. The sticks deliver killing strikes. The ends were excellent for poking into soft targets such as the throat or stomach. And, finally, their length, which was that of my forearm, made effective defense, even against an attacking sword. I learned to use them during my wandering days. They are a good weapon for a battle where one faces many foes at once, as I was sure to do if things went awry.

These were the best weapons I could hope to smuggle into the Choosing Hall. Swords and staves were not allowed. If I were caught, I would be killed and Gammin as well. It was a risk I had to take. What that meant terrified me.

We set off at the appointed hour. We were joined near the arch that reaches across the lane at the entrance to the Stone

Gate. Two Dryhm, hooded and robed in black, were waiting for us. From deep within a hood came a man's voice, flat and emotionless. "Come. The time grows near."

The Dryhm accompanied us to the Hall of Choosing. We allowed them to lead. It was far less unpleasant having them in front of us where we could see them. As we neared the hall, we were joined by other groups. By the time we arrived, we had a procession of about twenty people and five Dryhm. I could see other collections heading toward the hall from other directions, all moving so that we would reach our destination at the same time.

The boys were taken from us as soon as we arrived. The way it happened left little room for reaction. The entrance to the hall was beneath a covered portico supported by columns. Between each column, soldiers stood at what passed for attention in the garrison that occupied Twofords. In truth, they were quite a bit more soldierly than was usual for them, though nowhere near the standards of King Brand's army. Seemingly from out of nowhere, a score of Dryhm appeared and insinuated themselves quickly between each boy and his parents. The soldiers drew their swords. A woman's voice trumpeted above the startled clamor.

"Hold now! You are come to the Choosing. The Tax will be paid. Resistance will be met with destruction. Compliance will be rewarded with tolerance. Look to the Holy Ones. They instruct you. Obey quickly or die slowly."

Gammin was pulled away by one of the Dryhm. Another placed himself between us so that I could not see the boy. Marn and his wife were likewise confronted. All around me, others were dealing with the same situation. There seemed to be one Dryhm assigned to each candidate and one Dryhm assigned to each set of parents. The one assigned to me held its hand in front of my face.

"Hold. The time is come. The sooner you stand quiet, the sooner I will take you into the hall." It was a man's voice. I wanted to cut him down. Almost, the panic caused by the quick and unexpected separation won out. Marn's voice stopped my foolishness.

"We are ready. Take us in now."

I looked at my Dryhm, straining to see into the shadows beneath the hood. "I am ready. Take me in."

"First, the rules." He lowered his hand. "You will follow me through the door. I will lead you to your seat. You will stay there until the Choosing is finished. You will say nothing. If you resist in any way, you will die and your child will die. Others will die as punishment for your crime. Do you understand?"

It was an effort not to grind my teeth. "I understand."

"After the Choosing, when you are dismissed, if your boy is not one of the fortunate chosen, you will come here to collect him. Then you will leave this area immediately. Now follow me."

The Dryhm walked slowly to the entrance at the end of the portico. The door was shut and a line was forming. I could see Marn several places in front of me. The parties, usually one man and one woman accompanied by a single Dryhm, were admitted one at a time. The door opened briefly, shutting as soon as they passed through. There seemed a long wait between each admission. Soon I was to understand why. My escort paused as we entered the room, just beyond the pallid light of the doorway. My eyes adjusted. Here was a scene, if ever there was one, to create dismay.

The chamber was not large; perhaps a hundred could comfortably assemble, though there was never comfort in that place. I entered at the midpoint in the rear wall. At the front of the room, a fire burned fiercely in a stone fireplace that could have contained two men lying end to end. Gold and white flames danced madly as they ate the massive logs. Unlike most fires, this one did not create a sense of welcome or hope of warmth. It seemed that the flames sucked at me, pulling the heat from me rather than providing it.

On either side of the fireplace, the head, neck and shoulders of dragons protruded from the walls. These were carved in black stone, dark as ebony. They were not so large as real dragons, of course. The eyes of each dragon were magnificent amethysts. Flames rose from the fanged mouths casting light around them. I could see no smoke. Where the shoulders sprouted from the walls, their upper arms sprang outward, clawed talons raised to the height of their heads as if they were preparing to seize something on the floor in front of them.

Above the hearth, appearing to float on a torrent of flame, an image was carved in deep-set relief. The head and shoulders were draped in a cloak, hooded so that none of the visage could be seen. It was the Faceless, whom we do not name. This is not out of fear of summoning him, as Dauroth put about among his subjugated people. That was just a lie. The truth was simple. If the name of Ea is sweet to us and brings joy and hope, what shall the name of his adversary convey but bitterness and despair? The carving was twice man-high, filling the wall from the top of the huge hearth to the ceiling. Now and again, perhaps reflecting the flames that convulsed below, diamonds set in the shadows of the hood where the eyes should have been stabbed out from with startling intensity. The intended message was evident.

The black ceiling was supported by black pillars that rose from black plinths to equally black arches. The pillars were wrapped from the ground to the ceiling with the sinuous forms of slender dragons, two on each pillar. On each column, one dragon faced up, tail to the ground; the other faced down, tail to the sky. Snake-like heads came together at the center of the pillar, facing in opposing directions on opposite sides of the column. One of each dragon pair had emeralds eyes, the other rubies. Like the carving of the Faceless, they watched all those in the hall.

Cold benches of black marble, rough and unadorned, straddled the chamber. An isle split the benches in two parts at the center and led straight from where I was standing to a table on a raised dais that dominated the room. The dais was unremarkable; the table was not. The latter was made from a single block of obsidian that must have been as big as a wagon before they chipped it into shape. Except for its upper face, the builders had left the angular fracture lines, sharp as knives, from where they'd flaked off pieces in the making.

The effect of all this was disquieting and quite stunning. The Dryhm knew how to put on a show.

I was shown to my seat on the bench. My escort melted into one of the corners at the front. The room was not half full. There were an equal number of men and women, or as near that as makes no difference. Few sat alone. All looked apprehensive. Most of the people threw darting, worried glances at the carvings, only to look away again just as quickly. The place smelled of fear and despair.

There was no conversation. Sighs and sobs drifted intermittently from all parts of the room. The door opened and closed, admitting newcomers who were seated after being allowed to take in the alarming surroundings. Sometimes these unfortunates gasped or moaned. All of us traveled some distance down that center aisle, walking directly toward the hooded visage of the Faceless. Then the door opened no more and we sat listening to the sadness in the glow of the smokeless flames.

A gong sounded, soft when it was struck, rising in volume when it should have been decaying. When the sound should have been gone, we were cringing in pain and covering our ears. I was, like everyone else, insensible. The hall throbbed. The sound poured over us with almost visual perturbations in the air while the gemmed eyes of the dragons flashed in unison. Agony drove out all thought but the need to escape from that maelstrom of sound. Abruptly, the violent sound ceased as unnaturally as it had begun.

When I could think again, I saw six hooded Dryhm sitting at the jagged table. Behind them, so close to the hearth they must have been uncomfortable, a row of six acolytes stood motionless, their faces hidden. More showmanship.

We waited in what must have been silence, though my ears rang so that I could not tell. Without any apparent signal, the six acolytes simultaneously threw back their hoods, revealing faces and shaved heads. I ran my eyes over each, three boys and two girls. Uncertainty left me with cold realization. I knew the price the *drachem* had paid to keep his son off the Black List.

The middle acolyte in the line was Pruis.

All the children in Ehrylan, whether high or low born, were subject to the Choosing. No amount of money could buy an exception, but there was one way to elude the Gatherers. A child could join the Dryhm voluntarily, or, as was more common, a parent could volunteer their child. This was not seen among the loyal of Ehrylan, but occasionally, a family who had thrown in their lot with Dauroth and the conquering Outlanders would forgo the uncertainty of Choosing for the certainty of service in the priesthood of the Faceless.

The unfortunate Chosen were invariably sent off to far corners of the kingdom almost never to be seen again in their home towns. Those who joined the Dryhm of their own accord might spend their whole lives serving in the local community. They gained mastery over those who had been their friends and enemies, a mastery of fear.

The *drachem* had assured his son would stay close to home. He had provided his son the potential to rise into a position of power well above that of a rich merchant. It was an interesting gambit. I did not know the relationship between the merchant and his son. Perhaps the boy caused his father trouble or was in some other way an embarrassment. There was, at this point, no knowing and I had other matters to attend.

I barely heard the Chooser as she congratulated the six novices. My attention was held by the turmoil that chased its tail in my head. What would I do if Gammin or Marin were chosen? Could I allow them to be led away from me forever to serve the very servants of evil from whom I was sworn to defend them? Could I, for their sake, bring fire and destruction down upon Twofords? I felt the weight of that choice, my own cursed choosing. It was more real than the pressure of the daggers strapped to my thighs.

The gong sounded again, this time briefly, though we all waited with anxious anticipation for the ringing tone to swell. The six Dryhm sitting at the table doffed their hoods. None of them were familiar to me. Two were women, one of which sat at the centermost position of the table. Unlike the others, she wore a circlet of twined silver and gold that had been fashioned to resemble slender vines. She was the Chooser. She began by praising Dauroth and the Faceless, then moved on to describe what was about to happen.

I took stock of the situation. There were no guards that I could see. It was possible that several might be standing behind the rear-most benches. I gauged the distance to the dais and the time it would take me to cross it. The Dryhm would likely be on their feet or in the middle of standing by the time I reached them. Two I would have, for sure, and most likely the third before I would encounter opposition. I might be able to deal with two more before assistance could come to them from the back of the room.

That left the six novices and one Dryhm. It was not likely that the novices were armed. Their only hope was to entangle me. A dagger would be best for that close work. Which weapon for the Dryhm? For swiftness in dealing death or incapacitation, few weapons can beat a two-stick.

If everything went my way, I'd be facing six or seven after killing the first handful. Unless I got some help from Marn and the other parents. What likelihood that, I wondered, wishing I could risk a quick look over my shoulders to see if there might be other adversaries in the room.

The magnitude of what I was contemplating struck. If even the least of these thoughts were revealed, I would be killed. And all for what? The boys, if I managed to save them from this room, would live only a few more days. My heart cried out at the thought. Yet life in servitude under Dauroth would be a living death.

Did I have the right to make such a choice for them?

The Chooser called up the first set. Four boys filed in from a shadowy corner at the front of the chamber. A Dryhm arranged them in front of the dais so that their backs were to those of us on the benches. Another Dryhm followed behind. The two Dryhm stood sentinel over the boys. Each Dryhm held a short, cruel-looking whip. After an inspection of the document in front of her, the Chooser called out a name. One of the four boys stepped forward reluctantly. A cry leapt up from some parent.

"Silence!" roared the Chooser, erupting to her feet. The fires in the dragons' mouths leapt up with the word, and gemmed eyes throughout the chamber flashed. "We will have order. Or we will have death." As if on cue, the six acolytes chanted in unison, voices monotone, "Out of death comes order. Death and order are one." The Chooser swept the chamber with an ominous look before lowering herself into her high-backed chair.

There followed a series of questions, some asked by the Chooser, others by the five who sat next to her. The boy answered, hesitantly at first, and then with more confidence as the process continued. The questions varied depending on the child, and in many cases, only a few questions were asked before the panel moved on to the next candidate. It was evident from the questions and how they were asked that the Gatherers had specific knowledge about each boy. In every case, all four boys were questioned before a choosing was made from each group.

No one was chosen from the first two groups, the second of which contained one of my pupils. Hope soared within me; there was a chance that we would all get out of this alive. That hope was wounded when one of my pupils was chosen from the very next group. He was led off, forcibly, by one of the whip-bearing Dryhm. My last image of that wonderful youth was of his wide-eyed, open-mouthed face as he gaped over his shoulders at the benches, searching for his parents, hoping that help would come to him. I let them have him. I am responsible for his death as surely as the Dryhm.

His death, I say, though, as I have before told, his lot was not execution; more likely he'd have a place in Dauroth's conscripted troops. Dermen was a large boy, able to carry arms. Yet a death it was. He was taken before his time from his family, friends, and homeland. He would be bent and molded into someone that would suppress and even kill his countrymen at the whim of the despot who ruled the land.

The scene was repeated in the next group, the fourth, where another of my pupil's was chosen. I became certain that Gammin and Marn, both evidently in the last group, would be taken. The time was upon me. I must decide.

A Dryhm emerged from the corner. Marin and Gammin followed, just ahead of the two final candidates. As they took their places at the front, a single imperative ran through my mind. Decide now! Decide now! Now!

Cold realization flooded over me. I understood at last. Though it cost all I had and brought calamity beyond measure down on the community, I would not sit idly and watch Gammin or Marin be led away if they were chosen.

III.

The questioning began with Marin. He was asked no more and no fewer questions than any other boy. As in the other cases, the questions addressed his parentage, his various skills, and the like. The boy spoke cleanly, not stumbling over his answers as most had done, his voice not cracking or wavering. He was a fine young man. If left to us, he would become a strong and valiant man. If only he were left to us. I unclenched the fist that was pressing against my upper thigh.

When she finished with the woodcutter's son, the Chooser set aside the document she had been consulting and selected another. After inspecting the page, she peered at Gammin. Speaking in a voice that was slightly louder and almost mocking, she stated, "Gammin of the River's Bend. Who are your parents? My information seems to be incomplete."

This was an outrageous statement. No part of me believed

they were unaware of Gammin's background. The Gatherer was trying to humiliate the boy. She was playing with him as a cat toys with a mouse for amusement before devouring it. I forced my jaw to unclench lest someone see the fury on my face and be forewarned of the festival of death I was about to unleash.

If Gammin noticed the slight, he gave no sign. "I have none."

"No parents? Even a rustic knows everyone has a mother and a father. In your case, I should say a sire and a dam."

Her contempt ate away at my forbearance. I imagined what her face would look like as she felt the kiss of my blade.

"I do not know my father or my mother."

The Chooser expected this. She looked up into the audience. "Who stands for this boy?"

I got to my feet. "I stand for Gammin of River's Bend."

"Who are you?"

"I am Annen, long of Twofords and longer of Ehrylan."

"Ah yes. The teacher. We know you." She looked down at her sheaf of notes, glancing at them as if gathering information. She was play acting.

I wondered, as my mental control decayed under the stress, what it would feel like to run a sword blade through her torso so the cross guard slammed against her ribs. I wanted to look into her eyes and watch her miserable life fade as her blood ran out from a wound I inflicted. A wild music thundered in my head. Drums only I could hear pounded; unheard instruments wailed. It was the killing rage, the battle music. I heard it and knew death was near. It had been far too long since I had taken the life of one of Dauroth's possessions.

As if sensing my hostility, the Chooser looked up from her notes. "Have we not heard of your comings and goings?"

I did not answer.

"Answer me." She was seeking to exert control over me, to cow me.

"How am I to know the councils of the Dryhm?"

She considered, brushing the parchments here and there to

cover her discomfort, or so I judged. Then she said, "Yes. Quite so. You are ignorant." She eyed me, perhaps expecting some response. I gave none.

"Annen, late of Twofords, how do you come to stand for this waif? Your home is in the Stone Gate. Why render service to peasants."

The Chooser knew more than she was letting on, so I had to answer truthfully. And carefully. "Service rendered to those less fortunate is not a burden, Dryhm. If you walked in the light, you would know that. But to answer your question, I met Gammin some months ago. I took a liking to him and he, it would seem, to me. It pleases me to offer him my home and my teaching."

"It pleases you?" She tossed glances right and left to her colleagues. They shared a barely subdued laugh. "So we had imagined." She glanced at her notes again, then said without looking up until she finished the last syllable. "Sit, Annen of Twofords."

The boy did himself proud, adopting a manner that was brave without being brazen. I wondered at this. How did he come by such an ability? I had not taught him. If this were Chinenyeh blood speaking, we needed them on our side.

Almost before I realized it, Gammin's interview came to close. The Chooser moved on to the final two candidates. When she was done interrogating them, the Gatherers on the dais conferred. And then it was time.

The future of Twofords hung in the balance of my divided heart. I made ready to unleash death. I measured the distance to the dais again, visualizing the moves I would need to make to dispatch the two Dryhm flanking the boys. I set my mind like a trigger so that at either name, Marin or Gammin, there would be no thought, only action. It would be the first action in a battle that I could neither win nor avoid. I commended my soul to the Maker, asked forgiveness for my foolishness, and waited.

The Chooser rose.

"Of this final group, we find three that are of interest. We will take only one. The other two are too young to enter the king's service. Bagon is chosen."

The words did not make sense to me. I knew only that I had not heard either name for which I was waiting. I believe I gasped. At the same time, a woman's shriek filled the air. All heads turned toward her

"Silence! Contain yourself, woman, lest we take you too."

The Chooser glowered at us as Bagon was led away. When he was gone, she held her arms wide. The folds of her robe hung from them. Backlit by the flames, she looked like a giant, brooding bat.

"This Choosing is concluded. Go, but remember. We watch. We wait. We see. We know. We act. We overcome."

The acolytes echoed the chant in unison. "We watch. We wait. We see. We know. We act. We overcome."

Then, all together, the seven Dryhm and the six acolytes intoned, "We are the Dryhm. We serve the Faceless."

In spite of the delicate situation, I was amused. What a show! I did not smile as the cool breath of relief blew through my soul. I could not smile, for all through this final litany, the Chooser was looking straight at me.

Of the walk back to my home, I have almost no memory. The boys were safe; that thought filled me, pushing away everything else. The boys were safe for three full years. Next year was the Fallow. The cycle would start again with girls the year after that. The boys were safe for now. Safe for now. Safe.

I have been told that Marn and I gathered the boys at the appointed spot. We supported those who came back chasing the vain hope that the son, who was now Chosen, might, against all hoping, be returned. I recall the eyes of Bagon's mother, accusing eyes brimming with abandoned hope. The memory haunts me.

7. DREAMER

I.

The next day was filled with the traditions that we have in Twofords—the sharing of our food and our time with the bereaved. The community recovered quickly, as it had done in the past. Harvest was upon us. We worked all the harder in an effort to work away the painful loss of our young. There were crops to gather and an abundance of other activities that would not wait for emotions to heal and memories to fade.

The two boys matched my desire to instruct with their avarice for learning. There was a sense of urgency in all we did. The pace of our endeavors did not slow as we grew familiar with our new routines. A sense that there was much to accomplish and little time grew stronger with each passing day.

I lost more pupils from families loyal to the memory of King Brand. This hurt my heart, not my pride. Dauroth and his Dryhm had won a battle in the war to separate us. However, as I had been trained and as I was training the boys, I looked on the obverse side of that coin. What benefit might arise from the loss? It was there. I seized upon it gladly.

The reduction in students meant I had more time for my boys. The time we spent together was fertile for learning. That is not to say we avoided fun and play. Those we had in plenty. But, even in that fun, there was learning. From sun up to sun down, we trained and studied. Other mundane tasks blended themselves into the acts of teaching and learning—going to the market, hunting, even gardening.

At first, the training, both physical and mental, was limited to the two boys. This went on for about two months. As Snow Moon grew close, Marn asked if I would be willing to include Arica, his daughter, in the lessons. I was willing and said so. I left the final decision until after I had consulted with the boys. They agreed with a readiness that surprised me. As the snows began to fall on the peaks, the two pupils became three. Soon thereafter, the three became six.

Arica was fifteen—three years older than Marin and Gammin. She was too young to make the trek between Twofords and the Old Forest alone. Even a few years before, a young lady of fifteen would have been safe on that road. Lately, we had begun to see the rise of the youth gangs that eventually made many of our streets unsafe.

Marn brought his daughter with him when he had other errands in the city or the Shambles. We arranged certain days when I would expect her, maybe once each week. We tried to meet them at the gate to save Marn the trip, and, on our way back to the Stone Gate, we'd stop at the Step, Merelina's orphanage. The three children from the Bend quickly became an anticipated event.

That arrangement did not last long. Arica wanted more time with us. Another solution had to be found. As it turned out, one of the children from the orphanage in River's Bend, a lad by the name of Simon, expressed interest. He was little older than Arica, but big for his age. They would make the trek with Old Bilious. I doubted the dog would be willing or able, but he proved to be both. His health and vigor improved remarkably as a result, and he was an able protector.

So that was four, not counting the dog, who did not

participate in our learning sessions.

The final two members of our school came from the Step. One was a young girl called Breanna. She was small for her age, and unusually timid. The other, of course, was Max. He was also small for his age. Timid did not describe him.

Except with the five men under my direct command as principal, I had never taught others the arts of war. The open, unconcealed sessions with the children held little resemblance to the clandestine meetings with my men. I had to learn as I was teaching to be a teacher. Fortunately, I had been taught by capable instructors, not the least of which was my own father. I had excellent examples to follow. All I had to do was imitate those who had gone before me.

One might think Gammin and Marin would feel slighted at having to share our time with the others, particularly because, when the others were there, my boys did not receive much instruction from me. Such was not the case. The four additional students did not share all the sessions. At most, we saw them three or four times each week, and, when they came, it was only for a half-day. Gammin and Marin were with me almost always. As their training progressed, the physical part became increasingly difficult and arduous, often accompanied by bruises, sore muscles, and other similar injuries. The sessions when they could teach rather than practice became recovery times for them. That was as it should be.

We were consumed by our studies. We hardly noticed when the year turned at the rising of New Moon. As Wind Moon and Wet Moon—the third and fourth months—passed, the children began to show obvious signs of their studies. Their muscles became full and round and supple, as did their minds. They grew in their love for one another and we became, to my mind, a close-knit family. It was the first family to which I had belonged since I lost my own, and all my friends as well, in the year King Brand sent me away. I will never forget those children, even if I live ten thousand lifetimes.

II.

Days and nights became weeks and months. The children replaced illiteracy with literacy and untrained courage with calculated discipline. In matters of the mind, Gammin and Marin outpaced the others. This was not just the result of their more frequent and constant access to their teacher. They soaked up learning as dried sea sponges soak up moisture.

Gammin continued to be fascinated by words, both spoken language and reading. Marin was drawn more toward writing. He asked endless questions about historians. Who had authored which tale? Why was this or that story documented when some verbal tradition was not? Gammin would spend time reading the titles of my books to see which one he might want to look at. Marin inspected the books, looking at their bindings or the parchment or paper upon which the words were written. He would ask about the author. Gammin asked about the contents.

In the same way, Gammin was drawn more towards mathematics; he loved to test himself against problems I'd pose. Marin endured such learning and, while he did not excel, he was able to complete his lessons. For him, the joy was in the number, how they were drawn, keeping them neat and orderly without mistakes cluttering the pages. To him, poetry was math, an ordered, rhythmic arrangement of syllables to construct a whole concept. Several times, I caught him writing verse when he should have been figuring or reading.

I did not seek to influence the boys or the other children. There was little potential that any of them might grow up to be scholars or historians. My goal was to strengthen their minds so that their intellect might become weapons they could use for the good of the faithful. If one tended more towards drawing numbers neatly than adding them together, what of it? Ea gives to each the tools to complete their purpose. I sought to discover and to sharpen the implements.

It was not all work and study. We took breaks, some of

them quite long and eventful, though those occurred mostly in our second year together. Marin spent many days and nights with his family, so there were times Gammin and I were together alone, as we had been in the early days. Those were special times for us; I do not have the words to describe them other than to say that I often thought I caught glimpses of the love and pride a father might feel at having such a son.

The visits home started when, in the fourth month after Marin came to be a part of my household, I asked him if he missed home.

He answered me plainly, as was his way. "Of course, shinando. I miss my mother and father. Sometimes, I even miss my sister, even though I see her so often here. More than that, I miss the animals and the forest."

My heart sank, but he raised it up straight away.

"I miss all that, for sure. But so what? I'm here. I get to live with you and Gammin. What could be better than that?"

I spoke to Marn. We agreed that his boy should return home from time to time. We also agreed that it was time for the boys to learn what the woodcutter could teach them. There could be no better teacher in the ways of the forest than an Old One.

III.

There were, during this time, three dreams that revealed something very special about Marin. The first was the most spectacular as far as sheer imagery was concerned. Before the second and third dreams arrived, I did not know whether to make much out of it; we all dream and most of us have strange ones. Marin's dream was different. It brought the boys to my bed chamber in the time of darkness that is both very early and very late, which the Ehrylain call twinight.

They stopped at the threshold. Gammin called my name. I am a light sleeper and had awakened when first they set foot in the hallway outside their room. I had waited, listening, wondering what they were, literally, up to.

"Annen?"

"Yes, Gammin. Are you all right?"

"Yes, sir. It's Marin."

Sir? I did not ask the boys to call me sir. It was a courtesy, especially when more important matters were being discussed, and always when we were in training.

"Come in. Come in." I gestured to the two chairs I'd added to my room for just that purpose. "What has happened, Marin?"

The boys sat down, looking solemn and a little frightened. Gammin set the candle on a table between the two chairs.

"I had a dream, Annen."

I could have made some snide remark to make them laugh, a mild rebuke for not waiting until morning light. Something told me this was not the occasion for such things.

"I want to hear. But you must wait. Gammin, will you fetch Marin some water? There's a good lad."

I used the time to splash water from the basin on to my face. I sat down on the foot of my bed, as near to them as could be. Gammin returned with three mugs. He gave one to me and one to Marin.

"Right. Now tell us your dream, Marin."

"I dreamed of a battle. It was terrible. Everywhere I looked, as far as I could see, men were fighting and dying. I could smell smoke on the wind, not nice smoke like when you come home from a long hunt and you smell the fire from your own hearth when you are still a ways away. Not like that at all. It was a sick, oily smell. There was something else too, something I have never smelled before, not in real life, anyway. It was a wet smell, the smell of salt and sand. In my dream I knew it was the smell of the sea. That was a good smell."

Marin stopped and waited for me to respond. I wasn't sure what to say, so I asked a question, something that was sitting on my tongue. It just popped out.

"What do you mean 'not in real life'? Dreams are real, Marin, very real. And this one sounds like it might be more real than most."

He ignored my question, which was probably for the best. However, out of the corner of my eye, I saw Gammin's eyebrows rise momentarily.

"Go on, Marin."

"So I could see it and smell it, all around me, this great battle. What really caught my attention was the sound. It sounded like... it sounded like... like... I don't know how to explain it. It sounded like a mighty wind blowing hard enough to push rocks around. It sounded like a hundred wagons full of pots and pans were let loose from the top of a steep hill and all came crashing down at the same time. Like that, sort of, only continuous... continuously. Does that make sense, shinando?"

"It makes a lot of sense, Marin, and it is very accurate. I've been in a few battles myself. Everyone remembers the sound. After a battle, it is hard to remember what you did or how you felt at the time. But the sound stays with you. And the smell, of course."

Marin was visibly shaken, now much more so than before he started telling us about the dream. I began to realize there might be something important here.

"What else, Marin?"

"There was city on a hill, with a tall stone wall running round the base of the hill. But that is the strange thing, one of the strange things. I've never been to a city, other than Twofords—which everyone says is not very big. How could I see a city in my dream when I have never seen one when I am awake?"

"Sounds like Twofords to me," said Gammin. "There's the castle up on the hill. And there is a wall around the city. Maybe your dream just forgot to show the rest of the city in between."

"No," replied Marin immediately. "No and maybe yes. It might have been Twofords, but that's the thing. It wasn't. The city was big. And it was old. I could tell from the stone work, somehow. The walls were high and thick, much higher and thicker than here, in Twofords. Armored warriors were patrolling on top of the wall, shooting arrows, carting off injured soldiers. There were towers all along the wall, big ones, really tall, not like the ones we have on the walls around Twofords."

"Towers?" This came out more as an exclamation than a question. Both boys turned to me with startled eyes. "How many towers, Marin? How many?"

"That's another funny thing. There were eight towers. I don't know how I know that. I didn't count them, but, in my dream, I just sort of knew that there were eight towers, one larger than all the rest. The big one was set back from the wall a long way, maybe even at the center of the city, I am not sure.

"Even though the walls were thick and strong and the men were brave, I knew they wouldn't stop the attacking armies. That made me sad, not only in my dream. I am still sad." He stopped and chewed his lip.

Rhua, I thought, you carried this boy a dream of Tarabol? The implications reverberated behind my eyes like the drums of Arel. I felt Gammin's gaze and turned my head to see him staring at me, a thousand unspoken questions in his eyes. I saw concern on his face, as if he understood that what Marin had dreamed might be very important. One thing more I saw in his face, dancing in his eyes like starlight. I saw patience.

"The attackers were crashing against the walls. I also saw waves of grey-green water crashing over rocks that poked up through the sand on the shore. The waves were like flowing blocks of ice with crowns of white foam that danced all along the tops, and when the water ran back out after it hit the shore, some of the foam stayed behind, clinging to the rocks. But Annen, I have never been to an ocean. I've never seen an ocean beach!" The last two sentences were spoken such that each word had more emphasis and volume than the one before. His fists were clenched, his forehead and upper lip wet with sweat.

My heart was beating like thunder now. I watched the woodcutter's son. He was caught up in his tale, and I strove with myself not to disturb him.

"I am not sure, Annen. I may be confusing this. I think the

city was near the ocean, but it was also surrounded by all those men. I remember thinking in my dream, there are as many men in these armies as there are trees in the Old Forest and there is no way the city can stand against them. I began to cry. The city was beautiful and I knew that the people were good and the king that ruled there was noble."

Marin took a long pull at his water. He set the mug down on the table and toyed with it, sliding it from one hand to the other. He did not look up when he started to speak again, but he had calmed himself.

"As I stood there weeping for the city, I saw a man standing in front of me. He was looking out over the ramparts. That's when I realized I was up on the wall. I could see the fighting spread out below and the towers and… the sea. That is why the man was up there too. He could see. He was a warrior. I have never seen armor like he was wearing. It was black and silver, not like the stuff the troops from the garrison sometimes wear. It was much finer, not so … clunky. I don't mean fancy. It seemed of better make, the way something made by a wood wright is finer than something made by someone who is not so able. Anyway, his armor was stained and blotched with dirt and blood. He had a sword. It sort of dangled in his fingers as if he had forgotten it, but it looked like it was a part of him, as if he was ready to use it in the next blink of his eye."

A warm shiver danced along my spine.

"The sword was amazing. There was blood on it. I could see the smears, yet light ran along the blade and it shone like it was new-forged. Letters blazed along its whole length, on both sides. Something came to me, a phrase, I guess you'd call it. I knew it was what was written on the sword. The words rang out in my mind over the sound of the wind and the battle. *'Dan tahli meh ahn dan tahli noh.'* I don't know what it means. I thought it was describing the sword, or maybe even the man and the sword together. Have you heard that before, Annen?"

I drew breath through my clenched teeth. *Dan tahli meh; ahn dan tahli noh.* Yes, I knew that phrase. I had read it many times.

The question that shouted itself down the halls of my mind was: how did this boy come to hear those words, words in a language that had not been spoken by any nation or peoples for at least five hundred years?

"Yes, Marin. Yes, I have. It is an old saying, very old. It means, roughly, 'The sword of justice; the sword that gives life.' It speaks of a sword, a man, and philosophy. Well, not a philosophy exactly, maybe a way of governing would be more accurate. Go on."

I had to get him talking again. My tongue was tangled in a mouth gone dry.

"As I was looking at that sword, the man turned his head. His eyes were very green. There was a little scar beneath the right one. Anyway, he must have seen the tears on my cheeks, the ones I had shed over the city. He spoke to me."

Marin paused so long I thought he might not continue.

"What did Andur say, Marin?"

Both boys jumped at the name I used.

"He told me not to be afraid. He said there was no coming or going in this world or any other world that was not woven in Ea's will. He said I could never fall so far that Rhua could not lift me up. He said that no matter where we are taken, we could not be hidden from the eye of the Maker. But really, all he said was, 'Don't be afraid.'"

Marin fell silent. His stillness caught us in its net. We watched the shadows dancing to the tune of the flickering candle. The only sound was of breathing. My thoughts tumbled over themselves as I tried to piece together some meaning for the dream. I was sure of what the boy had dreamed, but I could not fathom why. When I came to myself again, the boys were waiting. It was my move, it seemed.

"Are you?" I asked, thinking that Marin would not understand I was referring to the dream words of Andur—don't be afraid. I wanted to get him talking again.

"Yes, a little," he replied. "Not afraid exactly. Confused."

"Why?"

"Not sure. Maybe because I saw so many things in the

dream that I have never seen. Maybe because it seemed so real. It still seems real. I can still see it all."

"I understand, I think. I've had vivid dreams before, and I have had dreams that scared my boots off." I was maneuvering for a way out of this, looking for time to think. "You wake up feeling like you are going to go on being scared forever. Those feelings pass pretty soon. The light of day chases them away so that you can't even remember what scared you."

I looked from one boy to the other then continued. "Let's cook up something to start the day. We'll watch the sun rise as we eat. Then we'll go about our day just like everything is completely normal. Which it is, right? Maybe later, when our spirits are as strong as the sunlight, we'll talk about the dream. Sound good?"

Gammin said, "Eating always sounds good! Race ya to the kitchen!"

Both boys erupted from their seats and bolted from the room. One of the chairs knocked against the table. The candle sputtered an archipelago of wax across the wood. I sat for a moment, looking at the little cream-colored islands. Then I went to see to my friends.

IV.

The morning passed without further discussion of "the dream," as it became known until another pushed its way to the surface and crowded the stage. After watching the sun rise, I took them out to the courtyard and set them to a stiff practice round. Sweating students asks fewer questions.

Arica, Simon, Max, and Breanna arrived as anticipated. The day passed as so many others, with work, play, talk, and food in the right proportions. If they noticed any underlying tension, I could not tell. Old Bil gave no indication that anything was amiss, and he was likely the most observant among us, if not the most energetic or wakeful.

The others departed for their homes; we three were left to

ours. I set Marin to cooking and Gammin to preparing the other necessaries of the board. It was not until our evening meal that they had a chance to ask me the questions that had no doubt consumed them throughout the day. Marin started it, speaking through a mouthful of barely cake and cheese.

"What I don't understand is, well, I've never seen a city like that, and I've never seen an ocean. But I can still see the images. How can that be?"

"I am not sure, lad. There may be more to this than a simple dream. Yet it may be nothing more, you understand? I think it is the former. I believe you dreamed of the Fall of Tarabol, the great city where Andur sat on his throne. You know the legends. Unless I am mistaken, it was Andur with whom you spoke."

"How can that be?" This question echoed his last almost exactly in content and tone.

"As I have said, I do not know." His face was crestfallen at my ignorance. I took a sip of canella before asking, "Do you doubt that you saw the sea? Do you doubt that it was a city, a great city, that you saw? You have never seen an army, yet you described the battle perfectly, sights, sounds, and smells?"

Marin did not answer. He had no chance. Gammin interjected, rolling his eyes, "Now look who's asking three questions at the same time!" We all laughed, though soon a quiet solemnity crept back in and enfolded us. It seemed comforting, so I tarried there, in the place where words have not yet been spoken. After a time, I sucked in a big breath and expelled it.

"Leaving all the other oddities aside, your discomfort would be enough to make me pay attention. We must ponder this thing, the three of us. I would not speak of it openly, however. Tell your father and your mother. They have wisdom to guide you. For myself, I believe you have seen the Fall of Tarabol, of which many legends and songs speak, though they are seldom heard in these years. It is a strange gift, and terrible, if I am right. Who among us can say they have seen bright Tarabol in the days of Andur's calamity and spoken to him on the walls as his fair city fell to the dark hoards?"

"Andur, the High King?"

My tongue responded before my sense. "No! Don't be foolish, Marin." He did not note the strong language. "Andur was never a High King. That is a false history Dauroth propagated. Andur was the king, the only king. There were no other kings under him or his heirs. They ruled the lands of the Crescent through others as do all good rulers, it is true, but Andur and his heirs were the only kings."

"Then it is not true that Andur subjugated the kingdoms of the Crescent and ruled over them?"

"Subjugated? No, that is certainly not true. He united the land, sure, but the unification stopped centuries of warring and bloodshed. The peoples of the Crescent benefited from the society he created. They were his people and he was their king. If the histories and legends speak true, he belonged to them as much as they to him. The kingdoms came later, after Andur's line failed. Some believe his line has only faltered and will return again."

I mused for a moment, considering what I had told them. I decided a clarification was in order. I was, after all was said and done, their teacher.

"Strictly speaking, one could say the people of the Crescent were subjugated because they became his subjects. But there were few battles where Andur's armies fought against the people of the Crescent. His fight was with Outlanders who had overrun the native populations—even then as now—and against Dauroth though he went then under a different name in those years. We fight alongside Andur in spirit if not in body. But all this questioning is folly. You know the stories of Andur and the City of the Eight Towers. I cannot believe your father would be so lax!"

My minor outrage was just theatrics, and they knew it. I knew they had no difficulty recalling the various times we had studied that subject matter. I did my best to glare at them. They had none of it, knowing me through and through.

"I had not thought of that! Maybe that's how I got the

image of the city, from the old stories."

"Maybe. Yet I think not. Don't focus only on the dream, my boy. Think also on how you felt, how you feel. Do you often have dreams like this?"

"No, never!"

"Is that not sign enough?"

There was a great deal more of this kind of questioning. They desired me to tell them all I knew of Andur. I spent the rest of the evening telling a tale that took us deep into the night. By the time I reached its ending, which was only another beginning, both boys were nodding in their efforts to stay awake. I told them of Andur and the victories he won that drove out the occupying Outlanders. I told them of how he ruled after, with wisdom in his right hand and mercy in his left. More importantly, I told them of how good King Brand had done his best to emulate these virtues during his own, much more recent, rule. I showed them illustrations in books and scrolls, some of them very ancient indeed. I was reading to them from a tattered, age-worn scroll when they stopped asking questions.

As I listened to the soft breathing of two boys on the edge of sleep, I thought how similar the situation in Ehrylan was to what Andur faced. If the lads had been more awake, I might have thrown this thought out to them, but they were in no condition for such a discussion. Their breathing grew deeper as I sat pondering my own thoughts.

In time, I rose and cleared away the remaining plates from the meal. Gammin, always attuned to me, roused himself before I finished the tidying. He put away the last of the items on the table, including the scroll, which he lingered over. I tousled his hair. He hugged me, then slapped Marin on the knee.

"Get up. It's time for bed!"

Marin opened his eyes, looked confused until he realized where he was, and answered, "Yeah, says you." He pushed himself groggily to his feet and lumbered after Gammin.

I watched them into their room, feeling very fortunate. I

had seen times hard and cruel in my life. I had more than once despaired. The days in which we now lived were little better than some of the worst I could recall. But, as I heard one boy pelt the other with a pillow, I thanked Ea for the gift.

V.

The difficulties with the youth gangs continued to increase as the months passed. The problem was most serious within the walls of Twofords. Outside, the farther one moved from the city, the lesser the gangs held sway. Within the Shambles, the gangs could not gather a foothold, a tribute to the organization of the seemingly unorganized. Likewise, River's Bend did well to limit the influence of the gangs; there were some significant skirmishes, but the miscreants discovered the villagers' mettle and troubled them little after.

Though we continued to exercise care, I lost any concern I felt for my students when they went in a group, something they did increasingly, especially in the second year. The six youngsters did not cower in the face of being bullied. When attacked, they would defend themselves. Please know that I am not boasting of my prowess as a teacher. Marin and Gammin were like that before they met me; Pruis had learned that fact at our first two meetings, as had I. There were a few encounters, most of which produced minor injuries and a little blood for the attackers. As they were not arrogant about their victories, my students gained respectful acceptance, not malice. It only occurred to me much later, after they were all long gone from my care, that my six had been a gang in their own right.

The respect accrued to Step. Merelina suffered very little at the hands of the gangs. There was some slight vandalism and, on one or two occasions, the theft of items left in the yard during the night. That was not much, considering. Perhaps even the gangs valued her efforts. I like that reason.

Marn and I were not incautious. We procured a small wagon and a horse to draw it. An ox would have been less expensive, but we judged the horse to be more versatile. The animal seemed to take an immediate liking to us, which made everything easier.

With the help of the children, we converted the dilapidated wagon into a poor man's carriage. There were no leather straps or chains to soften the ride. When we were done with the first iteration, the double-benched carriage afforded comfort for four and room for all six at a pinch. As the months passed, the students tried various innovations to improve it, some of which were successful. Arica and Simon used the carriage—which they named the Water Wheel for some reason I could never discover—to and from the city. Along the way, they picked up Max and Breanna from the Step. Old Bil dogged the horse's steps, sometimes even leading the way. I suspect he rode as much as he walked.

We had to build a paddock for the horse. This turned into quite a festival. Merelina brought Max and Breanna to help. Marn tried to lead the way but Gammin and Marin had decided this was their project. Dara, Marn, Merelina, and I were relegated to the role of advisors. Four adults watched from our make-shift table as the children worked. To their credit, the youngsters consulted us early and often.

Max managed the communication between the builders and the advisors. Whether he elected himself or whether the others appointed him was not clear. That day was the first time we noticed an interesting habit the boy developed. He would march up to us, chest pushed out importantly and chin high, the general of an army. There was nothing new in that, of course; Max always acted with bravado and a sense of grandeur. The oddity was that he brought his questions or comments in sets of two.

Max would come over to where we were sitting, a tiny tiger advancing on cornered prey. He would wait respectfully until we acknowledged him.

"Yes, Max? What is it?"

He would say, "Two things!" or, "There's two things."

The scene was repeated throughout the day. It became a

merriment between the older folks. When he broke the pattern and said, "I need a couple of things," Merelina quipped, "Arica must be teaching him new vocabulary."

The two-things behavior continued the rest of his life. It became such a fixture and so much a part of him that we started to participate, giving him two gifts when only one was necessary, or telling him things twice when it was clear he understood the first time. This was all done in good natured fun, to be sure. Max enjoyed the attention as much as we enjoyed giving it. He was a delightful boy, if a trifle obnoxious at times.

This was also a day Simon's talents stood out. The boy was able to estimate at a single glance how many nails would be needed for a section, or the number of boards it would take to build a partition. There was nothing new in this. Anyone who knew him had seen his talent with numbers. It made our hearts sing to see the reticent young man shine.

We drank a lot of canella that day, and treated any number of scrapes, cuts, and splinters. The paddock turned out to be sturdy. The horse spent many happy days there, as did Old Bil and, towards the end, rabbits that Arica brought. She assured me that there would only be two. One thing I learned: there is no such thing as only two rabbits.

VI.

The second dream occurred a week or so after we finished the paddock. This was in Wind Moon, two months before the anniversary that marked the day I met Gammin. The nights had started to catch up to the days in terms of warmth. This time, Marin waited until morning to tell me of his dream. I was forewarned. I awoke to the sound of hushed voices in the twilight. They were waiting for me in the kitchen when I came out of my room with the dawn.

"Another dream, Marin?" I sat down at the table next to him.

"Yes, sir." He looked down at his hands, which were clasped on his lap.

As before, Gammin got us drinks. I added a log or two to the coals in the fireplace.

"I saw the sea again, and the beach, but not from the same place, not from the city walls. I was standing on rocks that were piled above white sand. I guess it must have been an island. Maybe. It felt too small to be an island. Anyway, it was dead night. The moon was full, so bright it cast shadows. A man was sitting on the rocks. I couldn't see him, but I could see his shadow, plain as day. I was behind him, but there was none of my shadow, just his."

He swallowed and made sure I was paying attention. I tried to swallow too. My throat was dry. My thoughts flew straight to a conclusion I could not accept. Marin went back to staring at his hands.

"The man was using his arms to steady himself, supporting himself on each side. On the rocks. The moonlight was so bright I could see triangles of sand between the shadows caused by his outstretched arms and his torso. Perfect triangles, one on each side. It was amazing."

"What was he doing, Marin?"

"I don't know. I was just there, behind him, though I wasn't really there. You know how it is in dreams."

The boy looked at me for an affirmation that I understood dreams could be strange in that particular way. I knew what he was going to describe. I remember wondering whether or not I wanted this gift. My pulse quickened.

"He never really did anything, shinando. It was just his shadow, sitting there motionless, that was all."

"Nothing else?"

"Well, there was the sea... and the waves."

"What about the waves, Marin?"

"Now you ask, I guess that's what I remember most viv...vival...vividly." His eyes glinted when he found the word. I could see confidence returning. "The beach was a crescent. The moon was so bright I could see the waves as they broke far out from the shore. When they crested and fell over, the foam sort of drew itself out in long white lines that ran across the surface, the whole length of the beach and more, rushing towards us... him. The waves ran up the sand all the way to the rocks where the man was sitting. The water was so clear that I could see his shadow beneath it when the waves ran over the top. When a wave ran back out, there was a hiss that I could hear even over the sounds of the sea. That really stood out to me, over and over and over."

"Anything else Marin?"

I knew enough already. I just wanted to see how far this went. I remember noticing that my palms were sweating and my mouth was dry, thinking how strange that was. I licked my lips, uselessly.

"The stars. They were strange, not the stars we have here in Ehrylan. Some were really bright, two of them especially."

My hands clenched into involuntary fists. I responded much more vigorously than I intended. "Two stars, brighter than the rest? Where were they? Where?"

Marin looked up and his eyes opened wide.

"They were up to my right, up over my shoulder. I remember because, when I looked at them, I could see the peak of the rocks behind me, just below where they hung in the sky. Why, Annen? What does it all mean? Can you tell me?"

Gammin shifted. I had forgotten all about him. He sat across the table from us. He was watching Marin, the woodcutter's son; Marin, my pupil; Marin, the seer.

I took a deep breath, lingered over the exhalation.

"I can tell you what it means. It means that you have a gifting from Ea. It means that you are a seer."

Both boys exclaimed "What?" They spoke in unison, using exactly the same tone.

"It is a true dream, a dream of something that happened long ago."

I waited to see if they would respond, but they didn't. They sat there across from each other, mouths gaping.

"The other dream might not have been something that really happened, since the man spoke to you. Still, I think it was a seeing as well, now that you saw what you saw tonight."

Gammin spoke first. "What does it mean, being a seer?"

"You know the stories. Andur had Teryn, who dreamed that Tarabol would fall and Andur would rise to victory."

I let that sink in for a while, to myself as well as the boys. I went to a knee in front of Marin, taking his hands in mine. "It means that, from time to time, Marin will dream important things and sometimes see visions even when he is not asleep. Sometimes, he will understand them, other times someone else will interpret them, as Ea wills. It is a strange gift. I have never known anyone that had it, but the old stories are full of such folk. They show up when things get hard. I think it means your life will not be boring."

I did not tell then that it meant great change and trouble are hard upon us. Rhua does not raise seers for trivial matters.

"But... but... how do you know that, Annen? It was just a stupid dream, just a man sitting on a rock waiting for something. Not only that, it was just a shadow of a man. Was he even there at all? What was he waiting for? I just don't know."

"I do." In all the world, I was the only one who knew the answer to that question. I felt the tears coming. I was helpless against them.

"You do? What? Tell me! What was he waiting for?"

I looked him full in the face. Our eyes met as if we had come together in the center of a battlefield and were surrounded.

"I was waiting for hope."

I dissolved into tears. It took all my strength not to sob like a babe in the cradle. It is like that for us sometimes, when the past jumps out from behind a corner without warning. Moreover, it is like that when you catch the echo of Rhua, the power of Ea in motion and might. He made us. Our spirits celebrate his touch.

VII.

I told Marn, Dara, and Lina. They were not skeptical, since they knew of the first occurrence. I did not tell them how I was certain the dream showed something that had actually happened. They did not ask. I would not have told them if they had. That came later.

We discussed what Ea might be trying to tell us. I should say that we tried to determine what Ea had shown. The Maker does not try and fail. It is us, the creation, who fail. Yet even our failures are woven into the tapestry of his will. It is a wonder of wonders.

Nothing of great note happened as the weeks passed. The dream drifted away from the fore as Wet Moon came and went with its showers. Pleasant Moon rose, a signal that the hard weather had passed. Pleasant Moon is aptly named in the Southland. It is a time of soft breezes and sunshine, when both nights and days are agreeable. It is a month I will always hold blessed for the gifts it brought me.

One of those agreeable days, I was teaching my young friends in the Stone Gate. The courtyard was full. Gammin had just finished leading the other five students in a sword form called Four Rivers. They all knew it.

"Good," I said. "Gammin, Marin, to me. The rest of you, get some water and warm up with your staves."

There was a smattering of delighted squeals and tired sighs. Gammin and Marin waited in front of me as I watched the others move to the water barrel.

"Those four are looking better."

They nodded their heads at the same time and with the same motion. Sometimes they mirrored each other so closely it was unnerving. They looked nothing alike, yet their mannerisms could be identical at times. Other times, it seemed they might have been from different worlds.

"After they've rested, take them through Forest and Stream twice. Make sure the hand positions are correct, and watch Max's footwork. His steps are a bit long today."

"Yes, shinando," they chorused.

I gave them a short bow, which they returned more deeply before they went to get water.

I went inside, something I did not normally do during training. There was no harm in it; the boys knew what they were doing. Forest and Stream was still new to the other four. They'd be at it a while yet, and it would be slow going. I had time enough for what I wanted to do.

I opened what I hoped was a secret compartment in my chest. I did not believe the boys would come in my room without leave, and I certainly did not think they would go through the large wooden chest where I kept most of my clothes, but one never knows. I'd hidden two items there a week before, hoping to keep them undiscovered until the right time. Tonight was that time. Both items were wrapped in thin leather sheets and tied with rawhide strands. I took them into the front of the house and left them on the hearth.

Back in the courtyard, I watched sweaty young people with staves moving to the count of one leader. The courtyard was large enough, but just barely. It was never made for the purposes to which I put it. There had been several changes to accommodate six people with swords or stave, such as relocating the wood pile.

When they were done, I called them back into line. They knew that I would not speak again until they were settled, so that happened quickly.

"Good workout. Any questions? No? Attention!"

We bowed, each of them careful to go lower than I. I straightened up, waiting, testing them. I stepped out to the side, placing my feet apart, clasping my hands behind my back. The line held as the children waited for me. They were doing very well, and had developed excellent discipline for ones so young. They would need that discipline if they were to survive what was coming.

I moved off. Their line broke. Voices tramped over each other. I stopped near the doorway to the house, watching them. The children knew they had time now to do as they pleased. Free time in this safe environment was as important as the physical and mental learning. It was a time I liked to watch, though they needed space away from my observation. Today, I had to exercise patience, for I was eager to present the gifts. That had to wait until the other four had departed.

The children undertook the various activities that suited them. Gammin and Marin went off to one corner and practiced their staff form. Arica and Breanna were talking to each other. Simon and Max staged a mock sword fight.

It was nice to see those two together, each so different and yet so similar. Max was feisty and assertive, at times almost to the point of humor, since he was so small. His desire to be loved and accepted mitigated the worst effects of his aggressive behavior.

Simon was slow of speech and movement. He could move quickly when he wanted to, but his nature was to think before acting. This was not true where it came to numbers and counting. In these matters, he was quick as a snake. He could count seemingly uncountable quantities at a glance and could make sums and differences without thought. In truth, I do not believe he engaged conscious thought to count or do the simple mathematics. He seemed to know, intuitively, if that is possible. Because of his reluctance and slowness of speech and movement, Simon was considered bent by many, though his difference was less immediately observable than Temay's.

Max was quick and sure. Simon was slow and uncertain. Where Simon was tall and muscular, Max was slight. These were the differences. Yet both boys were without parents and had been since they were very young. Neither boy had any living relative; both depended on others for their survival.

At just under eleven summers, Max was the youngest boy. Little Breanna was not yet ten. Simon—the eldest in the group at sixteen—was a month or two older than Arica. Marin and Gammin had just turned thirteen.

I was watching Simon and Max, pleased at how they were adapting moves from the sword forms into their unstructured sparring. Arica came to me. She was a beautiful young lady, lithe and strong, her black hair tied back in a tail. She waited nearby, respectfully, until I recognized her.

"How are you, Arica?"

"Very well, shinando. I am enjoying the book you lent me."

"The Tale of the Lion? I did not lend. It is a gift."

The look on her face was magnificent. She had one of those smiles that put the stars to shame. The book was one of the better histories detailing the dynasty of which King Brand had been the last ruler.

"I thank you! I... " She looked down at her feet, then back up.

"Yes, Arica? What is it? You wish to tell me something? Have you stolen Max's heart again?"

Her face turned red as if by magic. "No, sir!" Then she realized I was kidding. Quick as a badger, she pelted me in the stomach. There was just time for me to tense for the blow. Her fist was tight and the strike was true.

"It's Bre, shinando, she wants to show you her dance. She's been working on it for days and... Will you watch it?"

I put my hand on her shoulder companionably and looked around for Breanna. She was standing in a corner by herself, trying to look as if she had not been watching us. She was even smaller than Max, and shy as a doe. I gave Arica's shoulder a squeeze and walked toward the little one. When I got to her, I squatted on my haunches and extended both arms wide.

"Does this pretty maiden have a hug for an old man?"

She dropped her head so low that her chin was pressing against her throat, but I could see the smile that decorated her face. Next instant, she flung herself into my arms.

I kissed her tiny cheek. "I hear you learned a new dance."

She clasped her hands across her abdomen and then brought them up so she was almost hugging her own shoulders. "Yes, shinando." Her mouth said one thing. Her body was shouting something different.

It was like that with her. She could dance, even at this tender age, like a snowflake sailing on the wide wind. When she was playing with the other children or even just moving from one place to another, she skipped and twirled with the steps of whatever new dance she was learning. But when asked to show the dance more formally, she became reluctant.

"What is the name of your dance, Breanna?"

"It's Corn Gathering dance." Her lower lip pushed out over the top one.

"That one? I like Corn Gathering Dance! Will you show me?"

Her eyes flicked up to mine, though her head did not move. It was a comical look, eyes up, head down, chin on chest, with lower lip protruding. I might have laughed for the joy of seeing it if the consequences had not been so high. Instead of laughing, I widened my own eyes and nodded an encouraging plea. Without hesitation, she turned on her heel as if dancing already and rushed, stiff arms at her sides, to the center of the yard.

If it had been Max or Simon or Arica, all of the students, Breanna included, would have lined up to watch. However, it was the little one. The rest knew that doing so would spoil everything. I saw them melt to the more remote spots, all save Arica who was allowed. It warmed my heart, this respectful society the children had built. Would that the adults around them had as much consideration for each other. There was hope here, in these children.

Breanna danced better than well. When she finished, she made a bow—not a courtesy, as we call them in Ehrylan—as if she'd been showing a sword or staff form.

"That was scrumptious! Will you teach me?"

"Teach you? That's silly, shinando. Corn Gathering dance is for girls."

"Really? Hmmm. I'd like to learn. If I swing you around, will you teach me?" She loved it when I held her out at arm's length and rotated in a tight circle.

"Yesssss!"

It was much later than usual when the four left. The gifts lay untouched and unnoticed on the hearth. I had learned a new dance. That was a gift to me, a reminder that patience, like wisdom, is its own reward. After I lifted Breanna into the Water Wheel, Arica came to me. She was always last to board, a steadfast shepherdess minding her playful flock. She hugged me tightly and for so long that Old Bil came over to see what he was missing. He stood between us and the horse, waiting without comment, his tail lashing my legs.

Arica said, "I thank you, shinando."

She dropped her arms from my waist and climbed into the conveyance.

VIII.

As was our habit, the two boys and I watched until after the carriage turned the corner. They would have time to make it home by darkfall, but only just. We vanished into various parts of the house, Gammin and I to our rooms to freshen up after the workout and Marin into the paddock to clean up after Sir Speedy, the horse. The boys rotated this duty when the others left too late to do it themselves.

I was sitting at the table when the boys emerged from their room, if not squeaky clean then at least acceptably refreshed. I was trying to look engrossed in some book I had selected at random from the shelf. They paid me little mind as they began to prepare for our supper.

"Not just yet, boys," I said, looking up from the book. I noticed then, only too late, that it was upside down in my hands. "I want to talk with you."

There was a short race to get the chair nearest me. Marin won, so Gammin moved around to the other side of the table, across from us.

"Do you know what today is, Gammin?" I thought he might say something silly like the day after yesterday or the day before tomorrow. He did not.

"This is the day I met you, one year gone."

"Yes, it is. I wondered if you'd forgotten."

Marin snorted. "Forgotten? Are you kidding? He's talked

about little else for a whole week." In reply, Gammin made a rude, vibrating sound with his lips and tongue.

"Well," I said, "I thought we should commemorate the occasion. Do you know what that means?"

Two heads nodded. Gammin said, "Yes, Annen, I know what it means, but I would not have known a year ago." He looked down, something that a year ago was common enough but now seemed odd for him. Then he added, "Back when I was more fragle."

He and I laughed. Marin looked uncertain.

"This is a great day," I exclaimed. "I want to celebrate! But if you keep looking at your feet, boy, you won't be able to see what is on the hearth." Two heads swiveled that way. Two chairs scraped the floor as their occupants shot out of them like arrows from a bow. Such was the respect they had learned that neither touched the packages, though they stood peering at them with eager eyes.

I left them suspended as I rose slowly meandered toward them. I sat on the hearth and picked up the gifts. "This one is for you, Gammin." I handed him the oblong package. "This one is for you, Marin." I offered the rectangular one to him.

Gammin asked, "Can we open them, Annen?"

"It would be a shame not to. Go right ahead."

He looked over at Marin. "At the same time, Mar?"

"No. It's your day. You go first."

Gammin began to unwrap his gift. He was not like me when I was young, or any of those with whom I ran in those bright days so long ago. He did not rip into the thing. No, he untied the rawhide and coiled it about his hand before carefully setting it aside on the stone hearth. Then, as if even with his cautious actions he might rip the tough stuff, he pulled back the leather wrapping a fold at a time. Another boy might have guessed long before what lay hidden in his hands, but I think Gammin did not. I believe that, until he saw the hunting knife resting across his palms, he was so concerned in the unwrapping that he quite forgot the gift.

I watched his face, identifying the parade of expressions.

He raised his head and eyes to mine and then to Marin's, then dropped them again to the knife. This was repeated two or three times before he spoke.

"I thank you, Annen. I... I... I don't know what to say."

"You just said it, lad. Now, if you will, take it out so we can see the pointy bit."

He looked startled, as if it were an unforeseen idea that fell on his toes. His fingers gripped the antler handle with something akin to eager hesitation. Slowly, carefully, he drew the blade; it emerged with the hollow whisper of steel against leather, a sound that was very familiar to me. The weight of the knife became apparent to him as it settled in his hand. He hefted it, measuring. His face split into a grin.

"It's old," he said. His eyes twitched back and forth between the knife and my face three times in quick succession. "It was yours, wasn't it?"

"Yes, Gammin. It was mine. When I was not much older than you, my best friend killed a deer, a big buck, high up in the Western Mountains. We brought it home and feasted our families and their friends. Our fathers were proud. We had ridden out alone and brought back meat. His father made everyone laugh because, every so often, he'd pound on the table with his hand and say, "Tell us again how you slew the mighty buck, oh, son of my life!" My friend would finish whatever was in his mouth and tell the tale again. It was a good day."

I lapsed into silence as I lived again the joys of that day. When I reached the other side of the haystack, the boys that were my current joy were waiting patiently.

"From then on, we rode with the men. I thought nothing more of it; it was a passing event. I told you once, Gammin, that I liked knives. My friend knew that as well. Later, on my birthday, he gave me that knife as a gift."

He was inspecting the handle.

He asked, "This is antler, isn't it?"

"Yes, from the antler of the buck my friend killed that day."

"Let me see." Marin held out his hands.

Gammin shook his head. "Not yet." He slid his knife back into the sheath. "Let's see what you got first."

"Oh! Right!"

He'd forgotten his own package in the joy of watching his friend. How different they were than I was at their age, how selfless. On the other hand, Marin was far closer to me than Gammin in his unwrapping technique. There was a single yank on the rawhide to untie the bow and one sweeping gesture to brush away the wrap. He held up the leather-bound book they'd concealed.

I watched for disappointment to take hold but saw none. It would not have been unreasonable. A book was something more akin to the likings of Gammin than Marin. He would discover that this was not what it seemed to be, much less in fact, and therefore much more. The cover was blank, so he flipped the book over. That side, too, was bare. He tipped it up and looked at the spine. Nothing there either.

"What is this, Annen? Is it a history? Or stories?"

"Open it. You will see what it isn't."

He did, looking at the first page, the second, flipping halfway, then leafing through to the last. There was no writing. They were entirely blank. Marin's face registering the question in his mind—what good is a book with no wri…

He lurched when understanding rushed in.

"This is for me to write in?"

For the second time that day, I was almost knocked over by a child. He flung himself at me. I was only starting to respond when Gammin thudded into us.

I was unhearthed. We fell to the floor in a heap. I landed on the bottom, which was just as well for them. The spontaneous affection turned into a wrestling match, with me outnumbered about five to one. This continued long past when my chest began to heave and when it became too rambunctious for the house. Marin managed set his prize somewhere out of danger early on in the struggle. It remained unscathed. As for the rest of us, there were scrapes and scratches, a bruise here and there. But it was worth it.

We had supper, though not until I had cleaned up again and put on a fresh shirt and vest. Gammin did most of the setting and cleaning for the meal, the knife hanging from his belt as it did from then on. Marin was of little help that evening; he sat on the hearth turning his book over in his hand, leafing through the pages, staring at them as if there were words writ there already, words that only he could see. Perhaps that was true. He asked me what he should write in it. I told him anything he wanted. That did not signify with him, so I elaborated.

"Maybe you should write things you want to remember. Things that happen. Poems, maybe?" He looked surprised at that, and pleased. "One other thing, the thing that made me think of getting it for you. You should write down your dreams, not just the significant ones, mind you, but any that stick to you."

His face contorted. We did not, as a rule, bring up the topic of his gifting as a seer. It was still too new and frightening. I wondered then, though now I know, whether those things ever grew so familiar as to be commonplace. They do not. When Ea's wind blows, the stuff of life moves. We gather the breeze like sails on a ship.

He did not say anything, so I continued. "This is your book. Write whatever you want. You can make up stories. The best part is you don't ever have to show it to anyone."

"But then why would I write it?"

"Ah, there's a good question. I think when you can answer that question you will know what to write and when to write it."

"You are so funny, Annen. You always answer questions with riddles. I think you don't even know you are doing it."

"Do I? Huh. I did not know I was doing it, and I don't do it on purpose. One of my teachers used to do that to us, to my friend and me. It drove us batty. I'll have to think about that some more."

"Fine. Think all you want. I am ready to write something." He moved off to get one of the quills we used in our schooling. They were fine quills; I tried to get the third or fourth feathers of the goose wing when I could. It might have been an extravagance. I wanted them to have the best tools.

"Not those," I called, forestalling him. "I've got something more for you." Gammin heard that and walked over from where he was putting away the plates. I pulled two items from one of the pockets of the vest I was wearing, handing Marin the first. It was a pen, shaped similar to the quills with which he was familiar. It had a steel nib that could be reused again and again. It was most definitely an extravagance for a child. Few of the scribes in the city would have such a pen. "And this." I gave him the second object, something that no scribe in Twofords was likely to own much less use. It was an inkwell, but far from ordinary.

"Is this...." He looked at it, wonderstruck.

"Yes, it's Dragon's Eye. The ink you keep in it will not dry up, nor loose potency. Look, see how the top is fit to the bottle."

The inkwell was fashioned as a small apple, so perfect in proportion that it seemed to be real fruit that had been changed by magic into Dragon's Eye. The stem, which was connected to the stopper, lifted off with a firm tug. So closely was it fitted to the hole that, when closed, no amount of shaking would spill the ink it contained. It had been, until this afternoon, on the writing desk in my room. The inkwell had come to me at the same time as the Dragon's Eye swallowers.

"It's amazing, Annen! I've never seen Dragon's Eye. Where did you get it?"

"I got it from a Stonethane, maybe twenty-five years ago. I saved his life, and his daughter's. The Stonethanes have traditions about that sort of thing, so he made me a gift of this inkwell for his life and a gift of some other things, Dragon's Eye things, for his daughter's life. He made them. No one else but a Stonethane can shape Dragon's Eye. They do not often give their handiwork to outsiders, but he was compelled by their customs to pay me something of equal value for the lives I saved. I did not want to take such treasures, but my refusal would have shamed him."

I realized I was rambling. Marin and Gammin were both looking at me with interested expressions. I did not often or willingly speak of my past. I had never told them of my time in the impossibly high mountains that border all the lands of the Crescent on their east side, cutting them off from the lands beyond as surely as the ocean isolates us from the west. The Stonethanes are a resilient people, and insular, keeping to themselves and holding to their own ways and traditions. I had come friendless and alone. When I departed, I left behind brothers and sisters.

Marin was staring at the blank pages of his new book. I said, "Why don't you go use the desk in your room? It's easier to write with nothing to distract you."

"No. I will stay out here with you two."

He wrote the rest of the evening and on into the night. Gammin and I played some games and talked with each other. When, after much yawning and rubbing of eyes, they went to their beds, I moved out into the courtyard and sat with a cup of wine, enjoying the moon and the pleasant darkness.

The breeze set the trees to chattering. I listened, wondering what one tree might say to another. A soft click told me the door was opening. Gammin came out quietly. He crossed the yard and sat on one of the other seats. He did not speak.

We listened to the silence. In time, I felt his stare and turned to see him gazing at me with his full attention, not looking in hope of attracting my attention, but watching. He had grown in the last year. The tale of our time together was written on his face. His eyes revealed most. Even in the darkness, I could perceive their color. They were grey, the eyes of the Ehrylain, though their shape was different.

As I returned his attention, he smiled and said, "This was a good day, Annen."

8. TOWER MILL

I.

Of my place as a principal in the resistance against Dauroth I told Gammin and Marin nothing. No doubt they would discover the truth as events escalated. They were intelligent children. There was no reason to help them to that realization, and I wanted to spare them as much pain as I could. I was conscious of the peril in which their association with me placed them. I could do nothing about that except to continue to be as careful as possible.

I did not take them with me to Mendolas. The principals from the Southland had agreed to meet, something that occurred only rarely. We were to perform a comprehensive review of our plans, troop strength, preparedness, and other like topics. The outcome, I hoped, would be a timetable to unleash the painstakingly prepared war for recovery of our homeland and our freedom.

Some principals did not share my enthusiasm, if I may use an encouraging word for such an egregious event as war. For several years, we had been caught up in the desire to prepare for every eventuality. To my mind, there was no hope of success in that goal, not according to the time-honored Precepts of War, which state that an army must not go to war unless they significantly outnumbered their opponents. There was no chance of this in Ehrylan; we had no standing army and were so outnumbered as to be insignificant.

Our hope lay in hope rather than strength. Each passing day carried risk of discovery and disaster. Better to embark now on a desperate enterprise than risk the unmasking of our efforts and lose before even setting out.

I intended to express my concerns to my counterparts, and try to move the reluctant toward willingness. Our regional representative, the senior, would take the recommendations to the Resistance council, the seniors from the three major regions of Ehrylan—the Northland, the Southland, and the Westland. If I were unsuccessful in Mendolas, the message would be that the Southland still did not have the strength and there was too much risk. Avoiding risk seemed to be the order of the day throughout the Resistance. That was foolish. We could not avoid risk if our goal was freedom. A man trapped in a burning hut cannot hope to avoid flame and yet escape.

I set out for Mendolas, a five-day journey down the Old Road through the Old Forest. Travel was not an oddity for me. I took trips from time to time, if for no other reason than to establish the comings and goings as a regular part of my industry. Some of the trips had no real purpose other than what I have stated, though I tried to return with either a new scroll in my saddle bag or gold in my pocket from the sale of books. I was in the habit of buying and selling books and scrolls, a common trade for a teacher, though even in this I had to exercise care; the older histories that showed Dauroth for what he was were outlawed.

Though I did not take the boys with me on this trip, I was not so foolish as to go alone. I traveled in the company of merchants and a healer. We hired guards, more for show than anything else. If a band of twenty bandits came upon us, four swords would not hold them off. However, the thieves and ruffians lurking in the unpopulated areas of Ehrylan preyed rather upon the weak than the strong.

I took Sir Speedy to bear me. He looked at me askance when first I put saddle and bridle to him. I took pains to do this well before the start of the journey. He was accustomed to it, if not delighted, by the time I needed him. The children rode him fairly often, mostly for adventure, but this was the first time I had sat his back. Whatever they did with him paid off handsomely. The horse saved my life. I would not have come back alive but for his bravery and intelligence.

We set out in the bright morning with fifteen people, nine horses, and four wagons. I took a staff and an ordinary sword I bought for the occasion; I left the better blade to wait for the time I might wield it again in service of a king long dead and a kingdom awaiting rebirth. I did not have a hunting knife, having given mine to the boy. I intended to purchase one in Mendolas. I had heard of a weapons smith who produced fine steel.

I took the boys to Marn's farmstead the evening before I departed. His holding nestled in the edge of the Old Forest, within a densely wooded valley created by the folds of a hill. We shared an excellent meal. I talked with Marn and Dara late into the night, long after the boys and Arica had said their good byes and gone to sleep.

In the morning, I saddled Sir Speedy and rode out to meet my party at the entrance to the Old Forest. I think seeing me emerge from its fastness lifted their hopes. As for me, it met my purpose. I was happy to have left Twofords and any inquisitive eyes that may have been focused on me the day before. If it were not known that I traveled to Mendolas with this party, so much the better.

There was little to do about the journey to Mendolas. Whether the armed guards kept the thieves away or some virtue of the Old Ones at the behest of Marn, we had no trouble from either humans or nature. We found way camps aplenty and rode, if not at ease, at least easily. For the first three days, the road stuck closely to the Silver River, and much of the time we could hear the water, especially in the way camps. Many of our party thought this a bonus. I, who had more experience with war than most, knew that the voice of a river could mask a sneak attack or an ambush. We had used a river's chortling to mask our own clandestine attacks when I was a boy fighting alongside men. My current comrades and I were spared these unsavory events. We came at noon of the third day without incident to Teryn's Crossing. There, an ancient bridge spanned the river halfway to our destination.

Our escorts proved trustworthy. They halted us before we came to the bridge and sent two of their number across to ensure there was no ambush. They raised two levels in my esteem for that. Under their watchful eyes, we came safely across and paused for a midday meal. After Teryn's Crossing, the road finally abandons the river for a time and climbs up an arm of the mountains. After meandering through the highlands, it begins a long descent into the valley beyond. Mendolas sits where the river deepens enough to be navigable by larger sailing craft used in the trades of commerce and war.

We came in sight of the city walls in the morning of the fifth day. The amount of traffic on the road had steadily increased. As the city drew close, we became part of a procession of wagons, oxen, horses, men, women, children, dogs, and the occasional soldier.

We came to the gate which, with the exception of the name, bore almost no resemblance to the gate of Twofords. This gate was much larger and divided in half so that on one side flowed those leaving the city of Mendolas and on the other waited those who wanted in.

I hung back to the rear of my party, brushing them all forward with some pretext. The gate warders spoke with most of the people entering, though many, presumably those with whom the warders were familiar, were waved through. When it came my time, I presented myself to the warder. He looked me up and down—I'd dismounted from Sir Speedy, which was the accepted protocol—before speaking. His voice was gruff and disinterested, but not unkind.

"Name?"
"I am called Ronl."
"Where from?"
"Twofords."
"Why're ya here?"
"To find a ship."
"You don't say? Ain't we all?"

He did not require an answer. His eyes lingered on my hands. They were, he decided, the hands of someone who could pass as a sailor. He admitted me to the city with a jerk of his head.

If any of my companions had heard me called Ronl, they would have understood. Many people traveled under assumed names. Annen the book dealer left Twofords five days ago; Ronl the ship's hand had arrived in Mendolas. To anyone but a real sailor, I could pass for an old novice looking for new work. What better place to find such work than a river port?

I did not look for my traveling companions. We had made our partings earlier that morning. There was no agreement to meet again for the return journey, each of us being on our own schedule. I was free of them. Up ahead along the gate road, the leader of our party was paying the remainder of the escorts' fee. I hurried up and added a few coins for the care they demonstrated. Then, I took myself away to find obscurity in the depths of the city.

Mendolas was not a small city. Situated at the upper end of the southernmost navigable stretch of the Silver River, the city had been the Southland's largest populated settlement for hundreds of years. It was an important trade center for the region, but compared to major cities such as Kingsholm, Neath, and Ehrynai, Mendolas was quaint at best. The people of those places thought of Mendolas as provincial.

I made way to my accustomed inn, the Hearth and Hound, and bespoke a room. A bed in a room with other travelers would have been cheaper, but I needed privacy. The innkeeper greeted me as a familiar guest and soon I was stripping off travel-stained clothing in preparation for a welcome towel bath. When I was clean, I assumed the garb of an out of work sailor on land.

Mendolas was not so large that I needed Sir Speedy. Despite my weary muscles, I walked. My only real task was to get a feel for the city. I intended to go nowhere near the Resting Bull, where the principals were to meet on the morrow. It would not be difficult. That inn was in Tower Mill, the next village over.

I made a job of inspecting the ships from the dock, as any prospective sailor would. There were other hungry-looking men engaged in the same activity. I talked with two of them, exchanging what news of the world we knew. There was nothing out of the ordinary, save that both of them commented on the amount of soldiers they'd seen in and about the city. My senses pricked up at that, as would be expected, but I stowed the anxiety. The likelihood that they were connected to my endeavor was farfetched.

After prowling the docks, I made my way to the marketplace and lost myself in the bustling crowds. I went into a few shops, places such as a sailor might frequent. I even bought a scarf of blue and yellow, the kind seamen use as hats, towels, and rags. While in the market proper, I saw six soldiers. It is not uncommon for soldiers to be employed in peace keeping. Six soldiers in this teeming marketplace did not seem out of place. None of them so much as looked at me.

Having grown bored with playing the sailor, I headed to the weapons smith. He had three knives of the type I wanted and several swords. All were well-made with blades of bright steel whose design spoke of an artist and whose build spoke of a craftsman. I wanted one of the swords, but I needed a knife. Besides, no sailor hoping soon to board ship would buy a sword of the kind he showed me, which were slimmer and less weighty than those used by sea-faring men.

I agonized over a splendid dagger with a blade that was dark and grainy rather than bright and shiny. I wanted desperately to own the thing, though I had no good use for it, having already a perfectly suitable dagger. The smith noted my interest, which proved he was not blind or stupid. Proudly, he claimed he had forged it himself. Few metal workers in the Crescent knew the secrets of forging this dark metal.

I selected one of the hunting knives. After haggling enough to seem like an out-of-work deck hand, I agreed to a price and handed over the coins. The knife sat well on my belt. It felt so good, in fact, that I tossed the smithy an extra mark. This was unnecessary and a little out of character for an out-of-work sailor. But I did not mind. Craftsmen, artists, and teachers should be compensated well for their work when it pleases.

II.

I was up with the sun. I saddled the horse and took my leave. The meeting was in the village of Tower Mill—which served the road and river—two leagues from the south gate of Mendolas. The inn, the Resting Bull, was built around a tower that stretched three stories above the second-story roof of the the building. The owner was friendly to our cause. We had met there before, though not in a handful of years.

The tower had a hidden stairway served by a trap door in the topmost room. This led to a door that opened on the roof of the inn. From there, a concealed ladder could be lowered to the ground or one could jump from the roof directly into the Silver River. The hidden escape route was what we wanted.

I had changed skins again. Ronl the ship's hand had arrived in Mendolas; Jerral the conspirator would appear at the meeting in the tower. Only one of the principals, Fothyr, the senior, knew me as Annen. I did not know their real names either. It was a simple precaution, one that served us that day when the dying started.

There was less foot traffic than I expected on the road. The paucity of travelers was the first real sign that something was amiss. Though I noticed it, I failed to identify it as significant. Other indications were less difficult to discern. Twice, mounted soldiers came thundering up the road in a gallop headed back toward Mendolas.

As I approached, I saw two foot soldiers near the outskirts of the settlement They were paying more attention to those leaving than entering. Beyond them, I could see two more soldiers near the inn, which was in the center of the village. My heart sank. I considered turning around. That would never do, of course, for it would bring attention to me sure as if I started to shout and dance. I had to ride forward to meet what was in my path.

My hastily defined intention, which could not be called anything so grand as a plan, was to move through Tower Mill without stopping at the inn. That seemed the best course of action. I had a backup story, to be sure, something about riding the road out to Rath in search of a wine supplier to provide for an inn up river.

One of the soldiers at the entrance to the village directed me to dismount. It was nothing personal; up road, other horsemen were leading their mounts. In any case, there was little I could do but comply. I led Sir Speedy into the village and past the soldiers near the inn, looking around as much as I thought any passerby might do. They took no notice of me. There were no soldiers on the far side of the hamlet. I started to wonder at this but soon my questioning thoughts were answered.

As I drew near the last structure, four soldiers emerged from an alley. They were dragging a man who was resisting feebly. The soldiers' attention was focused on him. If they had been watching me, they would have seen recognition spread across my face. I knew the man. It was Daen, the principal of Mendolas.

I looked back over my shoulder. The soldiers by the inn were nowhere to be seen. The two at the far end were too distant to be of assistance to those near me. That was enough. I led my horse toward Daen and, taking the reins in my left, dropped my right hand to my side where it would be closer to the sword which rode my left hip underneath my traveling cloak. I watched and waited as the distance between us lessened. Just a little closer. A little more. Ea, don't let them notice me until it is too late.

One of the soldiers saw me. He was behind Daen, facing me, the farthest from me. He growled some harsh words, warning me away. I was not listening. I was intent on one thing only. I whipped out my sword with the drawing cut known as Striking Dawn. The steel hissed out of the scabbard and, in the same motion, sliced across the neck of one of the nearer soldiers. I was too far away for anything but the tip of the blade to make contact, but it was enough. He collapsed with a spray of blood.

Sir Speedy skittered, frightened by the suddenness of my motion and the falling man; I had to let him go. I could not fight three opponents with one hand tied to a horse. Nor could I ride off and leave Daen. One does not abandon one's comrades without a fight. That was one thing. For another, he knew too much, far too much. I could not leave him—or myself—in the hands of the enemy. Either we both lived or we both died. I could fight for that. So I did.

Another soldier advanced on me. His sword was drawn and there was no fear in his eyes. I shuffled away, trying to look daunted and increasing the distance from all the swords. He followed, just as I hoped. I glanced behind me as if I were preparing to turn and flee. He took the bait and increased the speed of his advance. Turning my shoulder, feigning flight, I readied my sword arm. I snapped my head, shoulders, and hips around, using the twisting force to power my back-handed swing. Our swords met with the ting of steel and steel. His leapt from his hand and tumbled down the road with a clatter. The noise drew his eyes. It was the last thing he saw in this life. Two left.

Daen was struggling—feebly—with one of the remaining soldiers. The other was running back toward the inn, flailing his arms and screaming. His sword lay in the dust near Daen. I glanced at the other end of the village. The two guards there were starting to run towards me. There was not a moment to lose.

I called to Daen, letting him know I was there to help. He shoved his man away and staggered backwards. The soldier forgot him and readied to meet me. Then I was upon him. He avoided my first thrust. He parried my second and third attacks. The fourth ended him. As he slid off my blade, I looked back toward the oncoming soldiers. They had reached the inn, halfway to us.

"Come on! Run!" I put everything I had into that last syllable, yelling so loud that my voice cracked. Daen ambled past me toward the horse. The terrified beast stood watching us from several dozen paces farther down the road, stiff-legged and wide-eyed, shaking with fear. I measured the distance with my eyes. I could get to the horse and gallop away before the soldiers got to us. I had no such illusions about my comrade.

I rammed my bloody sword into its scabbard and sprinted past him, hoping I would not spook Sir Speedy. The horse shied but held his ground, mostly. I had to slow to a walk before he would allow me near him. Telling him what an incredible horse he was, I scrambled into the saddle and urged him back towards the action.

Two soldiers emerged from the inn. They bolted toward us. It was going to be four, maybe five, to one. And now I had lost the great equalizer, the advantage of surprise. But I had a horse.

I dug my heels into Sir Speedy's flanks, praying he would have the courage to obey and lack the wisdom to fly in the opposite direction. He jumped forward so eagerly that I nearly lost my seat. Daen seemed to have found strength. He was moving to meet us.

Having no idea how far I could push this animal, I sped past Daen and made a turnabout, dangerously close to the foremost soldier. Neither of us had a weapon out. He reached for his. We were two dozen paces from Daen, who had foolishly and bravely stopped, turned, and was preparing to come to my aid. As the first soldier came nigh Sir Speedy's rear, the horse launched himself back the way we had just come, toward salvation.

I was screaming at Daen to turn and run, but we were already upon him. He reached up with his arms, grasping at anything, everything. I reached down, grabbed whatever my hand touched, heaving mightily in an attempt to pull the man up and across the horse's back. My fingers found only smooth surfaces slick with sweat or blood. My hand came away empty.

Two soldiers were upon us.

I made a last grab for Daen. My fingers closed on cloth. I kicked the horse violently and he sprang away. I yanked up as hard as I could on whatever I was holding. A man's weight tore at my arm; for a short time, I held him off the ground. Then his arms closed about my waist and he began to pull himself up. I gave a final tug, then let go.

The horse was confused. His gait began to falter. The men behind us screamed and brandished their swords. Fear won over confusion. Sir Speedy raced away.

III.

It was midday. According to my aching muscles and weary mind, it should have been evening. We were hunkered in a steep-sided gully. There was water aplenty, though none of it was flowing. The moisture was a constant seep that left the bottom of the channel muddy. Sir Speedy was tethered farther up the slope in wooded seclusion, cropping whatever grasses he could find. He deserved it for the fine work he had done. So far. There was much yet to do.

We had tended our wounds. Daen had serious bruises where he had been pummeled and kicked, a large lump on his head, and a ragged cut on his cheek where someone had struck him. I had come away well enough, having paid more for victories where the odds where much less against me. Only my left knee bothered me, though I could not see what was amiss. There was no cut or bruise, but it was swelling and growing stiff. I had wetted what was left of a shirt from my saddle bag and wrapped the joint. That was the best I could do. The rest of the shirt had gone into various rags and bandages, some of which were stowed in the saddle bag for later.

Time was short. We needed to get as far as possible from anywhere near here, but we both needed a respite, and the horse too. We might lay low until darkfall, hoping to make our way through the forest or along the road under the cloak of night. The moon favored such a plan; it looked to be a fine night. In darkness we might avoid patrols searching for us. The same was true on the other side; the darkness would hide the patrols from us as well. Unfortunately, I did not know this country well enough to navigate off the road by day much less than by night. The slopes rising to meet the peaks west of us were exceedingly rough and torturous. There was a reason the roads were cut where they were. That left only the choice of traveling on or near the road, a fool's choice but the only hope we had.

As much to clear my head as anything else, I trudged down to a flowing creek and filled my water skin. I stayed concealed as best I could, which was pretty well in that wooded place. When I returned to Daen with a full water bag, he was rubbing the knot on his head.

I asked him "How are you?"

"I am as good as can be expected. Do you have a plan?"

"Not really, other than to move on as far and as fast as we can. We still have a lead on them, but that won't last for long. We'll go after you tell me what happened."

"Go? Where?"

"Anywhere but here. Do you have a better idea?"

He did not answer. I restated my request, more precisely this time, "What happened in Tower Mill?"

"We were betrayed. They came upon us just after I arrived. The others were already there."

"How did it happen? Do you know?"

"I know." I waited expectantly for him to continue. "Give me some water. If I am going to tell you this, I've got to have some. I haven't had a drink in... I don't know how long. This morning I think." I handed him the skin and he drank. Then he began.

"Benamen confided in someone, where he was going and why. The person he told was Dauroth's."

"The fool," I hissed, harsher than I should have yet less harsh than I felt. The exclamation rang like a bell in that quiet place. We looked nervously about until I carried on with my tirade with less volume. "What hope do we have if even the leaders cannot follow the rules?" Ben was one of the principals who always supported more delay. His term for it was patience. Thinking of him, distaste rose within me and I spit into the gully.

"There is always hope." Daen took another swig and handed me the bag.

"Yes. True enough," I said. "How did you learn of the indiscretion?"

"I had it from Fothyr who had it from Benamen himself. He told me before we parted on the roof. Fothyr went one way and I another. They caught me, as you saw. I don't know how he fared. It may be that they only followed me and missed him completely. One thing is sure. Ben may have been a fool, but he was no coward. We would all have been caught if not for him."

"How so?" Time was critically short, but I had to have the information. I had to know how deep this betrayal went, how much of our work would be swept away. "You say 'was no coward.' He is dead?" My question was based on concern for our network rather than any affection for Benamen.

"He's dead. I saw his body. It was broken on the crest of the roof, under the window. He jumped. There were three arrows in him that I could see. They didn't get him alive."

"Tell me what happened. Quickly!"

"You have to give me a moment. It's been… it's been a bad day." He collected himself, closing his eyes and taking several deep breaths. He put his hands to his face and held them there. I put a hand on his shoulder and said, "We will get through this."

He did not acknowledge the encouragement. Dropping his

hands into his lap and focusing his eyes into the distance, he told me at last what had occurred.

"We were all there but you—Fothyr, Benamen, Mynd, and me." Those were the other principals in the Southland. Fothyr was the regional senior; we took our direction from him.

"We heard the warning signal. That much worked. But it came too late. They were almost at the door when we heard it. Still, Mynd got away clean. At first, it was just a knock. Someone called through the door, telling Ben that something had happened to his wife. We were all looking at each other, trying to deny the truth. There should have been no knocks, no intrusions except you, and you have the password. That's when Ben told Fothyr what he had done. I was helping Mynd get the trap door open, so I did not hear that part. Give me the water, will you?"

I handed him the skin and waited, fingering my sword hilt. It was sticky with half-dried blood. Whose, I wondered? Which of the men I killed this day had left their blood to remind me?

"My thanks; that's good. I can go on now. Sorry I am so slow. It's hard to think about." He swallowed and started again. "By the time Mynd was down the stair, they were pounding on the door. Benamen was trying to stall them. I shoved Fothyr down the hole, none too gently I am afraid." Fothyr was a good deal older than the rest of us. It was rumored he had fought as part of King Brand's personal guard, though I did not believe it.

"He moved fast, the oldster. I think he slid down most of the stairs. I found out why, too, just a moment later; they were slicker than owl droppings. Anyway, it was just me and Ben then. I motioned for him to come over, but he waved me off and turned back to the door. That's when the axes started. Two or three. I thought the door would burst under their weight. Ben kept telling them he was looking for the key." Daen wiped his face with a grimy hand. I waited.

"There was nothing more for it, so I jumped down on to the stairs. I slipped and fell most of the way, out of control and in the dark. I heard the trap door shut. I didn't know if Ben was behind me or not. I didn't wait to find out. Fothyr was at the bottom of the stair, standing by a door in the dark waiting for us. Old fool. He told me what Ben had done.

"There was a loud sound, just outside the door, and right after that I heard the axes again. From the way they boomed and echoed, I could tell they were chopping at the trap door. It was time for us to go. Past time.

"We went through the door. It led to the roof, two stories above the ground and just below the tower. At first, we could not get it open. I thought it was stuck from disuse. But it turned out to be Benamen. His body was blocking it. His neck was broken from the fall and, as I said before, he was full of arrows."

Daen took another swig. This time he spit it out. He hung his head and shook it slowly. He looked like a defeated man. I wanted to comfort him but could not find the words.

"Fothyr and I closed the door behind us and shoved Ben up against it. Fothyr took Ben's dagger and jammed it in the crack. I doubt it held them even as long as it took us to put it there, but we had to try something." He stopped again. Another swig.

"Yes," I said, wanting to scream at him to hurry up. We needed to be away from here, but I needed to hear the story first.

"There was not much time. We decided he would jump and I would take the ladder. I knew the ladder was probably useless, but I do not swim. I have always been terrified of drowning." He looked at me again, wanting forgiveness. He knew, we all had known, that death was preferable to capture. It was imperative that we not allow ourselves to be captured; we had each made vows to that effect. Yet Daen had allowed himself to be captured. Few men can hold their tongue under the torturer's knife. Women do better. In my experience, nothing can be as strong as a woman. Their strength is wonderful and terrible.

"Fothyr jumped into the river. I heard the splash before I went down the ladder. That is the last I saw of him. From what

I heard the soldiers say after they caught me, he hadn't been found yet. I don't even know if they knew how many of us were meeting. Maybe not." The only man that could tell us was already dead, having paid the penalty for his indiscretion.

"Go on!" The words came out in an angry hiss. Daen's eyes flashed with indignation. He'd expected commiseration.

"The place where the ladder went down was hidden. I figured there would be a cluster of soldiers waiting for me, but there was no one. It led down into a narrow space between the inn and some other building. It might have been the woodshed. I could have gone either way, but, since the river was one way, I went the other. I wanted to keep away from Fothyr, you know?"

"Yes. What else?"

"You know most of the rest. I crept along, taking whichever turn kept me in the shadows or behind something. I got a fair distance too. I thought I was going to get away. A dog started barking at me. That started another one going. I tried to go back the way I had come. The soldiers burst around the corner, right at my heels, and that was that. They beat me until I stopped moving. Then they pulled me up and out into the main street, just as you saw."

"Nothing more?"

"No, nothing."

I gauged the sun. We had far to go. "Ready?"

"Ready? Ready for what?" His voice, though he kept it quite, was tending toward hysteria.

"Ready to go, Daen. We've got to get away. We can't stay here."

"You think we can get away?" He was balancing on his hands now, leaning forward so that his face was a finger's breadth from mine. I could feel his spittle on my face and smell his fear even over the pungent sweat that covered us both. I managed to keep myself cool. This was a bad spot, but I had been in worse, at least that is what I told myself.

"I am going to get away. Do you want to come or shall I kill you now?" I watched him take three breaths. They were quick, ragged. I grabbed a fistful of his tunic and pulled him even closer. Our foreheads collided. I hissed through my teeth, "I am not going to leave you here to tell them all you know. One fool is enough."

Truth to tell, I do not know if I could have killed him like that, in cold blood, even if it meant the continued safety of our conspiracy. I think not. If he had pushed me, I would have stayed and died with him when they found us. Fortunately, I did not have to make that choice.

"Come on, man!" I growled, shaking him with each word. Then I released my grip, tossing him backwards so that he almost slid into the gully. "Where is your spine? We are not fighting for our lives here. We are fighting for our people. If we have to die, let's die taking action, not waiting for death like frightened children. Are you with me?"

I saw understanding seep into his eyes. "Yes," he murmured hesitantly, "Yes. You are right. But what's the use? What matter where we die? There's no hope."

"There is always hope, Daen," I said, repeating his statement of only a few moments before.

IV.

I had a vague notion of heading toward the village of Stone Bridge, some three leagues distant. There, the road meets with a trade route from Rath, Ehrylan's southerly neighbor. If we were lucky and could evade the troops from Stone Bridge's garrison, we could cross the river at the bridge from which the village and garrison took their names.

Once we were back across the Silver River, my plans were as scant as my knowledge of the land thereabout. It was ten leagues and more from Stone Bridge to Teryn's Crossing. If we could make it that far, we could pick up the Old Road and take it all the way home. Ten leagues though the Old Forest without a road is a very long way.

I saw few alternatives. We might retrace the road north

through Mendolas. Or we could continue southward along the Rathian Way into Rath. The people in that region, whether Rathian or Ehrylain, hold to allegiance with the land rather than any king or queen. We would find sympathy enough to keep us safe if we went that way.

Of those two choices, abiding in Rath would certainly be more comfortable, safer. Yet waiting anywhere was a bad option. Now, more than ever, with the Resistance in crisis, Daen and I needed to be back at our commands. At least one of the principals was dead and we didn't know how much farther the catastrophe went. There were protocols for reestablishing leadership within damaged groups, but these would proceed more effectively if we, the established principals, were there to lead them. I judged that need to be the greatest. I would head north through the Old Forest until I struck the Old Road at Teryn's Crossing.

The Old Forest is often called trackless; this is not true. There were minor roads and hamlets within its wild expanse. It was home to many people. Groups of Old Ones, scofflaws, and other folk dwell throughout, some coming never out of the forest during their whole lives. I had lived with a family of Old Ones many years before when I came back to Ehrylan after my exile. I knew some of their ways. We might find help within the forest, though it was a risk. There was death as well as life under those trees.

We rode and walked toward Stone Bridge for the rest of the day, staying off the road when we could, picking our way among the trees. Occasionally, this was not possible due to the terrain and we had to take to the road. The risk thereof was not the travelers we met. They were few and kept mostly to themselves. It was the soldiers that gave us concern. They might come upon us quickly from front or rear or we might find them waiting in ambush. As the sun began to fall, we moved all the more warily, and it was a good thing too.

Sir Speedy heard them first. Something in the way he tossed his head alerted me. I halted him and then I heard it too—horses, three, maybe four, overtaking us quickly. We had been riding on the road, the forest thereabouts being lush and dense. I turned Sir Speedy and nudged him toward the trees in a walk.

"What are you doing? Hurry!"

I did not reply or even look back. The last thing I wanted to do was to kick up dust or leave an obvious trail for anyone to see. Sir Speedy ambled into the trees of his own accord. We were concealed by the time they came abreast us.

There were four soldiers on horses, fully armed. It may not be said that they were searching carefully, but it was obvious they were looking for something, someone. We waited until the sound of their horses had dwindled away. Only then did we emerge from behind the copse of mavramorn bushes. It was thick and prickly, pulling our clothing greedily. We did not mind. It had hidden us well.

I spoke quietly. "It's not safe to use the road now. They might ride back for Mendolas before darkfall."

Daen nodded. He said, "Maybe we should stop now. We could wait until twinight and use the road again. Surely they won't be out looking for us then."

That was not a bad plan and I said so. We had covered more than half the distance to Stone Bridge, not very far, perhaps two leagues of three miles each. Had we been able to move freely, we'd already be sitting supper in some homey inn. The village of Stone Bridge had to be avoided, festooned as it must be by now with alert soldiers angry at having been aroused from their accustomed lethargy. We needed to follow the road as long as possible, leaving it and cutting straight for the river as near the Stone Bridge as we could safely get. And getting across the bridge, if it were guarded? I did not have a plan for that. One thing at a time.

We crept west, as quietly as we could in the dense woodland where twigs crunched underfoot and birds took flight with unnerving regularity. I don't think we made even a third of a league more before we gave it up. We found a likely place to spend the night in a tiny glade set back from the road. I would have liked to have been farther but the forest simply did not allow it. There, in the shelter of another sprawling mavramorn bush, we made a camp of sorts.

I took the saddle off the horse and saw to his needs before resting myself. I set him to grazing the glade after feeding him handfuls of oats from the saddle bag. Sir Speedy had drunk water aplenty during the day, but for Daen and I there was little, only the one bag which, by now, was half gone. Nor was there much food. I had ridden out prepared for a morning ride, not an extended flight through leagues of empty land. The saddlebags held only the sort of supplies any experienced campaigner carries with him, half a crusty loaf of bread, a hunk of questionable cheese, and some dried meat, enough for two scanty meals for one person. I shared it out with Daen, who attacked it ravenously. As for me, I could eat nothing, though I was hungry.

Full dark was upon us when we heard the soldiers. They came from the direction of Tower Mill moving much slower than the previous group; there were no horses. We listened, knowing we were concealed by branch and by darkness. Snatches of conversation carried to us on the night breeze, mostly curses and complaints such as any disgruntled footman might make on an impromptu trek at such an hour. It was impossible to tell their number, more than five for sure, less than twenty. They were walking—not marching—without a lit torch in the soft light of the moon. I thought of Sir Speedy and looked to him with concern. He was standing alert, head up. That was all I could see in the darkness. The breeze must have long since told him what I was yet to discover. I do not think it would have changed much, that foreknowledge. It was already too late.

The sound of laughter caught my attention. There was some banter, but nothing else for a moment except the welcome tale of receding footsteps. Just when I had begun to breathe more easily, there came the sound of something heavy being dropped near the road. This was followed in short order by the haphazard crashing of at least one man pushing incautiously through the undergrowth.

It is something that has always bothered me, this question

of undergrowth. How can something be so named? I have always thought it should be called overgrowth since it blocks passage and generally gets in the way. But I digress and at the worst time. Perhaps it is well, a little mirth. There is much death before us. This was just the beginning.

I heard more than saw a man come through the opposite edge of our clearing. He was looking for something, though it was not us to be sure. He found the open space he wanted and squatted for his moment of personal necessity. Even then, all might have been well. He was no more than two dozen paces from us, but there was a large, thorny bush between us. We were certainly not the most important thing on his mind. When I heard the dog, I knew things were not going to turn out well.

Daen had been looking around nervously. He wanted to run into the forest, I think, but that would have been folly. At this point, they were still uncertain where we were; if we ran, they would know for sure. If this indisposed soldier detected us, there was only one solution. We had to eliminate him and his dog, quickly and quietly. Eliminate is an easy word for a difficult act. Killing someone, even an enemy, has never been easy for me. Before this night, I had never killed a dog. That was about to change.

Daen shifted his weight, making as if to turn and flee. I put a hand on his shoulder, pressing him down so that he could not rise without significant effort. He got the message and settled back.

I had not considered that they might be tracking us with dogs. From what I could see in the moonlight and from the sound of his bark, I guessed this was no hound, no tracking dog. It was a fighting dog. The animal did not act as if it was following a scent it had been tracking. Rather, it seemed to have just caught some new scent, something interesting. Sir Speedy, perhaps.

It was an ill chance that brought one of the soldiers off the road so near us in his moment of need, and a worse chance that the man was master of a dog. But not all chances were against us. The breeze was blowing into my face, which accounted at least partially for the dog's slow uptake.

The dog began to growl, low and soft at first, increasing swiftly to that rolling, articulated growl that indicates immediate danger. I pushed my cloak back and gripped the scabbard in my left hand. I gave Daen a stern look.

A man's voice called, "Fang! What is it?" At the edge of the clearing, a shadowy form was pulling his clothes into place and groping for his weapon. The dog started to bark staccato alerts interspersed with that ululating growl. "Ruff, ruff, ruff. Grooowwwlllll. Ruff, ruff, ruff. Grooowwwlllll."

That would bring the rest of the troop back upon us as surely as an alarm bell in a village square. It was time for action. I stood up and stepped from behind the bush, gripping the hilt of my sword, which was still in its sheath, with my right hand.

The dog saw me immediately. He took three bounds, each longer than the previous, and launched himself at me. The sword slid out of my scabbard of its own accord. I had no conscious thought of it, just as I had told Gammin the first day I had met him. Training breeds action without forethought. There was only the dog and the swift arch of the blade. The draw and the slice were one motion, Dragon's Tail. It was a different technique than I used earlier that day in Mendolas, but the result was the same. The dog fell at my feet. I looked toward the soldier.

Daen was moving toward him. Both men held drawn swords at the ready. I had a fleeting fear that there would be a sword fight with the ring of steel or iron, a sound that would bring the rest back all the more quickly. That did not happen. The soldier, who quite unaccountably did not yell or scream, took two steps forward and swung his sword. Daen stepped to one side and slid his sword into the man's throat. There was a gurgling sound. Daen struck again. The dead man fell back.

Daen bent down and took hold of the feet, dragging the body back toward me. He stopped in the center of the clearing and deposited his load.

"We'll never get away now," he whispered. "We've got to fight them when they come." That was the most sensible thing he had said to me all day, except the bit about hope. Perhaps he was better in a fight than he was before a fight. I had known men like that. It was no shame. We are who we are.

From up the road, a voice called out. They had heard the dog and were coming. There was little time to plan our ambush. I took a position near where the man had entered the clearing, careful not to step in the pile he had left as his last act among the living. By the smell, it was easy to avoid even in the dark. Daen settled behind a tree near the dead man. Our hope of success was in taking them from behind as they came in to investigate the body. I did not think they would see the dog. From where I was, the remains looked like a mound that might be any small boulder or bush.

If the others had come all at once, we would not have lived long. The first came off the road, plunging carelessly though the branches, pushing them out of the way with his sword. I let him go by and waited to see how many more would follow. He jerked to a halt as he saw the form of his companion. He looked right and left, then stepped forward and went to a knee. Another soldier stepped passed me. He saw his friend and hurried forward as well. A third man appeared. Three against two was enough.

I plunged my sword into his back, aiming for the spine. He fell forward with a gasp. The two men in the center jerked upright and looked back toward the sound. Seeing me, they lifted their swords. With near perfect timing, Daen stepped out from behind the tree, drawing the attention of the man nearest him who turned, leaving me to face the other. Both men began to shout for their comrades.

Quick as I could, I stepped away from where I had been and away from Daen. I wanted first to be able to see who else came into the clearing and second to distance myself from blades I was not facing. Small consolation it would be to vanquish my foe only to die on the point of a sword wielded by the man Daen was fighting. I managed to get the body of the man I had just killed between us. That put my opponent's back to the road.

He was not bad, that soldier. He leapt over his fallen comrade with his first attack. He came on like a windstorm. I parried a strike to my head. He followed up, slicing at my legs, then jabbed at my midsection. I jumped back, bending over his extended blade to keep from being skewered. As he recovered his footing, I risked a glance over my shoulder. Daen was holding his own.

Once more, my attacker put together a series of three attacks, this time middle, low, then high. I skittered around the first, which put me mostly out of danger for the two following attacks. I deflected each of them, more from the desire to lead him into thinking they were more danger than they really were than the need to defend myself against them. He was good, that one, but I was old. I had not gotten that way by losing sword fights. I might have tested him more, learning, but I had to prepare for the next wave who were screaming from the road.

He had attacked me in sets of three each time. I had yet to strike back. He came again, the sword slashing high, high, middle—two attacks to my head, the third to my stomach. When I leapt back to avoid the third, I brought my sword down on his arm, which was extended between us. He was unbalanced for an instant. Then he was dying.

A roaring fury bounded into the clearing. It was another dog. I was late getting my sword point up, else the ravening animal would have skewered himself. I took the brunt of him full on my shoulder. We went over together in a heap. He was mauling me before we hit the ground. My right arm was pinned against my body by the weight of him, my sword useless. He raked me with vicious claws, any one of which could have disemboweled me if it had found purchase. The dog's slavering maw groped for my throat. I could see its white fangs and its tongue. My left hand was at its throat, twisting and pushing in an effort to stay alive for the next breath.

Daen saved me. His sword chopped downward in a two-handed stroke on the dog's spine. There was a yelp, and then silence. For an instant. Then men poured into the clearing. As Daen's eyes met mine for the last time, he held up his dripping sword in front of his face and said loud and clear, "For Ehrylan."

I pushed the dead dog from on top of me. There was no way to tell how many had come against us. All I could do was face the blades that would kill me if I did not turn them. I saw Daen go down, crumpling as a shadow pulled a sword out of his abdomen. Without thinking what I was doing, I leapt to his aid, slamming into the man who was readying the blow that would assure my companion was dead. As he fell away from me, I slashed at him, felt the bite of my blade in his flesh. He tried to scream, but all that came out was a gurgling hiss. It was a sound with which I was familiar, the sound of a throat that had been cut. My blade, lucky for me and unlucky for him, had found a soft target.

There were three of them left as far as I could see. It was dark and my vision was blurred with sweat and blood. My chest was a riot, heaving so hard I could scarce focus my eyes. My arms and legs felt weak. I was shaking.

Behind me, I heard Daen's last breath. The rattle was unmistakable, a sound that stays with you, a haunting farewell. So he was dead and I was left to fight on. Was I fighting to die with him or fighting to live? To this day, I do not know. Sometimes, when the terrors that ride the night wind find their way to my bed, I dream of those nightmare moments. I see myself standing above him in a mist of exhaustion and blood as swords swarm and death feasts on the vanquished.

They came at me as experienced swordsmen would, one in front and one from each side. I did not wait for their attack. I focused on the man in front of me, raising my sword as if to meet his. At the last instant, I skipped to my right, bringing my blade across the face of the man there instead. He was taken by surprise, though he deflected most of my attack. The point of my blade flicked across his cheek. I heard him cry out, but I had no time for that.

I attacked the man on my left. He blocked the strike, countered with his own. I parried, jumping back to avoid a slice from the third man, the one that had been in front of me at the beginning of this round. Mostly, I avoided it. His sword cut into my abdomen. Pain, white hot and searing, rushed through me. I fell backward, tripping over Daen's body. I fought to catch my breath, but there was no time. They were coming for me and I was wounded, perhaps badly. Time was running out.

One of them jumped over Daen and struck at me. I ducked instinctively. A sword cut the air. I scrambled to a better vantage. There was a pause. Had they attacked me then, I would have died.

I claim no bravery for what came next, nor any pride for the tactics. There was no thought, no plan. There was only action. The two still on their feet were in front of me. The one to my right looked at his ally. I launched myself at him as soon as his eyes started to move. His sword came up, turning mine. I allowed the blade to slide down his. As soon as I felt it come against the cross guard, I ripped it back and up, slicing at the other opponent's body, the one who thought I was engaged with his fellow. There was a jolting crunch and I was only just able to keep my hand on the hilt as the body fell. Fortunately, it collapsed between me and the other attacker, blocking him from advancing.

The man I had just wounded started to struggle to his feet, his sword arm hanging useless at his side. Grasping my sword hilt with two hands, I hacked downward, hard as I could, aiming for the place where the shoulder joins the neck. There was a dull thud. I yanked my sword free of him and leapt back. Now it was one against one.

The last man flung himself at me. In my state, exhausted and wounded, it was all I could do to defend myself. Instinct saved me again, instinct that may be the result of long training. There was a flurry of blows, as blurred in my memory now as they were when they happened that night. We each advanced and retreated, dancing in lock step. I slashed at his torso.

Stepping forward, I brought the returning backhanded swipe through to his neck, expecting it to be blocked. I felt a thud. A roundish shape tumbled in the air between us. There was a red cloud of silence. The man stood headless as I gulped for air. Then the lifeless husk toppled backward and crashed to the ground.

In a daze, I turn this way and that, looking for the next attacker. But there was no one. Almost I dropped my sword in exhaustion. It dangled from my fingers. Blood ran down my arms. Pulling the back of my left arm across my face in an attempt to wipe it clean, I smeared the ichor from my sleeve over my cheek and lips.

I shook my head like a dog. My hair threw a spray of sweat and gore. One of the shapes on the ground, startled by the sudden motion, pushed itself into sitting position. It was the third of the three that had attacked me at the last, the one I had slashed across the cheek. He was young, likely still celebrating the first growth of wispy hair on his face. And he was crying. That face would boast a nasty scar from this battle if he lived. His right cheek sagged in a dither from eye to mouth. Another fraction and that mouth would have been much larger. He was no Ehrylain, just an Outlandish boy not much older than Simon. His fear had consumed his will to fight, if ever that had existed. Despite this, his hand groped for the sword that had dropped nearby. That is another irony of life; we will do things when motivated by fear that fear has stopped us before from doing. I do not understand this, but it is true. I have seen it many times.

I had had enough of killing. Sensing that he also had had enough death for one day, I stepped closer to him, though not so close as to be within range of his sword.

"Do you want to die?" My voice was edged. He did not answer in words. His head swung side to side as his eyes, large as saucers, followed my movements. His lower lip was trembling. "Then I will give you your life. Go and trouble me no more. If you have any decency in you, do not bring any others to me. I give you your life in exchange for mine."

He watched me, his sword hand shaking visibly. I could see he did not trust me. I stepped back two paces, then two more. He cringed at the sudden motion. His sword came round in a vicious arc. He jerked back, a child trying to get away from a frightening insect.

"Go!" I bellowed, or tried to. What came out was more like an exhausted bleat. Then I said, much more softly, "Why don't you get out of here?"

The frightened boy crabbed backwards. When he saw I was not pursuing, he rolled to his feet and took to his heels. That was the last I saw of him. As far as I know, he did not direct others to me. I thank you, Ea.

V.

I stumbled to Daen, hoping I had made a mistake, hoping he yet lived. He was dead as dead can be. I bowed my head for a moment, saying a prayer for him and for his wife and children, though I did not know if he had either. I thanked him for saving my life. More than that I could not do. Callused as it may sound, I searched his body and clothes to assure that there was nothing that could link him to the Resistance.

Before I tended my own wound, I verified that none of Dauroth's men were still alive. The moon was high and I found them easily enough. There were eight men and two dogs in the clearing. Two squads, I thought, two squads of four men, each with a dog. These must have been following the horsemen.

I went for my saddle bags. Sir Speedy was visibly shaken by the violence that must still, to his senses, permeate the air like a thick fog. I soothed him best I could. Since my hands were covered in blood, some of it dog's blood, my efforts did little.

I cleaned and dressed the wound in my side, using half the remaining water to wash it and to dampen clothing I cut into rags and bandages. The injury was not trivial, but I did not believe it would kill me before the morning. Even if it did, there was little else I could do. I had to get away from here as far and fast as possible. If I could come to the river, there was a plant I might find that would be of much benefit to me, but I would need the light of day to find it, and the strength.

I made a quick search of the dead soldiers. I needed food and water. Two of them had packs. In one, I found some food and a blanket. In the other was a rope that looked like it might have been a dog leash and some meat that was not fit for my consumption. All of them had water bags. I relieved them of these, using one, after smelling it, to quench my own thirst. The others I dumped unceremoniously into one of the saddle bags. That made me think of the horse's thirst, but he would have to wait a while longer. He would not drink the canella from the water bags.

I could not bury Daen's body though he deserved more respect than to be left for animals to despoil. Some would believe that lying among your vanquished foes is respectful. Either way, there was nothing more I could do and yet live to tell the tale, as I am doing. Digging a grave, even a shallow one, was certainly beyond me, as was dragging the body into more concealment. Also, burying him would proclaim for all to see that one who fought by his side had lived after the fight.

When I had done all I could think to do with wits addled by wound and weariness, I looked at the saddle. With the hole in my abdomen, I might die in the effort to put it on the horse. Yet there seemed no choice. I got him saddled in the end. It cost me much blood and more than a little pride. This was one of the times in my life that a kindness, that of taking off his saddle for his comfort earlier, created for me an unsavory debt. Still, he bore me away from that place of death and was ever after my steadfast friend. Perhaps I am counting the cost incorrectly.

I led Sir Speedy back to the road. More packs lay where the soldiers had dropped them. I searched a few. When I had food enough, I lugged them all into the clearing where I put them behind the mavramorn bush. What good that was, I do not know, but it seemed right at the time.

The last thing I remember is leading the horse down the road a ways until I found a likely spot and then mounting him, an effort that set my chest to heaving. I turned him off the road and pointed his nose toward the river, which was to our left. Bending forward over his neck, I murmured, "Find the water, sir."

I woke when the sun was starting to slide down the western sky fields. There was no momentary lapse of knowing where I was or what I had happened. The pain was enough to remind me.

I was lying beside a fallen tree. The trunk was large enough to conceal me and shelter me from wind. The horse was nowhere to be seen. I listened to the songs of birds and another song that was pleasant and familiar but something that, in my condition, I could not name. I passed out again. Next I knew a soft, wet sensation was pushing against my face. Sir Speedy, I thought, and opened my eyes.

It was dusk. The horse stood over me, dripping water onto my face from his velvety nose. He blew a snort and stepped back as I moved. It all seemed very dreamlike. I pushed myself up farther into wakefulness. The air was full of bird song, and I could smell the river as clearly as I could hear it. It was very peaceful

But this was no idyllic fantasy. I had wakened to a nightmare. My side was a raging torrent of pain. My right arm was scored with deep rips where the dog's claws had raked me. The arm had, quite by happenstance, protected my soft belly and preserved my life. The arm was worse than useless to me in my efforts to get up. My left knee was so stiff that I could not bend it and every hint of movement caused it to scream.

I managed to pull myself into a sitting position with my back against the log. The edges of the wound in my side were swollen. It was difficult to tell because of the blood, but the area looked an angry red. That was not a good sign. The forearm was worse. Unless I could get help and soon, the Red Death would kill me even if the wounds did not.

We managed, the horse and I, to get me on my feet. I used

him as a crutch. He supported me as I searched for the plants that might keep me alive long enough to find a friend. Such plants grow by the water. In the last light of day, I found what I needed a few paces from the river on a sandy flat. I might have found the ferns even in the dark by their smell, so strong and potent they were.

Water and plant I had in plenty, but little light. As darkness enfolded me, I bathed myself and cleaned my wounds. I made a paste of river mud mixed with chewed leaves, which I applied as best I could. This took all night. Several times I passed out from the pain, starting anew whenever I came again to my senses.

I repeated these processes—gathering and bathing, dressing wounds and sleeping—for I know not how many days. I managed to get the saddle off the horse early on. I did this in exactly the wrong way for the poor animal, simply loosening the girth and pushing the thing off. I remember a fever that drove me to pleading with Ea for relief, whether that came in death or deliverance. I remember sweat and chills and hunger and nausea. I was not conscious of the passage of time, only the endless cycle of bathing and dressing wounds, falling again into sleep.

Sometime later, I became aware that I was becoming aware. I noted the blanket I had thrown off and pulled it around me in the cold of twinight. I was not out of danger. I was terribly weak, the wound in my side an open sore. My arm was a mess; even where the flesh was undamaged, it was red and swollen, hot to the touch. I had seen men under the full care of a skilled nemen—the true healers—die from wounds such as these. For a wonder, my knee did not seem to hurt as much. One in three. It was a start. And I was still alive.

How I had remained hidden from Dauroth's men and why they did not find me I cannot conceive. The horse, or, perhaps it was me in a delirium, had selected a stand of bendbark trees that huddled back from the river a short walk. The trees concealed us well enough, it would seem. A steady stream of boats and ships sailed the river. It was already too late when I came to recognize the risk of the watercraft; they were close enough for me to hear the voices of their passengers.

My estimate is that two full days, perhaps three, elapsed from the time Sir Speedy delivered me to the haven by the river and the time I was able to think again. A further day was used up contriving bandages for my side and arm, filling the water skins with water, and stuffing the saddle bags with the river plant. Saddling the horse got the better of me and proved my undoing. The effort started the wound in my side to bleeding again. Mounting made it worse. I was almost as weak as I had been the day before when finally I was sitting astride him. I struggled to stay on his back.

I gave the horse his head. He had done well enough for us so far. In any case, I did not have the strength or awareness to guide him. I pointed him south, along the river. There were numerous paths. The one we chose must have been used by those who desired to come and go without detection from river or road. It was more circuitous than the trail running along the riverbank, but we were hidden by hillocks, groves of trees, and other convenient features of the land. Sir Speedy had no trouble following it once he knew what I wanted.

All that day we meandered downriver. I grew steadily worse. I found myself coming out of unconsciousness in the saddle more and more often. These were bouts of stupor that lay hold of me despite all my efforts to stay aware. Twice I woke to find myself lying on the ground with the horse nowhere to be seen. Each time I stirred, he appeared and helped me struggle to my feet. The second time, the blessed animal even lowered himself to the ground to ease the process, a maneuver I had seen battle-trained stallions perform, something never expected of this farm animal. I wondered where he had learned such a trick.

The efforts to mount left me exhausted and bleeding on each occasion. The wounds worsened and the Red Death took hold. I had no doubt that, if it could be seen beneath the coating of dried blood and filth, my abdomen would be laced with angry red lines. I only had a little longer to struggle.

I awoke on the ground a third time. It was dark. The horse was standing over me. Perhaps I had just fallen from him. Maybe it had been hours ago. After wondering if I could get the horse to lower himself again, I decided to give it up as a bad idea. I could not stay in the saddle; only luck saved me from further serious injury at each fall.

I struggled to my feet. It took nearly everything I had. I staggered the three steps it took to come to Sir Speedy's head, intending to speak with him man to man. I was that far gone. Reason had left me; I had only the determination to go on until I reached death. That became my goal—death before surrender. Just keep getting up. Had I been in a right mind, I would have stopped for the night, but that did not occur to me. I took the reins in my hand and began to walk.

I plodded down the path for what seemed like a very long time. It was likely only a few steps. The end was very near. I was talking with Ea, preparing him for my arrival, telling him of my hopes that there would be a bed there for me and a nice manger for the horse.

That is when I saw the light. I was so far gone by then that I was beyond even considering if the light might be a campfire surrounded by my enemies. My dying mind knew only that light meant fire and fire meant the possibility of help.

I remember telling Sir Speedy to hurry. I also remember him replying rather curtly that I was the one slowing us down. I took two steps toward the light. And that was all.

9. REVELATIONS

I.

Stars. Stillness. A voice above me. Arms around my neck. Water in my mouth. Coughing. Pain. Forgetfulness.

I was lying on something soft. I was listening. Opening my eyes did not seem important. What was I listening to? It became a game I played, listening and wondering. It was difficult to stay awake. What was I listening to?

Someone was chopping, a sound that made me think of cooking. I could hear that. There was a fire. That I could smell. There was another smell, something moist. Mud? Fish? I opened my mouth, intending to talk. All that came was a gasp. The chopping stopped. A voice, not mine—it was strong and alive and I was dead, surely I was dead—said, "Sleep. Here, I will help you to some water. That will be good for you. Then you will rest." An arm slid beneath my head and helped me to a water bowl someone was holding near my lips. Or maybe it just floated there. I drank and dreamed.

I was driftwood on the river. Stars above, water below. Drifting. There were others with me. They were talking. Were they drifting too? Stars above, water below. Stars above, water below. Drifting.

Someone was chopping. There was a fire. Was I remembering this or did it happen before?

I asked, "What are you chopping?"

My voice was weak, almost an inaudible sigh, the voice of a spirit. The voice that answered was strong and full, the voice of a person.

"I am chopping arrenil. You would call it waterboon, maybe starcress."

"Arrenil? Why?"

"I am making soup. Again. You drink a lot of soup. It has to be fresh each time. How do you feel?"

"I feel tired." My voice was growing stronger. "No, that's not right. I don't know how I feel. Arrenil? For soup? Who's hurt? I remember…There was…" I lapsed into silence until the chopping stopped. I heard what sounded like someone scraping something off a board. An aromatic fragrance filled the air. It was arrenil, the river plant that had kept me alive.

I opened my eyes.

This did no good. It was too bright. Everything was a blur. I blinked to clear my vision. Things swam into view. I was staring at the underside of a thatched roof. For an instant, I thought I was back again in the forest with family Brendel, the Old Ones with whom I had lived. Joy flooded through me—for an instant. Then I began to remember. I watched the man who was making me soup putter about the hut. Eventually, he knelt down to look into my face. He set his fingers against the underside of my left wrist.

"Let me see your tongue."

I stuck it out. Time was I would have done so playfully, acting as a child might, but there was no energy in me for that. There were only questions. The man, who looked a lot like Marn, examined it. He nodded and I retracted it. He put the back of his hand against my forehead.

"You'll live," he stated, almost as if the matter was inconsequential.

"Where am I?"

"Ah! At last. I was wondering if you were damaged in the head."

I tried to start my answer with "that remains to be seen," but all that came out was "I want to know where I am."

"You are in the forest, in the care of Pehter, son of Dehter, son of Loth, of family Naralyn."

This was good news beyond my wildest hope. I was in the care of the Old Ones. If they didn't kill me, I would be as safe with them as I could be anywhere else in Ehrylan. I realized, abruptly, that we were speaking in the Old Tongue.

"You are Pehtersa?" I tried to move, to sit up. Pain exploded throughout my body.

"I am," answered the Old One. He held a bowl to my lips, forcing me to drink and drink again.

"I thank you Pehtersa, son of Dehter, son of Loth, of family Naralyn. The Maker grant you joy of his will. I am Annen of Twofords."

My throat felt swollen. I tried to clear it. An invisible sword pierce my side like a blazing brand. I almost gasped, managing to hold it in and preserve what little dignity I might still own.

"I know who you are. The Maker's will lead you to joy."

"You know me? How is that?" Suddenly I felt tired, very tired.

He laughed. "Have I not tended you these four days and nights while you raved and fought again all the battles of your life? I know you, Calen, son of Colen. I know you."

The implications of what he said settled around me like a funeral pall. No man in Ehrylan had called me that since the day the king sent me into exile, more than thirty years gone. My life would not be worth two copper pennies if word spread that I was returned. I summoned myself to get up, but nothing happened. I had to get away. I tried to lift my hand. It was too heavy, like my eyelids. I had to get away. Now. I was spiraling down again into oblivion, sliding into sleep, defenseless sleep.

The bird was singing again. The song was sweet, stronger than the song of the grey wing. No. That was no bird. It was a woman singing. I opened my eyes, fool that I was. I should have listened longer. It was an enjoyable song and it ended when I moved.

"Welcome back, Calensa. It is time for you to have some soup. Pehter says he tires of feeding you, so you'll have to make do with me."

The Old Ones are a rough people, sure of themselves and their ways. They are exceedingly kind once they have decided you are not a threat to them or to those whom they hold dear. Usually. I recognized her words for what they were—rough, good-natured humor telling me that it was time for me to start the journey back up into the world of the living. I cast my muzzy mind after some reply. The best I could come up with was, "Patience is not one of his virtues?"

Her laugh was almost a bark. Light from the nearby open window danced in her eyes as she bent close to me. "Patience is a virtue that grows among rocks in the desert. Did you not know? We have no desert here. The forest gives us all, as the Maker wills it."

She sat herself in a chair by my head and picked up a bowl. I could smell the arrenil. Dipping a spoon, she held it to my lips. I took it into my mouth and swallowed. It was hot, thick as cream, green as leaves. As she dipped again, I held up my hand. This time it moved for me. "Thank you, nementha. I will try this myself."

Among the Old Ones, healers usually come in husband and wife pairs. Pehter I would have called nemensa. The tha for a female and the sa for a male were honorifics appended to the ends of Old One's names when speaking those names to their owners. It is a civility, their way of saying sir or lady, I suppose.

Comfort vanished as soon as I moved. If she saw pain scrawled across my face, the woman did not mention it. I would have very much preferred to use my left arm to eat, but that would not work for where she held the bowl. Not a coincidence. I reached up my right arm and took the spoon. The arm was heavily bandaged. The wrappings were clean and fresh.

It took a long time to eat and even then, I only managed to transfer a small portion of the soup into my mouth. Much of it trickled on to a rag the nemen cast over my chest and lap. Afterward, I was exhausted again. The woman retrieved her sodden rag and got up to leave. I gestured to her.

"Nementha, you know my name. Tell me yours." Exchange of names was important in most the cultures I had visited, but none more so than with the Old Ones. I did not wish them to think me a barbarian.

"I am Solea, daughter of Herea, daughter of Margrea, of family Naralyn. Pehter is my husband."

"I thank you, Soleatha, daughter of Herea, daughter of Margrea, of family Naralyn, wife to the fortunate Pehter. May the daughters of your house run in the light of the Maker."

Solea beamed and gave me a little bow. "May your sons meet them there. You are welcome here, Calensa. I go now. You should rest. Lelan is coming. There will be many questions. You must be stronger by then."

"Yes. One thing more, of your grace. My horse, is he safe? Is he here?"

"The horse is here. He is safe and, if I may speak for him, happy. You have much to thank him for. He saved your life."

"Saved my life? How?"

"Later, Calensa, son of Colen. Later. Now rest." She turned to leave.

"Soleatha." She was already half way out of the door. Her eyes told me to ask and also that it was the last question she would tolerate.

"Will you sow some patience among the rocks in Pehter's garden?"

The days passed in a slow procession of soup, sleep, and increasing mobility. I saw the wound in my side, cleaned and illuminated with light. To say that it was much healed is so drastic an understatement that those words cannot be used. The flesh along the right side of my belly boasted a thin red and black river, an arching line about a hand span long. The scar was still wet and sticky. Last time I saw it, I could have slid my whole hand into my belly.

After a few days, they had me salving myself. The morning of the second of those days, they made me fetch the salve pot from the other side of the hut. By the evening of that day, I visited Sir Speedy for the first time. He did look happy. Upon seeing me, he tossed his head and trotted across the paddock. I scratched his ears and stroked the middle of his muzzle, something he liked in particular. The paddock was clean and dry with a covered space at one end that was roofed by branches woven from adjacent trees, as was typical of the Old Ones. The manger was well stocked with fodder. Feeding Sir Speedy a carrot I had brought for just that purpose, I watched the horses in the adjacent paddocks and wished I had brought more.

The hut was not Solea and Pehter's house. It was an infirmary of sorts, where members of the family stayed when they became seriously ill. It is a custom among the Old Ones. Those near death do not tarry in the homes of their loved ones lest they die there and bring sorrow into the house where it does not belong.

I received visits from various members of the family, some of whom brought fruit or flowers. Others came to offer good wishes and blessings. I had, at first, little to offer in return for their hospitality. Eventually, I hit upon the idea of sharing out the items that had been previously bestowed me. This seemed to delight the recipients. It is difficult to predict how the Children of the Forest will react.

I took short excursions, playing—carefully—with the children, talking with the men and women I encountered. I enjoyed the easy, unhurried rhythm of their speech and their lives, falling into it with the satisfaction of a man eating a delicacy he has long missed.

I did not fail to pester the healers with questions about how I had come to be rescued, and, since I was in the Old Forest, how I had been transported across the Silver River at a time when Dauroth's men must have been on alert. To all such questions, the answer was something akin to, "Lelan is coming. The time for questions and answers will arrive with him." Such stubborn opacity is typical of the Old Ones.

I asked Pehter about my dream talk. Knowing that I had revealed my real name was bad enough. Not knowing how much I might have revealed about the Resistance was maddening. Even more maddening was Pehter's refusal to give me any information on what I had said during my rambling. It was simple. Lelan is coming. We would discuss it then.

Who Lelan was, I had no idea. He was not their king. The Children of the Forest have no king or queen. The families are independent and autonomous; there is no kingdom of the Children of the Forest. Be that as it may, Lelan seemed to hold the key to unlocking the tale of what had happened to me. I resigned myself to waiting until he arrived.

II.

I was sitting in a chair near the window, a pot of salve on the table next to me. My back was to the door, which was open to the breeze. The air in the hut was full of arrenil and whatever else was in the marvelous medicament I was rubbing into the scabs on my arm and side.

The morning was wearing away. It had not been particularly pleasant. My efforts to acquire information about Lelan had grown insistent. With each of Pehter's refusals, I became more petulant. As far as I was concerned, Pehter deserved my ire, if ire can be deserved. He had no need to be so close-lipped.

When I heard someone behind me in the doorway, I did not turn to face him. I felt him come through the door. I said, quite testily, "Are you trying to teach me patience?"

"You should know patience by now; you are the teacher." It was not Pehter's voice, not even a man's voice. But it was a voice I knew well.

"Gammin!" I simultaneously turned and rose from the chair so fast that, if the salve had not already worked so well on the wound, I would have ripped it open sure. The boy stood in the door way, Pehter behind him, Marin behind them both. There was a moment of stillness. I saw Gammin fighting the urge to fling himself at me. I flung myself at him.

The boy hugged me so hard that my side expressed an uncomfortable concern. He searched my face for signs of illness. There were no words between us though he said "I was worried about you," and I answered, not speaking, "It is fine now." Then Marin was there, all smiles and hugs. The morning had shown definite signs of improvement.

Pehter was pleased. He knew a joyous heart is a healing heart. He made as to leave us. I said to him, "Pehtersa, will you send some food for the boys? They are hungry."

"How could you know?"

"I know."

Then Pehter was gone, taking Marn with him. I was alone with my boys. I had not given thought as to what I might tell them about the causes of my injuries. Now the fact that I had to give an account of myself smote me square in the face. I could not lie to them, but neither could I tell them the truth. I bade them sit as I finished applying the salve, thinking it would give me time to think.

That was a silly request. They wanted to see the wounds. What was left of my injuries was unspectacular. After the viewing, I convinced them to take a seat so we could talk like civilized men.

I told them that I ran afoul of soldiers and that there had been a scuffle across the river. There were questions, some of them pointed and right to the points I wanted to avoid. Gammin told me I looked very thin. Marin told me I was pale. Just when Marn walked into the hut, Gammin told me that he had not known I was so fragle.

Seeing us disintegrate into laughter, Marn said sternly, "What is this?"

Marin answered him. "I don't know, father. They have this word that makes them silly. It's very strange."

Marn raised a single eyebrow. "Show me."

I pulled up my shirt again. Marn poked and probed with the sausages he called fingers. He gave my forearm the same treatment. When he was done, he wiped his fingers on a rag to remove the salve they had picked up from my skin. There were lots of rags in that hut.

"Your side. A sword cut."

"Yes."

"Your arm looks like you faced an animal, a dog."

"Right again."

He looked down at the floor. "Shinando, if I had known you were so inept at defending yourself, I would never have allowed you to teach my son."

I thought he was being straight with me. I was puzzled by the scathing—and accurate—accusation. When I heard Marin let go a half-suppressed snicker, I realized the woodcutter was teasing to hide concern.

We exchanged greetings. He stood above me as if I were an errant child caught in an indiscretion. He did not ask how it had happened. I assumed, incorrectly, that he had already heard the story from Pehter. We arrived at a place where I could ask some of the questions on my mind, one of which was how he had come to find out I was here. But one thing I wanted to know more than any other. I opened my mouth to ask him about Lelan. At just that moment, Pehter pushed the door open and peered in. That was the best he could do; the hut was almost bursting under the press of so many bodies.

"Come," he said, "We will share a meal. Then we will talk."

Marn was the first one out. Gammin and Marin waited for me. I made as if getting out of the chair was nearly beyond my strength. They were both on their feet in an instant. I said, "On three," and took their hands. "One, two..."

There was no three. On two, I tugged them both toward me with a burst of energy. They fell into my arms like startled kittens. It was good to be with them again. It was better to know they were safe among the Children of the Forest.

The formal talk commenced almost as soon as the last member of the impromptu council arrived later that afternoon. The boys went away to mingle with the other youth. I was escorted into one of the larger structures within the compound, a meeting place. The room was undecorated. There was a circle of seven chairs arranged around a fire pit. Against the walls at either end, two large tables boasted various objects.

There was only one person I did not recognize. He did not live within this group and had come in especially for the meeting. The newcomer was a dark man with deep-set eyes and black hair. He bowed to Bandoc and Fenali, the heads of this clan, nodded to me and Marn. I nodded in reply. He was, I decided, Lelan.

A small fire danced amid the stones of the fire pit. There was no need of heat; it was warm out. This was a formal gathering. Fire is required for such things. For us, the fires of our formal meetings represent Rhua, who is the wind and flame of love. Light poured through open windows. No one in the circle was in shadow.

Fenali was the clan's headwoman, the wife of Bandoc, the headman. She went to one of the tables and brought back a flattish stone bowl. Bandoc retrieved a water skin. They faced each other within our circle, across the fire from each other. She extended the bowl toward him. He emptied the skin into it. Even before I smelled it, I knew the liquid was linuvea. Whoever we were and from wherever we came, we all were about to be unified with a bond of truth.

Bandoc returned to his seat. Fenali sat as well. She said, "We thank the Maker." She closed her eyes and inhaled deeply of the liquid. It had been decades, more than half my life, since I had smelled that much linuvea. The fragrance breezed into every corner of the room. I could imagine how her senses must be exploding.

She drank deeply, not a ritual tasting, but a long, multi-swallow draught. Her eyes sprang open and she proclaimed, "I am Fenali, elder of family Naralyn. I will speak the truth."

Fenali handed the bowl to Pehter. He partook, saying after, "I am Pehter, nemen of family Naralyn. I speak the truth."

Each of us drank in the same unstinting fashion, afterwards proclaiming our names and our veracity. As the bowl passed from Pehter to Solea, I was considering whether I had the courage to say my true name. Something unexpected happened.

The darkling newcomer lifted the bowl to his lips and drank. "I am Vasudo of family Naralyn, and of the river. I speak the truth."

Not Lelan after all! Where was he?

Marn took the bowl and drank, proclaiming, "I am Lelan of family Trancal, watcher of the northern border, I speak truth."

Marn was Lelan? What was a watcher of the border?

It was my turn. I held the precious liquid to my lips, pausing to breathe in the joy. I drank deep and deep. "I am Calen, last of my line, a Justice of Ehrylan. I speak the truth." I passed the bowl to Bandoc.

Drinking, he said, "I am Bandoc, elder of family Naralyn. I speak the truth. Let this council begin."

We had been called together to discuss the important matter that had come to light as a result of my unconscious ravings—the existence of an organized, wide-spread resistance. To have revealed the Resistance was a very serious thing. I squirmed with discomfort at hearing discussed openly what had so long been hidden. I could not argue that these things were only the untruths of delirium, characters and events I invented along the paths of the fever. But it did not matter. The Old Ones were sure. That made it easier, which was a relief. I desired to share our need with these people, to entreat them to help us. We could not stand alone.

Bandoc stated that the revelation of an organized resistance was important news to the Children of the Forest. The elder believed he had news that would be equally surprising and welcome to me. It was time to cast aside some of the secrecy. As he put it, "Wolves that hide in separate caves are but lonely wolves. Together they live as a pack, which makes hunting and killing easier."

After the head man spoke, it fell to me to tell my story. I started hesitantly, unsure how far to go in this new trust. The lives of many depended on what I might reveal. It became easier as I continued. I found I could tell the story without revealing names and numbers. Much of what I said must have been known to them since I had, apparently, spoken so freely in my stupor. I began with my departure from Mendolas, took them through the rescue of Daen and the battle where he died. I left them where memory failed me.

Vasudo was called next. His voice was rich and sonorous, almost as if the river itself were speaking.

"I was asleep when I heard the horse outside my hut. I thought it was the soldiers returning. I was cross. I had told them already that I had not seen the man they wanted. This inquiry could have waited until morning. Concern that they might break down the door encouraged me to go out to them.

"Soldiers I did not find. There was only a horse with no rider. I could see the saddle by the light of the moon, and knew something was amiss. I went to catch his reins, but he evaded me in that infuriating way Brother Horse has, staying just out of reach. I had almost decided to let him go his own way when I realized that he retreated always in the same direction, back up the river path. He waited for me each time. I followed him, not trying to catch his rein. He led me straight to his rider, who lay in the dirt within sight of the ferry.

"He was injured, though I did not know how badly until I

got him back to my hut. He was beyond my ability to heal. I sent my son across the river with the horse for the healers.

"My wife and I treated the injuries as best we could. Much of that time was spent simply... unpacking him. Never have I seen so much arrenil stuffed into a wound." He shook his head, looking at me with an inquisitive look. There was nothing I could say. I shrugged.

"Pehter came, crossing the river in the last cover of darkness. He and my wife—she has more of the Maker's healing grace than I—worked on the man until mid-morning. Then the three of us took council. Though we knew nothing about the man, we believed he was the one the soldiers were seeking. Five times in the last three days the soldiers had ridden to the ferry to ask if I had seen anyone on such a horse. It would be disaster for the soldiers to discover him at the ferry. We could allow him to die, which was the easiest. We could give him to the soldiers. Or we could move him.

"Two of these choices were no choices at all." Vasudo's rich voice had begun to resemble that of a *faelyth*, performers who wander the Crescent singing, playing instruments, and telling tales. He was speaking with a rhythm, almost a chant.

"We would not let a man die for lack of care. The Maker commands us to aid even our enemies if we find them alone and injured on the road. This man was in my hut. We knew the soldiers wanted him. If they wanted him, we did not want them to have him. We arranged to bring him here, to the family. We knew he would not survive a ride through the forest on horseback or the longer journey across the bridge in a wagon.

"Pehter departed and sent Solea back in a wagon. She came the next day, carrying items any soldier might believe were intended for trade. After seeing to Calen's hurts and his comfort, she helped me conceal him in the back of the wagon."

"To my comfort? What does that mean? Did you drug me?"

Solea answered. "Yes, Calensa. With *nyremni*. It was necessary. You needed to sleep and we needed you quiet. You were quite vocal."

"I understand. It does not matter."

Vasudo pressed on to the finish of his tale.

"I ferried the wagon across the river. Pehter met us on the other side. The soldiers came again in the morning. They were looking for a man on a horse and asked, as before, if I had seen him. Since I had never seen Calen on that horse, I could tell them truthfully that I had not. It is important to speak only the truth." There was a murmur appreciation for Vasudo's cleverness.

"One of them had seen the horse's tracks and the wagon's. They demanded an explaination. The wagon, I told them, had brought me supplies. I showed them the two new blankets—we thank you for those, by the way—and the apples and nuts. As for the horse tracks, the wagon was drawn by a horse. I reminded them also that they themselves were not riding oxen and had come to me many times. I suggested, rather unkindly, that perhaps they saw signs of their own horses. They left me and have not returned. I fear that I have not made friends of them."

I did not recall any of these events he described. The use of nyremni, which is the essence of poppy distilled with some of the same ingredients as linuvea, explained much. Even a small amount of that drug will send a strong man into a long, forgetful sleep during which it is difficult to wake him.

Pehter spoke next. He had heard me call Marn's name several times in my delirium. That, coupled with other comments that put me squarely in association with the Bend, was enough to cause him to send for the woodcutter after consulting with Bandoc. He dispatched Solea to retrieve me and a messenger to Marn at the same time.

Bandoc spoke again when Pehter was finished. "Calensa of Ehrylan, that you are not alone. The Children have always interfered with the evil one's activities when we could. What you do not know is that we also have organized efforts. We are too few and therefore too weak to achieve his demise alone. It is our hope that, through cooperation, our two efforts, those of your people and mine, may each be the stronger. Together we may achieve our common goal to drive out the evil one and his armies from your land."

I could barely contain my excitement. "This is news beyond hope, Old One! The help of the Children of the Forest would be most welcome."

Bandoc smiled, but shook his head as well. "There is a catch, Calensa. This new cooperation will not prove easy to build. You will not reveal anything about us to your leaders beyond the fact that we exist. You will be the conduit for any cooperation that occurs—the only conduit. It is a manifestation of evil that this is as far as we can go, but you will understand."

"I do. It is how we run our own operation. You must know something also. I can no longer be an integral part of the resistance. I am damaged by all this attention."

"Damaged. Yes. I can see that. You have a gift for stating the obvious." The others in the room laughed at his attempt to be amusing. Among themselves, the Children of the Forest laughed and played in celebration of the joy of life. Even in times of stress, where attention was required to assure the smallest detail, they found a way to tease and smile. Yet there was one thing to remember. They killed with that same smile on their faces.

The meeting went on for some time. Bandoc gave me a message for the leaders of the Resistance which, in my case, meant Fothyr—if he was still alive. I agreed to return any answer they might have through Marn, who would never be Lelan to me. To my great relief, there was little talk of Calen and what he, I, had done after leaving Ehrylan so many years before. This may have been because they respected my privacy. More likely, it was because the Children of the Forest have little concern for the political doings of those beyond the forest, so long as they are left free from harassment. What King Brand had chosen to do to one of his subjects long ago in a world that no longer existed was of little consequence to them.

We talked until almost darkfall. When we were done, the whole clan feasted in celebration of the visitors. Gammin sat at my right hand as Marin sat at Marn's. The evening wore away in song and dance and storytelling. Vasudo told tales in the style of the *faelyth*, and received rousing applause. I enjoyed the evening until I grew fatigued and had to retire. Gammin stayed out with Marin. Though they were very quiet about it, apart from a few giggles and squirms, I awoke as they came in to the hut and lay down upon their beds. That was good; I was on the mend.

III.

I readied myself for the journey home. Also, I took great joy in watching the boys cavort with the younger members of the clan. I was not alone in this. There were many spectators among the Old Ones. Marin and Gammin contested with the other youth in games that amused us all. There were none to rival them or even give them a true testing with the staff except for one lad named Micah. That youth looked like he belonged in the Swamp rather than the Old Forest. He was a few years older than they. Even he was bested by my boys.

With the bow it was another story. In that art, though Marin and Gammin were sure shots, the Children of the Forest outshone them as the sun outshines a candle. Where Gammin could hit an apple on a stump, his opponent could hit that apple when it was flung into the air at the same distance. When Marin showed how quickly he could draw and shoot an arrow from the quiver, his opponent could shoot three in the space Marin could shoot two. When they saw that their skill was less, the Twofords boys cajoled the locals into giving them lessons and teaching them their secrets.

Marn spent his time with the other Old Ones. I did not try to insert myself nor did they invite me. When Marn did have some time, he called me over to the horse paddocks. We took the opportunity to give our animals a good brushing. The woodcutter was particularly interested in Sir Speedy, saying that he looked ten times the horse he was before. That was true though I had not noticed. Before, he had appeared as any wagon-bound animal of labor might appear. Now he looked almost like a small, shaggy war horse. Marn asked me what I had been feeding him; I replied that, for much of the time, he was feeding himself.

Gammin and Marin ran up, breathless and a little worse for wear, trailing a ragged line of other children behind them like goslings. Gammin stopped in front of me and leaned against the fence to catch his breath. He waited until I was done with the topic I had been discussing with Marin and said, "Annen! I've been wanting to show you."

"Is that so? Well, show away."

"We need Sir Speedy. Marin, Arica, and I taught him a trick."

"A trick," I echoed, trying to catch the tone in his voice and suspecting he was about to answer an unasked question.

"Watch!"

Gammin led the horse out of the paddock, explaining that it would be better if he were not distracted by the other horses. We followed obediently, Marn and I and the goslings.

He gentled the horse, then stepped back holding up both hands palms out toward the horse. Then, he squatted on his haunches, patted the ground, and said, "Down for Max! Down for Max!"

The animal stood stone still for two breaths. Then his head moved, ever so slightly from side to side. I would have sworn he was looking for Max if I had been asked. To the surprise of all but my boys, Sir Speedy blew noisily and lowered himself to the ground exactly as he had done for me a few days ago.

There was my question answered. How did the horse learn to kneel for his rider? Simple. An orphan and two woodcutter's children taught him so that their tiny friend might take his seat more easily. Wonderful. Just wonderful.

Next morning, with saddle bags full of provisions, we started for Twofords. I rode Sir Speedy. Marn rode the horse he used daily in his wood-cutting activities. The boys shared another horse.

That journey took five days though I would not have believed it possible to make such a distance in so short a time through the Old Forest. Of course, we drew no wagons behind us and did not ride in fear of outlaws. Marn knew short cuts that reduced the distance considerably.

On occasion, Marn took us from the larger tracks on to paths and trails that were hidden. These invariably led through country that was impassible only a step or two off the path. Many of these lesser ways took us to locations that held some value for a traveler—a water hole or stream, a hidden vale perfect for spending a night, or even just a splendid view of a mountain top or the slopes of a heavily wooded valley. Twice those little trails took us past rows of staked vines whose branches bore the beginnings of what would grow by the autumn rains into clusters of ripe grapes.

As the days passed I grew stronger. Marn and I spent the time discussing how I might reenter the city. That my absence coincided with the occurrences at Tower Mill, a location very near my stated destination, was of some concern. On the other hand, there was nothing to link those events to Twofords. We concocted a story that took these things into account. Once we'd returned to the Bend, Marn garnered the cooperation of his associates who would corroborate my story if need be.

I stayed three days at Marn's farmstead. He sent someone to investigate my house in the Stone Gate to make sure all was well for my return. The next day, taking with me the two boys, I walked to Twofords, and came again to my home.

Much had changed since last I was there. The moon in the sky was a different moon. Sir Speedy had grown from a farm animal into a traveling companion. Marn was a different man. Except for the moon, which had died and been reborn, I was changed most of all. When I had left Twofords, I was one of the principals of the Southland. The man that returned in the end of Middle Moon had been stripped of that responsibility by the events that occurred. Now I was a simple teacher.

More important than these changes was a realization that crowded out the sorrow at the deaths of my fellow conspirators and the pain and weariness from our labor. We were not alone. The loyal followers of King Brand had allies, significant allies, in the war against Dauroth.

10. STRIKING DAWN

I.

Homecoming was bittersweet. It was wonderful to see the Twofords' children again and Merelina. Yet I had to deal with the ramifications of the events in Tower Mill. Daen and Benamen were dead and had to be replaced. I was alive and had to be replaced. Fortunately, Mynd and Fothyr made it away safely. It took months, but, in the end, we rebuilt the framework of our Resistance. Decades before, I had been involved with the foundations of the network in Mendolas and Twofords, so the rebuilding was just that little bit easier.

The sweetness of my return was also lessened by the presence of the Dryhm. They became more active as the Choosing neared. The Tax Gatherers would arrive soon; they might already be in the Grove for all we knew. This was a Fallow year. There would be no Choosing in this region, but the villains would still come to haunt street corners and roam the countryside.

I saw Pruis stalking the various approaches to the Stone Gate, both alone and in company. It was difficult to be sure since the Dryhm were hooded, but there was something in the way the bully moved, an attitude of the head and shoulders. His interest was something to note; Pruis' animosity to us could not have decreased. The ascension to significance does not lessen feelings of entitlement and lust for power. It multiples them many fold.

On the brighter side, I thoroughly enjoyed spending more time with Sir Speedy. When the young ones were busy at their studies, I would visit him in the paddock. If there was time, and sometimes even when there wasn't, I brushed him or rubbed him down. I made sure he had the best hay and oats I could find and had always a good supply of carrots for him. Also, I gave him a new name. He was Avyansa.

Max called me on it. Arica, Gammin, and Marin were doing well with the Old Tongue and understood the change straight away. They knew more, much more, of what had happened to me than the others.

The first time I greeted the horse by his new name, no one commented. Perhaps no one noticed. Later, as they were leaving, I bade the horse fare well as I had always done with each of the humans. I used his new name. "Good bye, Avyansa. Come again and see me."

Max, speaking from his place in the homemade carriage, asked, "What did you call him, shinando?"

"Avyansa."

"There's two things I want to know about that."

"What and what?"

"What does that mean and why do you call him that?"

"You tell me, Max. What word in the Old Tongue sounds like Avyansa?"

Max pondered. The longer it took, the more his face showed the signs of concentration. He was like that; any test or challenge was an opportunity to shine, to show that he was bigger than he looked. Unlike others I have known who have this same trait, Max did not mourn failure. He moved on and looked for some new way to prove his worth.

Finally Max said, "I don't know, shinando."

"What is the word for fast?"

"*Avyan.*"

Avyan means fleet of foot or tongue, but fast was good enough. "And what is *sa*?"

"That's what you put at the end of a man's name to be respectful if he is an Old One."

"Yes?"

"Yes what, shinando?"

I gave him my "I am not going to solve this puzzle for you" face. He recognized it and went back to work. I watched his face mirror the contortions of his thoughts as he tried to bend them around the problem.

Max got it at last. "Avyansa is Sir Speedy!"

"Well done, Max. What else? You said you wanted to know two things. You must be *avyan*; it's getting late."

He answered me in the Old Tongue—or tried to. "Why now do you to call him those?" The attempt so pleased me that almost I teared up.

"I think the name sounds more beautiful in the Old Tongue. He deserves a beautiful name."

The horse was Avyansa from then on though I never asked any of them to follow my example. Fleetness of foot was never one of that animal's attributes; the name Sir Speedy was, truth to tell, an irony the children came up with on their own. Avyansa was not fast. However, from the first, he quickened to the bravery and wisdom of his kind.

Studies absorbed us again, though it did take some time. At first, our sessions were consumed in the telling and hearing and retelling of the interesting things that had befallen each of us since we parted a month before. Some of this took place at the Step, for the seven of us appeared there regularly to teach, help, and enjoy the company.

Merelina came to the Stone Gate in the first week after my return. That had not occurred more than a handful of times in all the years of our acquaintance. She brought Temay. He had pestered her incessantly, as only he could, about my whereabouts and wellbeing. I was happy to see them. Temay had been making improvements in his willingness to communicate with others; he was on speaking terms with Marin and Gammin, a major stride forward. To be on speaking terms with Temay meant that he considered you a friend. That was an award few could claim.

We enjoyed a dinner the boys prepared, fish on a bed of rice with vegetables. I was as stunned as she, but it was Lina who asked, "Where did you learn to make this?"

Gammin started to answer then stopped. His eyes flicked to mine with an unspoken question, "Is it ok?" I nodded, proud of him.

"We learned it when we went to get Annen in the Old Forest, from the Old Ones."

Gammin stopped talking and Marin immediately continued the thought. "It smelled so good we asked them if we could watch them cook."

Gammin spoke again. A gnat could not have winked between the time Marin stopped talking and he started. "They eat lots of fish there because they are so near the river." Marin nodded, popping a last morsel into his mouth, something he had managed to salvage from a plate that had appeared empty to me.

Marin finished it up. "Same as we do in the Bend."

They nodded in unison with that pronouncement.

"What else did you learn?" Apparently I had not spent enough time monitoring them when we were with the Naralyn. Then I remembered I had been in no shape to monitor anyone. It was they who had come to rescue me.

Gammin drew in a deep breath. "Oh, many things. We will teach you." He looked at me sternly. "You will have to study very hard if you want to understand."

Marin nodded agreement. Temay, who had not seemed to be paying attention, said, "Study. You have to do that if you want to learn, don't you? Yes, you have to study."

"I'll try. A man is never too old to learn."

Temay replied, "Never too old? That's not true, is it? No, not at all. What if you were so old that you were dead? You'd be too old then, wouldn't you? You couldn't learn then." He looked at each one of us in turn, folded his arms across his chest, nodded once.

I stood up. "I thank you for the wonderful meal. As your reward, boys, why don't the three of you clean up while Merelina and I go sit in the courtyard?"

I led Lina out under the summer stars. We took the goblets of wine we had been drinking. I did not use them often, but this had seemed a suitable occasion. I refilled them with pale Rathian wine. It smelled of apples to me. According to Lina, it was lemons.

We talked for a long time. I had to refill our goblets more than once. Merelina insisted I tell her more of what had transpired on my trip to buy a knife. I was just a teacher to her. She knew nothing of the Resistance, though, if given the chance, she would have joined in an instant.

I told acquaintances that I had fallen in with bandits on my return journey. It was a common occurrence in those days. Everyone knew someone to whom that same thing had happened, or so it seemed. I told Lina more of the truth. I would not speak falsely to her, even then. Soldiers accosted me and I had been seriously injured. I told her of my rescue by Vasudo, the ferryman, and the Naralyn in the Old Forest.

"You've lost a lot of weight." She touched my hand. "Are you alright now?"

"I am fine. I was lucky to be found by the Children of the Forest. They cared for me."

"We were worried about you, Annen. The children at the orphanage, they…" Her face, which had been troubled, changed. A smile bloomed. "There was an argument. Max wanted to mount a rescue party. Temay was furious. He said you couldn't rescue someone if you didn't know they were in trouble. He said we needed a search party, not a rescue party. It was funny, the way they argued about that." She laughed again, this time strong enough that she brought a hand up to cover her mouth. It was nice to see her laugh. I was sorry when she hid it. The moon glistened in her eyes, or perhaps it was starlight, and I saw a tear at the corner. She wiped it away with her sleeve, which was a faded yellow. Something Marin had asked me jumped to the front of my mind.

"More wine, Lina?"

"I think I've had enough."

"Perfect." I grabbed both goblets. "Don't go anywhere."

I walked casually to the door. Once inside, I hurried to my room and retrieved something from the table. I looked in on the boys, who were doing perfectly without us, and fetched wine before heading back out to the woman who waited for me.

As I handed Lina her goblet, she said, "How is Temay doing? Is he alright?"

"He was drawing. He has a fine hand."

"Yes. It's amazing the way he can draw from memory. I've never seen anything like it." She was going to say something else, something more about drawing, but she changed it. "The way he is opening up to those boys! He talks to them more than most of the children who live with us, children he has known all his life."

"Why do you think that is, Lina?"

"Oh, that's easy. Gammin treats Temay like he treats everyone else. Can you imagine how that feels to Temay?"

"Gammin is special that way. I do not know where he came by that. It is a good trait. Usually." I mused, losing my train of thought as I gazed into her eyes. "Marin, too. He is no slouch either."

"You are right. Marin is special too, but in a different way. You'd think he would expect to be the leader of the two. Most of the time, it's Gammin who seems to be leading, but not in a bad way. They treat each other like brothers."

"Like twins," I interrupted.

"Yes! Exactly."

We talked a bit longer about the boys and about the other children. Then, having waited unsuccessfully for a graceful way to turn the conversation in the direction I wanted, I said, "Lina, I have something for you from Mendolas. It's for you, not the children. Understand?"

She nodded. "You brought me something?"

I took the scarf I bought in the market out of my pocket. It was folded into a square the size of my hand. I held it out to her. "Don't get excited. It's not much."

Slowly, as if the scarf might fly away if she moved too quickly, she lifted her hand and took it. Me, I would have taken it by the corner and given it one quick shake, but not her. She laid it in her lap and unfolded it a fold at a time until it covered her from knees to navel. The blue and yellow were paled by the night, but they could be seen.

"It's beautiful, Annen. I love yellow and blue."

"I know." Bad as it was, that is all I could think to say. Then I wasn't thinking anymore because she had thrown her arms around me. "I thank you, Annen."

She was very warm. She felt soft and firm at the same time. She smelled good too. It was very pleasant.

I held her at arm's length looking into her eyes. There was not much light in the courtyard but there was enough for me to see her eyes. They looked like a storm on the ocean seen from the vantage of the stars. They were a combination of pale and darker blues mixed with swirling grey clouds.

My heart beat faster. Suddenly I felt very uncomfortable. I could not follow this path, no matter what treasure lay at its end.

I blinked as if breaking a spell and said, "You are welcome, Merelina."

I managed to get her back in her chair. We talked a while longer, mostly about the children and the future of the Step. During that time, she played absently with the scarf, now holding it, now wrapping it around her hand or arm. Later, as the boys and I walked Lina and Temay back to the orphanage, she wore it about her shoulders. It looked good, but I was troubled. What false hope had I sewn?

II.

I thought about the events in Tower Mill as my life settled back into the patterns I had come so quickly to love. I knew how fortunate I had been to come out of those situations alive. As is my intentional habit, I wondered what lessons I might derive from the experience, and how I might share them with the children. That made me consider how I had been teaching the arts of war. I had been lax.

I set out to remedy this at the earliest opportunity. On a day during the third or fourth week after I returned, I worked them strenuously for half our normal time. Then I sat them in a circle in the courtyard. I took a place as part of the circle, sitting between Arica and Bre. They knew that, by attaching myself to the circle instead of sitting in the middle of it, I wanted dialog rather than lecture.

"It's time for the next step in our training. We have worked hard on learning sword, staff, and bow. There is, however, a weapon much more valuable in combat than the ones you can hold in your hand."

Max exclaimed, "Hot oil! Rocks from a catapult!" He enjoyed the legends surrounding the great battles of antiquity almost as much as he enjoyed breathing.

"Not those things or even those kinds of things. The rocks and the oil are tools, right?" I paused to let that sink in. "Rocks and oil can be tools of warfare as well as tools of life, but that is another discussion entirely. What I was getting at is that rocks, oil, bows, swords, and staffs are all tools we use in the craft of war.

"We use those tools when we fight, but fighting is not about the sword or the staff or the bow or the arrow. Think of writing. That's not about the quill or the brush; it's about the story. Understand?

"If you fight with your sword, you fight as a beginner. If you want to fight like an expert, you have to fight with your mind."

Max perked up. "How about a master? How does a master

fight, shinando?"

Arica answered immediately. "With her heart?"

"Yes, that's true, but the heart can also get in the way. Emotion is one of the things you have to control when you fight. It is your enemy and your ally both. Anyone else?"

Silence. They were interested now, looking one to the others trying to figure out what I wanted. Let Arica or Max lead the way and the others were sure to follow. They were an interesting group. When one of them showed interest in something, they all were quick to take up the chase.

Gammin spoke, softly at first, then gaining volume as he grew more confident in what he wanted to express.

"A beginner fights with his sword. An expert fights with his mind." He paused, standing in the doorway to realization. I wanted to will him through it. "A master... fights with... nothing? No, wait, that's not it. With no mind! A master fights without thinking? Right?"

"Exactly right, *onando*." *Onando*, one who comes after, captures the special relationship between the respected *shinando*—the one who has gone before—and the student.

Marin looked at Gammin, eyes wide in wonderment. He was amazed, proud, and a little frightened, all at the same time. That was how I felt, too.

Simon asked, "How did you know, Gammin?" The excited chatter stopped immediately. Simon seldom spoke, asked question even less often.

"I didn't at first, but it sounded familiar. I remembered something Annen said about swords. He said that when you practice enough, you can do the moves without thinking about them. If you use the sword often enough, the sword uses you when battle comes. Something like that. I didn't understand it then. I am starting to, at least some of it. "

I needed to stop thinking of this one as a child. He was moving beyond that. Maybe he's was already there. I had to clear my throat before I spoke.

"What you say is true. But that is not what we were discussing." I saw in my mind an old man chasing six aberrant kittens, each frolicking in different directions. "We were talking about fighting with your mind rather than your sword. You've got to become experts before you can become masters, Max. And experts, as I said, fight with their mind."

We carried on from there. I described what I meant, trying to show how distance, timing, and intent were some of the more-important elements in fighting. I described how good timing and proper distancing keep opponents from surrounding you or coming at you many at once. This was their first real lesson in the Precepts of War.

My recent encounters near Tower Mill were perfect examples for this discussion I could not discuss this openly with all of them. I knew they could be trusted, but a secret is safest when it is known to none.

I did share the examples with Gammin and Marin, who knew much of what had occurred, though not why. After the others left us, I led them back out into the courtyard and took them through each of the two battles step by step, showing them how putting oneself in the correct position at the right time was so important.

I had been very lucky. The soldiers, all but two or three, had been relatively unskilled and inexperienced. Most of them were likely soldiering against their wills. If all of them had been half as experienced or motivated as I, things would have been different. It is conceivable that even then, with proper timing and distance, I might have squeezed by, but that is not likely.

Marin was intrigued when I mentioned Striking Dawn, the sword drawing technique I had used in my encounter with the first soldier in Tower Mill.

"Striking Dawn? What's that?"

"There are many different styles of swordsmanship; some call them schools. I have been teaching you the school used by the house of Brand." They did not ask me how I might be privy to such a thing. "The exercises and forms we do start with the sword out and at the ready, yes?" They both nodded, in unison as usual. "I studied another school, too. It is very different. That one is concerned completely with drawing the blade from its scabbard and delivering a death blow in the same motion. In the Common Tongue it is called the school of Sword Drawing, but it is not a school native to the Crescent."

With one voice, they said, "Will you teach us, shinando?"

What they wanted to learn was not taught until a student had become fairly advanced in the other uses of a blade. I had been watching them, knew they were not far from being proficient—but not yet skilled—in the sword arts I had taught them.

"I might, I suppose. It will cost you."

One said, "What?" The other, "Huh?"

"I said it will cost you."

Gammin demanded, "Cost us what?"

"Two things." I answered in my best imitation of Max. The desired effect was achieved. Both boys giggled.

Marin asked, "What two things?"

"I will let you know in time."

"But you'll teach us the style of drawing the sword?"

"Yes, if you like."

When I showed no sign of educating them on the spot, Gammin said, "Not today, though, right?"

"Right," I answered. "Now, I think, you will cook me supper."

"Is that one of the two things?"

"That depends."

"On what?"

"On how good the supper is."

Gammin swatted at me. I stepped aside. Marin's arms, surprisingly strong, closed around my middle, though not tightly. He was conscious of my wound. Without thinking, I twisted, swinging his body into Gammin, who was stepping forward to engage me. Gammin stumbled, went to one knee. I twisted again and peeled Marin off me so that he tripped over Gammin. Both boys looked up at me from the ground with startled faces.

"See?" I skipped out of their reach as they clambered to their feet. "Timing and distance. Timing and distance."

Turning my back to them brazenly, I bolted into the house, windmilling my arms and crying out like an idiot running amuck. Young boys, I have observed, love it when adults act like idiots. They grow out of that at some point.

We began the next morning. We had no other plans for the day, so we devoted most of it to the art of the draw. Much to the mutual disappointment of Marin and Gammin, we did not immediately charge out to the courtyard and start waving steel. I made them sit and listen to a fairly involved description of the whys, hows, and whens of the sword-fighting system I was about to introduce to them.

Most particularly, I was careful to inform them that this school was not meant for the kind of swords we use in Ehrylan. Our swords, for the most part, are straight and of middling width, about half that of a man's fist. The swords used in the archipelago of Telcanir, an island nation far off the coast of Arel where the system was developed and used, are slightly curved and only half as wide. The curve, slight as it is, makes them easier to draw. The reduced width makes them faster to wield. This was an important distinction for the boys to understand; care had to be taken when electing to use the various techniques. Some of them would not be effective when used with our broader, straighter, heavier blades. As always, the art of the skill was in the unminded use of the appropriate technique against the correct target.

For many days after, I had to endure experiments with bent tree branches. Eventually, we ended up with a matched set of two curved, wooded swords. They wanted to make one for me, but I told them I would not use it. I would stick to my old friend, who had served me well in the past.

That first day, after I finished lecturing them, I let them lead me out to the courtyard where I showed them the eight draws and two stances. It was a strenuous morning. We were exhausted as we cleaned up for lunch.

For afternoon studies, I gave them a pass on their

academics. That is what I told them as I brought out a very old scroll and set it before them on the table.

"This is a scroll that was copied long, long ago from an even older scroll that was recorded in the tongue of the people of Telcanir. I don't speak a word of that tongue. This scroll is a translation into the Old Tongue. When this was made, they did not call it the Old Tongue, of course, but that is another story and I do not want to get side tracked." The boys shook their heads in agreement that I should not become side tracked.

I opened the scroll. "Can you read that title, Marin?"

"It says…" he leaned over it, stared intently. "It says 'Mind and… heart…are… are… What's that word, Gammin?"

"It looks like *penentra*. That's 'joined,' isn't it, shinando?"

I hid the grin when they glanced up at me. It would never do for my *onandi* to see how pleased I was with them.

"You could say joined. Unified is better, maybe even solidified. They all come from the same root. Keep going."

They both bent over in the same motion at the same time, as if one was an image of the other in some strange mirror.

"Let's see," Marin murmured, "Mind and heart unified, no wait, are unified, that's it! Mind and Heart are unified in… in…"

Gammin finished it. "In the sword! Mind and heart are unified in the Sword."

They did not have to ask me if they were correct. They just knew it.

"Nice," I said. "Good work, boys. That is the literal translation. More commonly, one might say, 'Mind and heart are one in the Sword.' That is the core of this school of sword fighting."

Marin asked, "Isn't that sort of what you have been teaching us all along?"

"Yes." I could no longer control the smile. "Yes, that is something I teach. It is something I've learned, shall we say, along the way." I pointed down to the scroll. "So now you've read all the way through the whole title. Congratulations." Gammin rolled his eyes at my jibe, but I could see he was quite happy and not a little satisfied with himself.

There was not much useful content on the first two pages. Most of it was the writer establishing his credentials. Like so many before and after, she was a woman who claimed numerous victories, no defeats, and immutable wisdom developed from observations of rocks, trees, animals, insects, dirt, mud puddles, and the like. I let the boys labor over the translation; they learned, if nothing else, some new vocabulary. At first, Marin was enthralled. He was delighted to learn about someone who had written something so many years ago. However, as the text rambled on, even he began to lose interest. I was watching for that.

"Well done. I think that is enough. Why don't we move ahead a bit?"

Gammin advanced the scroll and came upon the first illustration. It depicted a female warrior standing on a beach in the act of drawing her blade. The sun rose out of a wave-tossed sea. A gull was winging across the sky toward the warrior. The caption read, "Striking Dawn."

I waited for the boys to figure it out.

Gammin got it first. Then Marin made the connection.

"Striking Dawn? That's the name of the technique you said you used on the soldier in Tower Mill!"

"Yes."

They wasted no more time with me. Gammin rolled out another page, this one filled with text. It took them some while to determine that the page immediately following the illustration did not, in fact, describe the illustration. Though they did not see it yet, Striking Dawn, in addition to being the name of a technique, was also the name of the first lesson of the scroll. Their efforts at translation revealed only the rudiments of the two stances we had already studied in the courtyard. I let them labor over the scroll, then made my way over to the bookcase and retrieved a book. It was much younger but still old and dog-eared.

"This book might help you with that scroll." I set it at Marin's elbow. The old book was another translation of the scroll, this one in the Common Tongue.

After they vented like sealed pots on the boil, they forgot me completely. It was rewarding to see them so absorbed, paging through the book, pointing here and there, sometimes referring back to the scroll to see how translations matched up.

Their hearts and minds were coming together in the study of the sword. I could see it happening. I wondered if Ea felt the same when the hearts and minds of his children joined in his perfection only then to find true rest and satisfaction.

III.

I was beginning to grow restless. There was seldom a day that passed where we stayed indoors morning to night. I was looking for signs in the boys to show they too were tiring, but I saw none. It was a surprise when Marin announced he'd had enough for the day. Gammin nodded agreement and looked to me for permission to close the book on the day's lesson.

I was pondering what I might make these two young food eliminators for supper. They were staring through the open window at the lane in front of the house.

"I could go for a walk," stated Marin.

"That sounds good," agreed Gammin.

That was a very atypical exchange for them. I looked in their direction to see what was making.

Marin asked, "How about you, Annen? Feel like coming out with us?"

"What have you in mind?" Something was afoot!

"I don't know." He rubbed his smooth chin.

Gammin said, "How about the Step? That would be a good walk. We could see the kids. That's catching two fish on one hook."

Gammin was not referring to Max and Bre; we had seen them only yesterday and would see them again tomorrow. It was a good suggestion for an evening's diversion. The children always enjoyed the boys when we stopped by.

Gammin said, "We could take them some of the apples you got at the market."

Marin said, "And there's more than enough cheese. We could bring them some."

Now I knew they were up to something. As far as Marin was concerned, there was never more than enough cheese. I decided to play along with them. They deserved their fun. What of it if it came at my expense? I was intrigued. What was under the covers here?

The streets had become dangerous enough at night that precaution was warranted. I strapped on my sword. The boys asked if one of them might gird himself with the spare. I declined the request. The sword was too big for them, and, more importantly, if push came to violence, I did not want them to fight with minds confused by the new learning. Better to take weapons with which they were comfortable and familiar. They accepted my decision without protest and took their staves.

Gammin paused to pluck a flower from a thorny bush in the yard. It was a passing curiosity. He was wont to do curious things, a tendency I had come to expect and to love. I passed the event over without concern and set a casual pace toward the Step. Twice along the way, we saw a group of Dryhm parading grimly down a street we crossed. They made no trouble for us, and I gave them little thought.

Lina was setting the tables when we arrived. There was the usual rushing current of children. Gammin and Marin absorbed much of it. After the fleshy tide receded, we added some of what we had brought to the board. There was plenty of room for the additional food. I felt shame when I saw how little Merelina had allotted for so many youngsters. I needed to do more.

In contrast to the lack, the children looked happy and healthy. How Merelina did so much with so little was a wonder. She was a blessing from Ea; the orphans seemed to recognize that. They usually behaved better than could have been expected.

The situation was a little better for her now. A couple of her charges were old enough to take a hand in managing the others. Also, Max and Breanna were being more helpful. Lina attributed this to the time they spent with me and the things we taught them. I believed it more likely that their close association with Marin, Gammin, and Arica was the explanation. There was a real love between those three. Max and Breanna saw it, recognized what it meant, and were working—perhaps unknowingly—to bring it about in their own home.

I had been considering Lina's plight and what might be done about it. I saw little hope within the city. Dauroth had accomplished his intent too well there, separating the people and driving us away from each other in the struggle to survive. There was still hope in River's Bend. That hope could grow into full flower if I could convince Merelina to relocate there. I had discussed my thoughts with Eanna. She was more than willing, seeing an opportunity to bring the children together in a larger community. Before that could happen, there were steps to take that would ease the process. Eanna told me what needed doing. As I sat that night among the children gracing the tables in the Step, I realized it was past time to start.

After the meal, Lina and I went out to share the beauty of the evening. We left the children to clean up under the watchful eyes of Gammin and Marin. Those two were never shy of work and their enthusiasm was contagious. Enthusiasm is usually contagious, which is why it is such a useful behavior.

As we took seats under a sprawling tree, alone for the first time, Lina said, "You are looking better, Annen."

"I thank you. It is catching from the boys. They've a lot of energy. Speaking of which, how are you, Lina? Holding up under the weight of your burden?"

"Burden? The children are not a burden." She smoothed her long skirts over her knees.

I searched for a way to wade into the subject I had in mind. The bank seemed steep and not a little slippery. After a few meaningless questions and answers, I said, "I've been speaking to Eanna about something important."

"Is that so." The words indicated a question. The tone did not.

I found that I was uncomfortable and was not sure why. Lina had a way of doing that to me. I put my hands into my pockets to keep them from fidgeting. That did not work, of course. They fidgeted there just fine.

"Lina, I am concerned for you, for the children, actually."

The expression on her face turned to surprised hurt. I had injured her, which had not been my intent. My hand squirmed deeper, came across some object in my pocket. It was soft. What did I have in my pocket? My face must have displayed the question in my mind. Lina sat up straight, abruptly.

"What is it, Annen? What do you think I am doing wrong?"

"What? You?" I was handling this badly. I would rather have pulled out my own hair than hurt Lina's feelings. "No, lady. This is not about you. You are the most amazing person I know. No one could do so well as you." I searched for better words but was distracted by the pliable thing I held in my pocket between my fingers. What was it? I pulled my hand out and opened it in my lap.

The soft thing that lay across my palm was, of course, one of the flowers from our yard in the Stone Gate. How it ended up in my pocket I did not know, though I suspected Gammin. I held it out to Merelina. She took it gently, as if it were made of mist, and held it to her nose.

"Lina, I am sorry if I was not clear. You need have no fear that I doubt the miracles you perform here. I was referring to the situation in Twofords. Things are getting bad here. Isn't it time we introduced the two sets of children to each other, those from Twofords and those from River's Bend?"

She was distracted by the bloom, but managed to pry her eyes away and looked at me. "You think I will have to leave here? Why? What has happened?"

"I do think that. I do not know why. Yet, I trust my intuition; it has saved me many times in the past. Right now, it is telling me a day will come soon when we will have to leave

Twofords. I see a haven with many children and two caretakers in a community where such folk are esteemed rather than disdained."

This was the gritty bit. Merelina was fiercely independent and, almost to a flaw, fanatically self-sufficient. If it were a flaw, it was the only one I could find in her. By suggesting the idea that she merge with Eanna, I might as well have slapped her in the face. That is how I feared she might feel. Once again, I underestimated her.

"I have been thinking the same, Annen. I wanted to talk with you about it."

Call me a fool. I wanted to go to my knees and throw my arms around her waist. I might have done so but, even behind my defenses, I felt attraction to her beating against the gates.

"What is it, Annen? What did I say?"

"Nothing, lady. I am just pleased you are open to the suggestion. I had feared you would not be, especially because of how you responded a moment ago. I thought I had offended you."

"Offended? No. Not that." She set the flower in her lap and folded her hands close to it. She took a deep breath and let it out slowly. "Will I tell you a truth, my friend?"

"You may tell me anything, Merelina."

"When you told me you had been talking with Eanna about something important, I thought you were going to tell me that you and she were… were to be wed."

"Eanna and me?" I was so astounded by this admission that I was speechless. For a time. Such a thing never lasts long with me; I am not a man of few words as well you know. I let the silence pass and used the time to think.

How could I tell this woman the truth? I had to arrest the seeds of affection that sprouted anew each time I saw her. No such effort was needed for Eanna or any other woman I knew. This was not because of any lack in Eanna; she was an astounding woman in her own right.

"There is love there, that of a brother for his sister. If I were to think of taking a wife it could only …" I stopped just in time. I had meant to say "it could only be you." I frantically sifted through the phrases that might end the sentence without causing more hurt. I thought of saying "it could only complicate matters." That was certainly true. I decided not to dance on the edges of the truth, so I gave up the sentence as a lost cause and started again.

"I could not take any woman as my wife, no matter how much I loved her."

Her eyes closed. I set my hand on hers. "No matter how long I have loved her." Her eyes opened and looked into mine. It was a look of such smoldering intensity that I almost threw away caution.

I saw the sea of storms there, a swirl of blue and grey. Kingdoms could have been lost over those eyes and this woman. I felt my hand tighten on hers. I watched it pull her hand up and hold it against my cheek. It was not lavender that I smelled on those fingers. Rather, strong and clear, it was the scent of a rose, the last surrender of the blossom in her lap.

I held her hand where it was and turned my head just a little, just enough that my lips brushed over it. Then, without letting it go, I tried to let her go.

"Merelina, there are things you don't know. Things about me. It is not safe to be the one I love. I hurt those I love with my love for them. That is all I can say."

I saw the tears forming. Not a cascade, she was too strong for that, just a glistening diamond at the corner of the swirling sea. I saw her desire for me, or perhaps it was love. I could not yield to what we both craved, and I knew this would hurt her again. I wanted to scream in frustration. I wanted to scream, yes, and I wanted to take her in my arms, press my lips to her ear, and say, "If ever I were going to love a woman, Lina, it would be you. It is you. It is you only."

But I could not.

"Don't cry, Lina. I… you…" I was stammering like a fool. Taking hold of myself, I said, "You are not unloved, Merelina," thinking that would ease her. Once again, I proved that I know nothing of women. She cringed as if I had struck her and snatched her hand back. She got to her feet.

"There is much I do not know about you, Annen. And there is much I know." I watched her fists clench and unclench. "I will go check on the children. They are too quiet."

I started to rise. She held out her hand, the one I had kissed.

"Annen, no. Will you wait for me? Please?"

"I will wait for you, lady."

She had composed herself by the time she returned. That made one of us. I was the more discommoded of the two. Something had passed between us, but I could not put a name to it. I was still wrestling with it; she had moved on past the trouble. She was strong in that way.

"Marin is telling them a story. Everyone is seated around him, even Temay."

"What story, Lina?"

"Andur and the Cave Bear."

Eventually, we came again to the subject of the two orphanages. We explored how we might integrate the two sets of children. Merelina listed the most likely obstructions that might mar the process. We discussed solutions.

We needed to start the process by introducing the two groups to each other. We decided to have outings in the countryside where both groups attended. We would also have visitations where each group visited the facilities of the other. This latter would have a benefit that Lina and I recognized but never discussed. If the River's Bend children saw the Step, they could not help but have pity on the children there.

We chatted about these and many other things, then sat in silence under the sky and stars. I had to resist the very real temptation to take her hand or put my arm around her. When at last we arose to make our way back to the house, I held out my arm to help her up. She took it.

Many of the children were still sitting in a circle and watching. Now, instead of Marin alone, there were eight young bodies in the center. They were doing Corn Gathering Dance. Three of the dancers were boys. At the front, next to Breanna who was leading, was Max. He was gathering as if it were a contest.

I joined them.

IV.

It seems foolish to claim I was unaware of what Gammin and Marin were conniving. Yet it is true. I had put away any thought of having another wife long ago. This was easy in the first years after the wife of my youth was so brutally parted from me, her and Connel, our son. At first, I had grief to isolate me. After, the struggle for survival left no room for romance. There came a time when I had healed of that hurt, or so I thought. I would not risk the danger of allowing my heart to seek comfort in a woman. Love is a steep mountain at whose peak is glorious warmth. From those heights, one can fall to into cold, deep and deadly. It was a mountain I feared and avoided. Through practice, avoidance became habit. Long habit eventually became my nature. I was a man for whom a mate was unthinkable. The consequence of my love was death, as so many who have suffered from it could attest if they were alive. This I have said before. As yet you have not seen it. But you will.

We left Stepholm—I'd heard Max calling it that, and the thought was still in my mind—much later than usual. It was full dark. The three of us were tired in that agreeable way that follows fellowship and good meals. We talked in low tones and short sentences. I asked Gammin about the rose. Gammin accepted full responsibility for the prank and told me he had put one in Marin's pocket as well, though that one he had not stripped of its defenses. Marin reached into his pocket and came out with the thing, feigning surprise. I knew he was pretending and both of them knew I knew. I might have pursued the matter further, but that is when the trouble started.

The trap was well laid in an area far from the gates. There were no guards to intervene, if they had been so inclined. We had intentionally taken a longer route that kept to larger streets where lamps burned the night through. This took us along the wall street to the gates, up Castle Road, which bisects the city from north to south, and then to the midway street that led to the area above the Stone Gate.

They came upon us as we made our way east along the midway, near the very center of the city. There was a stretch of the road where three or four of the lamps had gone out. Later, when I had time to think about it, I realized that the way layers probably extinguished the lights for this very purpose. Maybe they were never lit and the lamp lighter was in on it. Neither of those things mattered to the prey caught in the trap, but it does show how far into disrepair our society had fallen.

We had made it a third of the way through the lightless area when a figure stepped into the lane in front of us. He held a short stabbing sword. Pointing it at me, he said harshly, "Hold where you are and produce gold."

Sounds swirled all around us. We were surrounded. From what I could see, the figure was an older boy, a young man on the verge. I looked around hastily, as a frightened man would, turning head my left and right more than once though I saw what I needed the first time. Behind me, Gammin whispered, "Three daggers behind." Marin whispered, "Two each side. Daggers. One whip." Eight we could see. Eight to three. The whip was the worst of it, if the wielder was proficient. There would be more up front, hidden in the shadows behind the leader. Such man-boys do not leave themselves unprotected.

These were either ruffians newly come to the city or agents of Pruis' father. The local gangs had stopped harassing my students and friends. It was unlikely they would hit us now, when the three most capable were gathered together. I remembered Dryhm we had seen earlier that day, though they usually did their own work when the work involved evil.

"I said out with your purse! Or die!" The young man

brandished his sword. His voice was louder this time, more urgent. He was no battle-scarred veteran.

"As you wish," I said, trying to sound frightened. I needed the attackers in close where we could deal with them. If they kept distance between us, they would have time to recover from what we were about to do to the nearest.

I fumbled at my belt. The leather pouch in which I kept the day's money was on my right hip. I was careful that my cloak concealed the sword on my left. I could have given the pouch to the robbers with no great loss. Some would say I should have done so, for to do otherwise was to assume risk for no reason. But I am a stubborn man. I could not give up the memory of a time when honest people were free to walk the streets without fear for their safety.

I made a mess of untying the knot, looking up at the leader with an anxious face. He was moving closer, a step at a time, as greed consumed caution. Two figures lurked close behind him, one at each shoulder.

Pulling the bag from my belt, I extended it to him.

"Hold!" His voice was loud enough to make himself grimace. He did not want to attract the attention of the patrols that occasionally fulfilled their function in the city. I took the opportunity to drop the bag as if he had startled me as well.

What he should have done was command me to step well back. What he did was step forward quickly so that he was directly in front of me. Though he brought up his sword and held its point to my face, I could have killed him without much effort. My sword was twice as long as his.

"Pick it up, fool," he said.

I went to a knee, reaching out with my left hand, making sure the motion tugged the edge of my cloak away from the hilt on my hip. I caught up the purse and held it out to him. I looked into his eyes. He must have seen death in my face, for he flinched and stabbed at me.

That was just as well. He wasted precious time moving closer with the strike rather than running for his life. There was a chance he might still get out of this alive if everything fell into place. Otherwise, he would not live to see the sun.

I swiveled on my knee and drew my sword in the same instant, Striking Dawn again. It has always impressed me how the most rudimentary techniques are those that carry one to success time and again. One can do quite well in life if one just gets the basics right.

In other circumstances, I would have used Swallow's Flight, hacking his arm off with the cut and removing his head with the return. If I had been more concerned, I might have removed his sword arm, but I did not think blood was necessary. Blood on the streets has a way of bringing flurries of questions and swarms of inquisitive officials.

The blade of my sword slammed into his with a force that drove it from his hand. It skittered across the lane in a tangle of noise that would have brought the patrol if they had been anywhere near. I was on my feet before the cascade of sounds stopped. Gripping the young man by his tunic with my left hand, I hurled him back into the body of one of the figures behind him. I let the blade of my sword slide along his neck and ear, hoping it would leave a lasting memory of this night. As he crashed into his fellow, I made an aggressive advance and took a fighting position in front of the other henchman. Without even a look at his leader, he fled. I turned back to face the leader and his second. They were already gone.

I whirled to help the boys, but there was no one left to fight.

After withdrawing from the vicinity, we took a moment to collect ourselves. Then, with greatly increased caution and speed, we hurried home.

We arrived safe and sound. I sent the boys to their beds as soon as we got home though no real urging was necessary. I took a seat in the front room with my weapons near to hand. It was unlikely there would be reprisal, but long habits die hard even after years of disuse. I had a mind to watch for the remainder of the night. And to think.

I needed to consider this attack, to determine whether it was a simple attempted robbery or some other device of my enemies. But, fool that I am, what I wanted to think about was Lina. She was opening doors that had been locked for decades. I wrenched my thoughts back to where they needed to be and considered the attack. I decided that the hasty conclusion at which I had arrived during the situation was likely correct on both accounts. The attackers were likely newcomers to the city, and they were likely hired by the *drachem* to menace me. There was more. The fact that we had seen Dryhm twice that same night might have been a coincidence, but it did not feel that way to me. There was a missing link I could not discern.

Eventually, my thoughts having chased themselves in circles several times, I decided to allow myself some sleep. For caution's sake, I did not go to my room, contenting myself with the comfort of a chair by the hearth. I opened my eyes to morning light at the sound of boys stirring. By the time they came out, I had started water to boil.

11. ERRANTRY

I.

We did not tell Merelina of the assault straight away. To do so would have caused her concern for our safety and lessened her joy at our comings. She began to visit us in the Stone Gate more often, and, as her visits became a more regular occurrence, she learned what had occurred. I made it clear that she required an escort both to and from my home. I had no power over her and could not enforce such an edict. Nor did I try. Luckily, after a brief resistance, she came round to our way of thinking.

The escorting proved no burden. Much of the time we simply incorporated her visits into the routine of our training. Arica and Simon would collect her and the others on their way to my place. Marin, Gammin, and I would escort them back after we'd shared supper.

Temay was a frequent addition to these festivities and, in time, began to share in the studies, both martial and academic. This did him a world of good and we measured his progress now in leaps and bounds where before he had moved forward in fits and starts.

I enjoyed the visits so much so that I began to dread them. I could not allow my relationship with the lady to advance. Yet it was delightful to be in Merelina's company. How can I explain? My feelings would have been an excellent example of ambivalence had I needed to teach that concept to the children.

Merelina acted on our consolidation discussions. In the months that followed, we held outings in the countryside, parties really, where the children could run and play on ground that belonged to neither. The Twofords group got to know the smaller group from River's Bend. Old Bilious became something of a notable figure. After a lifetime spent waiting on the porch, he became the center of attention. How their noses stood up to the test is a mystery. The children from the Bend came to know the others as cousins who once were lost but now were found. Temay managed to capture their hearts straight away. I had worried that he might not be received well, but children can be very wise.

The third outing was held on the rolling fields that ran from the lip of land above the shore of the Silver River almost to the outskirts of the Shambles south of the city. Eanna brought with her Aldryn, the wood wright of River's Bend whose wife had died some years before. He and I had long been friends. His company was welcome and not unexpected.

That day is bright in my memory. Lina, Eanna, Aldryn, and I sat on a rush mat the children had made for us. We shared cheese and wine as the orphans frolicked from the river to the road. Old Bil suffered himself to play the part of a cave bear to Max's Andur. The dog did not always cooperate. Some of the best moments were when Max had to chase him down to force a fight. The antics reduced us to joyful tears.

These were sunny days, even when the sun did not shine. The meetings refreshed my soul, washing away the sweat of anxiety that often tainted my mood. The excursions did not detract from our training, though they did force us to work out a more exact schedule. The six core students still came and went as before, though with heightened awareness and caution. The addition of the new sword system, the school of Sword Drawing, is what really affected us. We had to find the time somewhere, so I slacked off on their book learning. The boys were already branching out into areas of their own interest. Study time lost to the new sword arts simply bled into their free time. They read or talked with me often until late in the night. There was nothing I enjoyed more. My heart—by which I mean my spirit, my soul, the real me that is trapped in this body—knew that I was doing the very thing Ea had created me to do.

I did not teach the art of the draw to all of them. Max and Breanna were too young. Arica and Simon were not yet advanced enough. It all worked out nicely, as so many things did in those happy days before war came again to the land.

As the anniversary of the day the boys had joined me in the Stone Gate neared, a thought was growing in my mind. The inclusion of the new sword school brought a need I would have to address before we could take the training to the next level.

I discussed my concerns with the woodcutter. We contrived a plan. When one of his associates ventured to Mendolas not long thereafter, he carried a letter. The reply came back with eager acceptance. The next time the man made the journey, I sent with him detailed instructions and a substantial purse of money. These were provided to the weapon smith from whom I purchased the knife back when disaster struck at Tower Mill. When the order was ready, I would ride out and retrieve the swords—as well as some other items—to make gifts of them to my boys and core family. Knowing that the making of a good sword is a long work, I settled me down to wait what would likely be a year or more. I swore Marn to secrecy, which meant I asked him not to tell anyone and he grunted something that resembled an acknowledgement.

The months passed as we studied, worked, and played. Teryn's Moon was reborn Harvest Moon, which shone in the relief of a Fallow year. Winter descended from the peaks during Snow Moon, as it tends to do in our part of the Southland, falling upon us that year like an enraged bear. We hunkered down in the warmth of our homes and used the inclement weather as an excuse to study and train all the harder. From Breanna to Old Bil, they kept coming through the wind, rain, mud, and snow. I continued to give them all I could and they continued to take it, returning to me a joy and contentment I had never experienced.

We met with Merelina and the children on a regular basis, sometimes at my home, more often at hers. The Step demanded repairs to keep out the unusually fierce winter. We kept at them, one by one. When spring came, a timid lamb chasing away the bear, the place was in better shape than it had been for years.

Then came the days where warmth bloomed from the sun. We filled them with purpose and merriment in balanced proportion. There is no stain upon my memory of the time between the day I ordered the swords and the second anniversary of Gammin's arrival in my life.

We began to hear rumor from the Badlands, as much of eastern Ehrylan had been known since Dauroth came. This was not because the land was treacherous. There was constant conflict between the peoples of that region and Dauroth's armies. The Badlands were held by an outlaw who knew no allegiance but to himself and his men. Little was known about him save his self-styled title, the Defier, and his reputation for brutality and intolerance. He did not suffer any to pass through his dominion, whether the traveler was simple citizen, loyalist, or Dauroth's man.

Rumors from the Badlands told of conflict escalating to all-out war. Early in his rule, Dauroth had built a stronghold there, Daur en Lammoth, Fortress of Sorrow. Whole armies issued from that terrible stronghold to suppress the Defier. The effort was mostly unsuccessful. The Defier avoided large-scale battles, preferring to engage his more numerous enemies in small skirmishes at unlikely places, a dog nipping at the heels of a bull elk. The Defier would strike hard at some exposed collection of Dauroth's assets, then dash back into the outstretched arms of the Great Mountains. The Defier had his own stronghold high up on the lower reaches of the mountains, an ancient castle known as Stormhaven. Large forces could not come at them there.

It was a good strategy. I shared it with my students, explaining the technique of attacking the end of a line rather than the middle, nibbling away at the extremities of a force much larger than your own. We spent an increasing amount of time reviewing and discussing the strategies of warfare. Much of our discussion had at its roots the various written and verbal traditions dealing with Andur's conquests.

Max hit upon the idea of acting out the Tales of Andur. The imitations started simply. The first few were simple re-enactments of the stories of Andur and his band of followers before they embarked on the ultimate task of unifying the peoples of the Crescent—Andur and the Cave Bear, Teryn and the Witches of Uruthron, Marden the Magnificent and the Raiders of Norlan. (Guess who insisted on playing Marden the Magnificent?) Over time, the play acting turned more original. Once that happened, the activities grew with a life of their own.

The events started as simple games that might take an hour or an afternoon. By the time the war brought them to a stop, these had grown into excursions that might take two or more of the group into the countryside for days at time. Max categorized the excursions as quests and gave them grand titles such as The Quest for the Cup of Justice, The Search for the Rod of Truth, and Nightmare at the Pikes. As far as I know, no cups or rods ever came back with them.

Max even made a quest out of my trip to pick up the swords. He called it the Quest for Mendolas. Bre was less grandiose, calling it Crossing the River, cute word-play on one of the sword forms I taught them.

When word came that the swords were finished, we were in

Snow Moon, near the end of the third year since Gammin had come to me. He and Marin were fourteen. It was high time they had their own blades, but the community had just survived another Tax. I could not abandon my countrymen to go retrieve a treasure. Twofords was especially hard hit, losing six beautiful girls to the fangs of evil. Arica was passed over. She was marginally too old. The fact that she was not even on the Black List was another attempt to drive a wedge between me, the city folk, and the villagers—so said Marn, the woodcutter, watcher of the northern border. We were too relieved to worry at that.

The swords had to wait. Almost fourteen full months had passed since I bespoke them; surely I could wear patience a while longer. I sent word to the smith, knowing he would understand. Mendolas was on the same hideous schedule. I made my plans for the next spring, and set myself to caring for those around me as best I could.

I thought to ride out to Mendolas and retrieve the blades with the coming of Wind Moon, the third month of the new year. The fourth month, Wet Moon, would have been drier and easier, an interesting irony, but my patience had fallen in tatters. The winter had been mild. Spring seemed to be straining to break through. There was snow on the mountains to the west of the river, but there was sun in uncommon measure.

Traffic between Twofords and the rest of the world was by no means an oddity during that time of year, though most people put off long journeys until after the beginning of Wind Moon. Had I been going north, I might have waited, but I was going south into warmer climes. Also that small voice was whispering to me that the calm before the storm was drawing to an end. It was time to make ready for war.

I had been growing my beard. I thought this small disguise some measure of caution against anyone who might recognize me in Mendolas and connect me with what had happened in Tower Mill. I do not fancy a beard, not on myself, but this I considered a good precaution.

As I say, I had thought to ride alone to Mendolas. When I informed the boys of my plan—without telling them why I was going—they said they wanted to go. That evolved into the idea that all of our core group should go. When I told Lina I wanted to take Max and Breanna, the look on her face dissolved any resistance I had. She was going to accompany us.

When we approached Max and Breanna about the idea, the young girl shied away in fear and would have declined. Max took to the idea like a fish takes to worms, exclaiming that he would see us all safely there and back and that the event would be known ever after as the Quest for Mendolas. Once Max had declared for the project, Bre said she would go, though she did this with her head down and her eyes closed. I gathered her in my arms and painted her face with kisses until she giggled.

Only Merelina required an explanation for the trip, though she did not ask for it. I did not lie to her. I told her that I was going to pick up gifts for the young ones and that the gifts were swords and knives. She accepted this with her usual grace and kept the secret safe. Gammin and Marin were too respectful to press me. When they hinted, I told them I was going to pick up a gift for Merelina, which was a truth dancing behind its own back.

My first concern was to arrange transport for the throng. I rented two horses of the right temperament for Gammin and Marin. There was a nice mare for Merelina who, I learned to my great delight, was an experienced horsewoman. She was looking forward to renewing her acquaintance with the art. I thought this looking forward business would stop after the first ride when her body began to report in. The other four would ride the Water Wheel, though Avyansa would not be pulling it. He was for me, and I for him. For the cart, I rented two stout, thick-legged horses. There was much switching back and forth between the riding horses and the Water Wheel. Arica was eager to ride and Simon was equally eager to learn.

After it was far too late, I took the time to consider what we were about. I saw how foolish it must have seemed to anyone not involved. But to Lina and the children, this was a wild adventure that promised loads of fun. Most of the children had never traveled outside of the Bend, and to go as far as Mendolas was as good as a journey to the moon.

Merelina had mentioned once how she would like to sail the river to the sea in spring. I could not pull the moon from the skies for the children, but I might be able to make that dream come true for her. More than anyone I knew, she deserved such a thing.

I did not hire men at arms for this trip. The seven of us could defend ourselves from the trouble we might encounter. Each of us, save Lina, bore a good bow. Max and Breanna could hit a target much of the time. Gammin, Marin, and I were able to handle a bow effectively. Arica had already surpassed my skill as far as I surpassed the boys'. We were set as far as distance weapons were concerned. I took my sword and staff, allowing the students their staves. And Gammin took his hunting knife; I don't think he would have parted with it if I asked him, but as it might serve its life's purpose on this trip, I had no reason to.

All of them would be better armed on the return trip.

II.

It was a crispy morning when we set out from the Bend. Old Bil looked at us mournfully. I could not tell if he wished to accompany us or whether he thought we might have been a bit touched in the head to be up and out so early. He looked at me with his one good eye and woofed. When I patted his shaggy head, his tail pounded a loud rhythm on the porch. Never mind about the drool.

We traveled at leisure. After the second day, Max, Bre, and Simon were farther from their homes than they had ever been. I think they were disappointed the forest showed no sign of changing its appearance in this undiscovered country. Eventually the novelty wore off, or else they just forgot.

The first night we made camp a short distance from the

road in a place Marn had pointed out during our return from the Naralyn. We were sheltered by the trees and a low rise behind which we clustered our horses and wagon. The horses we hobbled, with the exception of Avyansa. I would suffer him no such indignity, nor was it needed. I left him free to roam if he chose, which he didn't. There was less chaos than there would have been a year ago; Gammin, Simon, and the woodcutter's children were all now old enough to understand that work must come before pleasure, even when one is tired, sore, and hungry.

We pitched two tents, one for the ladies and one for the boys. I slept in the Water Wheel. Max had it in his head that we needed to mount a guard, which he did every night. Somehow, the little guy cajoled the three other boys to sacrifice some of their sleep for the effort. Though there was no real need, I stood a watch on three occasions, mostly to humor Max. I wanted time alone with my thoughts, which were tending toward the woman more than I cared to admit.

Max was acting on the training I had given him, and I was pleased. He did not know that Marn had spoken to the Children of the Forest. They knew what we were about and would be watching for us. Truth to tell, I felt as safe as safe can be—while we were in the forest. We saw no sign of them, yet we had no trouble either, not so much as a single tree fallen across our path. I let myself relax, which felt amazing.

We stopped just shy of the river the day we came to it. We could have crossed and made another league, but I wanted a fresh start in the morning. We needed a full day to traverse the pass sprawling between Teryn's Crossing and Mendolas. There was snow and ice up there, lots of it. We could see it, even in the darkness. I wanted to get as far down the other side as possible before making camp the next day. Tonight we would stay low, near the river. It would be the last night in the Old Forest.

I halted our cavalcade for a break when we were still a league from Teryn's Crossing. The old way mark was just visible underneath a tumble of stones and leaves if one knew where to look. I sent Marin and Simon ahead to scout the way. As I have said, a bridge is always a good place for an ambush. I could have relied on the Old Ones' protection, but this was good training for my students and it is better to be cautious now than sorry later.

The rest of us gathered firewood. Knowing that the wood we gathered along the way would be winter-wet, we had brought ample tender and a good selection of seasoned pieces to start our fires each evening. We needed to supplement these with gathered fuel. Yet it was not for our evening fire that we now labored. Rather, I had in mind to carry a significant supply with us into the heights. If we were stranded up there, fire could mean the difference between life and tragedy.

By the time the boys returned, we had a plentiful supply of wood, some of it fairly dry, which turned out to be a good thing. The high reaches were white with snow, as were the slopes just below them, including the shoulder we would be climbing the next morning. I had hoped that, with the mild winter, the situation would be better. As we had seen no one else on the road for three full days, I should have known it was not.

We camped in a meadow near the edge of the forest within sight of the bridge Teryn built. After tending to our horses, I made sure everyone repacked their packs and that the firewood and tools we might need the next day were accessible. I expected an early start; there would be no time to attend to packing in the morning. Then it was time for supper.

When all that was done, Lina and I walked to a boulder from which there was a nice view of the river below and a stupendous view of the mountains above. We sat listening to water sing and the converse of trees. Or we tried to. One by one, we were joined by inquisitive young ones who wondered what their adults might be up to.

Max was the first. He informed me that we needed to replenish the firewood we had used and that someone should look around to make sure we were safe. I sent him off to do just that. Even Avyansa checked on us. He wandered across the field, eating what winter grass he could find to supplement the food we had provided, until he came close. I said his name. He lowered his great head and blew. Lina and I patted, scratched, and caressed him until he was satisfied. Then he wandered back to his cousins. Lina grinned. When she sat back against the rock, she put her head on my shoulder.

Arica came last, with her bow in hand. She showed me the weapon, asking me to inspect the string. It was worn. Now that I thought about it, all the bows could use restringing. I told Arica we would purchase new strings in Mendolas, thinking she would go away satisfied. Instead, she lowered herself to the ground between us and our view.

"I've been thinking, shinando. We all have weapons, everyone but Merelina."

Lina tensed. I felt it where her side pressed mine—as often happens when two people sit together with backs against a rock so they can see the river, the peaks, and the glory of a setting sun.

Arica continued. "Do you even have a knife, Merelina?"

Lina still did not speak. She shook her head, and that only slightly.

"Why not?" Arica was seldom assertive. When she was, she took it to the limit.

Lina sighed. She looked at me with her stormy eyes for what seemed like a long while. Then she sat up straight and turned her torso to face Arica squarely. My side felt bare.

"The thought of using a weapon, of trying to hurt someone, doesn't seem right. Not for me." She turned her head back to me in a quick motion, looking at me with troubled eyes. The frown was a stranger to her face. "I am not saying you shouldn't... do what you do, Annen. I know the world they live in and I know you are helping prepare them for it." Her shoulders dropped in frustration. "For me, I do not think I can do it."

Arica said, "Not even in defense of the children?"

Ouch! Right to the heart, a perfect thrust. Did I teach her that?

"I don't know, Arica. I am too old to speak in absolutes. I don't know where I would find the courage to look someone in the eye and try to kill them."

Something about that statement rang true. Not the part about courage, because Lina was one of the strongest, most-courageous people I ever met. It was the idea of looking at someone in the eye that stuck to me.

I searched for better words. Frustrated once more with my inability, I said, "What about a bow?"

"A bow?"

Arica said, with excitement, "Yes! A bow. Exactly what I was thinking. Why not learn to shoot a bow?"

Lina looked concerned, cornered. "I don't know."

Arica pressed before I could stop her. "You can practice the bow as if it is just a hobby. You can shoot at apples. You don't even have to pretend it is for… the real thing."

Merelina's head bowed. A curtain of midnight hair slid across her face, hiding her expression from me. I did not need to see.

I glanced at Arica above Lina's head, telling her with my eyes that it was time to stop. She understood and sat back. I placed my arm around Lina's shoulder.

"Never mind, Merelina. You have more than enough to occupy your time. I'll concentrate on the weapons; you concentrate on the Step. That seems about right to me."

Wondering what we were going to do with the knife I had ordered for her, I kissed Lina on the cheek, pushing my face through the waterfall of hair. Even out here in the wild, it was clean and smelled of lavender. When I pulled away, gossamer strands clung to my beard. They were a bridge between us, a spider's web. The illusion was more real because the strands that stuck belonged to the grey streak at the front. I smiled and Arica laughed. Lina looked up. When she saw the mess I had made, a grin chased away her frown.

"Where's Max with the firewood?" I brushed away the web gently. "Arica, will you make sure he's not off somewhere stalking dragons?" The words were soft, playful. I made my eyes hard. The girl left us in a hurry. We were not disturbed again.

Lina and I finally had some time to watch. In the last true light of the day—the magic light—as the last rim of fading brilliance fell behind glistening ridges, Merelina took my hand in both of hers. "I thank you, Annen. I thank you for understanding."

I squeezed her hand, not liking how good it felt to be holding it. She settled against me again. I felt her warmth. That was both good and bad for me.

The next time the subject of archery came up, Merelina had changed her mind entirely.

III.

The morning dawned bright. Billowy clouds scudded across the sky, some low enough to engulf the highest peaks before they passed to the north and east. I noted them. One cannot ignore the sky and come safely through that time of year, if ever. The clouds were pure white against a blue sky and I quieted the whisper inside my head.

The road from Teryn's Crossing led across the valley floor for a league before it began to climb the north side of the ridge. The way became steep once it started to ascend in earnest. We had no difficulty until we arrived at the place where snow began to cover the ground in an almost unbroken blanket.

Until we had climbed so high, which was still low in comparison to the peaks towering above us, we could avoid the patches of snow and ice. Now, we were increasingly unable to determine a good route for the wagon. The road was not maintained. Run-off had cut deep fissures we could not hope to avoid without significant extra effort.

The wagon was the biggest problem. If a wheel were to slide into one of the run-off channels, it might break or become stuck. When we blundered across a runnel that cut the road from one side to the other, the wagon tended to jerk to a halt; the horses had to heave with extra effort to pull it across—and up.

We were greatly cheered when we crested the ridge. There was less snow on south side. A few of the young ones voiced their desire to stop and celebrate. Max wanted to stick a sword in the ground and claim victory over the mountain. I told him not to be boastful; we had not overcome the mountain, merely climbed to the top of one of its arms.

Those who wanted to stop had the right of it. It was past time we ate and the horses needed to rest. I knew a nearby spot just right for such activities. We pressed on and came there soon enough to satisfy all.

The place was a shepherd's ring, or some such thing. It was a flat spot set back from the road, encircled by a waist-high wall made out of stones of varying shapes and sizes. The structure was old, though it had been kept in excellent repair over the years.

Most of the space within the ring was free of snow. There was room for the horses if not the Water Wheel. The four boys and I tended to them first, while Arica, Breanna, and Merelina spread the meager feast on a rush mat.

When all was ready, we set to with a will. At first, there was little conversation, but a pleasant chatter started. I did not say much, contenting myself to watch the interplay between these characters who had become the major players in the story of my life. They were quite a cast. I felt very content at that moment, sitting beneath the peak southlanders call the White Tower. That is what I was thinking when the chill wind caught my attention.

I looked up at the sky and all thought of warmth and contentment bled away. The billowy white clouds had been replaced by the blurred muddle that come before storm. Merelina was holding her elbows across her body the way women do, the pose that reflects vulnerability and strength, but above all cold. A gust caught her hair, blew a dark river.

My mouth spoke though I had not meant to vocalize my

thought. "We've got to go. Now."

Marin and Gammin stood up. Simon and Arica followed. They scanned the surroundings for an enemy and found it in the sky. As the youngsters began to gather our things, Merelina looked at me, her eyes worried.

"What is it, Annen?" She started to get up, not waiting for an answer. I held my hand out to her.

"The weather is changing. You feel it, don't you? Look at the sky."

She nodded, looked up at the peak. "I do feel it. I was getting cold. I wanted to get my cloak but I was comfortable and enjoying the day."

"Me too, Lina. But now we have to go. It took longer than I anticipated to get up here, a lot longer. We are too high this late in the day. We need to get down as far as we can by dark."

She nodded again, laid her hand on my arm. "How far, sir?" Her voice was steady. She saw the danger and was not afraid.

In my mind, I thought "To the end, lady. I want you by my side until the end."

I said, "Twelve leagues to Mendolas as the crow flies. It is six to the river where we will be warm and comfortable. It is two leagues across this shoulder to the place where the road gets steep again. Another league will take us down to where we might be safe tonight."

Lina grimaced. "Six leagues to the river? Six hours?" She surveyed the sky again. There were not six hours left until dusk and we needed to stop well before dark to prepare for what looked to be a hard night.

I shook my head. "Six hours on a good road with fresh horses and no snow. Who knows what we will find on this road." I bent and picked up my things from the mat, and Lina's too. When I stood up, I said, "It may have been my mistake to make this trip so early in the year."

She looked at me with her stormy eyes and said, "You will see us though."

Standing beneath the White Tower with the wind around her, she looked like Magravina, the hero of legend who saved her people by leading them from danger into danger until they passed into a peaceful place beyond the mountains. It was only then that I recognized the similarity in their names. I met her gaze and saw what was in her eye. Her confidence made me feel strong. She had said that I would see them through.

I said, "I will."

The young ones seemed to understand our situation and, for the most part, saw it as one more adventure. This was especially true of Max, who was already treating the oncoming storm as if it were an adversary in his quest. Breanna was the exception. She was near tears with anxiety. She frantically demanded to know what would happen if we were caught in the storm and what we would do about it. With each sensible answer we gave, she became increasingly turbulent. Simon was of little help; in his usual understated tone, he mentioned that we had been caught in the storm already and were already doing what we would do if we were caught in the storm.

Breanna had shown this tendency before. In an instant, her timidity might be washed away by waves of emotion that wracked her so that she trembled and shook. When that happened, nothing would appease her. Lina, and Eanna too, claimed that the best thing to do in those cases was to let her cry it out. For me, I would have lifted her up and held her close if that had been possible. But it was not; when she became thus enraged, it was difficult to get near her without risking her own safety. Now, with the sun falling ever closer to the peaks and the storm brewing, I could not risk letting her get to that state. Everyone's safety depended on getting out of here quickly. We were not in trouble yet, not by a long bow shot, but the storm could bring it.

I nudged Avyansa close to the wagon and lifted the frightened child, setting her on the saddle in front of me. I held her close for many breaths.

"Don't worry. It's alright to feel frightened, because there is some danger, but we will be fine. Ok?" I nodded the way she was wont to do and made my eyes wide with the question. I kept nodding until she nodded back. When she met my eyes, her lower lip was pushed out and she was frowning, but there was a smile tugging at her mouth.

"Will you help me find the way?"

She nodded again. Her little hand came off the saddle and gripped my arm. She was so small and so shy; it was a wonder she had the courage to come with us at all. She had done splendidly.

I looked around, met Gammin's eye and Lina's. We seemed ready.

"Bre, Why don't you tell Avyansa to start?"

Her little legs kicked softly and she shouted, "Go, Avyansa!" And he did.

The road declined along the lap of the mountain. It wound around the beginnings of spur ridges that bordered dramatic valleys below and to the east of us. These ridges and their valleys were the reason the road had to climb to our present height; navigating them would have been tortuous. That was especially true now, for being shadowed for much of the day, they were still choked with snow. The road builders had decided that it was better to climb above those ridges than to walk among them. One benefit was that we were afforded an excellent view of the lands below. From time to time, we could see a glimmer of the Silver River far below. It was very beautiful.

When the sun touched the tip of the White Tower, we had only made it to the switchbacks that would take us down to the river again. We might have made a run for it, hoping to get low enough before the sun set fully and darkness made further progress untenable. Had I been alone and on Avyansa, I might have done just that. But not with Lina and the children. I could not risk such precious cargo. The gamble was unwarranted.

We stopped and took a position in another of the structures frequented by travelers on this road. I had sent the boys to find a suitable spot. They came galloping back, their shouts hopeful.

They found a haven that consisted of two structures made of undressed stones and rough-cut logs. The first, which had been used to shelter animals recently and often, was a sturdy enclosure with just room enough for our horses. The hut in which the humans spent their night was not quite civilized enough to be called a cabin. It was less well-built and finished than the other, showing how important animals were to those who regularly used the structures. Both consisted of a single-room, a well-used fire pit, and an open doorway. A hole in each roof was partially covered by a board that slanted across the opening to keep out the rain and allow for smoke to rise up and away.

The place was likely a summer home for some herder. It was quite a find. Breanna and Max went scouting and found a spring. The water drifted into a declivity someone had dug out and lined with stones, which lay everywhere ready to hand. The water was crusted with ice.

I set the boys to tending the horses. Arica and Simon prepared the fires. I would have preferred to see to this myself, since it was so very important, but I was trying to give away leadership where I could. One cannot develop leaders by delegating only unimportant tasks, or so I had been told in my younger days when they were trying to make a leader of me.

We hung a tent across each of the doors. As for the wagon, we cut boughs and fastened them over the open areas in an attempt to keep out the rain or snow. Better than that, we could not do.

As is typical in those mountains, rain began to fall in the late afternoon. In the spring or summer, light showers at this time of day are almost a daily event, so it seems to the traveler. However, this was no light shower. As darkness closed in, temperatures plummeted and the rain turned to snow. Anyone who ventured outside was preceded by exhaled clouds. By full dark, horses and humans were huddled in their groups, protected by rough walls and warmed by the heat of the fires.

That night I told stories from the days of King Brand. The young ones already knew the grand tales of armies and heroes; Lina and I had made sure of that. That stormy night, in the mountain herder's hut, I recounted the doings of simple folk from all the regions of Ehrylan—Southland, Westland,

Northland, and the central basin. Simple pleasures and pains are not often remembered in tales though they are the stuff of life.

I did not allow Max or anyone else to stand a watch. I tended the fires throughout the night, making sure none of the young ones fell toward the cold death that can strike so easily in these conditions. The vigil started as a group event, with the eight of us huddled around the fire. As each child showed the first signs of cold, I sent them off to the safety of their blankets. Sent them off, I say, though their beds were not three paces away.

Lina went first. She knew the others would come more willingly after, which is exactly what happened. She came back later, after the rest were sleeping. I had just returned from a protracted time with the horses. She took a place next to me, so close that our sides touched. This made sense because it was so cold. That is what I told myself.

We did not talk with words. Rather, in a very peculiar dialogue, we conversed with small touches and facial expression. For example, at one point and for no apparent reason, she very gently placed a small twig on my knee. I eyed it for a moment before picking it up and inspecting it. Then I placed it behind my ear as if it were something I was saving for a good whittle. I followed by setting a small pebble on the back of her hand, which just happened to be resting on my knee at the time. After a while, she plucked it off with her other hand and brought it to her lips, raising her eyebrows, silently asking, "Shall I put this in my mouth?" After considering calling her bluff, I shook my head. She pushed out her lower lip in the perfect imitation of Breanna. She motioned as if to toss the pebble into the fire. It was my time to push the lip.

Forever later, I saw her shudder again. The first time she had done so, I placed an arm around her and she snuggled close, laying her head on my shoulder. That lasted a long time and not long enough. When the next shudder came, I sent her to her blanket again. She rose and did me a courtesy. I stood and bowed to her as if I were a noble.

Dawn broke clear and bright. A carpet of new snow smoothed every surface, flowing across the landscape like a white water rapid frozen in place, which it was, I suppose. Gammin helped me see to the horses just after first light. It was our first time alone for some time, and we talked amid the chewing and blowing animals. I was going to miss that boy. I could see the man he might become, a friend worth having. Looking at him, I thought he could have run with me in my younger years, Marin by his side, if only they had been born a generation before. Then I laughed at myself. Who was I kidding? It would be two generations.

Marin joined us by and by. He was not too old yet to hug me, which he did. The three of us saw to the Water Wheel. We removed the boughs, piling them where the next traveler might find them. Then we inspected the harnesses and other tack so that all was in readiness when it was time to leave, though we did not yet fit the animals. We did not have to hurry. A little delay might be in order. A strong sun might melt the snow on the road.

Breakfast was waiting for us. So were the others. A cheer arose from the young ones as we came through the tented door. Soon, we were all eating and enjoying the cheerful conversation of comrades who have survived an adventure together. It was wonderful to hear each of the young ones describe the thoughts and feelings they had entertained during the long, cold night. More wonderful was the fact that we had come through it with no mishap. But I cautioned myself. We weren't in Mendolas yet.

After breakfast, I sent the others to pack their kits while I tidied up the remnants of the meal. I stacked about half the remaining firewood for whoever came after. There would be more storms.

Max climbed into the wagon as if it were a tower he was assailing. Breanna followed after him, her face screwed up with the effort and her knuckles white. I was very pleased when Max extended his hand to her, which she took with a grin. I helped Merelina into her saddle though she did not need assistance and crossed to where, as usual, Arica stood inspecting everything and making sure all the younger ones were accounted for. I extended my arm for her.

"I thank you, kind sir."

Just before I handed her up, she did me a courtesy, looking very much like Merelina with her dark hair and white smile. As I stood wondering whether she had been asleep all through the night, she did something that was only Arica, something Lina never did. She fluttered her eyelids at me faster than a hummingbird's wings. Gazing at her, I thought we had better keep a close eye on her while we were in the port. That we could count on her sensibilities, I was sure; it was the bedazzled senses of young sailors I was concerned about.

It was just past mid-morning when we set out. If we pushed hard, we might make it to Mendolas by the evening. There was no reason to do so. The weather looked to be fine and, barring any mishaps, we'd be down to the river by mid-afternoon at the latest. There were any number of excellent spots to camp down there, and the thought of one more night in the woods seemed good to us. I discussed these things with Lina and she was in full agreement.

That is just how it played out. We picked our way back and forth across the south face of the ridge, winding lower as the sun rose higher. About half way down, the snow began to retreat and progress became much easier, though still wet. By midday, we lost sight of the river, a sign that we were coming to the valley floor.

I became more wary with each passing mile. We were out of the Old Forest and could not count on its secret protection. By the time we reached the first spur trail that led to the water's edge, I had stopped and cautioned our company. We mounted guard and occasionally one of us rode ahead to spy out the lay of the land.

We arrived at the north gate of Mendolas by noon the next day after a good sleep and a morning's easy ride. This time when asked, I gave my real name. There was nothing to hide.

IV.

I took our company to the Silver Wanderer, an inn owned and run by a family loyal to the memory of Ehrylan. Since my plans required us to leave Avyansa, the horses, and the wagon while we journeyed by river, I needed a place I could trust. The Silver Wanderer was it.

We stayed in a complex of rooms joined by doorways. In each room, there was a bed, a couch, and a wash basin. The center room was biggest, with a large bed, several chairs, and a table long enough to serve at least six. This was certainly a cut above the accommodations I typically afforded myself, but I decided before setting out that this was going to be a grand occasion for Lina and the children. They deserved it, each and every one of them.

The rest of that day was spent getting clean, a task Lina and young ones set to as soon as we dropped our packs. I used the time, after cautioning the others not to leave the rooms until I returned, to visit the weapons smith. The term of delivery was yet a week away, so I was not expecting to take possession of the blades yet. I just wanted to see what I could see. I was surrendering to impatience.

The weapon smith recognized me. By the time I made it to the counter behind which he was polishing a blade, he had recalled the name I gave him. It was only later that night that I realized I had been wearing the knife I purchased from him, which might have helped his recognition.

"Ronl? Yes, that was it. Back from the sea? How did you fare?"

"Well enough. And you? How's the trade?"

There was the normal meaningless exchange as we sank through civility into the business at hand. He bade me examine the piece he was polishing. I lifted it, felt its heft.

"A fine blade," I commented.

"I think so."

I swung the thing a couple of times, listening to the pleasing whoosh as it cut through the emptiness, then set it back on the cloth in front of him.

"So what brings you back? Are you ready for a sword? If memory serves, you liked the ones I showed you."

"Quite ready. I've come to pick up two swords and five knives."

A look of eager pleasure bloomed on his face, then his eyes narrowed.

"So you are the one. I never guessed the mysterious customer from afar named Annen was you, Ronl." He wiped his hands on the front of his leather apron. "You must have fared very well. Good for you!" He waited for me to reply, which I did only with a very slight smile.

"Had I known Annen was a repeat customer, I'd have discounted the cost of the work."

"No need for that, friend."

"It's my policy. 'Keeps em commin back,' my father used to say. But we can talk about that later. Would you like to see your blades? They are ready for you. You can have them today."

"Can I? That would be splendid! I just dropped in to see you. I did not expect the swords to be ready yet."

"Not yet? Why not?" He looked scandalized. Then his face softened. "You are not a blade maker."

He wiped his hands on the leather again. Absently, he reached down and turned over the sword that was lying between us. I don't think he knew he did it.

"A blade" he said, "needs to rest after it is birthed, again after it is joined, after assembly as it were, though I prefer not to use such a vulgar term for sword birthing." He frowned at his own thoughts.

I nodded, not understanding, but enjoying him. He went on for some time describing the various intricacies of sword making until, stopping abruptly, he exclaimed, "Enough of that! I am sure you are impatient to see your blades." He vanished into a back room. He was more impatient for me to see them than I. He was keen in the way of true-born artists, those who work more for the recognition of their craft than for money it brings them.

He came back bearing two boxes. He had to set them aside because there was no space. The sword upon which he had been working was yet on the counter. I noted the way he slowed himself and quieted his impatience as he picked it up and moved to a stand at the back of the shop.

While he was at that, I looked at the boxes. They appeared to be very well made, though plain and unadorned. The wood's dark surface was polished to an impeccable sheen. I could smell the oil.

Taking his position behind the counter again, the smith set the smaller of the two boxes between us. He took a deep breath and looked me square in the eye. He was already beaming with anticipation of the praise to come. When he undid the brass catch and lifted the lid, I saw why.

The knives nestled on a cushion of plush red velvet within depressions that had been sculpted to fit them. There were three hunting knives and two daggers. The hunting knives were copies of the knife I had purchased, excellently proportioned for their intended owners, Simon, Max, and Breanna. Both daggers looked delicate, though they were anything but. The smaller of the two had an antler handle and a leaf-shaped blade of polished steel. It was for Arica, a woodcutter's daughter.

The knife in the center was a dagger of staggering beauty. The butt of its handle was fashioned to resemble flower petals of wrought silver that enclosed a sapphire. The blue cabochon sparkled with an internal star. The antler handle was fashioned as a thick flower stem. The leaf-shaped blade carried the flower motif to its conclusion. It was completely covered with distinctive bands reminiscent of ripples on water. It was Telcani steel.

All the items in the box were exactly as I had specified. The work exceeded my expectations.

"Acceptable, Ronl?"

"No. Not acceptable. Outstanding."

"They are, aren't they?" His statement was not a boast. He was admiring beauty the way he would whether it was the work of his hand or not. I could only nod.

"Pick it up!" He indicated Merelina's gemmed dagger. I shook my head.

I said, "I want her to touch it first."

"Ah!" he cried, "So you do understand!"

This time I thought I might.

He said, "She must be very special."

"They all are."

He lowered the lid and set the box aside, replacing it with the other. My first thought, as I gazed down at the two swords, was that they were as fine as my own. I was wrong. I did not know it until later, when I held Gammin's in my hand. They were finer.

The swords were not fancy. There were no gems and no engraving. They were purely functional and absolutely perfect. Shorter than mine, the blades were also less wide in proportion to the length. For both reasons, the weapons were lighter and more easily handled by the young men who would wield them. They would eventually acquire other swords to serve them, but these could be passed to subsequent generations. A sword maker once told me that a good sword will outlive its owner, as will a good hat.

I had already been away longer than intended, but we were a while more admiring the work. At last, I had to excuse myself. I began to pick up the boxes. He stopped me with a word.

"Wait. About your discount."

"Nay," I said formally, "It may be that I owe you."

He would not have it. To avoid arguing with him, I accepted what at first I took to be a trinket. Upon inspection, I saw it was another work of art, a silver rose no bigger than the last joint of my finger, with petals that looked to be tiny rubies. Equally tiny emeralds lay along the metal stem in three places. At the top was a minute hoop through which a chain could be passed.

"This is a master work," I said.

"I am branching out, into jewelry, I mean."

I made it back to my companions without mishap. They were excited to see me, inquisitive to know where I had been, and even more curious when they saw the two boxes. I told them that, when the time was right, they would find something for each of them in these containers, and set them on a table in the center room. I moved off to my room, then turned back.

"Max, stand a watch, will you? Don't let any of these villains near my treasures." The boy gaped at me, then circled the room with his eyes. He seemed perplexed. I watched him until I saw the grin invade his face.

After refreshing myself and changing into fresh leggings, shirt, and tunic, I was sitting on the bed massaging a sore foot when I heard a soft knock. Even before the door opened, I knew it was Merelina.

She came in. Her hair was loose and damp from washing. She had put aside her riding attire and was back to her long dress. Her only concession to decoration was the scarf. I thought of the silver flower and regretted instantly the foolishness that made me forget to buy a chain. The little rose would fit perfectly between her throat and the sunken collar of her dress.

I had gone too far, both in accepting the bauble for her and in allowing myself to feed the flame. In my mind, the rose was already hers though she did not as yet know of its existence. I knew the joy it would bring her. I told myself that I would do better at keeping my distance in the future. A man can lie to himself when it comes to women.

I thought to give her the little pendant on her birthday, which was the day after tomorrow. If I was right in my thinking, she had no idea I knew the date and I had it in mind to surprise her. Truth to tell, I wanted that very much. I do not recall how this thought came to my mind; I had known Lina for many years and the subject of birthdays had never come up. It may be that here, too, the machinations of my two boys had moved us forward. To be sure, I had set Gammin, Marin, and Arica to wheedle the date out of Merelina, but it was possible someone else planted that idea in my head.

Now, in the early evening of our first day in Mendolas, she sat on the couch, pulling her fingers through her hair as I pulled on a pair of buckskin boots.

"How are you, lady?"

"Clean and rested, sir. And you?"

"I feel like a new man."

"Did you accomplish your purpose? The boxes, I mean."

"Most of it. I have a surprise for you, Lina."

She smiled. "You always have a surprise for me, Annen."

"Do I?" I considered for a moment, leaving her in suspense. Perhaps she was referring to the food and supplies we brought to the children. "Well, this one is just for you, though we are all going to enjoy it."

She cocked her head to one side and waited patiently for me to get to my point.

"Listen, Merelina, I don't want to tell you what it is just yet, if that is alright with you, but I have to tell you this. We'll do whatever you want in the city tomorrow. Have you been to Mendolas before?"

"Yes, but not in many years."

"There's a fine market, far bigger than the one in Twofords, and we can show the youngsters around. It will be a good learning experience for them if we can keep Max from challenging soldiers to duels and sailors from stealing Arica."

"I think you are wrong there, Annen. Arica has eyes only for one man and that man is in this room."

The words brought a grunt out of me. "Huh. I had not noticed. If it is true, this is not the first time or the last a girl has fallen for her *shinando*. Is it serious, do you think?"

"Not at all. But do you say true that you had not guessed? Didn't you notice how she pressed me to take up the bow that night by the river? That's not like her."

"No, Lina, I had not guessed. I did think it queer how she acted toward you at Teryn's Crossing. She is usually so supportive and sensitive. Her heart will be as big as yours someday, lady, if that is possible."

Lina lowered her eyelids and smiled demurely. It was not a

show. She was honestly touched by the comment. It was an honest comment.

"I thank you for pointing it out, Merelina. I am dull-witted when it comes to women, as well you know. You are good for me."

The last words were out before I could stop them, speaking what my heart knew to be true. The problem was that I would not be good for her. If I allowed our hearts to go where they seemed to want, there could only be death, her death, and once again I would be left with the guilt and the sadness. There was an uncomfortable silence until I picked up the thread of our conversation.

"Tomorrow, just before sunset, we are going to come back here and get our packs, so they have to be ready. We are going on another journey, for a week, maybe more."

Her eyes widened and she opened her mouth to speak. I waggled my finger at her. "Not a word! No questions."

She spoke anyway. "Yes, your highness. As you command." Quick as a fish her hand shot out and grabbed the finger. Gently but firmly, she pulled it to her lips and kissed the end of it, looking all the while deeply into my eyes. I felt myself stir and fought to suppress it.

I made the children wait until after supper, which we shared with other travelers and a few locals in the common room. The food was similar to what we might have been served in Twofords, though I tasted the subtle influence of Rathian cooking in the sauces. We were, by and large, left alone. Who would brave the dangers of six children in search of conversation with a man and woman that, by their accent and appearance, obviously came from even further up the river out of the backwater of Twofords?

Back in the room, we decided the children would draw straws for the honor of going first. Max insisted that, if we were going to draw straws, we had better get real straws. That sent him on the Quest to the Stables. He could have gone alone, for this was a safe inn, but I sent Simon with him. The older boy would pick out perfect straws and was sure to come back with the right number. With Max, one never knew. He might come back with four stout branches.

When they returned, I asked Max to give Lina the straws. I took the shortest and kept it separate. The children drew from the rest. This, of course, set off a debate on who would get to draw first and in what order the rest of them would draw; I settled that straight away. I was done being patient. Arica had first choice, Bre the second.

On hearing my pronouncement, Arica fluttered her eyelids at me, made a courtesy, and said, "I thank you sir. I would yield my place to my younger sister."

I took a deep breath and chuckled to myself. Would this ever end? More than that, would it ever even start? "Fine by me, young lady." I gestured Breanna forward. Arica followed after her and the others worked it out for themselves. When they were done drawing straws, I handed Lina the shortest of the lot.

"Looks like you got the short stick." This from Gammin.

Shining her eyes at him, Lina said, "I have a differing opinion."

When at last it was time, Breanna came to us in her shy way, as if she were walking against a stiff wind while being pulled forward by an invisible rope. When she got to me, she stood with her head down, though I could see she was grinning with anticipation. I opened the box. When she caught the courage to reach out and take up the knife to which I pointed, she said, "This is for me, shinando? Mine? Really?" Before she touched the thing, she put her arms around my neck and cried until the shoulder of my tunic was wet.

Last of all, the place of honor, Merelina lifted the dagger out of the box as if it were made of glass. It settled into her hand and she felt its life. Her fingers tightened into a fist. She squeezed the hilt. I heard, soft as mouse bones breaking, the sound of her knuckles cracking. She said, "This is the most beautiful knife I have ever seen." She dropped it back on the velvet and put both arms around me. She kissed me full and firm, her lips almost touching the corner of my mouth.

Gammin and Marin inspected every hand span of their swords to make sure they were identical, which for them seemed to be very important. Once they got around to actually strapping the blades to their hips, I gave them the bad news. These swords were theirs only until we returned to Twofords. Once there, they must return them to me and win them in fair combat. This was another of those time-honored traditions. They had reached a level where they knew the basics and could use them. They would have had a place beside me and the others who fought under King Brand. They were not—yet—exceptional swordsman, but they were as good as any I had seen at their age.

12. SILVER SAILING

I.

After breakfast we ventured out into the city, probably better armed than any collection of men, women, and children in the vicinity. Even Lina wore her knife. It was concealed, after the fashion of the times, by a hanging fold of her dress.

We walked to and fro among the shops and streets, answering a multitude of questions from the bemused children, trying to let them explore without allowing them to venture too far out of our reach and protection. I purchased a few items we needed for the river journey, including the food we would eat. We found bow strings to replace those that had been worn to a frazzle by our practice.

We arrived back at the inn in time to say farewell to our host and our horses. I brought Avyansa a large carrot and others for the horses so as not to be rude. I think Avyansa knew he was the source of their luck. He whinnied when I came in and again when I turned to depart.

I said, "Don't worry, sir. We will soon be back and then we will travel together again."

Breanna reached her hand up toward his nose. Another horse might have nipped it or worse, but not Avyansa. He lowered his head so she could stroke his long face. She said, "Good bye, Avyansa. I love you."

It was a longish walk to the wharf. After the day's meanderings, some of the youngsters were becoming grumpy. As soon as one of them smelled the water, attitudes began to change. I led them right out along the dock where before I had paraded as Ronl the sailor. It took me a moment to find the ship I wanted. The Destra was a medium-sized river craft that plied the trade up and down the river between Mendolas and the twin cities of Arathai and Ehrynai. Those two port cities, the first in Rath and other in Ehrylan, faced each other across the mouth of the Silver River where it flowed into the Bay of Arai.

The ship was owned and mastered by a relation to one of my contacts in the Resistance. The connection was tenuous enough not to arouse suspicion. I had booked passage to and from the bay. Merelina would have her wish of sailing the river to the sea. Though our purpose was purely pleasure, the Destra was a working craft; our lot would not be a luxurious one. We would have only enough space on the upper deck to pitch tents or spread blankets alongside other parties who had paid passage.

Ea was smiling on us that day as he had on the whole journey. The Destra was kept in better repair than might otherwise have been the case in the effort to attract human cargo. She was painted blue and trimmed in yellow. When Merelina saw the colors, fortunate accident though they were, she began to suspect the true purpose of our visit to the docks. Elation spread across her face. The young ones caught the realization from her. Suddenly, I was at the center of a bouncing, squealing turmoil.

When I was free of their embraces, I saw we had been joined by a round, weather-beaten man of medium height. I was chagrinned at allowing someone to approach so closely, yet, when I took the time to notice, I saw that Marin and

Gammin were eyeing him with pleasant though serious faces. Hands rested on the hilts of their new swords, they looked like young warriors guarding a king's tent. They, at least, had not let their guards down.

"You'll be Master Annen of Twofords, I make no doubt," said the man, extending his arm. "Norbet is my name. I master this ship." I grasped his forearm and gave it a shake. He continued volubly, his bastardized Rathian accent so thick it was almost comical, "I'd not known it was a princess we was to carry. You're a lucky one, you are." He smiled at his own gallantry, not knowing the difficulty in which he put me.

"I am a lucky man, Captain Norbet. Good to make your acquaintance."

I introduced the others, though as master and captain, he had no need of the information. It was a civil courtesy only, or so I thought at the time, greatly underestimating the man.

Captain Norbet took us to our spot, pointing out that it was the best place on the deck for our purposes. The other parties had not been allowed to board yet. This avoided any unwanted contention. I set the others to making camp, as it were. Laying claim would be a better description. The captain introduced me to Garn, the first mate. He told the man that we were friends. I knew from the voyages of my youth that it was the mate who attended to all things, so I was doubly grateful. I knew also that the two men had more important things to do than talking to me. I excused myself as soon as was proper, giving the captain a gold crown, which was more than the agreed fare. He smiled at me toothily.

We had eaten a meal at the inn, hasty though it was, so tonight we were free of that chore. That allowed us to roam about the deck—as long as we stay cleared of the business of stowing the cargo and readying the vessel for departure at dawn. The falling temperature chased most of our company back to our spot where we huddled together and tried to stay out of the evening breeze.

I shared a tent with Gammin that night. He was asleep by the time I crawled in, one hand curled around the scabbard of his blade, the other tucked in a loose fist under his chin. I considered taking the weapon from him, which might save him some fingers if his sleep was restless. As I rummaged through my pack in the darkness, I decided not to. Better not to wake a sleeping falcon.

It would be poetic to say that we set sail at first light, but that would not be true. We bore no sails until almost noon, the captain being contented with the speed of the river. It was not until we met a wind off our quarter that the captain stamped up on deck and bellowed an order. The command was immediately repeated by the mate. Men scrambled aloft. Canvas billowed like clouds tethered to our masts, spars, cross trees, and who knew what else. Max refused to believe we could use sails to head so close into the wind until he saw it with his own eyes.

I told Marin, Gammin, and Arica that I wanted time alone with Merelina. They would make sure the others understood. Taking Merelina by the arm, I guided her to the back of the ship. Behind where the mizzen mast stood, the captain had installed a set of benches on a platform for his passengers. These afforded an unobstructed view off the back of the vessel.

We sat in silence. Perhaps by then Lina was used to my reticent manner or perhaps she liked to hear the emptiness in the same way as I. We watched the butt of the mountains sliding astern as we sailed west. Across the river, the kingdom of Rath ran south.

My silence was necessary. I pondered how I might best approach what I needed to say, looking for an introductory comment to open the door. Nothing came to mind, so I said, "This is a special day."

She smiled. "It is. I thank you. We all thank you."

"That is not what I mean and you know it."

Her eyebrows arched and she cocked her head to one side.

"Today is your birthday. That makes this a special day."

Surprise flooded her blue-grey eyes. "I had forgotten!"

"I did not forget, Lina. In fact, I have something for you, if you will have it."

"You have already given me a magnificent dagger and this trip, Annen of Twofords. What more is there?"

I wanted to take her in my arms and tell all about the what more, what every bone in my body wanted to give her. I could not do so without bringing death to her like a twisted dowry. Instead, I reached out and touched her cheek with my fingers.

"There is this."

In the same hand that had just touched her cheek, I produced the little gemmed rose. I had learned the prestidigitation from a traveling juggler when I was a boy. It had been a trick I used to amuse adults when I was a child. Now that I was an adult, it was a trick I used to amuse children. More than anyone, I think, it amused me.

The pendant was wrapped in a tissue taken from one of the purchases we'd made in the market the day before. I held it out to her.

A small cry escaped her lips. Reaching up with both her hands, she gently brought my hand lower so she could better see.

"Quick," I said, "before it blows away!"

One of her hands came up to hide the circle of her lips while the other plucked the packet from my palm. Her fingers made quick work of the covering, though she had time to look up at me and smile three times while she worked at it. I reveled in her unabashed happiness at this unexpected gift, even before she saw what it was. She was joyous at the gifting more than the gift.

"This is very beautiful, Annen. I want to tell you that I cannot accept it, but you'd have to cut off my hand to get it back." She set her arms about my neck and kissed my forehead. "I thank you, but…"

"But what?" Here we go, I thought.

"Is this seemly? I am only a widow who cares for unparented children. What will the neighbors say?" She had to avert her eyes from mine to suppress her smile.

"Unless they are sailing on this ship they will not have occasion to say anything, lady. But I will say this. You deserve far more, Lina. You are more special than you know. To the children," Surely I would not say it! "And to me."

She blushed.

"There is this also." I reached up and pretended to pull a length of braided leather thong from her ear. The strands were almost thread-like. I had purchased them yesterday and braided them as Gammin snored to his sword. Woven together, they made a good enough necklace, or so I hoped.

Lina claimed that the leather chain was perfect, even better for her than gold or silver, being more sturdy. She insisted on threading it through the pendant there and then.

We lapsed into silence. I watched the countryside pass and she alternated between looking at me and the rose. At some point, she placed her head on my shoulder. I could not bring myself to complain.

II.

We came to Ehrynai on the morning of the third day. The Destra could have docked the evening before, but the penny-wise captain dropped anchor for the second night a few leagues from the port, avoiding the heavy docking fee for at least one day. Lina beamed with pleasure at first sight of the sea.

The Silver River flows straight as an arrow for half a league where it meets the sea. At the spot where it first begins to lose itself to the arms of the Bay of Arai, Andur had built two enormous pillars, one on each bank. The paired monuments were true columns, not obelisks. They had been erected to commemorate the unification of the peoples on either side of the river, north and south. They stood many times taller than the tower at Tower Mill. Once they had been white. Now they were faded in the face of Dauroth's neglect. I made no doubt that he would pull them down when he got around to it, if we gave him the time.

Merelina was captivated even more than the children. She gazed at the pillars, first from the bow of the ship as we approached, then from the benches at the stern as the Destra glided into the mingling waters of the river and the sea. The vista to either side opened up and we saw the twin cities of Arathai and Ehrynai in the full light of a new sun.

We were two days at Ehrynai, the southernmost city on Ehrylan's coast. The mercantile activities left no room on the deck for the likes of us; we had to find lodgings in the city and return by evening the next day.

We packed our belongings before we reached the wharf, as did the other lots of human cargo. The captain did not stop by to pay his respects, though the mate did, asking if I wanted a man to see us around the city and help us to suitable accommodations. This was a kindly offer and generous, but I thanked Garn and declined.

After the Destra docked, paid the port tax, and navigated the maze of details involved in preparing for trade, we were escorted to the dock. There the captain met us and, though he was already looking haggard by the morning's haggling with the port bureaucrats, he took the time to greet us all by name.

"You be sure to keep both eyes on these two ladies, Master Annen. This here's not Mendolas. There's some about as might take the opportunity to make off with such prizes and sail away forever. For that matter, the younglings need a caution as well."

"We will take care, sir. I thank you for your warnings."

He eyed Gammin and Marin. "You've brought some young knights, so you have. I'd give 'e a warn about them too. There's many who'd pick a fight with them just because how they seem so able, if 'e take my meaning." He looked the young men up and down. "Aye, but the more I'm lookin' the more I am thinkin' they can take care of themselves just fine. Well, then enough said." He took a step back and opened his arms to all of us. "I wish 'e good day sirs and ladies. Take a care and have a laugh!"

He turned back to his business. Before I had time to speak to Lina, I heard him shouting, "Watch out, you ninny! That there's precious. Where'd e' learn your trade? In a stock yard?"

We took a room in a local inn, one of the three recommendations Captain Norbet gave us; we selected the one furthest from the docks, reasoning that the needs of sailors in port and those of families with children had little in common. Once our beds and meals were bespoken, we roamed the city before making our way back down to the docks. There we boarded a boat that took us over to Arathai, the northernmost coastal city in the kingdom of Rath.

The Rathian city was quite different than its Ehrylain neighbor. Where Ehrynai was dirty and worn, Arathai showed the pride of its dwellers. There was less litter in the streets in Arathai, and fewer drunks and shady looking characters wondering about. In Ehrynai, on many street corners and in most alleyways, one could find lurkers waiting for easy marks. We saw these too in Arathai, to be sure, but less often. The reason for this, I believe, was the presence of the Rathian military. There were Rathian soldiers aplenty. The king of Rath knew that Dauroth could not be trusted to keep the peace. He kept the border prepared for conflict as best he was able, though the strength of Rath is upon the water rather than the ground. Her armies were small, but her navy was top-notch.

We encountered no difficulties after the Rathian port warden saw what we were, a man, a woman, and their brood of children. Rathians do not view the Ehrylain as enemies but as subjugated brethren. We could have stayed in this city for a day, a month, or for the rest of our lives and been welcomed with open arms.

Both cities were gargantuan labyrinths to the inexperienced young ones. They saw for the first time what wealth can bring. For example, we saw what would have passed for a palace in Twofords, though it was but the house of some rich merchant. Simon wanted to know if that was where the king lived.

Eventually our feet brought us to the walls guarding Castle

Arathai. The high stone stood resolute grey against the hues of early spring. The castle, peering defiantly over the ramparts, watched the bay and the city on the far shore that was held by a ruler who could not be trusted.

Directly above where we stood, the walls were lined with armed men. Below these, between the mote and the wall, soldiers stood guard. On our side of the mote, foot soldiers patrolled back and forth in ceremonious synchronization. All were accoutered for war.

Taking this in, Marin asked, "What are they doing, Annen?"

"Guarding. What else, my boy?"

"Guarding what? Are they at war?" This from Gammin.

I started to form a scathing retort, then remembered myself. "Dauroth is at war with everyone, even his allies, I should think. This is where the king of Rath lives, and I know you have heard of Andur's orb."

There was a scurry of exclamations.

"You mean," began Marin.

"The Orb of…" interrupted Max.

"Here?" asked Arica.

I glanced at Lina. She was suppressing a laugh, her hand held up to hide it.

I asked, "Where else?" Max looked doubtful, so I added, "Gammin, where do the tales say Andur left the orb?"

"In Arathai, Annen. Every knows… that."

After Andur unified our people, he received a mighty gift from the Stonethanes of the Great Mountains, an orb made from Dragon's Eye. It was a symbol that the lands of the Crescent would henceforth be unified. The orb took ten years to complete and was rumored to be the most precious treasure in Andur's kingdom. It was impossible to move, so it stayed right where he left it. Many accounted this magic, though I discount that belief. When something acts according to the nature Ea gave it, the action is not magic but nature, completely natural, as it were.

It took some time to convince them they were standing in a place straight out of established legend, but it was worth the effort. It was good to connect them with the noble past.

Marin asked, "Can we see it, Annen?"

"There was a time when all the people of Andur's realm could come and see the orb. More than that, they could, if they wished, touch it and even stay within the grounds that later became this fortress. That ended when Andur's line failed, or rather when they lost his throne. I do not believe his line will ever fail. In time, his heir will rule with the justice and love Ea intends for his creation."

As I drew in another breath to continue, Breanna tugged on my tunic. "The Orb of Andur, shinando?"

"Ah, yes. Sorry. The Orb. No, we cannot see it." I repeated the part I thought most important. "That ended with the coming of Dauroth."

I convinced them that they would not be allowed through the fortified gate, nor would the keepers of the orb bring it forth and display it. With that done, and many a look back over their shoulders, we set out exploring again.

Before sunset we sailed back across the bay and returned to our lodging. For Merelina and me, it had been a nice day with pleasant diversions. For the children, the day marked a stupendous event. It was the first time any of them had been outside the kingdom of their birth. They had journeyed to a foreign port and returned to Ehrylan as world travelers.

III.

Later that evening, as we sat in the common room eating supper, Marin asked a question for which I had been waiting all day.

"Didn't you say that the Stonethane gave you other things made from Dragon's Eye when he gave you the inkpot?"

"Yes, I said that. It is true."

"I have been wondering why you are not worried about leaving such valuable things lying around unprotected when you leave. If the king of Rath guards his Dragon's Eye, why don't you? Did you hide it somewhere?"

"No, lad, not at all. I left the inkwell where it always was when it was mine. The same is true for the other things. They are swallowers, by the way, four of them. They have their own protection."

The young ones looked at me, expectant. They never tired of discussing Dragon's Eye, or of hearing more about my past. I glanced at Merelina. She patted her lips with a cloth, and took a sip of the excellent red Rathian wine, which smelled even better than it tasted. These actions helped me not at all.

I went on. "You've all heard in the tales. You know Dragon's Eye has special qualities. My pieces, the swallowers and the inkpot, were shaped by the same Stonethane, at the same time. One of their qualities is that they are not easily seen unless the owner wants them to be seen."

"You are joking, right?"

"No, I am not joking. It's the same as the orb, which hasn't been moved since Andur left it in Arathai." I was suggesting that being invisible and being immovable were both effective defenses. They weren't buying, or simply did not understand.

"Let me ask you something, Marin. That inkwell sat on the writing desk in my room every day from the time you came to live with me to the day I gave it to you. Did you ever notice it?"

Gammin and Marin turned to each other, considered, shook their heads at the same time.

"You were in my room many times. You both sat at my desk often." I questioned them with my eyes. They looked at me, mouths opening to gapes, then at each other again. I wanted to laugh but suppressed the urge. What was it about these children that made me so ready to laugh? It was a wonderful thing.

"The other pieces I have, the swallowers, they are in plain sight, not hidden at all." This last bit fell on deaf ears. The boys were beyond caring about my swallowers—the subject of Marin's original question.

"What else does the inkwell do?"

"I already told you. The ink in it will not dry up if you keep the stopper in, no matter how long you leave it. That was about it for me. That's plenty."

He looked disappointed

"Dragon's Eye is funny stuff. Each piece has different, hmmmm, characteristics, different attributes. The owner of the piece plays a part in bringing those qualities out. The inkwell might do one thing for me and two very different things for you. There is no way of telling. That is one of the things that makes Dragon's Eye so special."

The discussion continued until even the boys grew tired of talking about orbs, spheres, and the vagaries of kings. But the mystical and unpredictable properties of Dragon's Eye remained on their minds.

Later, when we were back in our room, Marin produced his inkwell and set it on the table in front of him. Like Gammin and his knife, he did not go anywhere without it. He stared at it, willing it to do something. When it refused to do something, the boy redoubled his efforts, even taking it into his hands and, at one point, holding it to his forehead. I had to stop him, though, like Merelina, I was on the verge of open laughter. I told him that he needed to take care. He would not be able to force the Dragon's Eye to perform. He must wait for it to reveal is secrets—something, I can assure you, it did.

The second night in Ehrynai we slept on the Destra, having retuned after a full day of enjoying the bond forming between us. I could have allowed myself to believe we were a family and had been so for a long time. Lina felt it too.

The ship set sail with the dawn. The wind was at our backs, which was fortunate since we were making the return journey against the amused river. The trip back to Mendolas took about twice as long. We fell into the steady, slow rhythm that can only be experienced as a passenger of a vessel.

These times were exceedingly pleasant. They seem to me now a restful interlude before the years of war and death that started shortly after we returned to the Bend. I was tempted to keep on sailing, away from the turmoil and sadness, toward the sunset, in search of a morning where war and death were but a memory. We were currently headed the wrong way for that, literally and figuratively.

One morning after the start of our return, the mountains looming, I lost myself in a haystack thinking of such things. When I emerged on the other side, I found that I had laid my hand upon Lina's. She had caught hold my little finger. The contact felt right. Too right. I started to pull my hand back, but I looked first at her, which required me to open eyes that had shut. She was looking at me, a soft smile lying across her lips, the one I saw when she was watching children play.

I smiled back and lifted my hand. I thought this would hurt her and she would frown, but she did not. Instead, she said, "Your beard seems to be settling in, Annen. Will you keep it?"

"Goodness, no, Lina! I am dreaming of the day I can scrape it off." After a thought, I said, "Do you think it suits me? Would you have me wear it?"

"You will do as you will, sir. I think it makes you look lordly, like some noble gentleman from the court of good King Brand. But for me, I would have the old Annen back, the one I have known these many years." It was her turn to contemplate. Then she said, "Still, you do look distinguished."

"That settles it," I said, "It's coming off as soon as we get back."

She laughed. Merelina was, when she laughed, even more lovely than when she smiled, if that is possible. My hand settled again on hers. I left it there, my fingers interlocking with hers. I am a damned fool.

13. UNMASKED

I.

So much happened in the three months after our trip that it is difficult to believe the events could have been crammed into so short a time. It seemed to us that we had entered a new day of hope and that our lives leapt forward into joy unlooked for. And these impressions were true; I will not say we were mistaken. The error we made was to believe the days would endure, that we would be left to enjoy them.

It was only a week or two after our return that the changes began. During that time, I had not seen Merelina. I would like to believe that this was unintentional, but it would be untruthful to report it. I had confronted my feelings and identified them for what they were. I was terrified by what I found. I faced a choice that would be difficult to make.

I could allow the relationship to take its course. There was no doubt in my mind that Lina felt the same affection for me as I did for her. Yet to permit the growth of our love was to accept that I would watch her die some horrible and undeserved death. I could not let that happen. The other course was to deny how I felt and remove my heart to a safer distance, in essence returning to the purely unromantic relationship we had shared in years past. I thought I might be able to bear the pain that would cause me, particularly in light of the fact that it would save Lina's life. Could I endure the guilt I would feel for the pain that would bring to her? Could I really hurt this woman like that? I had to choose between pain for us both or pain for one and death for the other. What do you do with such a choice?

You have already seen my error. That I thought I had a say in the matter seems humorous to me now, even after the pain and death that lines the road from that past to this present. The choice was not mine to make, for I had placed myself willingly into Ea's hands. Once you have done that with your heart, though it is a daily battle to be fought and lost over and over again, you can but hold to faith as your safety rope.

While I was busy holding the door shut, Rhua was brewing up a storm, and the storm started to blow in the second week after our return. I had set the date for Gammin and Marin to claim their swords from me. Merelina would be there. It would be the first time we had seen each other since our recent trip.

The thought of how awkward the situation might become filled me with anxiety. At first, it was a dull anxiety, but it came into focus as time passed. When the day came, it took everything I had to hide the affection I felt for her when Lina stepped down from the cart. I saw the hurt in her face when I did so, hurt that I caused. But I had other important work that day, work that might result in injury or death if I did not concentrate. I lost myself in that. I forgot, for a time, a woman who deserved to be remembered.

Merelina and the other students, including Temay who came to be with his friends on their special occasion, took their places in the courtyard. We brought out all the chairs so those who wanted to could sit. Both swords were lying across one of the stumps at one end of the courtyard.

I sent Gammin and Marin out and waited in the empty house until my mind was clear. In this at least I was a warrior. I forgot about Merelina and the trouble in my heart. I focused on the trouble I was about to give the two young men. They knew what to expect and what I expected of them. Above all, they knew that this was no mere show to display their skills to the onlookers.

When I was right within myself, I opened the door and stepped to the center of the yard. Crossing to where the swords rested, I put my back to them and called Gammin forward. His was the first test, since he was the most senior student, if only by a few weeks.

Before stepping to the center of the courtyard, Gammin bowed to me. He took the center and bowed again. This time I bowed back. If my head did not incline so low as to bow equal to an equal, it went lower than ever before.

"Are you ready, Gammin?"

"You must tell me that, shinando." It was the proper answer.

I took up both swords, handing him the one I judged to be Marin's. I was going to use the other. I could have exercised my own sword, but I was itching to try the blade from Mendolas. We bowed again and, at my word, took guarding stances. We began to circle.

He launched into an attack. I parried, stepping forward despite his motion, driving him back. He stumbled slightly, unused to the strength I used. Had this been a practice session, I might have let him recover. Instead, I let my momentum carry me forward to where he stood. He got his sword up in time. Trying to take the initiative, he swung low. I blocked his strike and hit him with my shoulder so hard it propelled him into the back wall. He smashed into the rock. The thud almost drowned out the gasps from the observers. Now they knew this was not a show.

As I closed the distance, Gammin ripped his sword across where my torso would have been if I were foolish enough to chase such a tiger. I brought the point of my blade to his throat. He was no longer there.

I jumped back to avoid an attack that never came. He was

crouching in a fighter's stance, balancing on the balls of his feet, the tip of his sword guarding his space. I met his eyes and held them. I launched into my offensive, driving him backward step by step until he ran out of room. With his back to the wall, there were only two things he could do. One of them was surrender and the other was too dangerous for this test. I elevated myself a level or two and disarmed him. His sword slid to a stop at the base of one of the trees, the blade singing.

He dove for it. I allowed him to pick it up and take the center of the field again. I slid back down to the level I had started in, only one level higher than his present skill. It was not my task to defeat him. I was assessing his spirit and his technique. Becoming master of the sword is a lifelong journey; all I needed to do today was assure myself that he was on the right path.

The circle of events repeated itself many times, most of them ending in his defeat or disarming, some of them resulting in my defeat. Obviously we never stabbed each other. I was the judge of when a defeat occurred. When I saw that he had maneuvered me into positions where someone at his level would likely be harmed or defeated, I stepped back, held up my hand, and said something like "good" or "well struck." When I saw that someone a level above him would prevail with the next move, I batted his weapon aside and said "No!" or "Not like that."

This was all a forgone conclusion. I would not have allowed this testing if both young men weren't more than ready. The true obstacle they faced was themselves. The only road to victory lay in one simple act. They had to keep coming back to the line to meet me again. But they did not know that.

I worked Gammin until he was about to fall from exhaustion. Then, I pressed him hard and fast, knocking him heels over cups so that he tumbled to a stop a full four paces from where I had hit him. I took my position and raised my sword. He pushed himself to his feet, stumbling with exhaustion, never taking his eyes off me. He came to his mark and raised his sword, ready. His face was bathed in sweat and his shirt clung to his chest like a wet sheet. The knuckles of one hand were raw. In his eyes, I saw what I was looking for. I might beat him, but he would never stop.

He had won.

"Done." I let the point of my sword drop. After a moment, his followed.

I bowed to him and he bowed back. Then I held out my hand. "The sword."

He extended it. I took the weapon back to the stump, setting it there to rest alone. Turning back, I presented him his sword, the one I had been using.

"Receive your sword, warrior. Well done."

Marin's testing went the same way. Gammin was the quicker of the two and used more advanced techniques. Marin was the stronger and relied on simple techniques perfectly executed. When Marin had received his sword, I let him rest for a moment. Then I asked Gammin to join him, telling him to bring his blade. I called them to attention.

"You are congratulated for your hard work and your achievements. You have earned the right to carry those blades. This does not mean that you have progressed beyond learning. You have only just arrived at the place when you can learn effectively. So now, receive your next lesson."

I lifted my own sword to the ready and gave them the barest minimum of time to comprehend what was about to happen. When their swords came up, I attacked, batting both blades aside and shoving Gammin away so that I faced Marin alone. In an instant, Marin stood weaponless as Gammin attacked me from my rear. Then Gammin, too, was weaponless. I stepped back to the center.

"Pick up your blades, *onandi*."

They bent to retrieve their swords. As they approached, I moved back two steps and held my blade at battle ready.

"Attack me, if you can."

I allowed myself to fight nearer my true potential. There followed a time where they moved this way and that. To each movement, I took a new position. When their swords shifted, I repositioned mine. It became apparent they could not attack without coming to harm themselves. When this occurred to them, they stepped back simultaneously and lowered their swords.

Lowering my own, I asked, "What have you learned?"

Marin said, "Even together we are no match for some fighters."

"I have learned," said Gammin, "that I have only just begun to learn."

"You have learned well, my friends. This lesson is over. Receive your accolades." The last sentence was a bit staid, but it was a nod to the traditions of my youth.

The congratulations went on for some time. I managed to avoid Merelina so that we only had a chance to speak after the other children were waiting in the Water Wheel. She purposely waited in the front room until they were out the door. Then she confronted me.

"Annen, why are you treating me this way? You have not spoken one kind word to me all day. Have I angered you?"

"No, Merelina, you have done nothing but be perfect."

"Then tell me what is wrong."

"There is nothing wrong."

Her eyes flared. "Would you lie to me, Annen of Twofords?"

"No. Forgive me. I am sorry."

Her hand came up. She placed it palm down with fingers splayed against my chest. Directly beneath it, my heart was pounding.

"Tell me what is amiss."

She was doing everything I would want a wife to do, standing up for what she felt was right, confronting my untruth, fighting for my affection. How could I not love her?

"Not here, lady."

She grimaced at me, showing her teeth in an imitation of an angry dog. Even through the hurt and frustration, I could see she trusted me.

"Then when?" Tossing her hair back, she said, "No, I will

not ask you. I will tell you, Annen of Twofords. You are going to talk to me and tell me what I want to know. Tomorrow. We are going to meet with Eanna and her children to celebrate what the boys achieved here today. Eanna is going to watch all of them while you and I go somewhere and clear the air, no matter how long it takes. Do you understand me, sir?"

"I will do as you say. But you must know this. I will not be able to tell you what is wrong with you. There is nothing to tell."

She rolled her eyes, brought both her hands to the side of her head, and growled deep in her throat. Then she spun on her heel and stalked from the house.

I was considering whether I should follow her out when I heard something behind me. I turned to see Gammin and Marin standing in the hallway. Their faces were startled. Ignoring them, I crossed to the front door. The cart was already starting down the lane. Old Bil peered up at me and barked once. Then he came to me and licked my hand before trotting off to catch his friends. I pushed the door shut.

Not knowing what else to do, I shouldered my way through the barrier the boys made and headed to my room with every intention of staying there the rest of my natural life.

As I shut the door to my room, I heard Marin's voice calling to me.

"So, party tomorrow?"

II.

Gammin, Marin, and I had finished breakfast and were starting to discuss what we should do when Marin's sister arrived with the cart. It was a tight fit with me in there. Poor Avyansa had to work harder than usual. He took us to a place near the border of the Bendwood. The river had cut a steep slope that fell to the shore of the river. It was a pretty setting though my stomach churned with the thought of what was to come.

It had rained during the night. I found a mostly dry log and attached myself to it, trying to become invisible. Eventually Merelina came to me. I expected her to arrive like a tornado, but she glided in like a summer breeze, settling on the log next to me and smiling amiably.

"How are you today, sir?"

I was completely unready for the ferocity of this assault. She seemed a different person than the day before.

"I am well. Merelina, about…"

"Yes, yes, about what I said yesterday." Her hand settled on mine. "Annen, I know something is bothering you, and I know you don't want to talk about it."

This was much better than I had expected! Still, it was early yet. Her statements did not explain why she was so cheerful.

"I asked you to come here today. You did. That is important."

"Did you think I would not come?"

"No, Annen. I know you too well for that. I know your heart. That is why I want to understand why you, why you…"

I saw the flush of blood rush up her neck. It was not untoward in the time of King Brand for the women of Ehrylan to speak first to the men they fancied, but it was not Merelina's way. Why should it be? What man could fail to love her if she favored him? Not Annen.

I lifted her hand and held it against my face, or maybe she did the lifting. I turned into it, kissed her palm.

"You want to know why I don't accept my fondest wish, lady. Has it occurred to you that you might not like the answer?"

"In this I feel that knowing is better than not knowing. If I understand the issue, maybe we can work it out together."

"Do not set your hopes so high." I started to say that I was cursed by Ea, but that was untrue. "I fear the pain I will cause you. Ea's hand is heavy on me. I am weary of its weight, yet he is my maker."

The children were playing together, paying us no heed. I still felt uncomfortable. This did not seem the place for such a discussion.

"Walk with me?"

"Gladly, sir." She already had my hand so I pulled her up.

Eanna must have known that we might wander off. She studiously ignored us as we left. I led Merelina to a path at the edge of the slope. It led down to the Silver River, which was narrow and shallow in these parts.

We clambered down that steep hillside like runoff from the recent downpour. There was much slipping and sliding. We came to the end of the path, or perhaps it was the beginning, winded and thankful to be once more in control of our feet. We paused under a large willow tree to catch our breath and peer out through the profusion of leafy branches. Just below was the shore, which was layered with rocks and pebbles of all sizes, shapes, and colors. Here and there, sprays of water bloomed, the breath of the river. I rested a hand on the trunk of the willow, wishing I could drink in its strength.

I jumped down the rest of the way to the rocky shore and turned back to Merelina. I braced myself and grasped her around the waist with both hands.

"Ready?"

"Ready as I'll ever be," she replied, hopping off the edge without warning.

She was feather-light and as graceful as a swan. Merelina could easily have made the jump without my help, and we both knew it. I had to step back to control her lithe body. I went with her and turned a full circle just for fun before setting her down. She voiced delight.

When the motion stopped, she tossed her head back and laughed. Her teeth flashed white in a quiet shaft of sunlight. As the laughter ended, her eyes closed, and she bent her head toward me. My lips brushed her forehead before I could react. I smelled the fragrance of lavender, faint and agreeable.

Merelina looked up at me. I saw the pleasure in her eyes bleed away to what might have been sorrow or pain. She sighed and pulled closer to me, pressing her head against my chest. I could feel the rhythm of both hearts.

Without lifting her head from my chest, she said, "Why do you fight it? Am I so undesirable?" Her arms tightened around my waist. My own, responding involuntarily, did the same.

"No, Lina. Never think it. You know how I feel about you. I am…" I considered my words, knowing that I had to get this right—for her sake, not mine. "I am not free to give you what I feel." I gently pushed her back and held her at arm's length.

"Tell me why, Annen. Don't I deserve the truth?"

A wisp of hair had escaped the captivity of the leather gather at her neck. It drifted back and forth across her face, dancing in the breeze. I gazed into her blue-grey eyes and drank the sorrow. In that moment, I, who had traveled the kingdoms of the Crescent and beyond and sat with foreign kings as they flaunted their riches and finery, realized the truth. She was the finest thing I had ever seen. I wanted her completely. That thought shattered me. I dropped my hands and turned away, unable to face her, unwilling to brave the truth.

"You deserve more than the truth, Lina. But what you ask is hard." I stammered to a halt. Words I was reluctant to say bound my tongue. With my back to her it was easier. I took three steps along the bank and noticed the river again as if for the first time. The water sang freely, its voice the antithesis of my own. Would that I could so easily tell my tale, the story she needed to hear. It was a chronicle of betrayal that I had never shared with another human being.

I turned. She was standing where I'd left her, watching me, hands clasped in front at her waist. But for the lack of fine clothes, she might have been a queen. The look in her eyes dismantled all my remaining defenses and there, in that instant, I decided to confess.

"You will be the first to hear. You will see why you must turn your heart."

"I judge what is worthy of my affection."

I shook my head and held out an arm to her. She stepped forward to take it. "Come," I said. "This is no place for such a story. I know a better."

I led her along the bank, listening to the rocks murmur beneath our feet. I wondered what they were saying, greetings or complaints. My imagination chased after the thought that Ea might have given all created things voices to be heard if only we, who style ourselves wisest, would stop and listen. Perhaps it was better that I made no mental preparation for the tale I was about to tell.

We came to a little-used track that led back up the embankment to a pair of large standing stones. These had been squared off and set to guard the entrance of what appeared to be a small cave. A third stone jutted ignominiously from the undergrowth a few steps below. The stones and the cave were mostly hidden by a stand of dense bushes that clustered close against the hillside.

Merelina hesitated as I moved up the slope. "Here, Annen? In a tomb? Surely not."

"A tomb is appropriate for the story I have to tell. This one was despoiled long before the grandmother of our father's father walked the earth. It's quite cozy, actually, or it was when last I was here." She replied with a look and followed after me.

The tomb was low and narrow. We had to bend our heads and enter one at a time. Two or three steps inside the entrance, the ground was dry. There was evidence of stone work, though most of the useful material had long ago been removed for use elsewhere by the pragmatic. Sunlight spilled over the area adjacent the entrance. The tunnel reached into the hillside for twenty paces. At the far end was a hollowed-out space that had been a burial chamber before collapsing earth had reclaimed much of it. Two lesser chambers, one on either side, opened off the tunnel close to the entrance.

The location was used to visitors. The remnants of two fire pits, ringed with stones brought up from the river, explained why the place smelled of old smoke. There was a pile of twigs and branches, some of which were green. Torch mounts had been hammered into the sides of the passage, though there were no torches in them that day.

I sat her by one of the fire rings, unable to ignore the

attractive way she curled her legs beneath her. Her eyes were so melancholy that I had to shut my eyes against them. Without forethought, I bent, cupped her face in my hands, and kissed her on the forehead where my lips had so recently touched. I sank to the floor beside her.

On the brink of the appalling storm men call war, we paused. I opened my heart to her. It seems to me now that Ea lifted us out of time and gave us a special world all to ourselves, a world where we were safe from intrusion and from the disasters that were upon us. I did not tell her all, and here I shall tell even less. Some of the tale is best left untold and much has been recorded elsewhere. But I told her the truth. In the end, she rendered her own judgment as you shall render yours. I ask no clemency.

III.

I waited until, distinct above the song of the river, I could hear the sound of our breathing. Then, gathering my resolve, I spoke.

"Merelina, I love you, not with the affection of a brother or a friend, but with all the longing and esteem a man can have for a woman." I kept my head down so our eyes could not meet. "I cannot give that love to you. It has not proved safe for those on the other end of it." I looked at her then for it would have been otherwise cruel. Her head was bent, her eyes fixed on the hands clasped in her lap.

"Your heart is given to another?"

"No." My throat trembled as I struggled to rush on, not wanting to let this lovely creature misunderstand, yet not able to articulate feelings I had never before vocalized.

"No?" She looked up, gazing into my eyes with a stare that stole my breath. Even in the half light of the tunnel I could see the pulse beating in her throat. I felt an almost crushing desire to place my lips there.

"There is no woman to whom I would rather give my heart.

But I can make no room for you there. It would not be safe. I will not bring death to you as I have brought it to all those whom I loved. I married once, Merelina, just before the first of the Five Battles. We were young. Our life as husband and wife knew no time of peace. We both thought I was the one who would die in the war. But we were wrong. Her name was Prescea. I would have you know it. She was like you and yet unlike, as sisters sometimes are."

I opened my mouth to describe the love we had shared, Prescea and I. Fortunately, common sense caught up with me. I shut my mouth and swallowed hard.

Merelina sensed my discomfort. "You do not have to do this, Annen."

"Yes I do. It is time for this story to be told. But there is no pain in that memory, Lina. That burnt itself out long since. Thanks be to Ea and to Rhua, the breath of his power. What pain there is lurks in my faithlessness and the failure of my mind, body, and spirit. I will tell you of those."

I was moved by what I saw in her face. Placing my palms on her shoulders, I kissed her forehead again, and then the tip of her nose, and the tip of her chin. I thought she might turn away, but she did not. I sat down, closer this time, so that I could feel her next to me and perhaps gather strength from her.

"Will you hear this, lady?" I hoped she'd say no. She nodded once.

So it began.

"My father was high in the king's councils. They were long friends and true. It was the same with me and Branden, the king's son, the prince."

"I know who Prince Branden was." There was a tang of indignation in her voice.

"Of course you do, Lina. I am sorry. Forgive the poor habits of an old teacher. Or maybe it is the old habits of a poor teacher? In any case, I had not yet passed into manhood when the first rumor of ancient evil came to Kingsholm. I had been raised at court, though my family is not... was not royal.

Branden was the best friend I've ever had. I accounted him my brother. He was as a son to my father. I was the same to his, to King Brand.

"Branden, as you know, was a warrior, a great captain whom men followed because they admired his valor. He was not devoted to the study of history or the sciences—as I was. He read a book only if it might teach him some tactic to win a battle or a strategy to win a war.

"We passed into manhood and assumed our places. He was by his father's side as they readied the kingdom for a war we could not win. I was with my father as he journeyed the width and breadth of the Crescent in search of allies.

"The time came to fight. My best friend was the prince, a potent leader already though he was not twenty at the time of the first great battle. He chose me to be in his command so that I could fight by his side, just as my father was by King Brand's side until they both fell at the Battle of Norbridge, the last of the Five Battles, the last battle of all." I had to stop to fight the tears.

"You fought in the Five Battles, Annen?"

"All but the last. I am going to tell you why we missed that one."

"You were in the battle of the Narrows? Even there?"

"Yes, Lina, even there. That was the fourth of the five great battles."

The largest of the battles fought during those terrible years were known collectively as the Five Battles, though there were perhaps as many as ten other major conflagrations. The Battle of the Narrows was the most ferocious, even worse than the Battle of Norbridge, which ended the war and the reign of King Brand. The Battle of the Narrows became the standard by which warriors on both sides measured themselves and other conflicts. One might still hear some hoary greybeard from the garrison boast in a tavern, "I were at the Battle of the Old Forest, I were. That were the first of the great battles as I recall. It were not so bad as the Battle of the Narrows, mind you, but it were terrible indeed." For the story he would tell, which might be as much fiction as truth, the old soldier's tankard would be kept full until the tale was told.

"I am sorry Annen. All these years and I did not know. I've heard that only one man in ten returned from the Narrows. You must have been... you must be very brave."

"Brave? No. I was scared, Merelina. Not scared of death, though. I was frightened that I might not stand fast when it was my time to die, that I might turn and run, letting down my king and my country and my friends. Valor is an illusion."

We listened to the murmur of the river for a moment. My thoughts were drawn back to a time many years before when I'd listened to a similar river in the company of another whom I loved. On that night, as we strained our ears and eyes to detect the approach of enemy forces, the air had been cold enough to freeze puddled water and snatch frosty breath from our lungs as we exhaled. It had been the last of the awful nights we spent contesting the Narrows. Though it was my turn to watch and Branden's turn to sleep, he'd sat up with me listening to the voice of the water and keeping the perimeter safe. The scant remnants of his force rested in caves and entrenchments, waiting for another day of war and blood and death. There was no surprise attack from our enemy that night. They were as exhausted as we. The next morning, Prince Branden led us through the newly fallen snow in a last, hopeless attack against an army that outnumbered us twenty to one.

But that was long ago. Now, in the half-dark of this small tunnel, I faced m past. It was an enemy that was far more daunting.

"After the Battle of the Narrows, King Brand came to me. It was full winter, a forced period of inactivity for both armies. He came to me, mind you. Think of that. He did not summon me. He found me in one his libraries, though no doubt his search was neither long nor difficult. His guards were everywhere, and I was well known to them. It was less than a moon since we'd returned from the Narrows, the prince, me, and a few of others. It was not one in ten that returned. It was one in a hundred. None returned unscathed. My arm was in a sling, and I still needed a crutch to walk. The prince was still confined to his bed, or at least to his rooms. He was never one to stay abed, even when wounded. I think he would have been up and about his work even then had not the healers set him to sleep among the poppies.

"The king looked well, considering. Like all of us, he was noticeably thin and wore the scars of many campaigns. He must have felt the weight of hopelessness, though his face did not show it. I started to tell him what I was doing. He cut me off, claiming that he knew already that I was looking for a way to come upon our enemy from the rear.

"The king was correct. I asked him how he had known, suspecting someone had been watching me."

He said, "It is nothing, boy. You sit here, newly come from a bed in the Houses of Healing, buried in maps of the lands beyond Norbridge where Dauroth's forces are encamped. What else would Calen Farseer be doing but looking for secrets where none are to be found? Only that. How is the arm?"

"Strong enough, my king," I replied. "It will hold a shield again, or else I will fight without one." Kings like that sort of nonsense.

"Ah, yes. Fighting. That is all the talk, isn't it? Truth to tell, your shield is what I wish to speak with you about. Come with me."

I started to put the maps and books away, but the king waved me off with a hand. "Nay lad. Landon will do that. Come with me now."

Landon was one of his guards, one of the…

I had to stop my tale. Merelina's face had gone pale. She shifted away.

I asked, "What is it?"

"You're Calen? Calen the Farsighted?"

"Ah." I sighed, knowing this was going to be difficult. I had been dreading it. "I wasn't thinking. I am a fool. But yes, that was my name back then, before I betrayed them all and led them to their deaths."

"My lord!" She struggled to her feet, the dress tangling her legs. I reached out and put a hand on her shoulder, pushing down gently. She ignored me and stood up as much as she could, which was not all that much in the low tunnel.

"Lord Calen. I did not know. Forgive me!" She was wringing her hands and shifting from one foot to the other as a man will when he is in urgent need of a tree.

"Of course you didn't know, Merelina. Sit down before you hurt yourself. You look silly standing there with your mouth open."

Her mouth snapped closed. Anger flashed from her eyes, which was exactly the reaction I wanted.

"Silly? Did you just call me silly?" She stopped wringing her hands and jammed them as fists against her hips. She started to draw herself up into a posture suitable for ire. Her head smacked into the top of the shaft with a muted thud. A blur of dust floated calmly down and settled at her feet. I waited until the air was clear again before I looked up into her flaming eyes.

I said, "You see? Far-sighted, indeed. I predicted you would hurt yourself." She opened her mouth and drew in a breath. I could feel the outburst coming, so I continued. "But you are beautiful when you are being silly. Very beautiful. Now please sit back down. I miss you by my side. And there is much to say. I have barely even started." I said this with as much earnestness as I could muster. I had known it would be difficult for her, if ever she were to learn my old name.

She raised a hand to her head and brushed at the place it struck the ceiling. Her feet shifted closer together, but she made no move to sit. I could see she was not going to make this easy, so I reached out, wrapped my right arm around the back of her knees, and pulled her sharply towards me. She collapsed into my arms and ended up sitting in my lap with her feet extended to the side. Before she could protest, I pulled her close and put my face against the side of her neck. She struggled for the briefest moment, but when I tightened my hold, she quieted.

I held her for a time, relishing the feel of her. I began to count our breaths, but soon lost even that thought and just sat holding her as we breathed the same air.

"Ok, Lina?" My lips moved against the soft skin at the side of her throat.

"Ok? Ok? No, it is not ok. Most definitely not!" Her words started at a normal volume. The exclamation ended as almost a shout. She tried to lean back. If she'd been able to, I thought she would have crossed her arms and lifted her chin. But I held her firmly. Gradually, her body relaxed, the way a water skin collapses from taught to slack when the water runs out. Where Merelina's tension went, I do not know, but I enjoyed that time immensely. Until I remembered what we were about.

"Merelina?"

"What?" She made that single word an accusation.

"My leg has fallen asleep."

"Good."

"It's all tingly."

"Good."

"Do you think you can behave now? Or do you need to go sit in the corner?"

"What corner?"

"Well, that's a good point. I guess you'll have to behave?"

There was a moment of silence before she answered, "Yes, my lord."

Now it was my turn to react. I tried to push back from her, but found she was clinging to me. I was pondering my next move when she spoke.

"Give me a moment, will you? This takes some getting used to."

"I can do that," I replied.

I felt her hold on me relax, so I did the same. She was out of my lap and kneeling with her back to me in and instant. I watched her shoulders rise and fall with each breath. Finally, she turned and resumed her original place across the fire ring from me. I noticed the distance with relief and distress. My arms felt cold, empty.

"You've got some explaining to do." Her voice was flat and

expectant.

"Yes. Exactly. Ready to listen? If you can, forget for now that I may have once been someone you heard about. Most of what you heard is likely just the mystery and fantasy that surrounded Branden as it surrounds any prince. Some of the mystique splashes off on those around him. Who wants to believe their future ruler keeps company with dolts and dullards?"

"But…"

"No buts."

"Yes, my…"

I cut her off, more savagely than I intended. "Don't say it, Lina!"

"Yes, my sweet Annen." Her eye twinkled. She knew there was room in my heart for her whether I would or not.

I began again. "Now where were we?"

"As I recall, the perspicacious King Brand had sought you out, despite his many and pressing duties, to seek your advice on an affair of state."

"Hardly. But listen and you will know the truth."

IV.

The king led me to his private study. He was forced to move slowly as I crutched my way along. I had never been there before, though my father had described some of the treasures therein, paintings and rare books, a sword and shield passed down from the first rulers of Ehrylan, an emerald the size of a large man's fist. The king gave me time to marvel at these things before initiating his business. He was wise, was King Brand.

He began by pouring wine. Then he motioned me into one of the chairs on the other side of a low table, across from his own.

"I need your help, Calen."

"Anything, sire."

"No, boy. Not anything. It will be everything. It is your life I ask of you now, your life, your wife's, your young son's."

He set his wine on the table, lowered himself into his chair. I saw a deep weariness crawl over him, one that had been hidden. I struggled to reply. The words could not overcome the frost on my tongue, so I waited. My eyes, betraying my thoughts, flicked to one of the swords that decorated the walls.

"Not that, Calen. What I ask of you will be harder than that. You must leave Ehrylan, this very night if possible."

"Leave, Majesty?"

"Yes. I have said this to no man, not even your father who is my dearest friend. But I say it to you now, a young man of bare twenty summers." The king leaned forward and grasped his cup, wrapping the fingers of both hands around its golden surface. There was a single gem on that heavy cup, a green emerald that served as the eye of a lion. He took a long swallow and continued his thought as if speaking to himself. "Only twenty summers, true, and near as many battles." Then, as if he had caught himself in the haystack, he changed the subject. "Drink up, boy! Or would you prefer warm milk?"

"Nay, sir." I drank two mouthfuls. I was used to his ways. He would get to the meat of this in his own time. But leave Ehrylan?

"I've considered this long and hard. I want you to know that before you start with your questions and your schemes. You will try to argue me out of this, for your way is ever to find some solution overlooked by others. You are successful, most often. Any king would be fortunate to have you by his side. I am twice blessed to have your father by me, thrice blessed with a son who is a hero in his own right. Ea be praised."

I opened my mouth to thank him for the kind words, but he did not let me speak. "Of a courtesy, don't interrupt me. This is hard enough without your prattle."

I took another sip, gazing at him over the rim of the cup. His beard was iron grey and his eyes the deep blue color of a mountain tarn.

"I've considered this. I am satisfied. It is best for the kingdom. But what I have to say cannot be said by a king. No king could admit what I believe." He stopped there to see if I had anything to say, which I did not.

"You must know, Farseer, that Ehrylan cannot win this war. Nay, don't deny it. A man who does not admit truth because it is unwanted is a fool. I am no fool. Nor are you."

It was his turn to take a sip. I watched in obedient silence. I began to see what he wanted of me.

"We are at the end. Were it not full winter, 'twould be done already. My head would be on a spike and covered in snow. My head and Branden's. And yours. And your father's. Yes, all my subjects and friends will follow Brand to his death." He raised the cup again and drained it. For a moment, he held it in front of his eyes. Suddenly, his brow rippled and his lips pulled back in a grimace horrible to behold. He slammed the cup down on the table. I saw the rim crumple in his hand. The lion's emerald eye bounced twice on the table and skittered across the surface until it came to rest in front of me.

The weight of his gaze pressed me down. It was difficult at first, then intolerable. At last I had to speak. "You wish me to take the prince away, somewhere safe, while you make your final stand."

The king sighed. "You are well named, Farseer. I thank you for making this easier. Yes, you must go with Branden. See that he does not return to Ehrylan though his heart will forever turn this way. For this service to me, this service to Branden and the kingdom, he will come to suspect you and perhaps even to hate you. You might even be branded a coward. This is what your king must ask of you though no king has the right. I do not command you to do this as king. I ask it as friend. You must judge which will sway your heart to the action. But either way, you and Branden will go."

I did not bother to protest. It was easy to see the logic in his plan. We could not prevail against Dauroth's overwhelming forces. Yet King Brand did not have the luxury of surrender; Dauroth was not interested in a vassal state, nor even subjugation. His goal was the destruction of hope, something he had pursued time out of mind. Dauroth was no ordinary man. He was not a man at all, though he was clothed in a man's flesh and blood. He was Everbourne. All the power of his mighty spirit was bent against the children of Ea. Dauroth, our ancient and inhuman foe, would not stop until all the works of Rhua, Ea's breath, had been brought low and set at odds with their maker. And now, in Ehrylan, only the devotion of King Brand and his loyal people stood between Dauroth and his goal.

The king told me his plan. I was to sail away with Branden, my family, and a cadre of sailors and warriors. The stated intent of our journey was to make final pleas to our supposed allies. We had to leave now, before Branden was well enough to resist. The excuse for such haste was the need to be off before winter made sea travel difficult. The prince could not be told the true goal, which was that we intended to remove him from the downfall of Ehrylan. As King Brand said to me at our final parting, a tree cannot rise again if all the branches, seeds, and roots have been destroyed.

The second prong of the plan was grim indeed. The king would make preparation for a final battle to be fought as soon as the weather allowed it. He would sally forth with no hope of returning. Not all his strength would accompany him to that last day of awful glory. Much of what remained of Ehrylan's army would be quietly siphoned off to disperse into the hidden places within the countryside, there to wait and prepare.

We talked for a long time. I learned many things that had before been hidden from me. I was torn with ambivalence, on one hand desiring to argue with the king over his plans for the last battle and on the other knowing that I must obey him and keep silent on the subject. When I edged our discussion to this topic, King Brand saw through my veil of words and shifted back to the issue of Branden and the impending voyage.

Finally, I gave in to disobedience and asked him outright, "Your Majesty, forgive me, but please allow me to discuss with you your battle plans. We can devise a course of action that yields victory for Ehrylan, or if not victory, then at least not sure defeat."

"Nay lad," he replied, not unkindly, though he sighed wearily. "Victory for Ehrylan cannot now be achieved by force of arms. Perhaps that was never possible. I do not know. But listen and look for wisdom in my words."

Despite his call to listen, King Brand lapsed into silence. I watched him as the fire crackled and hissed. Eventually he spoke, but his word was not directed at me. "Landon," was all he said, raising his voice little. Immediately the door opened. Landon stepped in briskly, his cloak swirling around his legs.

"Your Majesty."

"Bring more wine, and some food. I'll need another cup for myself, it seems."

"Yes, sire." With that, Landon, loyal servant of the king and member of his personal guard, vanished from the room, pulling the door closed behind him. At the time I did not think of it, but I believe now that this and much of what followed had been prearranged.

"Listen you now, young Calen. You earned your place at my side. Even so, there is much for you to learn. You believe I run to my certain death with no chance of success. If you will hear, I will tell you how we may yet together wrestle a future for the kingdom we love."

"I will hear you, sire."

"I am charged with the protection and care of the Ehrylain. These last years, I have seen the men and women of this land, young and old alike, give their lives to defend their homes and their king. I say this to you now." His voice became more intense. "It is not well that the people should die for their king. It is the king's privilege to die for his people."

I opened my mouth to offer any of an hundred rebuttals. The king silenced me with a look that was irrefutable.

"I will not lead my people, your father by my side, in a hopeless charge into the gates of death. Neither can I turn aside when duty calls home her price. We will make our stand, your father and I, when the spring sun opens the way to

Norbridge. I will make an end to this war. If you are successful, Calen, the seed of my fathers, whose blood reaches back to the years when the lands of the Crescent were united under a single king, will continue. When the time is right, bring Branden home to lead the Ehrylain again in to the field."

He lapsed into silence, The room felt empty without his voice to fill it. With all the theatrics and state craft that in part made him a good king, he made his voice soft again and finished. "Will you help me?"

"I will do whatever you ask, sire."

As the king opened his mind to me further, Landon brought a tray heavy with food. He set it on the table between us. He turned and moved toward the door without a word.

My father entered. He greeted the king and then Landon, putting a hand on the guard's shoulder companionably as they passed. He approached the table with his other hand on the ancient sword that hung glittering at his waist.

Our thoughts turned to the food, as usually happens when food is in the offing. A single cup stood empty on the tray after my father and the king retrieved theirs. I spared a thought to this, wondering why Landon, who was uncommonly meticulous in all things, would provide an extra. I concluded our company was not yet complete and wondered who else was coming. A soft knock announced the answer to my question. At the king's acknowledgement, the door opened. My wife stepped into the chamber.

"Prescea. Be welcome," said the king. He loved her as a father loves his daughter.

"Your Majesty, I come in answer to your call."

"Good, else I might have been cross with you. Take the cup, girl."

Instead of doing what the king ordered, my wife, who was in no way flustered or intimidated by him, picked up the flagon and refilled our cups before splashing liquid into hers. She lifted the cup to her lips.

"Hail, king and father and husband."

We drank to her words.

V.

Prescea and I were already on the ship when the king arrived. Connel was there too, our son who was two years old. They were below, making a dwelling of sorts in our cabin. Large as it was by the standards of the sea, the tiny room afforded so little space I came to think of it as our nest rather than our room.

I was on deck waiting, so I saw the king come aboard. He was followed by Branden, who embarked with the help of Merid and Gilmarun, two of his personal guards. King Brand started toward me with his son, supporting him as they moved across the deck. I hurried to help, the heavy cane for which I had traded my crutch clopping on the wooden deck with each step.

The king took us to the prince's quarters, opened the door, and ushered us in. He sat Branden on the cot and stood me beside him. I could feel the tension. The chasm of silence between them told me they had been arguing. I did not have to see far to see that, or to know why.

King Brand said, "Calen, I have for you a token. This may be of some help to you in the future. It shows how much confidence I have in you; when you forget that, look at it and remember."

He took a ring from his finger. It was old. A tiny scale surmounted its apex. There was a single stone—a new addition—the emerald that had until recently served as the eye of the lion on the king's cup. I knew, with no little dismay, what the letters inscribed on the ring declared and what the ring signified. The scales represented the balance of justice and mercy.

"Majesty! I…"

"Hush, lad." He held up a hand, shook his head. "No, I may no longer call you lad, for you are now the King's Justice. I give you right to speak with my voice. What you say will be law in Ehrylan, second only to my voice or my heirs'."

"Sire…" I was, understandably, quite unable to form a sentence. I looked to Branden for assistance. He averted his eyes, suppressing a villainous smile. Apparently he had known this was coming.

"Justice of Ehrylan, do not thank me. It is an ill that I do you with this honor. You are the first Justice in this kingdom since my father's father named Talesyn. There has been no need. Hard times have been upon us. Harder times are before us. You may rue this day, but I know that you will see justice done."

"Yes, sire, I… I… will try. I thank you, sire." These few words were the best I could manage. I was thankful to have uttered them intelligibly. The honor was so great and so terrible that I could not, in so short a time, wrap my thoughts around it.

The kings of Ehrylan had centuries before realized that blind obedience to the law sometimes leads to injustice. To mitigate this, the kings appointed Justices. The Justices were different than the other servants of the law. In them rested the power to hear, judge, and pronounce doom without question. They heard disputes, made judgments, and issued remedies as they saw fit according to the law and their wisdom. Even in the remotest corners of the kingdom, the people might have access to officials with the power and authority to right wrongs and see to their needs. It was a duty assigned only to the most trusted of the king's subjects. But it was a difficult and costly appointment, since the Justice sometimes had to execute the extremes of the law. It was a time-honored and ancient practice.

There was more discussion, but the years have wiped away the words from my mind, leaving only vague memories. Just before he left the ship, the king took me aside, where no one could hear his final words to me.

"Remember, Calen, Justice of Ehrylan, a tree cannot rise again if all the branches, seeds, and roots have been destroyed. I will tend the tree while I can, but my seed is in your care. Do not fail through the impatience of a young man. The seed must not be planted in Ehrylan until the soil is ready. Years. Maybe decades. You must be patient. Do what is right and you will not go wrong."

"If I do not know what is right, how shall I act?"

I thought he might simply turn away, but he spoke. "There is a saying among the Old Ones. When eyes cannot be trusted, heart speaks true. There is another saying, this one from my own father. Ea gave you eyes and a heart; you should use both." He gripped my shoulder, turned, and walked away. After a parting word with his son, he left the ship.

King Brand watched from the shore as we sailed away. He was flanked by Landon on his left and my father on his right. Behind them were several of the king's guard. Their cloaks danced in the wind. I thought that I had never seen a more noble assemblage. The prince and I watched from our place on the deck as our homeland receded and the people we loved shrank into the distance. And then, as the ship descended the back of one wave and rose to the crest of the next, I lost sight of them and saw them never again.

14. MANY PARTINGS

I.

The king's navy was much reduced after so long a conflict. However, it still controlled the port at Kingsholm and the waters thereabout. We were able to set forth without conflict or pursuit. We sailed north.

As we drew closer to Norlan, Ehrylan's northern neighbor, our vigilance increased. When we saw ships, we took evasive action immediately. We played cat and mouse with Dauroth's war galleys which, being rowed by slaves, did not depend on the wind. We were not a ship of war and must evade our foes, not confront them. Fortunately, each time we were observed, our vessel had the favor of the wind or the darkness to assist our escape. I suspect this was no accident, but rather the design and expertise of Enol, the captain of the ship, and Patrik, his sailing master.

My memories of the first part of our trip are sketchy. I have never been a glad sailor. I spent much of the time in our nest, for I was injured still and in no shape to gain my sea legs. It was an odd time for us as a family. Seldom since Connel's birth had the three of us spent so much time together. Never had urgent duty pressed so lightly. During this interval, we enjoyed our son. We could see his intellect and understanding grow almost by the day. Prescea and I talked much and listened much and did a lot of nothing. That was enough.

Though we sailed the winter through to spring, we were not successful in gaining aid. To Wyn, in the far north, we could not come because the ocean there is unnavigable in winter. We were unable to make land in Norlan; Dauroth's navy held blockades. In Rath, we saw open warfare upon the seas as Dauroth's galleys contested with the mighty navies of that kingdom. Branden wanted to find a way to land in Rath, but I remembered the real task to which I had been set. I spoke for caution and prevailed. Farther south in Arel, we did not encounter Dauroth, but her king would not aid us, saying that Dauroth was abroad not in Ehrylan only. He had his own shores to protect. And so we passed on to Sulan and Yar, the southern-most of the kingdoms of the Crescent.

As we sailed south, the days grew warm. The skies cleared. The sea changed from an angry winter gray to a deep green. My body returned to full health. Those might have been good days, had not the specter of war and the ghost of failure haunted our thoughts.

Branden grew increasingly discontent with my unchanging council. I wrestled with his desire to return to Ehrylan, advising always that we stay the course of our appointed mission. But my heart whispered otherwise, siding rather with his. He sensed my unvoiced ambivalence and was disquieted. He was, after all, his father's son and could not be easily fooled. The prince began to speak to me less, to avoid me when he could. King Brand had been right; I tasted the bitter truth of his prophetic words.

Hot nights followed sweltering days. Still we sailed southward. We watched for any sign of Dauroth's navy. The waters were as devoid of ships as the shores of vegetation. It was a barren land.

The main port and capital of Sulan is called Petras. I had

been there before. We were welcomed in the king's house, a palace carved into the face of a massive cliff. Visitors from Ehrylan seldom came so far south. News was always welcome. They knew our kingdom was at war with the Everbourne king. My father, with me by his side, had come in the same year the war had begun. As before, there was no hope of assistance. We were encouraged to replenish our water and supplies, and to stay as long as we liked. Our crew was allowed shore leave, long overdue. They were popular. The men of Ehrylan are tall and doughty, whereas the Sulanese are lesser of stature and more supple. Their skin is tinted by the sun. I am certain that, as the result of our visit, the seed of Ehrylan was well sewn in Sulan.

The King of Sulan—Ahmet was his name—cautioned us not to sail further south. That way lay only the deserts of Yar as far south and east as men had explored and returned to tell the tale. The coasts of Yar are subject to violent storms that strike in all seasons. The deeps are likewise afflicted. Those waters are known as the Turbulence. Few ships return that venture near those seas. Ahmet told us, and we knew from our own experience, that we would find no help in Yar. That kingdom comprised a nomadic people who roam the trackless wastes, living where no life seems possible. They move from place to place as the sands and the seasons shift. They take no interest in the world beyond their lands.

Branden and I held council. He spoke harsh words when I urged a southern course. He did not accuse me of cowardice, for he knew I was not afraid. This knowledge added to his perplexity. He asked me the same questions time and time again. How could I advise a continued search when all our efforts had been fruitless? Why was my suggested course always away from our people and our homes? I longed to answer these questions, but was bound by my honor to King Brand. I had already started to wonder how long being honor's slave would seem the more savory course.

II.

Out of duty to his father, Branden capitulated and bade the captain to set a southern course. We watched the weather carefully and looked for safe harbors into which we could retreat if the wind and seas turned hostile. We ran from oncoming storms and found shelter in small coves. Despite our caution, we were caught. Rhua stirred the wind and waters against us.

On the morning of the sixth day out of Petras, I came on deck and found the captain and sailing master eyeing the sky. The look in Patrik's eye and the set of his jaw told me this was no trivial matter. I saw them both sniff the air. The sailing master began issuing urgent commands. Immediately, as if they too had been sensing something to which only I was ignorant, the men on deck leapt into the rigging. The sailors who had been below taking their leisure followed.

The watch was hard at work taking in sail when a violent wind rushed down from the land. Though our sails were close reefed, the rigging jerked and groaned such that I was in fear it would be carried away. It was a mighty storm, coming on us suddenly with a ferocity I had never seen, save only in a woman's anger.

We were at the mercy of the wind. The tempest drove us far into the deeps where we lost all sight of land.

For more than a week, the storm continued unabated. Our sailors were scarce able to make amends when rigging and sails were damaged. Good men were lost overboard. The sky was black day and night; we saw neither sun nor moon. Huge waves washed the decks clean of anything not made fast. We lived then like prisoners, sharing our food and clothing among ourselves, sailor, soldier, and passenger alike. In a colder climate, we surely must have perished. All were wet, both above and below the deck.

Worse than all these physical discomforts was the fear that we were being blown into the Turbulence, a swirling monster of wind, water, and lightning that made all the seas in its giant vicinity perilous. Many of the guards and a few of the younger sailors voiced their concerns. These opined that it was already too late, that we were already in its clutches, a grasp from which no ship ever returned. Enol, when I questioned him, was quick to lay that fear aside. According to him, we had been too far north when this storm struck. Since then we had been propelled almost due east, as far as he could tell. This was little better, of course, for the eastern seas are wide beyond measure. No map I had ever seen told their tale.

I will not state that the ship began to leak. All ships bleed seawater even in the best of times, and these were not the best of times. We took on water at a frightening rate, as much from the waves washing over the decks as from the battered hull. Despite constant pumping, we were wallowing dangerously low. Branden, the members of his guard, and I took our turns and more at the pump chains, grueling labor that left our muscles exhausted and our hands covered with blisters. Try as we might, we could not forestall the water that invaded our ship. Eventually, we began to throw the food and cargo that could be spared overboard to lighten our load.

Finally, the storm eased and we saw patches of clear sky. One by one, frightened mice peering cautiously from holes in the wall, those who were not sailing the ship began to emerge from below. What we saw was frightening. One mast was broken halfway up and a second was missing entirely. The rigging was a tattered grave cloth clinging to spars that jutted askew.

At first, there was little attention to the ship, for all were spent to the point of death, and still we were slaves to the pumps. Enol and Patrik heartened what remained of the crew to their work. That first morning was spent running a thick rope around the hull, girding the ship to hold the timbers together more tightly. I had never seen such a thing before. I would have thought the master and mates were become fools or were having a jest with me, but there was no energy for levity, and these men were not fools.

We continued at the pumps for two days while the wood

wright and his mate went about plugging holes and repairing leaks. How they accomplished this I cannot say, for I was entirely exhausted after my tricks at the pump and usually went immediately to my nest.

The weather became so fine it was impossible to believe another storm would find us. The crew worked on the ship and its rigging. We all put out as much of our clothing and goods to dry as space would allow. No land was in sight. The stars were unfamiliar. We had no idea where we were. It was a bad situation, but there was much else to occupy us. The threat of drowning was more pressing than the thought of being lost at sea.

The fine weather continued for many days. A steady breeze carried out of the east, pushing us farther from home. It was some time before we were able to raise sail enough even to steady the ship and allow for steerage. A new mast was stepped in place of the missing, and the aft mast that had broken was extended. It was amazing to watch. Sailors have a power over rope and wood that even the mages of the Everbourne would envy.

During this whole time, the prince avoided me. He arranged our tricks at the pump so that we never met there. He sent messengers to me when he needed to communicate. This was difficult for me; I loved him as a brother. Prescea was predictably helpful, offering council when I solicited it and providing a nurturing spirit. Finally, though I had made no conscious decision to confront him, I happened to see Branden near his cabin. I followed behind and forced myself upon him. He allowed me in, dismissed the guard, and closed the door. I looked down at my feet, considering what I might say.

"Is there something you need?"

Frustration overwhelmed me.

"You ill-use me, Branden."

"You deserve it. I deserve better. What are you hiding from me, Calen? From the first you have set your will against mine, claiming that we must honor the wishes of my father. For love of you and respect, I let you prevail. You have always been able to discern the most sensible course. Look you now and see where you have led us, Farseer."

I would have lied to him, telling him that I hid nothing. But a lie had no hope of success. Branden was the hound of truth. And he knew me too well.

"The wishes of the king must be honored."

Rage settled over him like a death shawl.

"You lie like a Gryhm, even when you speak true."

The words pierced me, a sword skewering the angry love in my heart. The Gryhm were the worst of Dauroth's servants. Like Dauroth, the Gryhm were Everbourne. To be compared with those foul demons was a cruelness of itself. Branden saw that he had wounded me. True to his nature, he pressed home the advantage.

"You have not answered me. Since when has Calen needed to bend the truth? I ask you again. What are you hiding from me?"

There was such a mixture of hurt and urgency in his eyes that my resolve broke. I bowed my head and rubbed both hands against my face, perhaps unconsciously attempting to wipe away the guilt. Then, against the command of my king, I told him all, from the first to the last. I know I erred in this. I would like to believe that my judgment was impaired by long, sleepless nights and longer, tiresome days. But that is too easy. The truth is that my will was weak. My spirit, unwilling from the first for the task to which it had been set, was easily broken. I was not able to set my will against Prince Branden; he was made of sterner stuff.

There it is. He was a prince, the son of kings. I was not.

III.

The prince set a course for home. This decision was accompanied by no little risk. We were in unknown waters, had neither charts nor any idea of where land might lay, and were running short on food and water. It was a choice one might have expected from Branden. His audacious decisions had resulted in unlikely victories.

On the third day, the wind shifted so that it came out of the northeast. The bluster increased as the day wore on. Before the sun set, the waves had grown angry. The ship once again felt as if it were riding the back of an enraged bull. I took my concern to bed with me that evening. The reassuring words I gave to Connel and Prescea sounded hollow to my own ears.

I came on deck at sunrise, as was my habit. Once again, Patrik was inspecting the sky, this time with his mate, Dim. I made my way over, weaving through a bustle of crewmen. I did not have to ask what was so perturbing. A storm front stretched out as far as my eye could see. The leading edge was marked by an angry ridge of clouds that ranged from gray to outright black. A second layer of clouds roiled out from the first.

I asked Patrik what seemed to be the obvious question. "What is it?"

"That's a step cloud, Lord Calen, sure as I am old and damaged from my long life and evil ways." I was going to ask him what to expect from it, since he obviously knew something was afoot, but I didn't have to. He continued on his own. "I'll wager a king's ransom, beggin' yer pardon, sir, that we'll be in the bucket in… What do you think, Dim, fifteen minutes?"

"Nar," Dim answered, "you always was an optimist, to my view, sor. I'd say we've ten at the most." A shaft of lightning stabbed into the sea at the edge of the storm. An immense peal of thunder rolled over us immediately, followed by a stiff gust of wind. "Make that five if we're lucky."

Patrik began to bark orders in all directions, most of which were immediately echoed by the mate. This was a curious custom I had observed previously. I determined to ask the sailing master why it was necessary for his words to be repeated when they could be heard quite clearly by all involved. I never got that chance.

This storm was not as fierce as the one that had driven us from the coast of Yar, though it blew longer. We were at the storm's mercy for at least twelve days. The ship lost another two crewmen. One of the guards was washed away, though no one saw it happen. These losses detracted noticeably from the morale of the crew. The concern that Ea had raised his hand against us spread among the crew.

The night the storm finally broke, I awoke in the arms of my wife. Our son had slept with us since the beginning of the storm. He was curled up cozy as a kitten. What woke me was the motion of the ship, or rather the lack of motion. I listened, waiting for the renewal of the groans and snaps that accompany large weather, but heard only the precious breathing of those I loved most. I separated myself from the tangle of appendages and sheets and went on deck.

It was still dark. The wind was gentle. Exhaustion hung in the air, an almost palpable fog. I heard a noise behind me and turned to see Partik at my shoulder.

"It's over for now, my lord."

"Yes….aye. For now. But what next, I wonder?"

"She floats, we live. We live, we mend. We mend, she sails. What else is there?"

We floated on that quiet sea for days, nursing ourselves and the ship back to health. There was little else we could do. The wind, weary after so long a blow, vanished entirely. We were becalmed. It was strange to me that the word caused such an intense dread among the crew. Becalmed—it is a nice word, entirely pleasant. At the time, it did not occur to me that the dead are calm as can be.

We drifted aimlessly. There was no escape from the oppressively humid heat. Food shortages became a concern. We cut the size of our meals in half and then in half again. Water we had and it was fresh. The casks were brimming. Our crew had collected rain during the storm. Sailors are an odd sort, as any who have sailed with them are well aware, but I know of no other folk who are, on the whole, so resourceful.

IV.

The lookout was the first to see the pirate. The rest of us had been preparing for another storm. Ominous clouds darkened the sky. Even I recognized that we were in for it again. The storm became secondary to the new threat.

There was no thought of waiting for the other ship in hope of rescue; the few tales told in the Crescent of these distant waters invariably concerned pirates, savages, and dragons; only one of those used ships. We spread as much canvas as she would bear and fled before the increasing wind.

The other ship was bigger, faster. As she closed, we saw the emblem on her flag, a crossed cutlass and boarding pike. That left no doubt. We had braved the Turbulence, crossed uncrossable sea, and sailed right into a pirate tale.

They attacked just before dusk. I think they would have waited until full dark, but the storm was hard upon us. We had prepared our defense. Branden ignored me as he arrayed our forces. I positioned myself below the fore deck where he stood flanked by Merid and Gilmarun. That was as close as he would let me come.

The pirate came abreast of us. They deployed some sort of suspended bridge that pivoted down from a shortened mast. It crashed through our bulwark and plunged a spike deep into the surface of the deck. The bridge was wide enough for two men to move side by side and had tall screens that shielded them from our arrows.

Longboats embarked from the far side of their vessel, approaching from us all quarters. The boarding parties deployed grappling hooks and portable ladders to board us. Our men used pikes to hold them off. Our archers dealt death among them. We may have killed half of the longboat crews before an appreciable number stepped onto our deck. Yet, we were still outnumbered.

I saw two distinct kinds of men among the enemy. The majority were easily identifiable. Pirates look the same wherever you go. They carried long knives or short, broad, curving swords, sometimes one of each. The others were entirely new to me. They were brown men—darker even than the Sulanese—of extreme size, dressed only in breech cloths. Their skin was covered with blue and red tattoos. They were exceedingly savage, wielding bows, staves, or war clubs.

I had been driven back from the fore deck into the waist of the ship. I had no idea how long we had been fighting. From what I could see, our men were doing well. It was to be expected from the pick of the king's forces, men who had been at war for many years.

The storm had continued to rise. The ships, connected by the boarding bridge, bucked and rolled. It was increasingly difficult to maintain balance.

I was taking stock of the battle when I heard Prescea's cry. It rose to me from below, a harbinger of doom calling me to grief. I took a step toward the hatchway, then remembered myself and looked to the prince. The men on the foredeck were holding off the attackers who crowded in from below. Branden was directing the remaining archers. There was a fatal moment of indecision. Duty to my prince strove against duty to my family. I stood paralyzed in the midst of the raging conflict and the rising storm. I cannot recall the moment I came to a decision. Maybe that is best.

I fought my way to the hatch, hurled myself down the ladder. My boots thudded against the wood. A pirate in the passage turned toward me. Beyond him, lying inert, I saw the form of one of the two guards Branden had assigned to defend this section of the deck.

The pirate attacked first. Good for him. He held a long knife in each hand, and was better armed for an engagement of blades in this small space. But my sword was not yet encumbered. He felt the point of it before I was in danger. I shoved his body aside and stepped over the guard who was beyond any help I could give. Dead pirates littered the space between me and the door to my cabin. As I stepped around the last body and came to the door, a pirate stepped out.

My heart sank, for I knew what this likely meant. There was

no time for the agony which would so soon color all my days and nights. I ran him through before he had time to bring up his knife and rushed into the room. The second guard was there. He was dead, pinned against the bulkhead with his own sword. Another pirate lay in the center of the room, a crimson stain surrounding his torso. On the cot, I saw the worst. Prescea and Connel were dead. She held her dagger still. It was covered in blood.

The weather deck was littered with bodies. The dead lay on the deck and slumped in heaps against the gunwale. Groans of those whose end was near added an eerie quality to the raging wind. All around these unquiet dead danced the living, locked in combat. On the foredeck, half the length of the vessel from where I was, the prince and two of his guards were battling against what looked like ten men. Between us, from the waist to the bow, numerous collections of men hewed and hacked at each other.

My sorrow, though it would grow immeasurably stronger in the coming days, was obliterated by an inferno of rage. I do not know how long I had remained below, striving to come to grips with the loss of my family. When I came through that hatch, I had no recollection that I was fighting for the prince or for Ehrylan or even for my own freedom. Only revenge drove me, and maybe hate. I had no plan, no thought of self-preservation. I just wanted to kill as many as I could before I fell into death. There, I hoped to see my wife and child on the path ahead, where I might come again to them under the stars that shine forever beneath Ea's throne.

The deck pitched wildly. Untended sails snapped and shuddered as the storm freshened to what would soon be a gale. I spared no thought for these things. There was only death for me now. My mind, body, and spirit were united to that purpose. I stumbled toward the prince, killing pirates, slashing their unprotected backs as I passed.

One of the huge savages confronted me. He was almost a

full head taller than I, and proportionately as broad shouldered. He opened his mouth wide and pulled his lips back in a snarl. While doing this, he stamped alternately with each foot on the deck. In other circumstances, this might have been amusing. I was not concerned with his attempts to appear fierce. It was his weapon that drew my attention.

He held a wooden staff, as tall as he was. The end of the staff floated between us at the height of my breastbone as he shifted back and forth with his bare feet. He gave the impression of being very deadly. This was a style of fighting I had not seen. The Dryhm fight with staves, but they keep the weapon in motion, twirling and whirling and spinning it to confuse and distract their opponents. I had fought many Dryhm. This savage was something new.

This first experience was nearly my last. Without warning, he leapt toward me, striking upward in a sweeping motion with the end of the staff. I easily avoided that attack, and the downward strike of the other end of the weapon that followed. The third and fourth strikes, right and left, were unexpected. I was barely able to deflect them.

He shuffled back and demonstrated his foot and face ritual again. Then he launched into a second attack that was more ferocious than the first. An enormous wave struck the ship, pushing her rump around. The savage, closing the distance between us, was thrown off balance. I ran my blade through his throat. He fell twitching at my feet.

In my head, drums hammered a riotous rhythm to the accompaniment instruments I had never heard with my ears. It was the battle music, a familiar companion returned to visit one last time. I tugged the sword free, raised it above my head like an untrained novice, and charged toward the mass of attackers surrounding the prince.

My sword rose and fell in time to the battle music, a raucous thrumming only I could hear. Four pirates collapsed before I was noticed. Then there was no thought but the mindless fury of battle. I defended myself against one then two then three attackers. They drove me aft and I had to move carefully between the lifeless bodies. Three times I killed and three times other pirates joined the fray. Almost I was overcome, but in the end, exhausted nearly to death, I turned and turned and turned again to find no one facing me. No one, that is, save the dead, who accused me with the sightless eyes from which I had stolen life. Maybe now they could hear the battle music too.

Gasping for breath, I looked toward the prince. He stood alone on the fore deck against three assailants. They were in the defense; Prince Branden, though young, was mighty of hand and spirit. Of the guards that had been at his side moments before, there was no sign. There were only a few pockets of fighting now. I could not tell who was victor or who was vanquished.

A movement caught my eye. In the waist of the ship, back in the direction from which I had just come, I saw an archer reach an arrow from the quiver. His eye was trained on the prince. I threw myself toward him, screaming like a lunatic in hope of distracting his attention.

The archer glanced at me, then turned back to his intended prey. I summoned my last strength, but my body fell short, betraying me as had my spirit and my mind. I failed the ones I loved. I was three steps away when the archer drew down on his target. In the last step, my legs gave way. Perhaps the ship heaved as a wave pounded her, turning my foot awry. I've spent an eternity wondering.

The arrow flew just before I smashed into the archer. We fell to the deck. I lost all control. Forgetting my sword, I pummeled him with my fists until he moved no more. I continued pounding his bloody head and face until I remembered who and where I was.

I found my sword and pushed myself to my feet, only to fall immediately to my knees. I looked for my friend, saw him for the last time. He was sprawled on the deck unmoving, the arrow protruding upward from his torso. Forgetting weariness and sorrow, I arose and staggered toward them. I never made it forward.

An enormous roar broke over us. The ship jerked. The deck canted severely and stayed there. My foot, slipping in a pool of blood and sea water, skittered out from under me. I slipped backwards. The back of my head slammed the deck hard enough to release the stars that hide behind our eyes. A wave rushed over the slanting bulwark and took me in its fist. Helpless as a doll made of summer straw, I was sucked over the edge, drawn deep. I struggled for the surface, but that was only an action born of habit. I had no will to live.

The body will when the mind and spirit won't. That is what perspicacious King Brand used to say. I have no memory of gaining the surface or coming to land. I remember only the surge and press of the currents and the color of the surface of the water far above.

V.

The quiet brought me back from the sea of memories to the burial chamber and the realization that I had stopped talking. I had to shake my head to clear it. I blinked to clear my eyes. Lina was looking at me.

She had shifted so that her back was against the wall of the tunnel. We faced each other across the old fire pit. The air seemed full in the absence of the voice that had so long been speaking. There was no room for more words. I realized I had been speaking in the language of my youth, the language of King Brand's Ehrylan, the Old Tongue as it was known to a generation of youth that had never experienced true freedom. I cannot say when we had switched from the Common Tongue. Perhaps it was when I had begun the story.

"That is quite a tale, Annen. I am sorry for your loss, your losses."

"I thank you, Lina. They are your losses too. Branden was your prince. His men were some of the best in the kingdom. I am sorry to have let you down, all of you."

She came to me, wrapped her arms around my shoulders,

placing her cheek against mine.

"I would ask you a question, my lord."

Before I could even begin to feel irritation, I saw that she was not being mischievous. She was being quite earnest.

"Yes, lady?"

"You promised to tell me of how you were faithless, how your weakness brought calamity on those you love."

"Yes."

"I have not heard these things."

"No? Weren't you listening?"

"I heard it all, Annen. I heard more than words."

She shifted around and knelt in front of me, folding both my hands in hers. Her head was lower than mine so she could look in my eyes.

"You told the story of a man—a very young man—who did the best he could in an impossible situation. He survived and returned home to renew the fight. He has spent his life serving his king and his friends. I love that man and he loves me. Nothing except Ea will keep me from spending the rest of my life with him, no matter how many years or how few years that will be."

"Do you say so?"

"Yes, my foolish Annen. I say so. Do you hear me?"

"I do."

I started to form a rebuttal but found that my mouth was occupied in responding to a rather wonderful kiss. After that, there was silence again. It should have been an awkward silence, but it wasn't. It was enjoyable just to sit and feel her next to me. It always had been. Always.

I held her in my arms, the way I had dreamed for so long. It was better than I could have imagined. We were two pieces in a puzzle that fit together perfectly.

"Tell me two things, Annen."

"Two things? When did Max show up?"

"This is not the time to be funny."

"Yes, dear." She laughed, knew I was being facetious. "What would you like to hear, Lina?"

She lifted her head from my chest and pushed herself out of my arms. Taking my hands in hers, she lifted them to her lips and looked at me over the top.

"Tell me that you love me. I have waited a long time to hear it."

I was certain I had started my tale with that very declaration, but this seemed no time to quibble.

I looked into her stormy eyes. "Lina, I love you. I want you by my side forever. Wait, that's not right. I want to be by your side. Will you have me?"

"I will."

She let our hands drop. I saw that she was wearing the rose necklace. I reached out. There followed a time where we simply touched each other.

After a long quiet, she asked, "I said two things, remember?"

"I might grant you three if you kiss me again."

"The second is enough, sir. Will you tell me the rest now?"

"Lady, that would be a long story indeed. But I will tell you all you want. What would you know?"

"For starters, how did you survive the wreck of the ship against the reef? That's what happened, isn't it? What about the pirates? And, how did you get back to Ehrylan?"

"Ah. Just that, huh?"

"Yes, just that."

She placed her head against my chest. I caressed her. When I did not start the telling, she raised her face to mine. I stole more kisses, wanting to verify that the first had not been a dream within a dream.

After looking into her eyes and caressing her cheek, I finished my tale.

15. THE THIRD BATTLE

I.

From that day in the cave to the wedding was only a week. It might have been sooner, but there was much to be decided and more to be done.

Merelina, Eanna, Aldryn, and I agreed the two orphanages would be consolidated. The two ladies would share the responsibilities with their new husbands. Since the River's Bend facility could accommodate the new additions, the decision was easily made.

We kept the Step and the house in Stone Gate, hoping we might turn them into homes for the homeless. The relocation came off without a hitch. Not one child cried. They knew they would have more room, more food, and four adults. The children began to refer to the new situation as Bendholm.

The wedding ceremony, which was performed at the fountain in the Bendwood, took place at dawn. Aldryn and Eanna were joined at the same time; we doubled the fun and halved the labor. Marn and Dara stood for all of us, an unusual arrangement. That seemed fitting for this unusual situation.

Bewhiskered tradition dictated that four village elders stand for each couple. But we were not young or inexperienced. Marn and his wife would be good enough, so said the village elders. The four of us could not have cared any less. Marn took it more seriously.

After Merelina and I spoke in front of Ea, we drank of the spring from the same cup. When I had kissed my bride as her husband for the first time, Marn and Dara came to us. We withdrew from the celebrations. Together, the Old Ones told us the story of how their own elders had taken them aside to say these very same words.

"Now!" Marn was stern. He shook me at the first word to get my attention. "Hear the will of the Maker. Do not fear the wind or rain or the dark of night. Shelter each other under the wings of Ea."

Those were important words. There were others. I remember them. It was one of the best days in my life. Happiness and love seemed to float in the air, carried on shafts of sunlight. I can still see Lina dancing with the morning. She had flowers in her hair.

We bought the property next to the orphanage in the Bend. It had belonged to Eanna. It was in good repair. It took only half the work we put into it—Aldryn, Marn, Gammin, Marin, and I. The rest of the work was superfluous from my point of view, but Marn and Aldryn would not accept anything but perfection in their craft.

Once again, Pleasant Moon found me enjoying a new gift of unexpected happiness. The love of such an amazing woman was a hope I had not allowed myself to desire. The move to River's Bend was a desire for which I had not allowed myself to hope. I was twice blessed and many times more.

The house in the village was small. Since Marin returned to live with his parents, the crowding was not as bad as it would have been. What was sacrificed inside was regained outside. There was much more space for Avyansa. There was more room in which to train.

We had our pick of the yard, which was huge in

comparison to the courtyard in the Stone Gate. That is, we had our pick after my wife laid claim to a large plot. She told us in no uncertain terms that the plot was to be her garden. The students built a low wall of rough rocks around the perimeter of the plot.

Dara hit upon the excellent idea of using the children's enjoyment of crafts to better their lives. On some occasion when she, Aldryn, Lina, and I were lounging on one of the mats the children had made, Dara commented that the mat had proved useful and was well-constructed. She wondered if there might be a place at market for such things. Lina, Arica, and Eanna began to spend a few days each month in the Shambles selling goods the children made. It was a success.

This was as fine a time in my life as I can remember. I watched children playing in the yard. Neighbors visited almost nightly. I remember the way Lina looked at me when I caught her on her knees in the garden, wiping her brow with the back of a hand, gifting me her smile. I can see Gammin teaching her how to hold her knife because I wouldn't, not wanting to be her *shinando*, content to be her husband.

And the boy who started it all? He was not forgotten. Lina shared my love for Gammin. She gave of herself to him and was the mother he had never known. The three of us were a family. We were happy in River's Bend.

It was easy. It was fun. And it was too short by years and years. As quickly as it started, the interlude came crashing down around us. We were caught by surprise in the spring of our rebirth. You have heard time and again that war was on the doorstep. We lived beyond the door and didn't have this foreknowledge. The torrent of death and destruction we had long expected caught us unprepared.

I come to it at last, having tarried in the happy years as long as I could. I would enjoy better telling the tales of Gammin and his friends, how they made for each other the family that had been denied them, but that is not what I was commanded to do. I was instructed to make this history and to place within it the events and emotions that carried us to the precipice.

Hear now how the Ehrylain raised their heads and hearts, put down their rakes and shovels and mattocks, and lifted arms to take back what had been stolen from them.

II.

One morning, less than two months after the wedding, I accompanied Arica and Merelina to the Shambles. After we set out their wares, I continued on my own. For me, this day would be spent attending to the maintenance of our two properties in the city.

One would think an unused structure does not require the same level of care as an inhabited structure. I have not found that to be true. King Brand used to say it was better to keep up than to catch up. I intended to catch up on my keeping up. Gammin and Marin were to join me later, up at the Stone Gate. I took a pack with a few tools, some fruit, and a full water skin. My sword I left at home. Who needs a sword when mending a fence? My staff I left at home. Who needs a walking stick when riding in a cart? Caution and sensibility I discarded as well. After all, I was not using them.

I spent much of the day working at the Step. When I had accomplished what I had come to do, I set off for the Stone Gate. I stopped at the market and purchased a meat pie, having worked up more of an appetite than I had expected. That turned out to be a fortuitous meal. It was the last I ate that day and there was much exertion to come.

The house in the Stone Gate stood just as we had left it, empty and clean. I ate my pie and fruit while sitting on the hearth I had made with my own hands. Then I swept each room. I was in my room when I heard a knock at the door. I trotted down the hall and into the front room, throwing the door open as if there were not a thing in the world to be concerned about.

I expected to see Gammin and Marin. I was already forming the words to tease them about knocking. What I saw was the cruel point of a serpentine spear head. It snaked in as the door opened, hovered near my throat. A voice spoke from the yard, attracting my attention.

"Stand still, teacher. If you move without my leave, the girl will die. If you keep moving, the woman will die. Whether you move or not, you will die. Your life will be longer if you stand still."

I saw my wife. A Dryhm was holding her head back, a knife to her throat. Next to her was Arica. She was in the same predicament. There were at least ten Dryhm, maybe twice that, armed with staves. The one with the spear extended it so that the murderous tip hovered danger-close to my throat. The two restraining Arica and Merelina hauled back on their heads in an attempt to show me that they were serious. I had no need of such a display.

"Step out into the street, teacher."

I rummaged through my addled wits for an alternative but did not find one. I could save myself by stepping back and closing the door. Then I could fight them off as they found their way into the house. What would that gain but the death of two whom I loved? I could refuse to step out. If I did that, their next move would be to threaten Arica's life. After that, I had no move at all. Better to play for time.

I extended a foot. The spear tip drew back.

III.

The Dryhm formed a circle around me. Two of them laid hold of me, seizing my arms. Another stepped forward. He wore a large ring on his hand. His belt was formed in the image of a slender, fanged snake of gleaming silver. Those things, and the manner of his bearing, told me he was their leader. He moved without concern. Stopping a few paces from me, he stood silent as a statue as he surveyed the area. When he spoke, there was a mocking tone in his voice.

"All taken and no casualties. Your reputation is overblown.

Had I known that, I would not have inconvenienced so many of the brethren. Maybe one or two would have been enough?" The voice sounded familiar, but I could not place it. He spoke with an Ehrylain accent, in the flavor of a south-country local.

I did not know what to say. Something seemed forthcoming. "Your eyes are dark, and you cannot perceive the light. How can you see what is in front of you?"

"The darkness holds more than you could even dream. It's a pity you will not live to learn better. But know this."

He stepped closer to me, linking his hands behind his back in a good imitation of an orator. It was always about the show with Dryhm.

"Your cause is hopeless. The Dark One has but stretched out his smallest finger, and you are undone."

I struggled against the restraints, but it was no use.

"Soon," he continued, "all your plots will be laid bare under the eye of the Faceless. The people of Ehrylan know the meaning of grief. The time is coming. We wait now only for you loyalists," he stressed the word with a vocal sneer, "to reveal yourselves. We watch. We wait. We see. We know. We act. We overcome."

The other Dryhm repeated the litany in unison, "We watch. We wait. We see. We know. We act. We overcome."

"Before we go to your interrogation, I want you to know who has bested you." He lifted both hands to push back the hood of his robe. I was utterly taken aback by the face that was revealed. It was the *drachem*, Pruis' father. He laughed, scoffing the surprise that must have shown in my eyes. Looking back over his shoulder, he said, "It is time, my son."

One of the nearby Dryhm stepped forward, casting off his hood with none of the affected elegance of the leader. It was Pruis. Suddenly, a fool that has taken far too long to piece together a simple puzzle, I understood. I had never been able to figure out why the *drachem* sent his son to the Dryhm. Now it was obvious. He had not sent him away from his side; he had brought him immeasurably closer.

Pruis laughed his crooked laugh. His voice dripping with

malice, he said, "It is so good to see you like this. You are always so sure of yourself, so smug. But now look! You are a fox caught in a trap."

I held my tongue. I was thinking hard, calculating. I might be able to break free from the Dryhm holding me, but I could not save the captives from the knives at their throats if I did so. Care for Lina and Arica restrained me, not the Dryhm holding my arms. But time was running out. Gammin and Marin were on their way, walking into a deadly trap. I had to get this evil brood out of the area as quickly as I could.

"What do you want of me, *drachem*?"

"Of you? I want nothing except your miserable life. Oh, and any information you might have that I think is useful. I'll take that as well before we send you screaming into the darkness."

"Let the women go. If you let them go, I will cooperate."

"Cooperate? I have no need of your cooperation." He waved his hand dismissively. The ring glittered in the slanting sunlight of late afternoon. "As for them, they will serve their purpose in the sacred grove where the cold stone waits. If it pleases me, you may see them die. It would be fitting for you to see them spend their last few breaths suffering, and all because they knew you. Just that."

"You are a pig. You are a traitor to your own people. Ea will serve justice upon you."

"Ea is a dream within your nightmare. The darkness is supreme. I serve the darkness."

The other Dryhm echo back, "The darkness is supreme. We serve the darkness."

I did not see a chance to save my own life. If I could sell it to free Merelina, Arica, and the boys, I would do so. The sooner the better. I wanted this filth long gone by the time the boys arrived. Ea help me, I pleaded.

I was at the point of launching into a desperate struggle when the *drachem* spoke again.

"We will not tarry here bandying words. I am eager to put the knife to you. The moon is on the rise. It is a magic moon tonight. Did you know? It is a good night for sacrifices. The cold stone is thirsty. She is always thirsty." He pulled his hood up. "Bring them."

As he began to walk down the lane, Gamin rounded a corner several dozen paces away.

"Run, Gammin!"

I drew in breath to yell again. Someone cuffed my ear. The end of a staff slammed into my gut. Pruis stepped forward and kicked me in a bad place. I slumped to my knees, retching. Another staff slammed across my shoulders.

At the last blow, I lost control of my arms and fell face first to the ground. As soon as I was able, I lifted my head. The boy was coming toward us, walking as if he had not a care in the world. I wanted to call out another warning, but could not catch my breath. Merelina screamed. There was the sound of a sharp slap.

I pushed myself up. I would not have been able to do so without assistance. The two Dryhm hauled up on my arms. The other Dryhm seemed paralyzed as Gammin continued to approach. We all watched. Why didn't he see the danger? He passed through the perimeter of the deadly circle as if it were not there and strode right up to me. Didn't he see that Lina and Arica were prisoners?

"Annen," he said with a smile, "Are we having a party? You didn't tell me. Is it a surprise for me?" His voice was light, untroubled, as if he did not see the enemies close around us.

Pruis answered before I could. "A party, yes. And just for you, dog. On your knees before the mighty Dryhm!"

Gammin rolled his eyes and lifted his chin as if he were an actor on a stage. "You again? Don't you ever get enough? I've beaten you twice already. One would think two beatings from someone so much younger than you would be enough."

I expected to hear protests from the other Dryhm, but they stood in silence, a wall of evil between us and freedom. If one good thing can be said about the Dryhm it is that they know discipline.

Pruis stepped forward. He had grown in the last two years.

Gammin held his ground. He had grown even more, though he was still more than a fist shorter than the older boy.

"Care for another go?" asked my tadpole merrily.

Pruis raised both hands and pushed violently at Gammin's chest. Gammin turned his torso just a fraction. The hands slid off harmlessly. Pruis stumbled after them. Gammin laughed.

"I thought you Dryhm were supposed to be good fighters."

Pruis glared at him. "I'll kill you this time, you....peasant."

Their eyes locked. Pruis' chest heaved. Gammin's breathing was controlled.

Pruis broke the stare and looked at his father. "Dark one, allow me to kill this peasant. He insulted me and insulted the Dryhm. He must be punished. May I be the finger of the Faceless?"

The *drachem* considered, looking from Gammin to Pruis. He glanced at me and smiled. "That will be well. Let the teacher's punishment start here." He gestured to the Dryhm holding my wife. "Kill the women if he moves."

A hooded figure tossed his staff towards Gammin. It clattered on the stones at the boy's feet. He did not bend to pick it up.

Pruis glared at him with disdain. "Second thoughts, dog? Have you caught prey too big to swallow? It is too late now. There's no one to rescue you this time."

Still Gammin did not move. What was he playing at? Then what Pruis had said hit me. No one to rescue him this time. Where was Marin?

"So be it. I will kill you where you stand." Pruis lifted his staff.

"Your days of hurting others are done." Gammin's voice was emotionless. "Now back off. I will not bend in front of you when you are armed. You are coward enough to strike me before we start." So saying, he took a step back, putting the staff at his feet between him and his opponent.

Pruis looked indecisive, then moved off a few steps. Gammin picked up the staff. I watched Pruis as he readied himself. His grip was good, his stance assured. He looked as if he knew what he was doing. He had almost three years training with this weapon. Dryhm were experts in the use of the staff though their style was very different than the one I had taught my students. I wondered with growing concern if Gammin was underestimating his opponent. That would be a deadly mistake.

Pruis began without warning. He stepped toward Gammin, his staff spinning in the bewildering arcs and changes in direction that were typical of Dryhm staff work. Gammin stood his ground with the end of his staff pointing at the advancing opponent, eye high. Pruis leapt forward. His staff whistled toward Gammin's head. The younger boy was no longer there, having skipped back two paces.

Pruis' attack continued. Gammin had to move again, twice in rapid succession, farther back each time. He was nearing the edge of the circle. The Dryhm would not move for him. In fact, they might restrain him. Gammin had the same thought. Next time Pruis charged, he slipped sideways and skipped past the older boy to take a position near the center of the battle area. So far, so good. But why didn't he strike his opponent as he moved past? Sweat trickled in my eyes, burning. I could not wipe it away. My arms were held tight.

The scene repeated itself. Pruis advanced, his staff a blur. Gammin retreated to the edge of the circle, only to skip aside at the last moment and take position at the center again.

Pruis jeered. "What's wrong, dog? Scared to fight when there's no one to rescue you?" He launched himself into a third assault.

This time, Gammin did not retreat. He slid sideways past the other and delivered a low strike at Pruis' knees. The young Dryhm expected such a move. There was a loud bark as the staves collided. This was followed by two more when Pruis swung twice in rapid succession, high then low. Gammin parried each attack.

They separated, each to a position near the center of the circle, staves at the ready. Pruis was breathing hard.

"Are you ready to die, Pruis?" Again Gammin's voice was quiet, devoid of emotion. "Would you like it quick or slow?"

Pruis advanced. His body twisted and turned like a spinning top. Gammin retreated, countering the strikes. His staff met Pruis' three times as he shuffled backwards. Clack! Clack! Clack! Gammin at last launched his own attack. His staff smashed into Pruis twice, maybe three times as he marched forward, pushing the older boy back past the center of the circle. Pruis stumbled and fell. Gammin backed off.

Finish it! I drew breath to scream at him, but could not. If I moved, the ladies would die. I watched as Gammin relaxed. He let a hand drop from his staff and set one end against the ground. He leaned on it as a man might at the end of a hard road.

"Did you fall, Pruis? You're not hurt are you? I wouldn't want to hurt a dying Dryhm. That would be cruel."

Gammin was taunting him. I began to hope and to wonder what would happen if Gammin won the fight. What were his chances of surviving if he overcame the *drachem's* son? Not much. This was a day when all my hopes could be lost. I had to think of something.

Pruis regained his feet, his robe and his dignity equally soiled. His face wore a new look, a calculating stare with a grim set to his thin lips. He was done with searching for the quick victory over an opponent he'd thought less skilled. Before, the contest had been only for Gammin's life. Now Pruis realized he had to fight for his own life. He spun his staff, snapped it to a stop in a ready position. The change in his demeanor was as obvious as it was drastic. Did Gammin see it? Did he know what it signified?

Pruis slipped forward, half a step at a time. Gammin stood his ground until they were within striking distance. There was a flurry of action while they fought back and forth, staves swinging through the air when targets were missed or crashing together when strikes were blocked. Pruis countered a blow to his midsection, swinging the low end of his staff up and around to strike straight down towards Gammin's head. There was loud snap as the attack was blocked. Pruis levered the other end of his weapon beneath Gammin's guard and caught him square in the stomach.

Gammin's head went down as he was doubled over by the force of the blow. Pruis swept his staff low, taking Gammin at the knees and tossing him off his feet. He landed on his butt with a gasp. Pruis waded in for the kill, his staff a twirling distortion. Gammin rolled; the end of Pruis' staff smashed against the ground.

Gammin used his position on the ground to deliver a sweeping attack to Pruis' ankles. Pruis fell in a heap over his outstretched hands, his staff clattering next to him. There was a moment of soft sounds as both combatants climbed to their feet.

Gammin was visibly discomfited. He held his elbow close in to his ribs and hunched like a man who has been struck hard in the stomach. Pruis was limping noticeably, favoring his right side. They squared off again, the center of the circle between them, the look that heralds death in their eyes. They were both breathing heavily.

This time Gammin attacked first and paid for it. He looked slow and stiff. Pruis avoided the attack, striking Gammin in the upper arm. Gammin cried out and stepped back in what could only be viewed as a retreat. I saw fear in his eyes and I was afraid.

Pruis saw it too. He smirked, lifting his chin jauntily. He stepped forward without raising his staff to a ready position, disdainful now of his opponent. Gammin responded by sliding back again, retreating out of striking distance. Pruis was having none of that. He thrust himself forward, his staff a blur.

Instead of slipping further back—something we all expected—Gammin drew his back foot close to his front foot, then sprang forward. There was nothing fearful or tentative in the move. I saw victory in his eyes and realized the wonderful truth. His retreat had been a sham!

The end of his staff flicked up. His shoulders turned and his arms extended in perfect sequence so that the weapon reached out to its maximum range at the moment of maximum power. There was an awful sound of bone cracking. Pruis staggered back. His staff clattered to the ground as he fell backward over tangled feet. His head struck the stones of the lane with a sickening wet sound. It lolled to one side. I could see his face. He would not move again.

There was an instant of eerie quiet when the only sound was Gammin's heavy breathing. I was looking at Pruis. The end of the staff had struck him right between the eyes. There was a third eye there now, a ghastly red depression peering out from a forehead crumpled with unnaturally jagged angles.

The *drachem* screamed, shattering the reverie. "Kill the boy! Kill him now!"

Several things happened all at once. The Dryhm near Gammin broke from the circle and rushed toward him. Before they covered half the distance, the air was split by a wild hiss followed immediately by two muffled impacts. Sssssstttt! Thud, thud. There was a gurgling scream from where Lina and Arica were being held. Both my guards looked in that direction. I did not need to look; I knew the sound of arrows when I heard them.

This seemed to be the right time to do something. I did something I had never done before, something I had seen Gammin do the first time I met him. I collapsed as if my legs had been cut from under me. My captors' heads crashed together. For the merest fraction, their hold on me lessened. I twisted violently and rolled away.

I got to my feet, weaponless. I was groggy. My limbs were slow and heavy, the effects of the blows I had received only a few moments before. My abdomen was an aching ball of fire. No matter. It was time to fight. If I lived, there would be time for hurting.

The guards squared with me. Their staves went up. I saw my death coming. Then I heard it again. Sssssstttt! Thump. Thump. Both attackers staggered. As I jumped back, one of them looked down at his chest and brought up a hand to finger the black point on the end of the shaft protruding from his heart. The other fell forward, shrieking around the arrow in his throat. I stole a look around. Gammin was in trouble, facing three assailants. Sssssstttt! Thump. Sssssstttt! Thump. Two of the Dryhm menacing him collapsed.

I looked to my right and saw two grey-clad archers beyond the circle. Already their arrows were nocked and they were looking for new targets. Something about the way they moved told me they were no ordinary men. Ea! I ask for help and you send Silanni? I decided then and there that I needed to ask for the Father's help more often.

I spared an instant to survey the battlefield while I picked up one of the staves from my fallen attackers. The rest of the Dryhm were moving to engage us. The *drachem* was kneeling over his son. Merelina and Arica were heading toward Gammin, but Dryhm were rounding on them. A robed figure stepped in front of me. My looking was over.

I was in no mood for the tactics of fighting. Sheer, brute violence guided my hands as we exchanged a set of blows. My mind was consumed with the welfare of my friends. I was torn. I could not help Gammin and women at the same time. How would I choose between them? Where did my duty lie?

Even in that desperate time, my mind asked, "Do I have to make this choice again?"

I had not been attending my opponent well enough. His staff arced in, striking me on the arm. The pain brought me back to proper attention, and I focused on the destruction of the enemy in front of me. The other end of his weapon was arching toward my head. I ducked under, buried the shoulder he had just struck in his chest, and tumbled him off his feet.

I came down hard on top of him, drawing the length of my staff across his throat. Setting my hands on the shaft to either side of his head, I bounced viciously with all my weight. There was an ugly noise. His eyes bulged. In the moment of disorientation that followed, I jumped to my feet and drove the end of my staff into his exposed throat. I delivered a second tap to his head, as hard as I could. Then I turned to see what my indecision had cost.

I had forgotten about Arica. She may have been a beautiful young woman, but she was also a warrior, and a good one. She was engaged with a Dryhm. They were fighting furiously. Nearby, Merelina was holding the knife I had given her at the ready, waiting for the opportunity to use it on that same attacker. Behind them, Marin was locked in combat with another opponent, putting it to him soundly with a bright sword that gleamed like lightning as the strokes fell. Marin! Oh, Ea, beyond measure you answer your children when in need they call upon you! There were two figures locked in battle near where I had seen the Silanni. One was a Dryhm. The other was a man with an axe. Marn? Ea be praised! I turned my back on my friends and looked to my boy.

Gammin was beset by two opponents, one of whom was quite large. He was being driven back under a withering attack by the larger attacker. I started toward him. There was a final Ssssssttt! Thump. The larger Dryhm crumpled. Gammin shifted without hesitation and took the offensive against the smaller opponent. The figure staggered back as Gammin struck him.

I looked toward Arica and Merelina. They were coming towards me, their attacker lying in the dirt behind them. Marn was walking towards me, his son at his right hand. The Silanni were nowhere to be seen.

I turned back to Gammin and saw that he needed no help. His opponent was on the ground, cowering. Gammin was raising his weapon for the death blow.

There was no need for more death; we had won the battle.

"Stop!" I shouted. The command echoed back from the walls of the Stone Gate, then all was quiet. The only sound was lamentation, which drew our eyes as the flower draws the bee.

It was the *drachem*. He was on both knees beside the body of his son. His shoulders were shaking with the force of his sobs. His hood had fallen to the side, revealing his face. The lack of noise seemed to stir him from his grief. His head turned, and he peered at us with eyes full of hate. Rising shakily to his feet, he stood over his dead son. He drew a crooked knife from his belt, a flame of gleaming metal. His eyes explored the carnage, travelling from one body to the next.

Then they lit upon Gammin.

"You! You killed my son." He took two halting steps toward the boy. I did the same, readying my staff.

"You killed my son!" He hurled himself at Gammin, raising the knife above his head as he gathered speed. His other hand reached out, a claw grasping for vengeance. Gammin slid into position, his staff held in front of him, ready for the fight.

I swung my staff the way a child hits a walnut with a stick. I used every muscle, leaning into the effort and bracing myself with a good stance. My weapon slammed into the *drachem* where the hip bones embrace the abdomen. The staff drove in with the weight of the impact, and the *drachem* tumbled, rolling to a stop near Gammin's feet. He landed face down on top of one of his hands. The blade of the long knife protruded above his back from the space between his shoulder blades. He jerked twice, blood welling in thick spurts from the wound each time. His feet scrabbled against the ground. His other hand reached out toward Gammin's feet. Then he gasped and died.

Only a fool runs with a knife.

The only Dryhm left alive was huddled shaking on the ground at my boy's feet. He was young, no older than Gammin or Marin. His gaze was fixed on the *drachem*, and he was sobbing. As much as I hated Dauroth, the Dryhm, and what they represented, I could not kill him in cold blood. I cast about in my mind for some idea. Then it came to me. I saw it all at once, as if my eyes had opened upon some vista seen from a high mountaintop.

It was time for me to come home.

"Bind his hands."

Without waiting for a reply, I stepped to where the *drachem* lay. I pulled the arm from under his body and saw what I wanted. On the first finger of his hand, now stained with blood, was a ring whose insignia was a ravening wolf's head with ruby eyes. I severed the hand and brought it to the last remaining Dryhm. Marin and Gammin were still working on the bonds. I waited until they were done, then put the grizzly thing into the pocket of his robe.

I let the silence consume us while I gathered the hate and anger, the hurt and suffering, the indignation and wrath that I had consumed in the last forty years. I allowed them free reign so that they must show in my voice and in my eyes.

"Hear me, Dryhm. I am going to give you your life, but only because I need a messenger. Go back to your sacred grove and your cold stone and your foolish elders who worship the dark. Show them that token."

I gathered myself, looking at my friends and allies one by one. I knew it was time. At last, after more than thirty years of waiting, I spoke the words.

"Tell them this. Calen, son of Colen, is come again. There will be justice in Ehrylan."

As the young Dryhm staggered off into the night, Arica came to me. I thought she would throw her arms around me and bury her head in my chest, but she didn't. Instead, she looked me up and down with dispassionate appraisal and said, "So that's what it is like." Her eyes were too hard for a woman of her gentle character.

"Yes," was all I could say.

"Is it always like that?"

I thought for a moment, glancing past her to Lina. My wife had a smile for me. It gave me the strength I needed, pulling me back to my duty and my friends.

"No, dear heart. Not always. Sometimes it's difficult."

Marn put his hand on my shoulder. "You teach better than you fight. Your students stand on a field of victory. They do you honor. I will do the same. Hail, *shinando*." He bowed his head to me.

A little embarrassed, I looked over at Gammin. He was troubled. I thought I understood why, but I was mistaken. I did not understand at all. The boy—no, the man—had already realized something that did not occur to me until later. Life as we had known it was over, and there was no going back.

He stood in front of me in his usual place. He was not now so much shorter than I. He was almost man-high already, though he had still more yet to grow, more out than up. "Time to go, Annen?"

That jarred me back to reality. "Marn, where are the Silanni?"

"The archers have gone on to cover our retreat."

"Will we see them again? I would thank them."

"You will not see them again. Do not fret. They know you are thankful. It is they who will want to express thanks. Their bows will bear new notches from the Dryhm they killed."

"Fine," I said, dismissing them from my mind. "We've got to get out of the city. For good. If we hurry, we won't have to fight our way out. Can you think of a place where we will be safe for a while?"

"I know a place and a way to get there; there will be no more fighting. Leave the Dryhm weapons here. You will not need them." He stepped past me toward the shadows.

I started to follow, then stopped. Even if all the Dryhm in the world were on our tail, there were important responsibilities to accomplish.

I cupped Arica's cheek. "I am so proud of you." I wanted to say more, but nothing would come. Her hand came up, touched the back of mine.

I turned to Merelina. I took her hands, brought them to my lips, kissed her bloody fingers. She pulled them back, but only to draw my hands to her own lips.

"I thank you, Marin, bravest of friends." I extended my arm and grasped his, forearm to forearm, warrior to warrior, equals.

I turned to Gammin. "I thank you, Gammin. You saved me. You did so very well."

16. A SHELTERING PLACE

I.

Marn led us through streets, often turning in a course that kept always in the shadows. Had I not known this city, I would have become lost or disoriented quickly. We were tending toward the city's east wall; that much was obvious. We came to a small house that squatted in the concealment of an alleyway.

Not bothering with the gate, the woodcutter stepped over the low partition that enclosed the yard at the rear of the dwelling. The boys were quickly over and across. I stopped to help Arica and Merelina; both were standing in the yard by the time I turned to assist. I followed them through the doorway.

There were sounds from elsewhere within the house. Marn gave them no heed. He led us without comment down a hallway and into a windowless room filled with crates and clusters of discarded furniture. The room was lit only by a suggestion of light from the hall.

Against one wall was a pallet of chairs. Marn crossed to it and knelt. He reached into the space behind the stack. There was a distinct sound. When he pushed, the pallet, pile and all, shifted along the wall revealing—though it was barely visible—a half-high door.

Marn opened it. The space beyond, which rose to the level of my waist, was empty. The woodcutter reached up and pressed a surface within the little closet, simultaneously pushing down on its floor. When he withdrew his hand, the entire surface at the bottom of the enclosure, a square as wide as a single pace, popped up a finger's breath. Marn slid it back.

Looking up at us from his crouch, Marn whispered, "Stairs. Go down and wait. Silence."

Without further explanation, he urged us through. Marin went first, then Gammin and Arica. I went next. I felt my wife's presence behind me on the stair. The way was very dark; I could not see Arica though I knew she could only be a few steps below me. I counted many stairs. Though steep, they were dry.

I came to a floor, moved away so Lina could follow me and Marn after her. I felt the others near and heard their breathing. A stink of sweat and blood, the coattails of battle, filled the unseen chamber.

Lina came against me, a gentleness already more welcome than the feel of a sword hilt or a good book. My arms drew her closer. Though I heard no rumor of his coming, Marn pushed past us. The oiled complaint of hinges cut the silence like soft thunder. Immediately the smell of water and wet stone filled the air. Someone's hand groped for mine. I took it, giving Lina my other.

Once through the door, I had to bend lower to navigate the passage. We shuffled less than twenty steps, all told. After a single corner, we emerged into a larger space. Water lapped stone and there was a moist tang that could be tasted as well as smelled. I extended to my full height and waited.

I heard a heavy door close, and a bolt being shoved home. There was the sound of steel against flint. A glow of tender swelled into the steadier flame of a candle. Our eyes blinked against so sudden a light, small as it was.

We were in a chamber. I could not tell the size. The light

did not reach into all four corners. Marn, holding the candle, looked at each of us. I think he was counting to make sure we were all there. He nodded and held a finger to his lips. He gestured us closer and we crowded in against the light.

"The way is not far. One hundred eighty seven paces. Three bridges, the first as soon as we leave this room. There are no railings. Do not fall." His stern look was warning enough to describe the danger.

"After the third bridge, we will come to a room like this one, a waiting place. Arica will go up first, and then me. Then Marin, and next the tadpole. There will be a signal for each person; you shall hear it. Annen, you and the lady will come last. You two, who are strangers where we are going, might have to stay in the waiting place for a long time, as long as a day maybe, more if things are not well. We will not know until we get there. No talking."

Marn set the candle on a slab next to the door and replaced the flint and tender in a hollow nearby. He crossed to the far wall and selected torches from one of several crates. Returning to the candle, he lit one and handed me. The other flared as he blew out the candle.

In the brighter light, the whole rough-hewn chamber was revealed, as was an opening in the far wall. Marn led us through that opening into a low passage beyond. I took the place at the end of our procession. I had to keep my head down through the entire journey that followed.

We came to a set of wooden planks spanning a canal filled with dark, fragrant water. The three crossings came and went without incident. We passed closed doorways that gave no hint of what lay beyond. After the final bridge, we followed the passage for thirty paces. Though I had lost sense of direction, I kept count of my steps and knew we were coming to the end of our trip. It was no surprise when Marn halted us and slid open a door in one of the walls of the passage. He ushered us through and came after.

We were in a room similar to the one that lay less than two hundred paces behind us. There were two doors, a low slab with candle and tender, and boxes lining one wall. Marn snuffed his torch in a bucket of sand near the slab. Taking up the candle, he lit it before extinguishing my torch as well.

"The way out is like the stairs you descended in the city. Once through this door," he indicated the door at the far end to the chamber, "ten steps straight, a left turn, and ten steps straight. That will put you at the foot of the stair. Do not tarry. Go through the door at the top. No talking. No noise."

Like the stairs you descended in the city? So we were beyond the walls. That was good. But how far beyond and where?

Marn concluded his quiet instructions. "Make yourselves comfortable. We may be here a while."

He reached up and grasped a rope that hung down the from above. He tugged it twice and let his hand fall. There was another rope next to the one he pulled. The end of it terminated in a slender piece of wood the size and shape of the handle of a hammer. That dangled within a hollowed out block of wood the size of Arica's head.

Marn looked at us expectantly. When we did nothing, he motioned right and left with his arms, indicating that we should sit along the walls and seek what ease we could find there. He crossed to the boxes and brought out a water skin and a lump of dried figs. I could smell the fruit even from across the room. It was a familiar odor that called memories with startling intensity. My stomach turned. I shuddered. I do not care for figs, not at all.

I sat. She dropped next to me and grabbed my hand. As we waited, I considered how desirable it would be to vanish with her into the Old Forest or depart with her into Rath or Norlan, even to set sail for the lost islands of my youth, far and far across uncrossable oceans south and west. I knew I could not. The bonds King Brand set upon me were as binding as the promise of a dragon. I could not shirk them. We must live in our hopes rather than our fears. In hope, there is life and the will of Ea. In fear lives only death. I clung to hope.

Yet fear I had also, though there is no good in it. What peril had I brought to these friends whom, in all the world, I loved the most? The lives they had before today were ended as surely as the lives of the Dryhm we had killed in the city. Pondering this, I realized what Gammin had seen straight off. With that thought came another memory, the recollection of the night King Brand commanded me to take his son away from Ehrylan and out of danger.

My eyes darted to the boy. He was looking at me, as almost always seemed to be the case when I looked his way. Is that it, I wondered? Do I send him away? Would he go?

I could not go, and I knew Merelina would not part from me. But Gammin? Should I send him from my side so that he might live to fight for Ehrylan when at last its people found the will? I began to drink of King Brand's cup. He had faced this same decision, would have been about my age at that time. I began to see him in a different light. My understanding grew a thousand fold in the coming days, as did my doubt and uncertainty.

Merelina whispered in my ear, her voice barely audible even at that close a distance. "What is it, my love?"

I raised our hands to my lips, kissing hers.

While we chewed the grist of our imaginings, Marn passed around the water skin three times and the figs as well. I accepted the water each time; I was very thirsty. I would not touch the figs until Lina broke off a small piece and held it out to me. I shook my head no; she nodded hers yes. She was right, of course. She knew about my figgy aversion, something I brought back from beyond the sea. But she knew that eating something—anything—would help in a multitude of ways.

There came a musical noise from the hollow block at the end of the ropes. The suspended hammer handle twitched against the block a second time. Marn rose. He extended his hand to Arica. Crossing to the door that was still closed, he slid it open and went out, beckoning his daughter to follow.

I inspected those that remained. The boys were doing the same. Marin looked as if this were an adventure such as those he had with his fellows during the last years. Gammin looked worn out. I wondered how many Dryhm he had killed. As far as I knew, he had never killed before. Taking a life, even in battle, is a difficult thing, and never more so than the first time. Perhaps as important, he had ended a long-standing enmity that had been unjustly visited upon him. There was no doubt. He was a boy no longer.

The sound of a bolt, muted by distance and corners, came to us from the passage. It was followed by Marn. He moved about the room making sure all was left as it should be. Crossing to the candle he whispered, "I will put it out. Else you, Annen, must put it out when you come."

I pulled a finger across my throat, knowing that neither the boys nor Merelina would mind. Marn blew across the wick and darkness sprang out of every corner. There was no sound of movement. Whether Marn remained by the door or took a position elsewhere was a mystery. He could move that quietly when he had the desire.

I felt Lina's hand on my cheek. She gave me a tender kiss that spoke of the love that bound us together as one. Before it was finished, the signal came again. Bonk.... Bonk. There was no sound of anyone rising. Marn's whisper came from the entrance to the passage. "Remember, Marin next, then Gammin. I go."

There was nothing but the warmth of Lina next to me in the dark and the sounds of breathing. A rustle from where the boys sat told me they were standing. I felt Gammin lower himself next to me. I heard Marin drop next to Merelina. I considered for a while what might be the right thing to do, then did what I wanted, setting my hand on Gammin's knee. His hand settled on mine.

The signal came again. Marin departed without a word.

Now that there was no one to spank me when I violated the no talking rule, I whispered in Gammin's ear, "I know how you must feel. It is all right. It will pass."

I felt him nod.

"I am very proud of you, Gammin."

"I know," he answered.

I waited for more from him, but nothing came. He was as mute as the darkness. When it was his time, he left us without a word.

I began to wonder what we should do next. When the signal came, it would be Merelina's turn to go. I did not care to send her into the unknown danger above, yet I was loath to leave her here without me. I was considering options when the signal came, answering my unasked question without a doubt: Bonk.... Bonk. Bonk.... Bonk. Two sets of two. Marn was a clever fellow.

Merelina and I stood up. Hand in hand, we went to meet the future.

II.

We came off the last step into a large storage closet, stooping to get through the twin of the half-door we'd used in the city. The smell of cedar and fresh linen was prominent and oddly reassuring. Marn was standing in a doorway that led to the next chapter of our lives.

"Wait here." He pushed past me back down the stairs into the darkness. I thought I heard a bolt sliding home, though that was likely my imagination guessing what he might be up to. He emerged not long after, closed and locked the little door, and pulled a large chest in front of it.

Looking at Merelina he winked. It was not a common thing for him to do. He raised his eyebrows as if he were asking a question and stated, "You are well."

"Yes, Old One. I am well, thanks to you and yours."

"Welcome to *eldehrah*."

"The sheltering place," I repeated. That is mostly what *eldehrah* means in the Old Tongue. More strictly, it means a place where one waits in safety before setting forth on some difficult encounter or journey. In Ehrylan it is said that children wait for birth in *eldehrah*, their mother's belly.

We followed him into a room filled with our companions.

Arica and Marin were seated at a long table. Gammin was standing bare-chested in front of a wash basin doing what folk normally do in front of wash basins after fierce battles followed by head-long flights through darkness and underground tunnels.

When Gammin finished, Marn refilled the basin with fresh water and gestured to Merelina. She did strip off a layer of clothing. That was all Marn and I saw, for being men of sound upbringing, we averted our eyes as soon as we realized what was happening. I suppose I could have watched with no ill propriety. She was my wife, after all, and I had by then a comprehensive knowledge of what lay under the wrappings.

A knock called Marn to the door. He answered it without concern, leading me to believe that we were reasonably safe. A young girl presented him a serving tray laden with a steaming pitcher and clean towels. Marn took the tray and gave her back another with an empty pitcher and towels s red from the blood they had wiped away.

When Lina finished, Marn disposed of the water in the basin and refilled it from the pitcher. He motioned for me to take my turn and produced a shirt from a chest. It was then that I noticed that the boys and Arica wore clean shirts. Lina was donning one as well.

After we were all clean and somewhat refreshed, no one seemed to want to break the silence. I believe they were waiting for me to speak. I could not find my voice, though I had many questions. I wanted to know how Merelina came to be in the clutches of the Dryhm and how Marn and his rescuers happened upon me in my time of need. I was not past believing that Ea had transported them there in an instant to answer my pleas for help, but that was not his usual way. Sometimes I think his joy is in our efforts rather than the results they bring.

The girl came again after a time, trading a tray of food and drink for soiled towels and empty pitchers. Marn placed the tray on the table. We promptly ignored it. Shortly after, there came a single rap on the door. It opened and the last person I expected to see walked through.

It was Koppel, a vendor from the Shambles. He was one of the people from whom I bought some of the more difficult to obtain plants and herbs—such as tenur root. He nodded to me in passing. It was to Merelina that he spoke.

"You are well, lady?"

"I am."

"The rest of you, any hurts that need tending? Nemen Nellyth is with us."

Wounds. I had not even considered them. I ached where I had been hit—which seemed to be my whole body—but it was not serious. Gammin I had seen with his shirt off; apart from some angry bruises, he bore no wounds that I could see, not on the outside. To the others, for my shame, I had not given thought before this moment. They were all shaking their heads, so my oversight had not been harmful.

"Good. A dozen servants of the dark lay dead and you with not a wound. Would that we had an army of such warriors." He held his arms wide. "Let me welcome you all to Eldehrah, the sheltering place. I think you know it better as the Shambles."

The Shambles! Of course. It only made sense, now that I had time to consider. If we were outside the city and had only walked two hundred paces, we could hardly be anywhere else. What a fool I had been not to see it right off.

"You are safe here, or as safe as you can be." He turned and addressed me. "This will not last long, given what has happened between you and the Dryhm. You have set a spark to tender long prepared, Calen Farseer." His face showed an expectancy, as if he thought I might react to the name. I did react, inwardly. When I showed no sign, he was more direct. "Do I name you rightly?"

"You do."

Koppel went to a knee and bowed his head. "How may I serve you, lord?"

"Lord? Who? Me? I am no man's lord. Koppel, stand up, please."

"Aren't you a Justice of Ehrylan, lord?"

"I... am." I was caught off guard by this, having sailed away without ever serving as Justice. "Koppel, I desire no mastery. Justice serves the people. It is my place to serve."

"Truly spoken, lord. You will lead us until Prince Branden comes again."

"Lead you? You seem to be doing well enough without any help from me. As for Branden, he will not come again. I saw him dead on the deck of a ship some thirty five years ago."

"Sad news, though not wholly unexpected. I had hoped you were a herald sent to prepare the way. Yet, if he will not come, who should the people follow if not the prince's companion, whose word by decree of the last king is law in the land?"

I did not want to admit it, but he had a good point. I have never wanted mastery and am not a good leader. I am not patient enough. I cannot tolerate fools with grace. Rulers do much tolerating. I was searching for something to throw up in defense when Marn, as was his habit, came to my rescue.

Marn picked up the flagon and began to fill cups. "Leave off, Koppel. Let this rest until its time is come. I am hungry. If you will not sit and eat with us, get you gone until we are fed."

Koppel asked Lord Calen's leave to sit and eat with us. I gave him what I hoped would be my first and last command as Lord Calen, abjuring him to call me Annen which, as he and everyone else knew, was my name. This was all foolishness as far as I was concerned. It is useless to cling to the past when fighting a foe in the present.

The food was cheese, bread and a simple porridge of oats, raisins, and other things besides—things we ate at the breaking the night's fast. I had lost track of time. Night was speeding to morning. I discovered I was famished, so I set to with a will.

It is not the custom in Ehrylan to discuss matters of great import at the board. Our meal talk is usually concerned with good things, the small pleasures and victories that had occurred that day. However, we all had questions and answers to be shared out.

Lina spoke first, describing how she and Arica had been

confronted by a swarm of Dryhm while selling the children's wares near the south gate. They were surrounded before they knew what was happening. With so many Dryhm and the guard at the gate so close, there was little any of those nearby could do, if even there was a will for anything to be done. They were hustled through the gate, in the direction of the Step. Someone met them about half way; Arica said it might have been Demus, one of Pruis' gang.

As soon as the leader of the Dryhm had spoken with Demus, the boy ran off. The group of Dryhm and their captives turned and headed toward the Stone Gate. Just before entering the Stone Gate, the Dryhm stopped and conferred with another newcomer. That person also ran off immediately.

I asked, "What I want to know is how the rest of you came to the rescue at just the right time."

Gammin answered. "We saw what happened to Merelina and Arica from the Old Road. It was Marin who noticed first."

I was going to bid Marin speak. He started to talk before I could.

"It was all a coincidence. We were coming along to help you in your old house, remember? It all seems so long ago now. I saw the Dryhm pour out of the gate and turn into the Shambles. Even a single Dryhm entering there... here, I guess... is strange, but there must have been fifteen or twenty, more than I have ever seen in one place. Anyway, we were still a ways off. By the time we got close enough to see anything, they were going back into the city. We thought we would turn off and ask Arica what was going on. We found out she and Merelina were what was going on." He stopped. Gammin took up the narrative.

"We talked about what we should do. You know, whether we should go for help or split up with one following and the other going to get help. We knew the two of us wouldn't be much help against twenty Dryhm, so we decided I would follow them and Marin would go for help. He knew his father was in the Shambles, so he went to find him. I followed the ladies." He gave a quick look at Arica, who appeared pleased at being referred to as a lady rather than a girl.

"I stayed pretty far back once I figured out where they were going. There's not much worth going to on that part of the wall street, other than the Step. I came closer than I meant to when they stopped to talk with Demus. It was him, by the way. I would know him anywhere. I had to hide quick because they turned around and started coming back toward me.

"After they crossed the market street, I was sure they were headed up to the Stone Gate. That meant they were looking for you. Why else would they go to the Step and Stone Gate? I decided to go tell Marin, then head up there to help if I could." He concluded with a little nod of satisfaction, and started to point to the half-eaten round of cheese. Marin was already reaching to pass it, and after that, the bread.

The woodcutter spoke next.

"I was with Koppel at his stall, which is not as deep in the Shambles as we are now. It was lucky my boy came quickly. Koppel and I were just leaving to address the situation. Though Marin was swift, Koppel has eyes and ears everywhere within the Shambles. Not even the sun can shine here but he knows before the shadow is cast. Or so it is said."

"That is indeed said," interjected Koppel, "and it cost me much gold to put about that rumor. But know this. Before the Dryhm were taking their captives back into the city, we had heard of their coming. We were already acting when Marin came to us." Koppel turned to the woodcutter. "From what I have heard, Marn, your son has this day proved he is no longer a boy."

"Eh? What?" replied Marn, taken aback. "Oh, yes. I see. Well, a man he may be, and I will not argue, but he will still be my boy no matter how old he gets or how many Dryhm he sends into the darkness." His hand reached out and grasped his son's shoulder, shaking him with rough affection.

After banishing the twinkle from his eyes, Marn continued. "Koppel sent men into the city. You saw two, Annen; others went elsewhere in case Gammin had been wrong in his assumption."

"The Silanni?"

"Archers," corrected Marn.

I glanced sideways at the woodcutter, wondering what he was saying. Then I got it. He was not going to confirm or deny that the archers were Silent Assassins.

"Please thank them for me, Koppel. I have been in many tight spots but never has such help come to me so unlooked for and in such good time. We owe them our lives."

"Your gratitude is enough thanks, Lor…. eh… Annen."

"Much has been said of the magic of the Silanni. The tales do not exaggerate."

Koppel chuckled. He sipped hot canella from a little clay cup glazed with blue and brown. It must not have been sweet enough for him. He spooned honey into it and stirred before replying. Maybe he was thinking. "Many things are said of the Silanni." He sipped again, added, "Most of them are true."

Gammin, caught up in the excitement of the topic and the memory of having been so near the legendary creatures, contributed, "I heard they can walk on water and see through walls."

Koppel replied without hesitation, "I have heard that too. It is nearer the truth that they can see through water and walk on walls." He paused to let the table appreciate his wit, then gestured dismissively. "It is not permitted to speak of the Silanni more than is required. Return to your telling, Marn."

"I have not told much," grumbled the woodcutter. "We sent Marin to help if he could, or to come back and tell us if things changed. He had his sword with him. I knew he could use it. Koppel dispatched the men. I took up an axe and hurried after the boys. My haste was such that I gave little attention to passing unseen or unheard. It is well that the Dryhm left no rear guard, else my coming might have been delayed.

"The archers came there before me through the secret ways. They were watching for me. One of them saw me coming a block away and held up his hand to caution me. In time, he waved me up. I approached though he would not let me near him. He moved to another spot before I got to him. Where he left me was a good vantage point. I could see Marin and Gammin, who were also hidden, and behind them the other archer. I don't think the boys knew any of us were there."

"Too true," said Marin. "We were trying to figure out what we needed to do. We knew Arica could fight, and Annen, of course. We figured Merelina could take care of at least a couple of those Dryhm if she got the chance."

Lina's hand, which was resting upon mine, twitched. My eye turned her way and caught the back end of amusement as she chased it from her face.

Gammin took over the story with unspoken agreement from his friend.

"I had my knife and Marin his sword. We were trying to figure out what to do, which was hard considering we couldn't talk for fear they might hear us. The odds were bad, but we had the great equalizer, as shinando calls it. Surprise, I mean," he added the last as an explanation for Lina. "And we knew Marin's father was coming, or at least that he knew where we were.

"Pruis' father started talking about sacrificing on the stones. He was about to take you away. We had to do something."

"So Gammin just walks round the corner like he was strolling through River's Bend," said Marin. "That took me by surprise. The Dryhm, too. They just stopped and watched him come. I missed a lot of that part. With them looking in my direction, I had to pull back around the corner again. That's when I saw father and knew we were going to be all right."

I interrupted. "Wait. Are you saying Gammin marched unarmed up to a circle of Dryhm without knowing anyone was there to back him up?"

"Marin was there," replied Gammin. He used the familiar tone that always made me feel old and stupid, as if I had missed something so obvious even a blind man could see it. "And Arica and Merelina. And you, too, Annen."

I thought he was going to stop speaking, and he thought so

too. Then something occurred to him. "None of that mattered. I'd walk barefoot across the deserts of Yar to save you, Annen. Don't you know?" He held my eyes. I could not break the contact as joy collected in them and started to run down my cheeks. What is joy but happiness unfettered?

Marin started speaking. I was thankful for that. "When I looked at my father again, he was pointing. I saw someone, or almost saw him. I started looking for more, because I know they never work alone. I wasn't too surprised when the shadow down the lane moved a little. He came to me quick, holding up his hand to silence me. When Gammin captured the attention of everyone, the archer told me to stay put until the action started. He did not speak. He never said anything. He just used his hands and somehow I understood."

Marn, nodding in agreement, said, "The archers, there were two, only went close enough to get clear shots. Marin and I waited until after the first volley, then we rushed to help. I think they fired three times. The first two were over and done before we came up to them and the third flew over my shoulder. After that, it was blade and bough."

I watched Koppel inspecting each of my companions. When his eyes turned to me, they met mine. He toyed with his cup and said, "Quite a tale. I thank you. I have a part in this as well. I will speak.

"It was here in Eldehrah that these events began this morning and to Eldehrah you have returned. I do not say you have made an end today. This is but the first ripple in a wave that has been long awaited." Koppel rose from his chair and started to pace. His hands moved constantly as he spoke, belying restlessness he could scarcely contain.

"Some of what I tell you now I was going to say only to… Annen, but the rest of you have shown courage and loyalty in the face of death. Those deserve honesty in return, though you bought it at a great price. You have sown the seeds of destruction for the lives of every man and woman in Ehrylan." He stopped pacing and put the knuckles of his fists on the table, leaning on them to stare down at us.

"I do not say this is bad. I have been waiting for a day like today." He gathered himself. I recognized the look on his face.

"I am Zefram, son of Stam, of family Lemadon. I and my brothers fought with Brand the Just in the Battle of the Old Forest."

I cut in. "On the left flank! That's where the Old One's arrayed, on the rise beside the men from Mendolas. That was... Byrea's division. She fought under the river hawk's crest. Your people were valiant indeed! You did not break ranks even when Byrea was pushed back. Without your support, we would not have won the day."

"Aye, Calen Farseer, you were there too. You were a boy, not much older than yon young lady." He pointed at Arica with his chin. "I was not much older myself, truth be told. I never saw you, nor the prince either. The rumor of Brand's house, with Branden at the king's right hand and Colen at his left, put more enemies to flight than we killed there. Half of Dauroth's forces turned tail and ran that day." Koppel was beaming, the memories of bygone victories shining from his eyes.

"That may be what was said by some," I replied, "but I know the real story. The Old Ones saved the day. I can tell you this for sure. Colen, my father, was at the king's right hand. That was his place. The prince wasn't anywhere close to them. Branden and I were cutting our way to the right flank. It was a vain hope, but there seemed no other."

"I am sure this is all very nice," broke in Marn, his voice a pail of cold water on the embers of our remembrance. "If you ancient warriors will stop talking about your victorious past, we can get back to the war that is upon us."

That was quite a mouthful for Marn. I grinned at him, and he grinned back. Merelina had a glint in her eyes that I liked very much; it made me feel warm and not a little manly.

"As you say, Marn," said Koppel. "I have told you these things so that you will know, you who are not of the forest, that I have fought against Dauroth since the beginning. I will not stop until the end, his or mine. There are many and many among the Children who share my goals. That much you know. What you have not known until now is that there are men and women here in Eldehrah who are ready to fight and die for the cause of their freedom. We are not many, but we are who we are."

There was more talk. Heads began to sag. Battle makes one weary, and flying for your life even more so. The young ones were nodding in their chairs. We urged them to beds freshly laid in rooms close by. At first they would not go, but each eventually roused themselves to make a grumpy trip down the hall. This I have noticed. The young resist with great indignation when elders encourage them to bed. Yet, upon having to rouse themselves enough to stumble there later, they display resentment equal to or greater than before.

Arica went first. After that, Marin soon followed, taking Gammin with him. Merelina and I were not immune to weariness, but there were important matters that could not wait until dawn.

The garrison would retaliate for what I had done in the city. It was possible the folk of Twofords would be the victims, but we thought that unlikely. I, who was at the center of this storm, had removed myself to River's Bend. The village, we predicted, would bear the brunt. In this we were completely correct.

Koppel sent messages to his people. Marn sent Dara instructions to retreat into the forest and send any that would come to help. I sent, by trusted hand, two coded notes I composed on the spot. They contained among their few words a phrase I had never written before, a phrase that meant "War is upon us." The notes went to Aldryn and the butcher in Twofords, two men who had been, before Tower Mill, my seconds. They would mobilize the men in their commands—about thirty warriors each. They would also notify others in the Resistance, including the other principals.

After more than three decades of waiting, the Southland was girding for war.

III.

I awoke in the still of twinight to a tapping on the door. We had not been abed long, perhaps two or three hours. Merelina's arm was draped across my chest. It fair broke my heart to move it. When I did, she murmured, "What is it, love?"

"I will find out."

Climbing out of her warmth, I picked up the sword Koppel had given me and crossed to the door.

"Yes?"

"My Lord Calen. You are called to council. It has begun."

I never found out who said those words, but they began a day of great sadness. I dressed as quickly as I could, not waiting for Lina. She climbed out of bed as soon as she saw that I was not coming back to her. After kissing her brow, I turned to go.

"That will not do, husband."

"What?"

"You will have to do better."

I made no answer save the one she wanted, then left her to follow when she would.

I met them in the room where we had held council. Marn, Koppel, and two men I did not know were arrayed around the table. I took a seat.

Koppel spoke, catching me up. "The Dryhm are moving. My men say they are headed toward the south gate."

"What will you do?"

"Nay, lord. What is your will?"

I started to form a retort but thought better of it. This was no time to argue about who should command. What could be said to this man, who had been the leader of his efforts for decades and yet so willingly stepped aside for someone he deemed more worthy? I asked, "How many?"

One of the newcomers, a man dressed in black, answered. "We count twelve."

"Twelve. How many do you have, Koppel, ready to fight and near enough to help?"

"We are twenty-three, ten men, five women, and eight youth who can hold their own. I do not count you or those in your party. With myself and Captain Sheal, we are twenty-five total. The call has been sent. They assemble as we speak."

"Excellent." I did not ask him of the Silanni. I knew they did not fight in open battle. Their way was to strike unseen and get away unseen.

I addressed the man in black. "How long do we have before the Dryhm come to the gate?"

"We must move soon. Fortunately, they may be delayed. The gate will be difficult to open. That will give us a little more time."

The grove was on the west slope of Castle Hill, in the northern section of the city. In better days, the wooded vale had been a park accessible to all folk. The Dryhm had taken it for their own. For the Ehrylain, to enter it was punishable by death.

The Dryhm would not move quickly. They were, as I have mentioned more than once, partial to showmanship. Maintaining their dignity was important to them, part of the image they sought to project. Rushing, no matter the reason, was not part of that image. It would be a steady, mournful march that brought them to the gate, not the fast dash that would better serve their purpose. My guess was that they were intending to strike River's Bend just before dawn, maybe two hours hence.

"Best not to meet them at the gate," I said. "That's too close to their reinforcements and there are too many eyes to see where we come from. We need to get ahead of them, somewhere up the Old Road. Can we do that without being seen?"

"If we start now."

"Good. We'll try to get to a place beyond sight and hearing of the city walls, yet not so far as the Bend Road. There is a place where an old stone wall…"

"I know it." Koppel cut me off. "It is a good place for an ambush. We have planned to use it in such a time as this."

Without realizing it, I was falling into the behaviors I had observed Prince Branden and other commanders use in times such as these. I accepted Koppel's words without reply and turned to the man in black. "Your name?"

"Lothel, lord."

"Lothel. I am Annen, not lord. You said twelve?"

"Yes... Annen. We counted twelve. There may be more by the time they come to the gate."

"Koppel, would you know if others joined them?"

"I would be told. Such a message may be on its way now, but twelve is the number as we sit here."

I nodded again. "I don't want to leave our base unguarded."

Koppel agreed. I searched for sign of relief in his face and did not find it.

"So twelve Dryhm. Let's estimate half again. Not because I doubt your estimate, Lothel. You understand? That makes eighteen. You have archers, Koppel?"

"Yes. Five."

"Fine. We will reduce them by five before they can respond. Let's make that three. That leaves fifteen. The archers will get a second shot, I think, so take two more, being conservative. That leaves thirteen. Hmmm. If we took eighteen, that would make us even at the high estimate and put us five up by the time they can fight back. That leaves near half your twenty five to stay and prepare the next wave. Do I have that right?"

"Yes, Annen," replied Koppel, thinking. That was good. I needed him to think.

"I'd not council you on how to use your own men, but will you leave Sheal here? A good commander in the rear can be worth two in the front, especially if things go ill with us, or if more enemy come from the city."

"I had thought to have him with us, but what you say is true. He shall stay." Koppel paused, frowned. "He shall stay and make ready. This is but the first stone in a landslide."

"Right. So... what? We should not all move together, nor at

the same time. Teams of six? That should work. Distribute the archers in each team, except mine. Marin and Gammin can both shoot. They will be with me. Do you have bows for them? Yes? Good. See to it. That will make the odds even better for us."

They were all thinking now.

"Spread the teams along the wall, out of sight. Wait for my signal to shoot. If it goes the way I intend, I'll be talking to them, the Dryhm. I will pull my sword and yell. That's the signal. Two volleys, quick as you can, then charge. Let the two teams nearest charge first, the third team to follow where they're needed. If I go down, Koppel, you have command."

I looked around the table at each of them. When my gaze came across the second man I did not know, I said, "My apologies, sir. Please forgive my discourtesy. I am Annen."

"No offense taken. Urgent matters spawn urgent talk, or so my father told me. I am Sheal."

"Ah, the captain. Good. Do what you can to prepare Eldehrah. This sun will see great things begun, but our lives will get far worse before it gets any better. There is still the garrison to deal with. That's about three hundred twenty swords and forty cavalry. Hopefully, we will not see them today. If you get word that troops are on the move, send a message."

"Yes, lord."

I turned to Koppel. "That's about the best we can do in so short a time." So short a time? We'd had thirty years. "Remember, plans are just dreams that break in the wake of battle. Go and do as you will. I will follow, but first I must have a care for my wife."

"I thank you, lord. You bring us hope."

I pushed back from the table and stood up, the others doing the same. I was buckling on the sword when a movement made me look to the door. Gammin and Marin were there.

Marin asked, "Leaving without us, father?" His voice was equal parts question and accusation.

"You shall fight at my side, Marin, the son who is become also a man."

Gammin demanded, "And me?"

"That is not for me to say."

What Gammin and Marin had done yesterday was amazing. This morning would be different, the odds better but the field more crowded. Though no battle is a small thing, this looked to be a small battle that would school those who had not fought such an engagement before.

"Our army would be the stronger for your arm, Gammin of River's Bend. I would be glad of your company. Will you fight by my side?"

His face turned from distress to joy in an instant. "There is one condition," he said.

All motion in the room stopped. You could have heard a fly fart.

"What?" I was amazed at the temerity.

"I will wear shoes."

I looked down at his feet. They were clad in the boots he had worn yesterday. The boots were caked in blood, but appeared functional to me. Bewildered, I glanced at Marin for help. He was snickering. That connected it for me; I saw the reference to what Gammin had said earlier about going barefoot to save me. I rolled my eyes, imitating him, and walked out of the room.

I saw Arica as soon as I crossed into the hallway. The look on her face told me she needed to talk. Knowing there was no time, I took Gammin by the elbow. "Go with them. They may start leaving without me. Make sure someone stays behind to guide us. It is you, me, Marn, and Marin in our team, and two men whom Koppel will provide. Six in all. Make sure they give you and Marin bows. You need a sword. Come back, or send someone to show me the way. I won't be long. I have to talk with Merelina and Arica."

He hurried to catch up with the rest. I turned my attention to Arica.

"Lady."

"Sir," she replied, doing me a courtesy and continuing the game. Then she reverted into one of my students. "What is going on, shinando?"

"War. The first battle. Maybe the second, depending on how you count. The Dryhm are headed toward River's Bend. We go to meet them."

"May I go with you?"

"That is your decision, or perhaps your father's. I will not stop you. You are valiant and skilled. We could use you. But there is a greater service you could do that would ease my heart. I would not leave Merelina here alone. Will you stay with her?"

Arica showed surprise and a little relief. "I will do as you ask, Annen. But I am not afraid. Well, maybe I am."

"It is no shame, lady. No one doubts your bravery, least of all me. You will show your courage again many times ere we come to victory."

I needed to press on, but I could see she had more to say. "Yes, Arica? Speak to me."

"I just want to… to thank you, Lord Calen, for all you have done for me and the others."

I replied with what was quickly becoming my standard litany. She said the same words, at the same time, a kind-hearted mocking. "My name is Annen."

She went on. "You will always be Annen to us. And more. Sometimes, though, one must be more formal to show what is in one's heart. Yes?" The last word was spoken as a bald-faced imitation of me.

I was going to stoop and kiss her on the forehead when she stood up on her toes and kissed my cheek. After a firm hug, she started to go.

I called to her. "Do something for me?"

"Anything, shinando."

"After I am gone, see if you can find some lavender, or maybe a rose. Take it to Merelina. Tell her I love her."

Time was so short. Every moment I delayed might cost a life. Yet I had another task that could not be ignored. I found

Merelina sitting on the bed, hands in her lap, waiting. She was fully dressed and ready to go, the knife at her belt. The lamplight caught it just right so that the polished jewel in the hilt sparkled like a star.

I gathered her into my arms. She was trembling.

"Never fear, Lina. All will be well."

"We are going?"

"I am going."

She started to push away from me. I held her. "Please don't. I like the feel of you in my arms."

She relaxed back into me. I tangled one of my hands in her hair, something that was becoming a comforting habit. She pressed her cheek even more firmly against my chest.

"What of the boys and Arica? Will you take them?"

"I will not take Arica, though I cannot stop her from coming with me any more than I can stop you. Marin walks beside Marn, and I will have Gammin. Arica stays here with you, if you will stay."

"I will do as you bid me, love."

As we breathed the same air, I felt her heart beating. She said, "I am afraid. Not for me, at least, not on the surface. I am afraid for you, afraid you might not come back." Her fingers dug into my back. I could feel her fighting tears. I thought they were tears of frustration rather than fear, but I am no judge of women. "The last husband I sent to war never came back."

"It is just the same with me, Lina. I fear for you, wherever you are, wondering if you are safe."

"I do not know what you would have me do, what my place is. Am I to wait here so I can mend your garments and tend your wounds when you return, if you return? Is that what you need me for?"

That last statement gave me the key. I knew Merelina was fully aware of why I needed her. It had nothing to do with mending my clothing.

"No, Lina. I've mended my own clothes for years now. Besides, I sew better than you. I was taught by sailors, remember?"

Indignation splashed her face and vanished just as quickly when she realized what I was attempting. I continued before she could form a retort. "I need you because you are part of me. You balance out the horror of the rest of my life. Just that. You make it all worth it. Without you, I am alone, no matter how many are with me. That is why I need you."

"What can I do?"

There it was! Merelina needed a mission.

"Take care of Arica. She will need your strength. Also, others will need support. You have a special way with children; it will serve. Ea did not bring you here to sit and wait. Help them if you can, especially in preparing for the days to come. War is upon us, Lina. Everything is going to change. Learn what you can of these people. I don't know enough. Go among them where you can, and just… be you. That will be more than enough. It has always been enough."

Her head came up. I saw the smile I needed. I carried it with me into the fear and into the darkness.

Gammin was waiting for me. I put my hands on his shoulders and looked into his eyes. I saw no fear there, which was good, and yet no eagerness either. That was better. I tousled his hair, thinking I would not be able to get away with that much longer. There were so many things I wanted to tell him that I found myself unable to speak. He seemed to understand.

"Come on," he said. "You are late."

He led me out of the house and through the maze of narrow cart paths to the outskirts of the Shambles. There, in a small barn, the teams had been organized and briefed. The first, led by Koppel, had already departed. The second was just leaving as we arrived.

I greeted the two members of my team that I did not yet know, a boy about the same age as Gammin and a man of slight build who looked like he was more used to selling shoes than fighting. I tried not to allow his appearance to rush me to an unfair opinion. The boy was working with Marin, adjusting a quiver. Marin had a bow limbered across his back. It was nearly as tall as he was. He handed its twin to Gammin as soon as we entered. I had trained them to the long bows of the Old Ones as well as the shorter bows used by the Ehrylain. They would be effective with either.

I did what I had seen my father and Branden do, moving among the members of my team. I talked with each of them, making sure the mission was clear, showing resolute confidence. I asked Marn and the other man if they had any advice or knew of anything that was worth sharing. With the younger ones, I made a show of inspecting their weapons and making sure they hung in the right places, something one should always do before going into combat.

I explained the plan. When the Dryhm came to the place of ambush, I wanted us to be in the road, waiting. Bait. It was the four of us for whom they were looking. If we were lucky, they would mistake the man and the boy for Lina and Arica. Our main goal was to keep the Dryhms' attention away from the wall.

17. THE BATTLE OF THE BEND

I.

We arrived in time, but only just. Koppel had posted a rear guard, so we did not surprise the company as we approached. I stationed my team. The moon was gone. It was the dark before first light. There was no sign of the men waiting in ambush.

In their arrogance, the Dryhm made things easy for us. We could see them from half a mile away, marching as they did with lit torches. I believe they had yet to grasp the magnitude of our determination, thinking still that we were but a handful of misbehaving villagers. We just needed to be disciplined as a lesson for others to see. It did not occur to me how foolish it would have been for them to send a single dozen against the same party that had, just the day before, beaten eighteen or twenty.

The enemy saw my team, as we intended, before the light of their torches touched the first tumbled stone from the broken wall. Their overconfidence drew them on. They stopped ten or so paces in front of me. I had intended to let them speak first, but I felt very vulnerable. It is a condition that loosens my tongue almost every time.

"Do you come for me, servants of the Faceless? I am here." I tried to count them. There were more than twelve.

"We come," said a voice from the midst of the pack. Those between us parted to let him through. "We see you. We know your crime. You and all your kind will die."

"That is true, Dryhm. We all will die."

He processed this. I think he was surprised by my agreement. "You come to surrender?"

"Surrender? Hardly. I come to offer you your lives. Return to your grove and trouble me no longer. If you do that, foul slave of the darkness, you may live to see the light of day."

A movement that might have been laughter spread through the pack. "It is you who are about to die." He raised his voice. "Beg for a swift death, and I may yet give it."

I set my hand on the sword. "I have given you your chance." I yanked the blade free and cried, "Now comes death!"

The Dryhm surged toward me. My heart hammered as I waited for the arrows. Why didn't they shoot? At last I heard the sound. Five arrows hissed through the air closely followed by the two Gammin and Marin loosed. Dryhm began to fall. Others charged. I stepped to meet them. The second volley dropped more of them, but I could not see the effect. I was fighting.

So short was this conflict that the familiar musical rhythm of battle could not form in my head. I finished my first opponent, who was a skilled fighter, and turned to find another. It was a tough search. We had overwhelmed them. The man in my team was hacking at an opponent who had his back to me. I stuck my sword into that back at the same time Marn chopped into him with his axe. I could not see any Dryhm standing.

After the moment where we all looked around to see who was hurt and who was standing, the celebrations and congratulations started. Several men slapped me on the back. I could tell the more experienced in the group. They were inspecting the downed opponents, looking for survivors. Of these, four were found; all of them had been felled by arrows. They were all beyond saving. We sent them into eternity.

I counted the dead. There were fifteen. None of us were injured. I was just beginning to relax when I heard someone from beyond the wall. Heads turned. A man hurried out of the darkness from the direction of the Shambles.

"Koppel! I have news." From the look on his face, we knew it wasn't good news.

"What is it, Delnen? What has happened?"

Delnen pointed in the direction of Twofords. Cold silence washed over the elated men and boys as they saw the glow of torches.

"How many, Delnen?"

"At least fifty soldiers from the garrison. Cavalry, too. Six horsemen."

There was a murmur of dismay.

"Eldehrah?" I asked, "Did they attack Eldehrah?"

"No. They did not stop."

"That is good," said Koppel. He turned to me. "It is still dark enough. We could get away."

"We might, but what of River's Bend? The soldiers will go there after they see this."

Koppel winced. "It is as you say." He thought for a moment. "We could meet them here, or maybe ambush them somewhere else along the road."

It would be folly to face so many with so few in open combat. Much better to strike quickly and withdraw into cover, drawing them into another ambush. If we did that, we might be able to cut their number in half, which would make the forces almost even.

There were two obvious locations that provided cover, each about the same distance from our current position, the Old Forest and the Bendwood. If we retreated south to the forest and the soldiers continued west to River's Bend, we would not be able to help.

"We'll make a stand in the Bendwood. We can set up a two

stage ambush there, but we'll need some time. Are you with me?"

"Aye, lord." Koppel began to give directions to the team leaders, men I had not even met. There was nothing I could do about that now.

I told my team what I was thinking and asked them to make ready. Pointing to the other archers, each of whom was moving among the inert bodies, Gammin asked, "What are they doing?"

"Fetching their arrows. You should do the same." His face went blank for a heartbeat. He steeled himself and, grabbing Marin's arm, went to do as I had directed.

We had to move fast. Unlike the servants of the Faceless, the men of the garrison marched briskly. Fortunately, one of our men had thought to extinguish the torches dropped by the Dryhm; it was possible we were as yet undetected. Koppel sent a message back to Eldehrah.

By the time the sun was fully above the horizon, we were under the shelter of the trees. Koppel left a scout to watch the approaches to the wood. I sent a messenger on to River's Bend with instructions. I had no authority over them anymore, but Aldryn—who would be in command there—would see the sense in our plan.

We arrayed Koppel's men half on each side of the Bend Road. I would like to have been deeper within the wood, but I did not want to give away access to the spring. I felt sure the soldiers would take this opportunity to deface it. The spring was only a symbol, but men have died for symbols time out of mind.

The plan was to shoot into the oncoming troops from within the cover of the trees along the road. The first targets would be the leaders, if they were apparent, and the mounted troops. If the enemy responded as I hoped, some of them would charge into the woods in pursuit of their harassers. At that point, our archers would fall back to predetermined locations, leading the soldiers into a trap where they would be waylaid by the rest of our men. In the event the soldiers came in pursuit with too many men, our men would fall back toward River's Bend where, hopefully, thirty freedom fighters waited. On the other hand, if the soldiers failed to pursue, the archers would shoot until they ran out of arrows and call the rest of us forward to make an attack on our attackers.

The plan put Marin and Gammin at the front of the action, something about which I was not pleased. I could think of no reason, other than my love for them, to remove them from that duty. Doing so would only damage our slim chance of success. I swallowed my concern and went about making preparations, wondering if my father felt such things about me when I was newly come to war. If so, he never showed it.

We heard the alert from our forward scout. The soldiers were approaching the forest. The scout joined Koppel's forces across the road, just as the messenger I had sent to River's Bend had come back to me. Weak as we were, we were at full strength.

The enemy captain sent a mounted patrol along the road. We let them pass, knowing they would not return if they went all the way through. There was a long wait; we never saw that patrol again. The commander must have grown weary of delay. His company appeared in the wood. This was utter foolishness. Who sends a whole force to investigate missing scouts? Perhaps I am being too harsh. The Twofords garrison had not encountered armed and organized opposition since before most of them had been born. Many of the soldiers in the garrison had never lifted a weapon in defense of their lives. But, oh, how that was about to change.

I saw almost none of what I just described. I waited in hiding with the rest of my men. My first experience in this battle was the cry of soldiers struck with arrows and the curses of their companions. Next came Gammin, Marin, and the other archer in our group. They were moving very quickly, as can be imagined. From the sound, there might be as many as a dozen men chasing them. Either that, or a herd of crazed elk. We were in for a fight.

Gammin came out of the trees and around the edge of the

small hillock behind which I was crouched. He saw me and stopped dead in his tracks. I nodded. My hand dropped to my sword. He grasped his own hilt. For the first time, I drew steel in battle with Gammin of River's Bend.

Three soldiers blundered past, then three more. The men behind us would deal with them. I stepped out from behind the hillock and saw four shapes converging on me.

I raised my sword to meet the first attacker. He moved straight to his attack. I blocked that one and then an attack from one of the other soldiers who had taken a place to my right. That left me open to the next stroke from the first soldier. There was nothing I could do about it. As I cut downward toward the second man's middle, I heard a cry to my right. The first soldier dropped his sword, double over. I saw the end of Gammin's blade. It was red.

Now there were three in front of me, all with swords at the ready. There was nothing I could do but die if I stayed where I was. I stepped back, hoping I would not trip over Gammin. That did not happen. Instead, he darted into the bad spot I had vacated and took a ready position. He was now in my way and I could not use my sword to help him.

One of the soldiers lifted his weapon. The other two waited to see how Gammin would respond, ready to kill him when he did. Gammin began to parry the blow. In desperation, I grabbed the collar of his tunic and pulled him back as hard as I could. He tumbled off his feet somewhere behind me. A soldier's stoke split the air where he had been standing.

I whirled, cutting at the corner of the line. That man parried my first blow and died as he raised his weapon for the counter attack. I was dragging my sword out of him when one of the two remaining soldiers attacked me.

I skipped back, came up hard against a tree. I no longer had my sword. It must not have come free. The soldier advanced and, raising his sword high above his head, started a descending strike that might have split me in half had it landed. I jumped toward him, under his attack, and caught his wrists against one of my forearms. He bore down on me, growling in rage, and we were locked for a moment. I reached to my waist and pulled my knife free, slicing him from navel to ribs. Feeling the warmth splash over my hand, I was filled with a vicious hate that I felt from the tips of the toes to the roots of my hair. As he dropped his sword and fell to the carpet of leaves, I was gazing down at memories kept fresh in my nightmares, seeing the first man I had ever killed with a knife. For an instant, I was back in the forest of my youth, fighting a party of invaders come to lay the foundations of evil.

I came back to myself in the same instant. Gammin was fighting the last soldier, who was larger and seemingly more experienced than he was. Gammin was on the defensive, retreating at almost every strike. Behind him was a knot of men locked in fierce combat. A single soldier broke from their midst. He headed directly for Gammin. Forgetting the blade at my feet, which belonged to the man I just gutted, I rushed to retrieve my sword. If the oncoming soldier had intended to face Gammin, I would have been too late to help. However, the soldier passed the boy without a glance. He was rushing to meet me.

My sword was underneath the man it had killed. He had turned face down in the throes of his death struggle. I rolled the body over to get to my weapon. The hilt was wet with blood and other liquids that have bad names and worse smells.

The oncoming soldier attacked me savagely. His first strike was a two-handed hack that knocked the sword ringing from my hand. I jumped back to avoid the second strike and dove forward under the third. I rolled to where I thought my sword might be and groped for it. My hand came up empty. Jumping up, I faced him. I circled away from the weapon that hovered between us.

The soldier jabbed at me twice. I jumped back twice, desperately trying to get to the spot I thought my sword had fallen. At last I saw it, nestled deep in the tangled branches at the base of some overgrowth. I made a fake in the opposite direction and threw myself at the bush. He was on me before I had a chance to extract the weapon. I had to take my eyes off it to watch his approach. I kept groping for the sword as I looked at his face. At the last instant, my hand found the hilt. I lifted it to deflect the oncoming strike. It was not a good block; the impact jarred my arm, wrist to elbow. But his blade did not cut me.

I was forced to fight from the ground, defending myself against a rain of blows that left no chance for me to form an attack. The soldier lifted his sword high for a downward cut. I saw the point of a blade erupt from his chest. His back arched, and he fell to his knees in front of me. I sliced at his neck and twisted away from what I knew would follow. Rolling to my feet, I saw Gammin pulling his sword free. He appraised my state before turning to the fight behind us. Without waiting for me, he hurried in that direction.

Keep moving. Move fast, breathe slowly.

I wiped the hilt of my sword clean. It was a common weapon. The hilt was not expertly made. The grip consisted of leather on wood, which becomes slick when wet. The pommel was almost non-existent. It was the kind of weapon one hopes one's opponents are using. If I had my own blade, none of this would have happened. I know these are only excuses.

The fight was over by the time I arrived. We took a quick accounting. There were ten dead soldiers. We had lost a single man. My original five were safe and sound. The boy had a cut on his arm, something Marn was seeing to. The man that had looked like a seller of shoes now looked like a warrior. He had acquitted himself well. Marin was unscathed, at least physically. His customary smile was nowhere to be seen.

Telling the others to wait, I made my way back to the Bend Road. I saw several bodies, each with an arrow protruding from them. Koppel was waiting for me. He also lost but a single man. He told me the other soldiers, now numbering some thirty, had marched down the road toward the village. There was no sign of horsemen. We agreed to follow them with the intent of falling upon their rear. Deciding to meet back at the spring, we parted.

II.

By the time we met at the spring, Koppel and I had reports of the action at River's Bend. The soldiers of the garrison were heavily engaged with the men, women, and boys from the village.

I reminded everyone to check their weapons, then led them down the road at a lope. One of the younger men volunteered to move in front of us in case there was a trap. We came unmolested to the place where the Bend Road let on to the village green. It was chaos. The ring of metal on metal punctuated the shouts and screams that filled the air.

We paused long enough to suck in a few quick breaths. I pointed our men to several places where the field seemed to be falling into the wrong hands. Looking at Gammin, I said, "Are you with me, Gammin?"

He drew his sword and shook it in the air, crying, "I am with you!"

I raised my voice so the others in our company could hear me and said, somewhat unpoetically, "Run screaming into battle!"

I did so myself.

Directly in front of where the road emerged from the wood there was a group of soldiers. One of them looked like he might be the leader. I led Gammin and whoever might be following toward them. There was a brief, bloody action. I killed one man and wounded another. Then I came face to face with the man I had thought was the leader.

He was dressed in black. Around his neck was a silver torc, the ends of which were wolf heads with gemmed eyes. On his forearms were silver guards that glistened in the morning sun. His hair was black, as were his trimmed mustache and beard. He looked at me in a way that made me feel like a slave at auction.

Apart from being well dressed and handsome, he was a very good swordsman. He might have beaten me two times out of five, but today was not one of those times. Our contest lasted what seemed like a long time. I was lucky my companions kept my back free of other assailants. By the time he fell to me, I was exhausted and dripping with sweat.

I sucked air in great gulps and turned to see where I was needed. As it turned out, the battle, or that phase of it, was mostly over. The tide had turned when the men from Eldehrah fell unexpectedly upon the backs of their enemies.

The field had turned from chaos to carnage. Fallen soldiers and villagers were everywhere. Groans of pain and screams of anguish rose like an uncomfortable fog.

In my weariness, I had not even thought of Gammin when I heard him call my name.

"Annen! Are you well?" He ran up to me, jumping over bodies along the way. I made a mental note to tell him that was risky.

"I am. Good to see you. You're fine? Yes?"

"Yes, shinando. Marin and Marn are also fine. The man that was with us is still alive, too, though he is wounded. The boy, I think he is dead, or no, wait." He pointed. "There he is. He is up and walking, at least."

I nodded, still breathing hard.

Gammin said, "You are leaning on your sword, shinando," referring back to the admonitions I had given my students countless times about not leaning on their swords.

"So I am," I said, and went right on leaning.

Gammin looked down at the leader.

"I know him, Annen. He was the man that led the training. You remember, I told you I used to watch the soldiers practice? He was the teacher."

"I remember, Gammin. It makes sense. He was a good fighter." I looked around the field. "In fact, everyone I crossed swords with today had some skill. He must have been a good teacher."

"Maybe," offered Gammin. "He was their teacher, but he was never their shinando."

Koppel walked up. "Victory, Annen. You have led us to victory. The men are saying you are a hero."

"That is foolishness," I said. They did not know that what had happened—all of this—was my fault. A man is not a hero for helping rescue his fellows from the danger in which he has embroiled them. "I am no hero, Koppel. You know that. You were with me the whole way. If anyone is the hero, it is you. You were ready when we needed you."

He looked at me quizzically and shook his head. Someone called to him. He excused himself, touching my shoulder. I had known the man less than half a day, and, already, he felt like an old friend.

We picked our way across what had been the village green, weaving through the bodies, stopping here and there to help a wounded villager. Twice I dispatched a badly wounded soldier. I was heading toward Marn when Gammin spoke.

"Annen. I would talk with you."

This being an odd statement for him, I stopped and gave him all my attention.

"Yes, of course."

"This fighting, the fact that I have… killed a man… more than one man. Does that mean I am a man?"

Suddenly, as if a trap door had opened above me, I felt the emotional weight of all that had happened to the boys, as well as Arica and Merelina. I lifted my right hand—my sword hand—and placed it on his shoulder.

"No, Gammin, not at all." I forged ahead through the disappointment that contorted his face. "Manhood is not in the killing. Manhood is in how you deal with the killing, how you face it and how you react to it after. These are in your head and your heart, not in your hand. Understand?"

"I think so." He did not look convinced. Who could blame him?

"Gammin, you were a man long before this. You are still young and have much to learn, but you've been acting like a man the whole time I have known you."

"Is that true?"

"Yes, lad, it is true."

Mischief crept into his eye. "Then why do you still call me

lad? And sometimes boy?"

In spite of myself, I laughed. It was a single exhalation and not very loud.

"You know why."

"Sometimes it feels good to hear what we think we know."

"It is because I do not have a son of my own, but if I did, I would want him to be you. It is because I am so very proud of you. Most of all, it is because I want you to know and remember those things all the days of your life. It is because I love you."

He nodded and started walking toward Marn, who had just appeared a few paces away. I felt emptied, hollow, as if someone had knocked the wind out of me. There was no time to deliberate on what had just happened. Marn took a place in front of me, hands on his hips. He greeted me. It was not until he greeted Gammin and was asking after his welfare that I noticed the four figures accompanying him. They were Marin, Simon, Max, and Breanna.

First things first. "Hail, Marin. You are well?"

"Passable, shinando. I've come to no great harm. And you?"

"I'll make it. One thing, though. I want to get my own sword."

"You can have mine!" Max held up a sword that was three sizes too large for him. Breanna was holding out its twin with noticeable difficulty. Her eyes were blazing.

"I thank you, Max." I went to a knee so I could look him in the eye, or more nearly so. Actually, this put me below the level of his eyes, but it was better than talking down to him. As soon as I lowered myself, Breanna came close and leaned against me. I put an arm around her. "Where did you get those?"

Aldryn answered as he came up to us with quick steps. "I ordered the villagers—the ones who could not fight—to take refuge in the forest across the river." He eyed Max. "These three came back. When they saw we needed help, they came running and picked up swords from the fallen. That's the story I got." He armed sweat from his brow. "Are you well, Annen?"

"I am. A moment, Aldryn." I looked at Max and Breanna. "You fought?"

Max stuck his chest out and exclaimed, "Yes we did!" Breanna dropped her eyes and put her head down after a short nod.

"With those swords?"

"Oh, no, shinando. We picked these up after. We'll use them next time." He grinned. "We used some branches from the forest. Simon cut staffs for us with his knife. I didn't kill anyone. Did you, Bre?" The little girl shook her head, still eyeing her feet. "I tripped up some of the bad guys, and someone else killed 'em. I would have fought better if I had a real staff or a sword. Next time!" Breanna nodded.

Ea! What had I done to these sweet children? "You two, I am very proud of your bravery. Do you understand?"

Max answered, "Yes, shinando!"

"I am not happy you disobeyed Aldryn's orders." I tried to glare at them with my sternest look. It was no use. I scooped Breanna into my arms and kissed her cheek. Releasing her, I grasped Max by the shoulders and gave him a warrior's shake.

I stood up. "Simon. I am glad to see you. How did you fare?"

He dismissed my question and proceeded to the explanation. That was his way—no wasted words. "Aldryn told Eanna to take us into the forest. We went with her. That was last night. We started talking. Max said we were trained and should fight. He said Aldryn had ordered those who couldn't fight into the forest. We could fight. We wanted to help. It sounded like the right thing to do. Some of the other villagers wanted to help too. So we came back. Like Max said, I made a few staves. We watched for a while, trying to get the courage. Well, I was trying. I had to hold Max back. When we came to the battle, I picked up a sword from one of the fallen soldiers. And I used it."

He gripped the hilt of the sword at his waist. I had not noticed it. Simon was older and bigger than Marin and Gammin. If they could fight, there was no reason he couldn't.

"Are you all right?" He knew what I meant.

"I am."

Something occurred to me. "Simon, were you watching when the soldiers came out of the wood?

"Yes, shinando."

"How many were there?" I knew he could no more resist counting something than I could resist kissing Merelina.

"Thirty two."

"Excellent! We thank you, warrior. I am glad you are with us." He smiled, something that was unusual. He was a solemn young man and not given to strong emotions.

I turned to Aldryn, gripping his forearm. "I thank you for waiting, friend. Nice work. You got my message?"

"Yes. We were ready, or more ready than we would have been."

"Your people fought well. It must have been nearly equal, and they were against trained soldiers. You must congratulate them."

"They would like to hear that from your lips, Annen."

I ignored the veiled request and ran my eyes over the chaos that had replaced the village green.

"There is a lot to be done. You have men watching the approaches? Good." I grabbed Marn's shoulder, continuing to run from any speech I might have to make. "Let's find Koppel. We have plans to make. There is work to be done. I do not think we have much time."

Koppel was gathering his men, seeing to the wounded. Of the original fourteen, two died in the Bendwood and three more on the village green. Aldryn did not fare as well, loosing twelve of his thirty and about half of the villagers that had returned with Simon. Many of the survivors were wounded so badly they would not be able to fight again if the need came today. I thought it might. I was in a mind of the horsemen. My concern was that they had ridden back with the news and that more troops were on the way.

Prisoners were treated for wounds and bound humanely. Aldryn secured them in a stable and left it under guard. The fallen from the River's Bend and Eldehrah were gathered into the forest. After we were done counting the human cost of this first course, I told Koppel and Aldryn that those who could no longer fight should be taken across the river. No one argued with me. That was a good start. They understood.

There is worse to come, much worse. The garrison could not sit back and ignore what we had done today. But that is only where the worse started. Dauroth would not ignore our temerity. He would send armies against us, real armies. It had taken all we had to defend against a fraction of the garrison.

Someone asked, "What can we do against so many?"

"You won't like my council. We cannot win here against a the rest of the garrison." I let that sink in. "We should not meet them in open battle. Our victory can only be measured in how much we reduce the enemy's strength and how few we lose in the process."

They were nodding agreement, though hesitantly. I could not blame them. Let's try to lose slowly is not a good strategy.

"We must abandon River's Bend."

I prayed they could see the sense in living to fight another day.

Aldryn said, "That is my thinking also. It will be a sore thing to lose the village. Yet it is better to lose our buildings than our families."

Koppel nodded. "A village is people, not structures. Buildings can be rebuilt if the people survive."

Aldryn opened his mouth to say something, but at that moment a horseman emerged from the Bendwood.

"Koppel! News from the city."

"What is it?"

"The garrison is on the move, headed this way. At least a hundred strong, with cavalry."

I do not often curse, but I did then. Ea forgive my errant tongue.

"Where were they when you left?"

"Filing from the gates."

I interjected, "Any news of rebellion within the walls?"

"No." The horseman replied with a curious look. He could have no notion of what had long been planned.

I was a little curious myself. If my message got through—or the backup messages Aldryn sent as part of the protocol—we should be hearing reports of a significant conflict. More than one hundred loyalists should have been executing plans that had been waiting for years. I told myself that Torlan, the principal who had taken my place, must be waiting for the garrison to leave the city. That must be it. Or must it? Hope and doubt contested in my heart. I pushed them aside, turned my thoughts to where they needed to be.

In Dauroth's armies, squads of eight were the unit of choice, with cavalry equivalent to one horse per squad. One hundred foot soldiers meant about twelve horsemen. If Branden led that force to attack a village, he would cover every approach. Since there were three routes into River's Bend, there would be three companies of thirty to forty foot soldiers, one to each approach. Any one of those individual companies would be larger than our whole force. Things were going to be tough.

"The garrison will send scouts on horseback, armed and ready to fight. Post archers in the wood and between the water and the trees. No scout survives. That is important."

Bend Road was the main route into the village, through the center of the Bendwood. The way lay open to a determined traveler on either side of the wood, someone who, for his own reasons, desired to come to the village by paths less trodden. On the north and south sides, the Bendwood was bordered by the Silver River. Between the water and the trees, as the villagers say, ran swathes of low, rocky dunes that were difficult to traverse, but by no means impassible. The folk of the Bend knew the best vantages and easiest paths; it was unlikely any from the garrison had given much attention to those areas.

"And after that, Annen?"

"If I am right, they will send men through each approach. We might defend one with the force we have. But for what?

The other two would flank us and cut us to pieces. I think we concentrate on the south approach between the water and the trees. We kill as many of the soldiers as we can, then will fall back to the docks and over the river from there. Do you have boats?"

"Enough for thirty men and their gear.

There was more to contemplate, more than I could hope to address. We needed someone like Prince Branden who was a master of strategy. He would have found some bold move that cost the enemy twice what I could contrive and cut the price we paid in half. But the prince was not here. Only Annen was here. Still, I had a sword, and I was not yet finished spilling blood. That made me think about the weapon at my hip and something else besides.

"Marn, is Dara safe?"

"She is well, friend Calen. She is in the forest. Will send for her or fetch her myself when it is time. Spare no thought for her."

"Calen? Why do you call me so? My name is Annen, which you know full well."

Marn looked at me with a toothy grin. "It is not Annen who stands now before me. I see Calen, of whom many tales tell, a great warrior sent by the Maker to lead us into the deliverance for which long we have prayed."

This was too much. I wanted to scream at him, but there was no time. "Where is Gammin?"

"Here, Calen Farseer, ready at your side where you asked me to stand."

I did my best imitation of him rolling his eyes.

"If you will, come with me. I am going home. I want my sword, and there are other things I would not leave behind. You will want a few things, too, I think."

I handed Koppel the sword he had given me. "I thank you for this blade. Aldryn, if you will allow me to council you on what is yours, some of the better weapons from this field should be sent across the river."

"As you wish, Annen," answered Aldryn. "Those who have

gone do not know how to use weapons or are too old or young to use them. Perhaps a sword in the hand will give them courage to face death if it comes near."

"I was thinking of the wounded. In days to come, they may look to take up a weapon again. I would not have them search in vain. Also, I have in mind to send a teacher or two."

We paused to take in the lines of our home, the fresh-cut angles and the well-tended garden. Once inside, Gammin went immediately into his room and began to rummage. I gathered the items I knew would be missed the most and the few things we could not do without.

I took down my sword and Gammin's. After a second consideration, I lifted down the spare for Simon. I found a pack and stuffed what I could carry into it. As I was doing this, I chanced to see Merelina's blue and gold scarf. Wrapping the swallowers with it, I took also a book she had given me, and, almost as an afterthought, a shawl she loved. Everywhere I looked I saw something I knew was pleasing to her. I would have taken them all, but it was not possible. Last, I took from its hiding place the ring King Brand gave me, a ring only a Justice of Ehrylan could wear. Unworthy as I was for that honor, I jammed it unceremoniously onto my finger. I went out onto the porch and waited for the young man who would never be my son, no matter how much my heart yearned for that connection.

When he came, I handed him one of the money pouches I had picked up. As I stowed mine in the pack, it resounded with the familiar sound of metal coins rubbing elbows. When Gammin stowed his, it made a different sound.

I watched him. Gammin was the future; I was the past. My wants and desires had to be balanced against what was good for the kingdom. I did not think that Gammin and Marin dying for a small city was what was best for Ehrylan. And I realized what duty required of me. It was much more difficult than fighting.

"It was a good house, Gammin, and a fine home. I am glad you were here with me."

"I will always be with you, Annen."

I slapped him on the back, my face masking what I felt in my heart. I did not think our time together would extend much longer. We stepped into the afternoon sunlight and walked back to where death had already feasted. She would banquet again before the sun set.

I felt the weariness that had been accumulating in the background. I could not remember the last time I had slept a full night. Was it one or two nights since? No matter. The tasks at hand cared not a whit if I were exhausted. Gammin, in the way the young have that belies hardship in the face of adventure, seemed alert and ready.

Wishing I felt as well as he looked, I asked him, "Where do you think Max will be?"

"In the thick of things, wherever he can do least good and get in the way most."

This turned out to be a good guess. We found the boy helping to transport the wounded. Max was carrying the light end of a man Gammin and I would have had difficulty moving. With Simon at the head, Max had a booted foot hooked under each arm. It was all he could do to keep the man's rump up off the ground. The look on his face would have been comical had the situation not been so dire. Breanna was trotting alongside, toting various articles that belonged to the patient—a scythe, a hat, and a ravaged water skin that would never be used again.

We fell in beside them. I asked Gammin if he would take over this load and then come with Simon to find me again.

"Max, I need you, and Breanna, too. Let Gammin take over. Are you strong enough, do you think, Gammin? He looks like quite a load!"

Max handed over the feet and stood puffing. Bre carefully piled her cargo on the man's chest and abdomen.

"I need your help."

"Yes, shinando. What can I do?"

"It's both of you I need. I've been thinking of Eanna and your fellows in the forest. Who is protecting them?"

"I don't know. They are protecting themselves, I guess."

"Ah. I was thinking of sending a couple of the warriors to make sure they are safe. Any ideas who might be good for that?"

"You are asking me?"

Pushing at his arm with her hand, Bre said, "No, silly. He's telling you... and me. He wants us to go back into the forest."

"That's right. I do. I want you to accompany the wounded and stay with the villagers in the forest. Make sure weapons go back with you. I want you to show as many of them as you can how to use them. Can you do that?"

"Teach the villagers to fight?"

"Just so, if you can. If you will."

That was all it took.

III.

We appointed team leaders and took positions. The battle plan was to fight and fall back, to cross the river in an orderly fashion with the a guard defending the retreat. The rear guard was not likely to make it across alive. It was not possible to determine who those unfortunate men would be. I knew my place was to be one of them.

More than a third of our small force was forward-deployed to waylay the soldiers and horsemen as they came through and around the Bendwood. There would be no attempt to stop them. The archers would let fly their missiles until it became too dangerous and then flee into the wood and back across to meet us.

The enemy scouts were eliminated. I heard of six, which seemed to me a logical number, two horsemen for each approach. The enemy split their forces. It was judged that sixty foot soldiers were coming along the Bend Road. Thirty foot soldiers and five or six cavalry were flanking the wood on either side. So far so good. We could meet their south flanking force and, if we moved quickly, evade the rest before they could cross the green.

Our forward positions inflicted real damage. I saw a few horses that afternoon, but none bore riders. The archers told of thirty-five confirmed hits. In most armies, I would divide such a number in half and use that as a more likely estimate, but these men were not given to boasting or speculation. By the time it got to us, the force that attacked along the south flank numbered twenty men at best.

After the first assault, in which we fared well, we retreated before them, inflicting what damage we could along the way. As we fell back, we were joined by those who had been positioned for just such a purpose. By the time we came nigh the village and saw the mass of troops bearing down on us from across the green, few of the soldiers in the south-flanking arm were alive. Those fled back into the main body of their fellows to the north.

Three of our men went back for fallen comrades. Had the enemy charged then and there, none of the three would have made it to the boats. For some reason, perhaps to hear the report of the defeated soldiers, the advancing lines halted. Before they began to move again, five men limped past me. Two of them were carrying unconscious figures.

I sheathed my sword and helped with one of the unconscious men, coming nearly to the docks before I stumbled to a halt. The enemy was moving again. I could see what they intended. I sent the men with orders for everyone to retreat across the river. The oncoming storm of metal and men had changed direction. Whether the enemy commander had seen enough to know we fought like cornered tigers and wanted to face us no more, or because we had never been the real intent of his charge, I never discovered. Whatever the reason, the seventy or so soldiers that remained on the field seemed to have forgotten us. They were advancing on the structures in the village.

I saw them in front of me, a wave of soldiers, unbroken

and unopposed. Many of them had torches though the sun was still high. The flames were not meant for illumination. The village of River's Bend lay directly between us. The homes of my people were defenseless before them. My home was defenseless. The enemy was going to burn our village, and there was nothing I could do about it.

Something inside me broke. Koppel had said that a village was people, not structures. But there was more. A community is also an idea, a goal, a shared life. The soldiers were not attacking structures with their flames; they were attacking our way of life. I lost all control, I, who have fought more battles than I can count. This could not happen! I could not stand by and watch. I yanked my sword free, spread my arms to the heavens, and screamed until I thought my lungs would burst. In my head, I heard the battle music begin. The rhythm raged at twice the speed of my resting heart. It pounded a tuneless melody with a crash of unheard drums. It sang as if thunder and lightning had been given voices. I could feel it beating, pulsing, driving me. My eyes saw red. I began to stalk heedless, laughing, toward the unbreakable line of my enemy. My steps quickened. I was running to meet them. The village would die. She would not die alone.

Truth to tell, I did not know where I was going. My only thought was that I wanted to be among the enemy, hurting them, killing them, making them pay for the rape of River's Bend. Almost forty years of anger and emotion overwhelmed me. I abandoned myself to it and drank deeply of the throbbing battle ecstasy.

I saw soldiers in my path. They were lifting swords. I swung at one, hitting him, and kept running. There was a knot of several men standing in front of the bakery. One of them must have thrown a torch because the flames were already crawling up the wood. I ran, lifting the sword above my head with two hands as every boy does. I was screaming, the drums in my head driving me incessantly. It seemed to me that the men I was attacking turned in slow motion, dream like. I saw surprise on their faces as hands went to sword belts. Then I was among them, slashing, stabbing, spreading death as far and as fast as I could.

Someone swung at me from behind and missed. I had already started for a group of men who were standing in front of the next building. They were laughing at the destruction. I stabbed at one of them, pulled my sword back and stabbed again, this time at a different stomach. My sword slid through cloth and flesh. I heard the lightning singing. It called to me. One of the soldiers hacked at me. I twisted away. I parried a third sword, and a fourth. There were too many of them. They were all around me. The end was near. I laughed and swung again, my sword biting into flesh as silent drums pounded.

Someone jabbed at me. I skipped back. I stumbled and fell, tripping over a body. A blade ripped the air right where my head had been. Next to me, a man cried out, cursing. Rolling to my right, away from the body and away from the men, I saw two swords stab at where I had been. There was a man above me lifting his weapon for a downward stroke. I slashed at his knees with all my strength, felling him like broken tree, and crawled to an open spot two paces away.

As I pushed myself to my feet, expecting to be struck down at any moment, I heard that sound. Ssssstttt, Thump! For an instant I thought Ea had sent the Silanni to rescue me again. Then pain erupted in my thigh. I staggered, looked down to grab the arrow that had hit me and pull it free. There was nothing except torn leggings and blood. It had been a glancing blow. I looked up again, searching for someone to kill, someone I could pursue into the afterlife there to punish him for all eternity for hurting the paradise that was Merelina's River's Bend.

There were four men in front of me, all brandishing swords. Though they looked toward me, none of them were looking at me. They were gaping over my shoulder at something that must have been behind me. A dozen paces behind them was an archer, one of their allies and my enemies. He was trying to get a clear lane so he could shoot me again. I dropped.

The hiss of arrows tore the air above me. Three soldiers went down. I turned, knowing the men could not have been felled by the one archer. Four of Aldryn's archers were nocking arrows two dozen paces back toward the docks. A gang of angry soldiers swarmed around them, and they had to defend themselves.

The enemy archer had a clear shot. He drew his arrow in a smooth, practiced motion, hand to cheek. I saw him smile as he released the death on his string.

I have heard many descriptions of what happened next. Few were accurate. I've heard that the man emptied a full quiver at me as I blocked shot after shot with my sword. One blind singer in a tavern so far north that the word summer has little meaning told me that Calen the Far Sighted caught each arrow and dropped it until, after the last, the archer fled in terror. None of this is true, of course.

As the man let fly, I jumped to the side. It was not a big jump. I jumped as soon as his lips curled. I swept my sword around, not in hopes of batting away the arrow, but in sheer desperation. Two finger's breadth of steel between you and the point of an oncoming arrow is infinitely more comforting than none at all. As luck would have it, the sword struck the arrow, deflecting it.

It was said that I walked, carefree as a cloud, toward the man as he loosed arrow after arrow at me, each one finding the same fate as the first. The truth is that I did walk, but not because I was calm or cool. It was because my leg hurt, and I was exhausted beyond caring. The archer was more than a little put out as I stalked toward him. He may have, as the tales tell, shot another time and missed me. I cannot say. Whatever the case, he hit me again with his last shot in the same leg. He was shooting low. He should have corrected his aim. I took his head off.

I pulled the arrow from my thigh. Warm blood spilled onto my hand and I knew I was going to die. I heard the unmistakable sound of sword play behind me, audible even over the roars of the billowing fires, audible over the thunderous drums that played an insane rhythm in my mind. I turned, saw several figures moving my way from the docks. Some of them were engaged in heavy combat. Others were running, calling my name. I stepped toward the fighting, wanting to help where I could before I bled out. The first step went fine. When my weight fell on the wounded leg, I collapsed in a heap.

Climbing to my feet, I wondered why the men were disobeying my orders. They should have been safely across the river by now. We were too few to overcome the enemy that had come against us. To try and do so was only folly.

Two soldiers stepped toward me, swords raised. I parried the first, stabbed at the second, hacked at the first, and parried the second. I needed to move into a more advantageous position but was anchored by my wounded leg. I paid the price for remaining in one place too long.

The first man cut me as I was engaged with the second. The blade sliced into my left arm above the elbow. I slashed at his neck. My sword bit deep. Blood spewed. Before I could spin back to face the other man, a sword hit me on the top of my back, near where the shoulder met my neck. I stumbled, dazed. When I stepped on the left leg, it collapsed under me and I fell.

I was flat on my back, staring up at the sky, thinking my long journey had ended and the longest journey had finally begun. It was a blue sky. Clouds floated calmly across it. I wanted to reach out and touch them. But I did not have the time. There was something important I was supposed to be doing, but I could not grasp it.

For an instant, as if I had blinked, the sky was hidden from view. A man fell across me, lifeless, knocking me back to my senses. It was one of the two men I had just been fighting. He was so heavy I could hardly breathe. But why was I still having to breathe? I was dead, surely.

Two men stood above me. I did not know either of them, but my mind said they were friends. I recognized them as villagers. One of them reached down and pulled the dead body off me. He stood guard while the other knelt next to me.

"He hit you!" His eyes went to my left arm, which was wet and dark with blood. He gently probed my neck and shoulder, looking carefully at his hand when he pulled it away. There was no blood on his fingers.

"Show me." He helped me lift my torso and turned my shoulders. He looked at my back, touched it, pushed at it where the sword stuck me. "No blood. No cut. Must have hit you with the flat of his blade as we cut him down. Come on. We have to go."

He stood up, looking right and left, front and back. He extended his hand to me. I took it, and he pulled me up.

Flat of his blade? Go? It wasn't over?

It wasn't over. I sighed, looking around for my sword before realizing it was in my hand. I shook my head to clear it. If I were still alive, I needed to be able to think. I might be able to take a few more of Dauroth's servants with me into death. Very gingerly, I placed weight on my left leg. I had to concentrate, but it held. I realized numbly that one of them must have tied a tight bandage around it. When did that happen? Had I passed out?

I staggered half a step and a step toward the nearest opponent. He was several paces away, farther from the docks.

My rescuer shouted at me. "What are you doing?"

I ignored him. I concentrated and was able to stagger a step and half more. I tried to lift my sword. It was very heavy.

"Annen! Come on! We've got to get out of here."

I still didn't understand. If these men had come to fight, why weren't they fighting? I staggered another pace. I had to stop and catch my breath. The soldier I was trying to get to saw me, started to come towards me, stopped, and turned away. My rescuers came abreast of me, one on each side.

"Annen," one of them screamed in my face, shaking me, "You are going to get us all killed. You've got to come. Now! We can't hold out much longer." He gripped my upper arm, the one that had been cut. The pain, immediate and intense, cleared my head.

Get them killed? Get out? What? Then it dawned on me. They had not come to fight; they had come to rescue me. By refusing to follow, I was putting them in jeopardy. I looked into the man's eyes and nodded. They each put an arm around me and half dragged me toward the dock. The waiting boats were fifty paces away.

Some of our men saw us. Three of them got to us and formed a protective arc, but it looked to be in vain. There was a gathering of soldiers between us and the docks. They swarmed towards us. I shrugged off the supports and hauled my sword up. It took all my strength, but if felt wonderful. Ea. Let me kill another, just one more for my people, your people. Just one more.

My fist of protectors met the onslaught. Steel rang. One of the soldiers leaked through the protective cushion around me. I tried to lift the tip of my blade. He could have killed me as easy as thought, but he staggered past and kept going. Away.

The five protectors had cleared a space in front of me. They were fighting fiercely. Several soldiers were headed our way, though most of those between us and the docks were dancing about and cursing. They had stopped paying attention to us. I saw why.

Dark shapes darted and plunged in and out of sight near the river. Everywhere they went, soldiers screamed and struck low with their weapons, down below their waists. One of the dark shapes leapt up, and I heard a rolling snarl. Dogs! Someone had loosed dogs on our enemies!

The villagers did not keep dogs of war. I wondered whose they could be until I saw my mistake—a mistake I should have heard. There was no barking. The animals weren't dogs; they were wolves. And I understood. The Old Ones do not come willingly into open battle, but, when they do, they bring their allies.

I stumbled in the direction of a group of village men that seemed to be overmatched. I tried to lift my weapon, but it was too heavy. Someone, a friend, seized me none too gently and dragged me back toward the river. I tried unsuccessfully to make my feet move fast enough to keep up.

The village of River's Bend was engulfed in a maelstrom. Huge flames clawed the sky. Soldiers were converging on us from all parts of the village, which had become too hellish for even their evil dispositions. Some of them were abandoning the fight and fleeing around the calamity they had made.

The space between me and the docks was clear of any live opposition. Marn stood near the edge of the river, his hands gripping Marin's and Gammin's shoulders. Those two looked to be shouting at the woodcutter. Each of them held a long bow. I saw Marn nod and lift his hands. The boys, for so I shall still call them though they had already proved otherwise, lifted their bows and nocked arrows without undue haste, just as they had been taught. To each side, other men were doing the same.

My last strength gave out just as I came nigh Marn. I fell at his feet, unable to rise or to defend myself. The woodcutter stepped over me and took up a belligerent posture, his gleaming battle axe at the ready. I heard him shout something, but I could not understand what he said. A wild roaring in my ears obliterated his words. It was not the battle music. It was death come to call.

Hands grabbed me, man-handled me into a turc. The men who had been dragging me pushed the craft out into the river and piled in after.

I fought to raise my head. The roar in my ears was turning the world pale. My last sight was of Gammin, Marin, and the other men around them. They were shooting arrows into the enemy.

Colors bled to pale and paled to black.

18. AFTERMATH

I.

I was dreaming. Something smelled wonderful. Young ones were playing at swords, using practice weapons made from woven willow branches. They were laughing. Simon smacked Gammin solidly. Gammin staggered back as if mortally wounded. He dropped his weapon and held both hands over his heart before falling theatrically to the ground where he flopped like a fish. Simon whirled back to the others and raised his practice sword to ready position. He shuffled a step closer to Marin. The woodcutter's son feigned terror, dropped his weapon, and fell, flopping, to the ground. Simon squared off with Arica. She held up her hands, surrendering. Seeing this, Max strode boldly forward and took an opposing position in front of Simon, who was at least a head and a half taller. Max raised his weapon. Breanna came forward, taking a place next to him. She raised her sword. It was Simon's turn to act terrified, fall on the ground, and flop like a fish.

I turned my head. Merelina was next to me on the lover's seat the carpenter had made for us. Her head nestled against my shoulder, and her knees were pulled up so that she reclined against me. Her hands cradled my upper arm tenderly, gently, firmly. She was happy, laughing so hard there were tears in her eyes.

Something smelled wonderful and I knew I was no longer dreaming. I opened my eyes. I did not know where I was or how I had come there, but I knew my wife when she bent to examine my face. I moved my hand, and she took it, kissing it. I wanted to kiss hers but could not pull it to me. She laid a wet cloth on my forehead after wiping my face with it. It was warm and wonderful. It smelled like lavender.

Lina turned away. I thought she would leave me. I tried to call to her, tried to stop her, but I could not. Don't go, I thought, please don't go. She sensed it and turned back to me. I tried to mouth the words "stay with me." She must have understood because she sat, very lightly, on the bed next to me. After looking into my eyes for a while, forever, not long enough, she very gently set her head on my chest. She gathered my hand to her lips, holding it there. I wanted to tell her how much I loved her, how proud I was to be her husband. But I could not. Yet it was so important. I had to tell her, had to make sure she understood. I could not.

They said I was three days unconscious. It was mostly induced, I think. When finally I regained my senses, my mouth was redolent with the cloyingly sweet taste of nyremni. It was necessary, they told me. I needed to sleep. When I asked the nemen how much of the drug she had used on me, her answer was, "Enough to kill a horse." When I asked if I had been babbling, she told me I had not. The problem had been that I insisted on going back to the battle and could not be convinced it was over.

During the next days, I saw much of Lina, Gammin, and Arica. One of them was with me almost constantly, even when I was asleep. I had a fear of being alone. I needed a loved one by me. I was fortunate, being surrounded by those who loved me. Only Marn and Marin were absent. As the days wore on and my awareness expanded beyond my own needs, I grew concerned at this and spoke to my wife of it, asking her if they had been killed. She assured me that, as far as she knew, they were alive and well. Gammin made the same assurance. Though I noted the careful phrasing, I did not press for a more complete answer. If I could not trust that young man and my lady wife to know what I should be told and when, I was doomed. I did not feel doomed, not just yet.

By and by, I came to recognize where I was. The bed upon which I lay was in my very own room in our house within the Stone Gate. I wondered how I had come to be back in Twofords, in my own home, surrounded by those I held most dear. You are no doubt wondering the same.

I learned what had transpired from Aldryn, Koppel, Lina, Gammin, and Arica. Each of them told me different pieces of what happened after I lost consciousness. I did not see these events, but I believe the men and women who related them to me.

This is how Twofords was liberated.

Early that first morning, as soon as Koppel departed to the location of the first ambush, Sheal doubled the watch on the gates of Twofords. They did nothing to interfere with comings and goings, but every passing was noted and reported. The Dryhm began to issue from the south gate before dawn touched the sky. There was, as promised, difficulty getting the gate open. Koppel had friends.

As soon as the first contingent of the garrison headed south, Sheal sent the messenger. That man, as has been told, arrived just in time.

Riders thundered back into Twofords. They rode straight to Castle Hill where the garrison commandant kept his abode. The rest of the garrison was assembled. Such a gathering was seldom seen in Twofords. The lack of practice was evidenced, on this important occasion, by slovenly performance and general disarray.

Sheal's watchers reported another development within the

walls. In almost every part of Twofords, city folk—Stone Dwellers, he called them—were seen gathering in furtive groups. Whether these groups were friend or foe was not initially apparent.

About forty soldiers were stationed at each gate, which left about sixty back at Castle Hill. These figures did not account for the mounted troops that remained. Horsemen were difficult to track as they moved quickly.

They were the first to be eliminated. One by one, sometimes two by two, the horsemen were brought down by arrows from concealed positions. Sheal's scouts saw that it was the Stone Dwellers who had gathered in groups of five or six that were responsible. That's when Sheal realized for which side those men were fighting. And that, he told me, was when he began to hope.

When their horsemen did not return, the commandant sent other soldiers, sometimes in small groups, to investigate. This was exactly what we wanted. The investigatory troops were eliminated in the same manner as the horseman for whom they had been sent to look. By the time the garrison commander knew he had a problem inside the walls, his force had been reduced by more than twenty soldiers and horsemen. He lost even more when he sent messengers, accompanied by armed parties, to each gate.

There came a lull in the activities within the walls. Sheal received the report of our victory over the first wave of soldiers in River's Bend. Arica requested a bow. Sheal told me that when the bow and a standard quiver were delivered, the woodcutter's daughter said, "I will need more arrows if I am to fight very long." After Sheal mentioned this, he looked at me strangely and said, "I thought she was a young girl, but she looked amused. It seemed odd to me at the time. Now I understand better."

The lull was just an inhalation before the real battle for control of Twofords began. The loyalists in the city were assembling for the first concerted attack. At the same time, the commandant of the garrison gathered his own men around him on Castle Hill. Whether he did so for his own cowardly defense or because he was preparing to sally forth was never ascertained.

When they were ready, the loyalists fell on the remaining troops at Castle Hill. There was a short, bloody action. There were few prisoners. The commandant was not one of them. This outcome might have been very different if the soldiers had taken a defensive position within the castle. However, once again, the arrogance born of long and brutal mastery worked against Dauroth's men. They were caught in the open, gathered together, unprepared to fight for their lives.

Once the castle was taken and the commandant deposed, the loyalists split their forces, attacking the gates, north and south. The results were the same. The more numerous and prepared rebels overwhelmed and destroyed the fewer, disorganized soldiers.

Just like that, the city was in the hands of the Resistance. The townsfolk realized what was happening. Those who were for freedom joined the cause. Those who were for Dauroth were killed or detained.

Of the Dryhm there was little sign. They had lost thirty or so. Their total numbers had never been known to us, so no one could judge the threat they posed. A heavy watch was set on the grove. Any Dryhm who appeared was shot down without warning or hesitation. No one who fought for the light ventured into the grove until later, when the Old Ones came.

It is easy to believe, when reading these words in an arm chair with a steaming mug of canella at one's elbow, that the whole takeover had been absurdly simple. But it was not simple. One must count the cost to the village. The battle of the Bend had drawn off much of the garrison, evening the odds in Twofords. River's Bend paid the price for the first freedom of Ehrylan.

Once the city had been taken, Sheal met with Torlan, the leader of the Resistance in Twofords—the man who led the insurrection. Though neither had any inkling of the other previous to that morning, the glow of victory lubricated their acceptance and cooperation. It is easy to be magnanimous when you've just thrown off the heel of your oppressor, even when the other boot is about to kick you in the face.

They knew more than a hundred foot soldiers had set out and that some number would reappear. They laid plans together. Sheal's watchers gave plenty of warning so they were not surprised when the troops came back. What did surprise them was how few soldiers retuned.

I wish I had been there to see it, but I was still in the Old Forest, heavily sedated and under the care of nemen. Almost sixty soldiers returned to Twofords, or tried to. They found a barred gate and a city held against them.

Torlan did not have the strength in troops to sally forth. He had to be content with securing what he had taken. His duty was not to me or the men and women with me; his duty was to the city and to the Resistance. Tired and bewildered, the soldiers were left to fend for themselves. They retreated to the open space south of the city, between the river and the walls where our children had played not many weeks before.

There they made such camp as they could. Weary and disheartened from their losses in the Bend and from their city being taken from them, the soldiers posted only a minimal guard. The ragged company might be forgiven this unfortunate oversight. Their officers and senior commanders had been among the first to die. The remnant were left to perform—in the most-difficult conditions any of them had seen—without the leaders that had always made the decisions.

Sheal attacked the encampment that night. The sentries were easily slain. Silent killings continued until someone discovered what was happening and sounded the alarm. As the camp rose, a swarm of arrows leapt out of the darkness. Before the first soldier carried his sword beyond the fire-lit borders of their camp, it was too late. The last engagement of the first battle for control of Twofords and the River's Bend was over.

One of the members of that raiding party was a woodcutter's daughter named Arica. Sheal observed her skill. To hear him tell it, she dealt with half the soldiers by herself, shooting arrows with no pause between arrows and never a missed target. Arica told a different tale. The truth, I think, is somewhere between the two.

Merelina, with no particular martial skills, had been forced to stay behind. This aggrieved her. True to her style, she addressed this with me as soon as I was strong enough, requesting that I teach her the arts of the bow. I gave her my word that I would do so. Seldom has any promise been more pleasurable to fulfill.

I was brought to the city near dusk the day after the battle of the Bend, only two days since the Dryhm took me captive. Those who had taken part in the fighting were in favor of appointing me to command the city once I recovered. There was talk of installing me on Castle Hill. Gammin suggested he would prefer to stay in his old room if the place had not been despoiled. He said that would be my preference. Lina agreed. As luck would have it, the house in the Stone Gate had not been bothered. Somewhat less fortunately, the bodies we left there had not yet been removed. This reminded everyone how rapidly events had unfolded.

Torlan appointed his team leaders to be responsible for different sections of the city, five in all. Where possible, the leaders gained authority over the sections in which they lived Torlan did not attempt to exert any control over the Shambles. This he left to Sheal. The two got on very well, and their friendship grew as the days passed.

My home in the Stone Gate received unfair treatment. The street was cleared of carnage before I was brought there. Moreover, the whole house, inside and out, was cleansed almost unbearably. Someone fetched beds and other furniture so that Merelina, Gammin, and Arica had places to sleep. The kitchen was stocked with all manner of good food. And last, but certainly most disturbing, an honor guard was posted both at the Stone Gate and the entrance to the house.

Koppel proved his worth during this time. Recognizing the effective relationship between his captain and Torlan, Koppel allowed Sheal to continue as intermediary. Koppel controlled

Eldehrah, as he had always done though we hadn't known it. Once I was well enough, I was forced to take over from Torlan, who was only too eager to divest himself of so public a position of service. Koppel and I worked together, acting through Torlan and Sheal as much as possible. But that was later, after I was out and about.

The second day after my return to consciousness in Twofords, Sheal and Torlan came to me, asking what was to be done. I had no qualifications to be an advisor in this area and told them so, but they insisted. I sent them away with a request to return later. Then I did the most sensible thing I could have done. I consulted with Merelina. Between us, though most of the ideas were hers, we decided the following.

First and foremost, thanks had to be given to Ea, both publicly and prolifically. The prohibition against worshiping the Creator had to be reversed. Immediately. There was to be no attempt to force worship upon the unwilling, but all opposition to it was removed.

Next, help had to be sent to River's Bend. Lina suggested this, though she did not get her way entirely. She was for a full scale, massive rebuilding project, to commence right away. She was quite firm until I pointed out that, within a week or two, Twofords was likely to be surrounded by a sea of Dauroth's soldiers. Those men would either use the rebuilt structures for their own purposes or burn them again. That sobered her enthusiasm. She saw the right of it and adjusted her focus. Instead of rebuilding the village, we needed to extend a hand to the residents of the Bend and open our gates and homes to them: men, women, children, horses, mules, cows, pigs, chickens, and all.

On a less-human front, we needed to prepare our city for full-scale war. We had to lay up stores and create plans for siege. This included significant attention to the walls and gates. We also needed to know what was happening in the rest of the kingdom.

I prompted the destruction of Eldehrah. The structures provided cover at the base of our walls, cover that could be exploited in the inevitable siege that was to come. Merelina counseled that everything useful from the Shambles be brought into the city. The materials salvaged would be useful if the siege went on for the long-term. I did not think this likely since we had so few to defend our walls. We could be overwhelmed by only a modest army.

This was an extremely difficult issue for the hundreds of people who lived in and around the Shambles. To offset this, we encouraged mingling between city folk, those from Eldehrah, and the Bend. It had been the lifestyle for time out of mind before Dauroth arrived. Once they were reminded of that fact, the resistant townspeople usually developed a new attitude.

II.

As Lina and I discussed what needed to be done, it occurred to me how much I desired Marn's council. I asked again where he and Marin were, for they had not been to see me. There was a great fear in my heart. It was possible they had been slain and, at the request of the healer, this news was being withheld from me. Happily, that was not the case. Lina told me that Marn and his son were reconnoitering, one of several teams sent out, each to different locations in southern and central Ehrylan. The mission was to discover if the rebellion was widespread and how Dauroth was responding.

Marn and his son returned. I exercised my patience, wanting to let them rest and refresh themselves before I went to them. They did not give me the chance. They came to me. They were much the worse for wear.

The sentinel at my door sounded the alert.

"Lord Calen, Marn of the Forest is here with his son. He requests an audience."

"Let him in."

I knew full well that was not what Marn said. Gammin, Lina, Arica, and I were sitting in the front room. The shutters were open to the fresh morning. We heard every word. Request had not been one of them, nor had audience.

As an afterthought, I added, "Marn, his wife, and his son and daughter may come and go as they please, at any time."

"I understand, lord."

Lord. There it was again. It was all horse poop. These people were trying to rebuild the civilities of King Brand's court right here in Twofords. I neither needed nor wanted the honors they were focusing on me. It was nonsense.

Marn pushed through the door, followed closely by his son. They were travel stained and looked at once both dusty and muddy, dry and wet. There was a pronounced aroma of horse in the room.

Marn looked at me and grumbled. "You are putting on airs."

"Hardly. The only airs I have put on arrived just now with you."

We stared at each other hard, each looking the other up and down, toes to pate. One of us smiled first, and then he was in my arms and Marin too.

"I was worried about you, Marn, and you, Marin." I tousled the young man's hair. I could not resist.

"We are fine. I was worried about you, Annen. The last I saw you, three men were holding you down while another two were trying to dam the blood from your leg. We could not convince you the fighting was done."

"I do not remember that. I am not sure I believe it. The last thing I recall is seeing Marin and Gammin shooting from the bank. I think I passed out, maybe from loss of blood."

"Yes, and it was a good thing for us. You would have capsized the turc otherwise."

"Well. I thank you, all of you, for saving me." Smiles all around. "Have you eaten?"

His gaze swept the table. It was strewn with the remainders of the meal we had just eaten. "Nothing such as this."

"Sit. We'll refill the plates."

Marn shook his head. "We will clean ourselves first, if we

can find water. Where are we to stay?"

"With us, if you will, Marn of the Forest," answered Merelina. "There's plenty of room."

"No there isn't," replied the woodcutter, "You must be full up already. And I would not sleep under a roof in the city, if I had a choice."

"Exactly my thinking. Why don't you stay in the courtyard?"

Marn saw there was no way she was going to allow him to stay anywhere else. I don't think he really wanted to. He was just being him. We relished it, having missed him mightily.

Arica had put every kettle and pot in the house on the hearth to heat water as soon as they appeared. There was not as long to wait as there might have been. Marn passed the time by inspecting the courtyard and generally staying out of our way. He was, perhaps, conscious of his uncleanliness. On his way out, he plucked a half-loaf from the table and a hunk of cheese. True to his word, he did not sit at the board.

Gammin and Marin vanished into their old room to catch up. A bowl of porridge vanished with them. I busied myself with finding some clothes that might do for the woodcutter and left Gammin to forage for Marin.

Earna had thought of us as she was preparing the orphans for their exodus into the forest. She had packed a few things for us that she knew we would need. Those, and what Gammin and I had gathered, were the only items from our former lives that we had. Everything else had been burned with the house in River's Bend. The housewares we were using now, plates and mugs, chairs and tables, were all donations. This was not the first time I had lost everything; my past, it seems, has a way of erasing itself.

A trip to the market was in order. I had not yet left the Stone Gate, though there was mounting pressure so to do. Lina said she would go; I asked Gammin to go with her. Quick-eyed Marin saw what was happening. She was escorted by two warriors. The swords they bore had tasted blood, had drunk of death deep and deep. Youth could no longer hide behind their eyes.

How quickly they grew up.

As the woodcutter began to tell me his tale, Arica started down the hallway toward the courtyard. I called to her.

"Will you join us, lady?"

She looked back over her shoulder. "I will gladly, sir." She fluttered her eyelids at me in that way she had, faster than bee wings. She did me a courtesy and glided toward us, hands clasped in front of her, without seeming to take steps.

Marn looked back and forth from the young lady to me, bewildered.

He said, "What have you done with my daughter? And who is this... person?"

"May I present the Lady Arica, she of the Forest and the Stones?"

Arica inclined her head toward him.

Marn shook his head. "You've been letting her read those tales from Andur's time. She will be useless if you do not stop filling her head with that sort of foolishness."

Ignoring his barb, she settled into a chair between us. Marn grabbed her, pulled her to him, engulfed her in his rough embrace. She squealed and squirmed exactly like Breanna, then gave in and hugged him back.

I winked at her. "You were saying, Marn?"

He cleared his throat, a man who used few words preparing to speak many.

"I cannot say we held them at the river. Once the soldiers saw we were showing our backs, they left us alone. They were frightened of us, content to let us depart. You were in the last turc but one. Once you were away, we followed quick as we could. A few of their archers let fly, but our archers were better, your son and mine included. They soon left us in peace, those that were still standing."

Your son. The words cut like a knife and made me feel wonderful.

"You were in bad shape. It seems to be a habit of yours, teacher. You must have missed the lesson about dodging when you were training in Brand's court."

He stopped, appeared to reconsider what he was about to say. "I would taunt you as I did in the forest with family Naralyn and in the Stone Gate, but I will not do that again. Back then, I had not seen you single-handedly put an army into disarray. Now I must ask your forgiveness, Annen. It was wrong to say such things to you. I knew not then what now I have seen with my own eyes."

"I do not remember. There is nothing to forgive."

He nodded and went on.

"We had to tend you on the bank, across the river from the burning village in full sight of the soldiers if any had been looking. We carried you to the villagers. There were sentries posted; they were armed, though I am not sure they knew how to use the weapons. Still, they were sharp-eyed. Old Bil was helping them. I did not know that old dog could still see. It was Max who set them to guarding."

Good old Max, not yet thirteen and running the camp.

Scouts were sent throughout the land to see how Dauroth was responding. No one was more suited to the task of venturing into the Old Forest than Marn. Moreover, there was an element to that enterprise only he could carry out. Someone needed to carry a message to the Children of the Forest. Dryhm were unprotected in the grove.

III.

Merelina and the boys returned from the market laden with the supplies we needed to provide comfort to our friends. Prices had already increased, though there were no shortages yet. Truth to tell, the city was burgeoning with goods; all manner of things that could be lifted and moved flowed in through the gates. The shortages would come later, on the heels of Dauroth's armies.

The prices occasioned a family meeting. I was summoned into our bedroom. When Lina closed the door behind us, I saw that she had cornered Gammin too. I knew something was afoot. I just didn't know which one of us was the sore toe.

"Prices were high, husband," she said.

I sat on the bed. My leg was still cantankerous, and I eased it when I could. She took a place in front of me with her feet spread shoulder width and her hands on her hips. This stance, her battle stance, was familiar to me. I began to wonder what I had done wrong.

"Go on," I replied.

"I did not bring enough money with me, foolish as it seems."

Ah! "I am so sorry, my love." I reached for the money pouch on a nearby table. "Here! You know where the purse is. It's all yours. You know that."

She shook her head impatiently. "Not that. I have no cause for complaint on that account, husband. We share all that we have. What I did not know was how much we had. Gammin?"

Gammin looked like he was caught between a she bear and a mountain lion trying to eat her cub. He took a pouch from his belt. It was the one I had given him in River's Bend. He undid the knot and tugged it open before spilling a small part of its contents onto the coverlet. Gems scattered, red and green and blue. Some were finely faceted, others fresh and completely unworked. Gammin's fingers could not close around what was left in the bag.

I did not know what to say, not being sure yet what was amiss. I looked up at Merelina and tried to put on the face that Gammin showed me when I was being obtuse.

"You do not like gems, my love?"

"What I do not like is finding that I am walking around with enough wealth to buy half the kingdom!"

"Hardly. At least not in that bag. There are others."

"Others?" Her voice was rising in intensity with every statement.

I stood up. "Lina, if I have wronged you in any way, I ask forgiveness." I took her face in my hands and kissed her forehead before placing mine against it. She was tense a moment longer, then I felt her hands slide up my back. She raised her face, so I pulled back and gazed at her.

"Imagine how you would feel, you great, slow-witted, pack horse, if you were in our places. When I asked Gammin if he had a scepter, he looked in the bag and found…. That!" She pointed to the glittering pile.

I laughed. "Sorry about that. I had forgotten I gave it to him. I wanted to make sure you had money in case something happened to me."

"You forgot? Are you so much in the habit of distributing bags of jewels that you could forget such a thing?"

I saw this was going to be all right.

"Lina, money is a funny thing. I've gotten out of the habit of thinking of this… of my… of the hoard as my own. Someday, when there is time, I will tell you the story of a man I met. It is his story and it taught me a lot."

Gammin broke in on me, which was probably a good thing. I might have told that story then and there.

"You brought them back with you, didn't you, Annen? From across the uncrossable ocean and all that."

"Correct. After the ship wreck, I came to a place where gems were so common they were of little account, other than for use in art. Now that I think about it, they did not use money at all in that land. Art—the act of bringing things out from within—was their treasure."

Gammin said, "If you had all this, you could have… Wait. I see. You couldn't. And besides, you did."

Merelina's eyebrows arched. "Is that so?"

I prompted him to go on, wanting him to share his insight.

"I was going to ask why you didn't use all that wealth to take care of the poor and the orphans. But I realized, if you had, you would have attracted a lot of attention, something you could not afford to do. And then I realize that you had been doing a lot for everyone."

"Not a lot, maybe not enough. But some, yes."

Lina took my arm in her hands and pressed against me. That was nice. One thing about her—or maybe it's two. She may have been in those days quick to ire but she ran quicker to forgiveness.

"Why didn't you hire armies to put out Dauroth?"

"Think. Bringing in one set of foreigners to cast out another is a losing proposition. Yes?"

"You are right, shinando," he said, nodding. "Do you really have enough to buy half a kingdom?"

"Not nearly as much as that. But we do have enough to help our people during this war. If we are victorious, we will need a lot to get the kingdom up and running again. I am hoping that's why Ea gave this wealth to us. I've done my best to preserve it." As an afterthought, I added, "And much as I'd like to, I can't start paying for everyone's needs by flinging jewels at every problem that comes up. If we did that, jewels would become pretty stones again, just like they were in the place where I got them. Understand?"

He nodded.

"Gather that up, will you? You should probably not carry that bag around. But why don't you keep some for yourself?"

"I thank you, Annen, but no. It would not be right. You give me plenty."

Once again, I was proud of the young man. So was Lina. She kissed him on his forehead as we turned to go back to the others. Gammin embraced her lovingly.

There was one task none of the townsfolk were brave enough to undertake. No one volunteered to attack the Dryhm stronghold on Castle Hill. There was no shortage of those willing to mount guard outside the grove, but few would venture under the eaves of even the outermost trees.

Koppel came up with the solution. He knew the Old Ones hated no one more than the Dryhm. That hatred was returned in full measure and there was great enmity between the two. Therefore, at Koppel's request, Marn sought the aid of his kindred.

A delegation of six men and six women arrived at the city a

day or two after Marn returned. They brought six wolves. According to Torlan, the animals were remarkably well behaved. His words were, "The wolves were as calm as well-trained dogs but they weren't friendly. No one wanted to pet them. The Old Ones did not leash their pets. They didn't have to. The wolves obeyed any word spoken by their masters."

I did not bother to correct him. He thought the wolves were some kind of pet. That is not so. The Old Ones—maybe even the wolves—would have found the idea humorous.

Marn told me later that these twelve were members of the families that lived nearest the Bend. Some of them had been involved in the battle there and all had seen the wanton destruction. Even that could not increase their desire to confront the Dryhm in their seat of power.

As far as I know, there is no recorded eye-witness account of what happened in the grove. Sometime in the night, flames sprouted in the center of the grove and continued to burn until well after dawn. Only the structures and machinations of evil were burned. Few trees were harmed.

The Old Ones told no tale of what transpired save that there had been twenty Dryhm alive in the grove the night before and now there were none. The paths had been cleared of several deadly traps. Care should be taken, they said, in case one or two had been missed. The Old Ones questioned a few of the Dryhm. They discovered message birds had been sent to Dauroth and Mendolas.

The eighteen children of the forest returned to their homes without fanfare, which is their preference. They received ample thanks for their efforts and an invitation to return whenever they liked, and all their kin besides. The two-footed accepted a meal of simple foods. Torlan told me that, when he offered to feed the wolves, the leader of the Old Ones replied, "Your offer is kindly meant, but there is no need. Our friends have eaten well."

19. PARTINGS

I.

A messenger arrived summoning us to council. I did not intend to go. My wounds were still healing. I no longer had a place in the Resistance. That's what I told Marn, anyway. The real reason was that I suspected what they would ask of me. It was something for which I did not have the stomach.

He chastised me. "You must go among the people. They would see you. There is much talk."

"What is the talk? Are they frightened?" They should be, I thought to myself.

"Most of it is about you, my friend."

"About me? Why?"

"Surely you cannot be so stupid."

"What are the men saying, Marn?"

"Some say you are Teryn come again. Others say you are Andur himself, reborn to lead us to victory and freedom."

"Ridiculous. No man is reborn. That is the curse of the Everbourne. Andur was not Everbourne, nor was Teryn."

"No, indeed. You are Calen the Farsighted. If ever Ehrylan

crawls out from under the oppression of Dauroth, your deeds will be every bit as much the stuff of legend as Andur's or Teryn's."

"Now you are being foolish, my dear friend."

"I saw what I saw."

"What did you see, Marn of family Traneal, watcher of the northern border?"

"I saw lightning with a silver blade. I saw a storm with the face of man sweep across the field of battle like a scythe through wheat. I saw one man charge a hundred and come back alive."

"You exaggerate. By that time, there could not have been more than seventy."

"You jest to reduce the import of the things I say. I do not jest. I saw a teacher leading men into battle. And I saw men follow that teacher without question because they knew he was their leader. You must not rob them of that. It is their right. They fought for it. And for you."

"You speak of rights, Marn. I have no right to rule in Twofords."

"Maybe not. But you must honor the men, women, and children that followed you into death. You must lead them back out."

I thought hard about that last point. Finally, I said, "I will do as you ask. But you are right. If we come out of this alive, woodcutter, it will be the stuff of legends. Why are you laughing?"

"Because I see how funny it will be. I will be a name in those legends, Marn the woodcutter, forever associated with Calen Farseer. My sires would be proud, I think."

"Your sires could not help but be proud of you, brother. But as I have told you before, those closest to my heart have a way of finding death when they travel at my side."

"If we die, we will die in such a way that our children and our wives can be proud. Is there more than that?"

"There is a little more. But say not Marn the woodcutter. Say rather, Marn Wingfoot. In our company shall be Marin

True Heart and his sister, Lady Arica Sure Hand. As for the others, they shall be Merelina the Wise and Gammin who needs no other name."

The facetious drivel put me in mind of Simon, Breanna, and Max—the rest of our merry band of players. They had played their parts. And how many more, people whose names and lives I did not know nor ever would? So many had sacrificed so much to get us even this small distance up freedom's road. I felt a great weight on my shoulders, thinking of the part Marn the Wingfooted would have me play. He was right. If others could give so freely, why shouldn't I?

"I will go with you, Marn. But you will have to go slowly. I am limping."

For a wonder, he smiled.

Marn went to get his wife, taking with him the young ones. He was not one who could stay long under a roof. Marin, Gammin, and Arica came home first and went to their rooms after bidding us a good night. Merelina and I were not yet abed, for that would have been discourteous. We were sitting in the courtyard, passing the time in silence. I was holding her, my arms wrapped around her torso. She was close against my chest. I could feel her heart beat. She was humming softly.

It was into this paradise that Marn and Dara came. I did not hear him until the door to the courtyard opened.

"Are we disturbing you?"

"Not at all, Daratha," answered Lina. "We were waiting for you."

They crossed to where we were sitting and took the two chairs. We made as to get up.

Dara motioned to us. "Stay and sit with us a while?"

Marn said, "We are in the mind of your company." He slipped an arm around Dara's waist. She smiled warmly and put her hand on his thigh.

We chatted about recent events and what might come after. At first, there was much interchange of thoughts and ideas. Gradually, rain fading to mist, the talk subsided, then stopped altogether.

We said nothing for a long time. The trees spoke with the wind, and it was enough. I had been staring at the cluster of stars called the Warrior, lost in thought and memory. I came back to myself as if waking from a dream. Without moving my head, I shifted my eyes to Marn, thinking that perhaps he might have fallen asleep. But no. He was looking at me, staring with eyes that were fully awake.

Lina stirred.

"Come. We keep our guests from well-earned sleep."

Lina led me to our room. I slept all night with my arms around her. Each time I awoke, she was smiling in her sleep.

As always, even in the worst of times, morning came. I made sure to rise first and prepared the board, then sat waiting for the others. The morning went nothing like I intended. It started fine, with Lina coming out first, wearing her blue and gold scarf across her shoulders and displaying for me the smile she had born all night.

The three young ones came out next. From the looks of concern on Arica and Gammin and the look of fear on Marin, I could guess what had happened. Gammin started to tell me straight away. I stopped him.

"Let us wait for Marn and Dara."

"No. I don't think we should wait. I am sorry. I mean no disrespect."

"I thank you for letting me know." I turned to Marin and Arica. "Would one of you please give my respects to your parents?"

"We are here." Marn's voice proceeded him down the hallway. "We were up with the sun, same as you. Something's happened."

I answered for us all. "Unless I miss my guess, Marin had another seeing."

There was a chorus of yeses followed by the movement of many feet. The woodcutter's children went to him. Gammin came and stood by Lina. It took a moment to get everyone seated and served with a cup of juice or canella. Gammin eyed me the whole time with uncharacteristic impatience. From that alone, even without the signs from Marin and Arica, I knew this was something serious.

It was not like the first time when Marin had been mostly confused, nor the second when he had been surprised. This time, he was visibly shaken, distressed. He looked frightened more than anything. He was hanging his head as I fetched the drinks. I could see he was pale. There was a sheen of sweat on his brow.

His voice was timid, almost quavering. "I dreamed about Twofords, and about Gammin and me." He tried to swallow, found his throat was dry, took a swig.

I thought of something my mother told me. One should never scold a child for being frightened; one should never let a child be frightened without picking them up and comforting them. Marin was not in any way a child, but there might be something I could do for him. I wanted to tell him that Ea did not send dreams to his seers to make them fear, but I did not know if that was true. I knew little about being a seer and less about Ea.

"Tell us what Rhua brought you."

He took a deep breath and wiped the sweat from his face with the palm of one hand.

"I dreamed you were on the wall above the north gate of the city. Twofords, I mean, not the city from the first dream, not Tarabol. This was Twofords for sure. It was raining. The sky was dark with clouds. I could not hear you, Annen. You were talking to the people in the city, encouraging them. You had a sword in your hand. You used it to point several times. You turned your back on us, on the people below you, and looked north toward the Swamp.

"There was a huge wolf coming. It was the size of a mountain. Or maybe it was the shadow of a wolf, or a ghost wolf. I don't know. The body was blurry, like a cloud. Its eyes were red and blazed like fire. Froth and foam, maybe blood, fell from its mouth when it snarled. Another wolf was coming up from the south." Marin was wringing his hands. He shook his head and lowered it to hide his face. "I was afraid, Annen.

The wolf was coming for me and for Gammin. I was afraid."

He stammered to a halt. I could see the effort he expended to stop the tears. His hand was shaking. Dara drew breath to speak, but Marn placed a hand over hers. She remained silent.

Marn said, "Go on, son. Fear is not unmanly. What he does with his fear defines the man." He looked at Dara and Arica. "Or the woman. Tell us what you did with your fear."

"That is the worst part. Annen was up on the wall, only now he was standing on the top of huge scales, like the balances they use at the market. When he saw the second wolf, he opened his arms wide and shook his sword. He threw back his head and laughed like he did in River's Bend before you sent the men out to bring him back. Lightning split the sky all around, the wind kicked up, and the skies opened. I mean, it had been raining before, but now it was really coming down.

"The storm didn't seem to bother the people in the city, or Annen, who was on the scale up on the walls. I could see the wind tearing at his clothes. He just ignored it and kept shaking his sword at the wolf. All the people below took out their weapons and shook them, too. Gammin was there. We did the same as everyone else, shaking our swords at the wolves and screaming. Here is the bad part."

Instead of telling us straight way, Marin took a swallow from his cup. He wiped his mouth on his sleeve, something he would not have done in front of his mother in a normal situation.

"Annen pointed at Gammin and me. The lightning blazed and a ring on your finger flamed up so much it hurt our eyes. We hid our faces. But we could still see you. You pointed to the river. You said something. We could hear it, even though all the people were shouting at the wolves. You said, 'The tree must rise.' Gammin and I did not know what that meant, but we knew you were telling us we had to leave, that we were not allowed to stay in the city.

"You pointed west toward the river. We could see all the way to the sea, as if we were standing at the peaks of the Western Mountains. A fleet of ships was sailing southward.

The ships were made in the likeness of leaping wolves." Marin looked around the table, perhaps hoping we would stop him with questions. No one did. He swallowed again, producing a sound that was somehow thick.

"Then we were looking closer to the city, down near the shore of the river. There was a group of men standing on a dock. I know there is no dock there, but there was in my dream, a big dock too; it was right here on the Silver River where it is too shallow for anything but a small boat. You were there, father, in that group of men, and you too, Annen. You were talking to us, telling us to get on the ship and get away. But there was no ship. It was just a turc. There was someone underneath a covering, a friend, I think, or an ally.

"Annen and father were urging us to go, but we wouldn't. The people would think we were cowards. You would be ashamed of us. All the time, the wolves were getting closer, and I was more afraid. You said something strange, something I did not understand. That is when I woke up."

Merelina said, "Tell us what you remember. Or even what you felt."

He nodded and swallowed hard, wiping his face again. I heard Gammin say, "It's alright," though I am not sure he spoke.

Marin grimaced. "You said:

> Water and tree.
> Stone and darkness.
> Storm into storm.
> Home and home again.

"I don't know. That may be wrong." His frustration stopped him, spurred him on once more, to the end. "But I know this. We have to leave Twofords."

Marin looked down at his feet. When he lifted his head again, he turned to the side and looked at his father and mother. I saw a single tear drop from the corner of his eye. It fell to the ground and, for some reason, the memory of the first day I met Gammin pushed its way to the front of my mind. And I knew. I saw.

We waited for more. None came. One by one, each of us offered encouragements. These gradually turned into opinions or thoughts. The real effort was to keep talking until the dreamer felt better.

No one needed interpretation about the wolves. The ravening wolf was Dauroth's sigul and it was a fair guess even without the dream that he would soon be upon us, north and south. That's how the major road ran. With a falling heart, I was sure as I could be of what I was supposed to do, two things that were not in accord with my will or my desire.

I was to take a place at the head of Twofords' armies. The reference to the scale and ring were reminders of my responsibilities. The role of Justice was not intended to be one of martial responsibilities, but I had to try. While I was never a leader of men, I had been around the best leaders of our time. I would imitate them as best I could. I was relieved the seeing had not shown me sitting behind a desk planning a schedule for waste disposal or food distribution. I would rather face an enemy with a sword in his hand than an irate neighbor in whose garden my rabbits had defecated.

The second duty was far more difficult. I had to send Gammin and Marin away from Twofords in the same way and for the same reasons King Brand sent Branden and me from Ehrylan. I did not infer from this that Gammin was in any way a prince of Ehrylan. Brand was an only child. He died without issue. This I had seen with my own eyes. The conclusion was that the two young men had some important part to play in the rebuilding of the kingdom. The first move in that game was their flight from Twofords.

Thinking about such a parting sent lances of anxiety through my heart. I knew only too well how it felt to be flung aside just when the kingdom and its people were at their uttermost need. Perhaps King Brand had felt the same. If so, I experienced now every bit of his agony and owned it for myself.

II.

A fresh wind blew moist against my skin. Clouds were gathering. Marn felt it too. I could see he knew my thought. It was time his son and my young falcon were gone. I was impressed with his sympathy. Then I realized he did not need to imagine my unease; he felt it himself. This man was a father who was about to cast his only son into the wild world, a world full of evil and hate. In that same moment, I remembered that it was not only a world of hate. There was much good in it. Life had taught me that lesson recently. I smiled the worry out of his eye and clapped him on the back.

"Come, friend Marn, let's go to market and see what we can find to send away with our boys."

We spent some long while on the market street buying the things a hurried traveler might need—dried and salted meats, dried and fresh fruit, crusty bread baked into thin traveler's loaves, and cheese, of course. New cloaks and gloves were an excellent purchase, and, for good measure, two new sets of flint, steel, and tinder. We found excellent travelling packs with sturdy straps, and other things as well. Once we had finished spending, we found, to our amusement, that there was little room for anything else in the new packs, large though they were.

The first drops fell on my upturned face as we left the market. By the time we arrived at the Stone Gate, the sporadic drops had turned to rain. The wind had picked up dramatically.

We found the house empty save for the silly guard and Avyansa, who had resumed his place in our paddock some days before, this time with the company of Marn's other animals. There was no reason for us to be taken aback by our missing families. We all had duties. It was likely they had gone to see Eanna and the other children.

With that thought, my mind turned to Simon, who was silent and brave, a young man who never boasted and seldom laughed. And Breanna, so timid, yet so valiant, trying to lift a sword almost as long as she was tall. How long since I had seen their faces? I missed them, all of them. I had been too long away from them and completely remiss in my lack of effort to go and see them.

At this time of day, my students might be anywhere doing anything. On the other hand, it was raining steadily now; they would be under a roof. That should make them easier to find. I corrected my thinking. Sensible people would be inside under a roof. But that merry band? Who knew? They might be playing stick ball in the mud.

With Marn at my side, I went to find them. Eanna was out in front, putting the new orphanage in order against the unexpected rain. She gestured for us to proceed inside. All in all, it was a nice place, a cut or two above the Step, though not nearly as well-made as Eanna's complex in River's Bend. The front room was large and open, filled with what was now a single family of dozens of brothers and sisters.

Gammin and Marin were hunkered down in a corner of the main room, the rest of their training partners sitting in a semicircle around them. Many of the other children were clustered as close as they could get to that central group. Marin seemed to be the center of attention. He was telling some sort of story to Temay. The latter was listening as well as he was able, nodding vigorously now and then, interrupting more than occasionally. Whatever the subject, it must have been interesting, for none of them noticed Marn and me. That allowed us the rare opportunity to observe them at their best.

Eventually, we were noticed and the place erupted into pandemonium. After surviving the squirmy stampede, we hugged, kissed, and patted our way to something resembling calm. There were greetings all around. Everyone asked to hear my story first-hand then rushed to tell their own before I could start. That was just as well; my tale was not one fit for children.

By and by, Eanna came in and began issuing instructions. The older children got up to help her, as well as some of the younger. Once she had orchestrated their efforts, she made her way over to us. Just like her charges, she was interested in hearing from me first-hand what she had heard from others before. She told me of her adventures during that difficult period. Old Bil had played a significant part and came away rather better off than he had been before.

Gammin was staring at me. I could read the look on his face. It was time to be going. I nodded at him. He rose to his feet, followed closely by Marin. They spent a long time making their partings with everyone. Only Marn and I suspected why. This might be the last time any of them ever spoke.

I will not tell of the conversations we had as we walked home in the pelting rain, or of the private times we shared in our last few hours together. We discussed much and spent as much time in silence. I tried to give sage advice such as my father had done to me so many times, even when I was grown enough to have a family of my own. I felt very much like I thought a father would feel upon sending his son away in such a situation. As for Gammin, his feelings did not show, and he did not talk about them. His face displayed nothing.

I showed him the new pack and what we had placed in it. He added items he had gathered that day. He had his knife and his sword. I pressed a purse into his hand. He tried to hand it back. I would not take it. He made as if to drop it; I did not let him. There was not much in it, only as much as a man might carry on a long journey, and I told him so. That seemed to do the trick; he accepted it.

Almost desperate to show the love that was breaking my heart, I sat the boys down for a last lesson. I begged them to remember the Precepts of War. I stressed that the principles are not only for war; they are principles of life. That was the deepest meaning of the words *Dan tahli meh; ahn dan tahli noh*. The sword of justice; the sword that gives life. These words can also be translated as the sword of justice is a life-giving blade. And conversely, the life-giving blade is a just sword.

There was something I wanted to do with the boys before they left, a ceremony of sorts. A boy customarily performed the ceremony with his father, a girl with her mother. I had already discussed it with Marn. I asked that he join us. It seemed right that the four of us, who had shared so much, should drink the parting cup together as a group. We had lived that way, even if our beds and larders were in different locations.

Gammin, Marin, Marn, and I, gathered in the courtyard. It was where the boys and I had lived, studied, and played. Marn and I had erected a temporary shelter there to protect against the rain and wind.

I placed the swallowers in a square on a leveled-off stump. Marn brought out his water skin and a fat candle that he set in the midst of the square.

It was Gammin who understood first. "Are you... Are we...?"

"Yes. It is time. You may be a little young in years, but you are long in trials and experience. As I said to you on the green, you've been acting like a man for quite a while. This is mostly to show you that we recognize it."

Marin was looking at each of the three of us in turn, over and over. Marn stopped that by saying, "Sit now and think about what it means to be a man. I tell you what my father told me. Being a man means that you have real responsibility to others. You can no longer be motivated only by self-interest or your own wants and desires."

As Marn's voice ceased, all three of them turned to me.

"I tell you what my father said to me, and what his father said to him as far back as our line, or so it is told. This is also what King Brand said to us, for, as you two, Prince Branden and I went through this rite together. Being a man is not enough. You must be a good man, the best you can be. Everything you do is an indication of the man you are becoming and a reflection of the man you are."

Marn filled the swallowers from his water skin. The welcome aroma filled the courtyard with life. The linuvea sparkled like starlight, pale green in one swallower, pale blue in another, silver and grey in the other two. The colors switched from one container to another so that what before had been blue was now grey and what had been grey was now green.

Marn picked up the swallower nearest him. The rest of us did the same.

"Marin, you are my son," said the woodcutter. "I see that you are a man. You are my brother, also. I am glad of it." His voice grew huskier and moister with each word. Tears scurried down his cheek and hid among the profusion of his beard.

I wondered what I would say to Gammin, longing to call him my son, knowing he was not. It was my time to speak. I didn't have the words. I opened my mouth and let come what would.

"Gammin, you came to me, a boy who did not know his father. I have loved you as my son. You are a man and still I love you as my son."

Together we lifted our swallowers and drained them. I was the last. The instant I finished my draught, the candle wick flickered to flame with a soft woosh. None of us had known that was going to happen; Marn would have lit the candle as the final step in the ceremony. Fire represents Rhua, who is also Ea, and the wind.

You never know what to expect with Dragon's Eye.

Night was upon us as we left the Stone Gate. Marn led us to the same house we used the night all this had started, the house near the wall where a hidden tunnel would take the young men away into the wide unknown. The storm hid us from any eyes that might be about; it could not now be characterized simply as rain. Wind tugged at our cloaks, blew droplets of water past the protection of our hoods.

As before, we entered the back door by way of a deserted ally. Once again, there were sounds of others in the house though we did not see anyone. Marn repeated the process of getting us into the tunnel. He led us down and down, through the doors and tunnels into the small chamber where we picked up two torches. He took us through the tunnel until we arrived at one of the doors we had bypassed on our previous journey.

All this while, as though we had said all that could be said, no one uttered a word.

Handing his torch to his son, Marn took out a key and unlocked the lock. He pulled it open. It swung smoothly on well-oiled hinges. Unmistakably strong, the smell of the river wafted out. In the light of the torches I could see the first few steps of a winding stairwell descending from the doorway.

Marn nodded to his son. The young man took a long last look at his father's face. He glanced at me, nodded, and stepped through the door. The torch was in his right hand. His left rested on the sword hilt. I wanted to tell him how much he looked like a hero from a long-forgotten legend.

The woodcutter grunted something underneath his breath and stepped back.

Gammin looked up at me. His eyes were wide open, the same look I had seen a hundred times. A thousand. Maybe a hundred thousands. He blinked, holding back a tear, but that may have just been my heart's fancy. He reached out and touched my hand. I opened my mouth to tell him how much I loved him, but I could not speak.

Pushing Marin before him, Gammin started down the steps that led I knew not where. Just before the stairway turned out of sight, he stopped and looked back.

"I thank you. I am going now. Goodbye, father."

He turned his head and stared into the receding blackness of the stairwell, then back at me. One last wide-eyed look. And finally, he smiled. It bloomed on his face, sunlight racing across water. I thought my heart might burst. Then he was gone.

I fought the urge to rush down the stairs after them.

The Beginning.

ABOUT THE AUTHOR

John Day lives and writes in northern California's San Joaquin river delta. Before retiring to write full-time, he spent decades working in the Tech industry. He enjoys music, martial arts, animals, and language. He relishes the outdoors and spending time with his incredible Labrador Retriever.

A Justice of Ehrylan is his first published novel.

More information is available on the author's web site:

jdouglasday.com

OTHER WORK

<u>Annals of the Everbourne</u>

Book II- *Warriors of Ehrylan*
Book III- *Battle for the Southland*
Book IV- *Everbourne*

Made in United States
Orlando, FL
28 July 2024